To Rose—
You blossom even
in the heart of
your family!

Warm Regards,
Elisabeth Lee

For Glory

Web site:
http://www.For-Glory.com

For Glory

A Carlyle Hudson Novel

Elisabeth Lee

ISBN-10: 1-4196-5046-7

Library of Congress Control Number: 2006909005

Publisher: BookSurge, LLC
North Charleston, South Carolina

To Marc, prairie wizard and keeper of my heart.

1

I deal with other people by keeping secrets. Bottom line: I do not like people knowing what I do for a living, how much money I make, my age, or marital status. The answers—gamble, six to seven figures (depending on how well the cards fall), fifty, and not interested in marriage—always raise more questions. Even well intentioned people seem to feel entitled to that information, which irritates the hell out of me. So I lie. It entertains me, keeps my energy positive and my creativity high. In the rare instance that idle curiosity turns into some sort of friendship, I'll buy you a drink, confess the truth, and see how you take it. Most people are good sports. Once they know me, I think they understand the lies. They think of it as misdirection. I think of it as acting. All good poker players act. I am a very good poker player.

Right now I have two problems. I'm on a losing streak and I'm in Kansas.

I never expected to stay. It was, after all, Kansas. I had sworn never. Never, never, never. Except for the odd visit over a long weekend around a family ritual like Christmas or a birthday ending in zero—my mom's, not mine. I avoid zeros. And birthdays. And until now, my mom. The hell of it is, she died, and now I'm here. In Kansas. It looks like I'll have to stay, for a while anyway. Until the cards change. Until I can figure out how to leave. Kansas. Damn.

We would have had Christmas a few weeks ago: mom, her sisters, and me. It had become a ladies-only event in the last few years, the result of sundry break-ups, separations, divorces, disappearances, hospitalization, and death. Bottom line is that men did not last with the women in our family. We think of ourselves as bigger than life, something like a unified force of nature. When we aren't *at* each other. Or depressed. Hudson women tend toward depression. Before anti-depressants, the antidote was to pick up and leave. *Ms. Hudson has left the building.* Poof. Gone.

But I skipped the Hudson Christmas this year. I took Chas to a private Costa Rican villa I rented for the holiday. He was alone and I owed him the fabulous view of the Pacific and there was a casino in town. But that's another story.

Damn Louise. I wasn't ready for her to be dead. I should have been here for Christmas, for Christ's sake. Talking, for a change, laughing, enjoying keeping company. That's what we call it, "keeping company;" *hanging out* has the wrong feel. People Louise's age did not hang out, thank you very much. She left me with a house I am damn well not going to live in and a business I certainly don't want. But I'm getting ahead of myself.

I had been back in San Francisco maybe ten days. The trip hadn't exactly paid for itself. Too little time on the beach, too much time at the tables, losing. But a reasonably good time with a good friend. I'd had enough time to sift the spam from my email, pay bills, reconnect with friends, and break up with the latest man after two days' of steam and massage up in Napa. I was in the middle of figuring out whether to be depressed or happy about it when the phone chirped and my aunt Luce told me Louise was gone.

"She left? Just like that?"

"Let's try again, Lyle," she said. "What is the first thing I said when you answered the phone? Think about it."

"How's the weather? Shit." *How's the weather* is family code for *somebody died.* "Dead?" I stopped breathing. I was confused. Someone in the room was moaning and making choking noises.

"Lyle, sweetie? You OK? Listen up…"

"Luce, I can't. Can't…" Words would not come. "I'll call you back."

That was weeks ago. Lots of blank spaces since then, gray air. Luce handled arrangements. Louise had insisted on cremation. No viewing. A service at her Episcopal church. There was no rush. I changed my life and left San Francisco, everything I needed in the back of my car. Flying might have made more sense, but I wanted time alone, wanted to have the car with me, my car, not some creepy rental out of KCI.

My car is an Infiniti G35 Coupe—Liquid Platinum on the outside, soft leather and rosewood within. 298 horses push her to Mach speed on the prairies. She's as quiet as a purr, guaranteed to get attention. Valet guys love her.

I traversed the Sierras and arrived in Reno with some difficulty. The G35 isn't a car of choice for driving in snow, and a winter storm was dropping in from the north. I-80 would be closed all the way to Salt Lake. And I wanted to take Route 50 due East, two lanes, begging for the solitude of the high desert and the absence of semis on a long haul. I'd have to wait for the plows so I dropped in on my friends at the Peppermill hotel-casino, not so much for the ambience as knowing I'd get comped—a free stay for reliable players, whatever "reliable" means in a world built of cards.

I finished fourth in my first tournament there three years ago. Risked a dime to enter and added a zero to it in five days, well, nights of hard work. World Poker, no-limit-Texas-hold-em before it hit television and the web and everybody decided they'd be the next champion.

The storm forced me to stay three nights with cold cards. I lost about $3,000 a night.

When the road was mostly clear it took two slow days to drive across a couple deserts and pass through the Rocky Mountains. The G35 wanted to run, but I couldn't. I talked to Louise, tried to come to terms with her abrupt departure. Luce had said they didn't know why she died. "At home" was all she told me.

Too late for Denver, I pulled off of I-70 on the descent from the Eisenhower tunnel and cut over to Central City where the casinos are cut into the canyon. But my luck was worse than sour. I lost $5,000 in an hour and called it quits. Walked away from the free room and got back in the car. I'd drive straight through to Lawrence.

Driving that car, I was locked in a solitude that scared the hell out of me. With the sun rising over the Flint Hills I howled, I raved, I begged the Deity to let me wake up. The daughter in me expected to have time left with Louise for us to build a relationship. Even this late in the game, it was my dream. And now, nothing. I felt numb. The constant weeping terrified me. Truth is, part of me was just getting started.

The service went well, considering there was no casket, no cemetery. In our shock, we behaved ourselves. Mostly. Hudsons don't do death well; we take it personally. Lack dignity, blurt things out unexpectedly. Mutter under our breath. We brood and drink a lot, both before and after a funeral. Which is not cool when you're taking antidepressants. The hangover is not bad at all, but there are a few…gaps…in the memory, and I have to tip-toe around, sleuthing out what I might have said. Due to the degree of shock we were experiencing, for Louise's funeral we went easy on each other. Behaved ourselves in the presence of patient Father Bob. Tried to take it slow. Which is how I ended up staying at my mother's house with my Aunt Luce.

My aunt's name is Lucille Hudson. My mother's name was Louise. She and her sisters all had names starting with L: Louise, Lucille, Loretta, and Lenore. Except for mom, they gave their daughters L-names, too. Tribal tradition. Maybe not a tribe, a clan? But we feel like a tribe and all like the word. Hudson women are sensitive to words. More on that later.

My name is Carlyle Hudson. My aunts called me Lyle, so I ended up with an L-name after all, just like the rest. These days, every one of us has silver hair. Mine is silky, quite long, and reaches well below my shoulder blades. We share another trait, as well. When the men disappear or leave or die, we take our name back, become Hudsons again. It suits us just fine.

So here I was, in Kansas, and all bets were off. It

was spooky to be in that house without my mother, like visiting a museum of my own past. The physical evidence of the woman, the things she touched and lived with, everyday things, seemed wrapped in time, artifacts of a lost world. Which indeed they were.

It's a big old house and stands in the middle of a shady street in Old West Lawrence. A large Victorian, red brick, with a porch that wraps around the front of the house, it was built in a time before air-conditioning when families sat outside and drank lemonade and fanned themselves to keep cool. The ceilings are high, the windows tall, and over the front door is a stained glass fan light that spilled dollops of light on the wood floor every afternoon. The silence and peace of the place suited my mother. In a house like this, she once said, you don't rush. So slow down, please. If the house spoke, it was with her voice.

After the funeral the days passed slowly. Most of my time was spent throwing out casseroles left by well meaning neighbors. I often found myself standing in the front room at the large main window, looking out across the porch at my car parked by the curb. To park in back, off the alley by the door would have meant I was moving in. Looking at the car out in the street reassured me, let me know I was just visiting. I love that car, love to drive, and I was brooding about leaving when Luce walked in from the kitchen.

Of my three aunts, she seemed most different, most herself. She has the basic Hudson build: 5' 7", not lean but not in the neighborhood of plump either. Luce always moves with the confidence of good health and has the grace of a much younger woman. You'd never know she's seventy. Unlike her sisters, Luce wears her silver-blond hair short, an inverted bob with longer pieces of hair in front that tended to waviness. It makes her look both sleek and playful. When she tosses her head to make a point, her hair always goes back to where it belongs. Luce likes to wear a small, colorful scarf around her neck that can be tied up to keep her hair back. The woman is groomed!

I grew up being curious about her and felt she was curious about me. That, too, was something I thought about as we sat together. Wondered. Mutual regard deepened into a closeness that still means a great deal to both of us, though we'd rather be bludgeoned than talk about it. My eyes were practically closed when Luce cleared her throat. Just get it out, Luce.

"Now, Lyle," Luce began, in a voice as quiet as if she were speaking to herself. "I want you to know I have no expectations. You take time, decide what it is you want to do." With the house, she meant. Oh, God, the house.

"And you can do that pretty much anywhere you want, go back West—" My aunt did not like the words *California* or *San Francisco*. Refused to say them. It's that word-aversion thing I mentioned earlier. "—or take some time in Mexico, whatever. That's OK. But I want you to know, and I'm sure you do, that this house is yours and always will be. I'm going to look after the house, pay bills, sort things out at the shop, and help with the legalities of your mother's estate. I have talked to the girls—" she referred to Lenore and Loretta, Louise's twin sisters "—and they are fine. Louise's will was clear on what she left to them, and they're happy, if that's the word for it. Lenore was pretty broken up; she thought she'd be the one to leave stuff to Lou."

This was a pretty long speech for Luce. She was not much on lengthy pronouncements. At this point, she stopped speaking. I suppose she was full of feeling for her sisters, the living and the dead. She cleared her throat and continued.

"So, there is no need right now to go through closets, attics, cedar chests, you know—stuff in the house, generally. Nor the shop, either." Mom left me the shop, too. A bridal shop, for God's sake! What was she thinking?

"I'm going to stick around, as I said. My place is fifteen minutes away. We can talk things over whenever you want."

"Luce, I..." My voice got husky. "I do want to leave, you're right. But I just can't decide. It makes no sense, you know?" I walked over from the window and sat down, hands clenched. "They don't *know*? They don't know what killed her? No apparent cause? She was a healthy 72 –year- old woman! How could she just die? No flu, no stroke, no heart attack? Just die?" By then I knew the details. Luce had found Lou lying peacefully in her bed. But is still made no sense to me. I set my jaw and turned around. "I don't think I'll be leaving just yet."

My aunt regarded me with her sharp, gray-green eyes, smiling at me with them. "So stay." The words hung there. "I'll take Lou's room for the time being, and you can keep yours." Luce lived in her own house across town, but was offering moral support that I needed just then.

My room is not really *my* room, but it is the one I take when I visit Louise. Visited.

"Good. That's settled, then." We moved to the kitchen for tea. Earl Gray, raw sugar, two percent milk. We sat at Louise's table and stared at the teapot, waiting for it to steep.

"About Glory," Luce began.

My eyes widened in disbelief, the sudden realization that I had been set up, *bushwhacked* by my aunt.

Again. If I hadn't been so pissed off, I might have smiled at her technique.

"No! No Way!"

"There was no provision in the will, you know. I suspect Louise expected to outlive her." This said quietly while pouring our tea with a delicate, opinionated hand.

I stood up, slammed over to the wall between the back window and the fridge and beat my forehead rhythmically against the wallpaper. "No, no, no, no, no!" It wasn't that I hated the dog, exactly. But she set my teeth on edge. A purebred, small-boned, Smooth-haired Fox Terrier, white with black eyes that are full of fire and black, goofy ears, Glory is tightly wound. Affectionate, yes. Obedient, for three seconds. She barks and runs at everything that moves, passers-by, squirrels and birds, wind, rain. She's been known to climb trees. The damn dog erupts without warning and always makes me jump. I saw myself rapidly disintegrating into a perpetual nervous state with the beast in the house. Hell, my training in the self-control of Aikido, a martial art specializing in higher awareness—not to mention the years of dedication to working out—counted for zip in the face of one small dog. I groaned.

Luce, oddly, didn't seem to hear. Maybe my aunt was going deaf.

"Carlyle. Come and drink your tea before it gets cold." The full name an indication of her impatience with my head-banging. "Sit." I sat. "Glory is sweet natured. That dog loves you. Surely, at least while you are here you can look after her. No need for histrionics."

"OK. OK. Don't go judgmental on me. I apologize. It's just...she doesn't listen to me the way she listens to you." Luce met my wheedling tone with a knowing silence. A direct stare over the mug.

"She...she..." I raked a hand through my hair, at a loss. I did not want to reveal the true source of my resistance to the dog. I released a breath, giving in to my vanity and not willing to explain myself picked up the mug, drank my tea, and looked out the window at Luce's yellow Chevy truck, an unexpected burst of color against the bright snow and bare trees, vintage 1965. February in Kansas. Oh, joy.

A few days later, having successfully postponed a visit from my Aunt Lenore and Aunt Loretta who were increasingly insistent about stopping by, cheering me up, and inundating me with yet more casseroles, I was driving around town, re-orienting myself to streets and neighborhoods. I have lived in so many places that city streets superimpose themselves. I take a left turn that worked in Denver, for example, that gets me nowhere here in Lawrence. Unlike some men I have known, I have no compass, no GPS device lodged in the cerebral cortex or wherever the hell they keep it.

I took the small dog with me. She, too, was suffering from cabin fever. The relentless cold kept her indoors when her natural inclination was "Out." As the day was a brittle 17 degrees, I popped her into the sweater Louise had knit for her, and warmed the Infiniti's passenger seat for her before we took off. So, maybe I liked her a little.

Lawrence is a picturesque little place. Reminds me of Boulder thirty years ago. Even in the gray of late winter, it held a quiet charm. In the middle of the day the students were back in class and off the streets, so I did not have to pray at intersections. Life was good. I was close to smiling. The dog sat contentedly in her sweater, looking around. The woman at the drive-in window at the bank sent her a dog biscuit along with

my receipt, and Glory ate it daintily, leaving not a
crumb.

On our way back from a visit to Clinton Lake, a
quick drive by because of the cold, we parked at a place
I know overlooking the lake which was on its way to
freezing over. I took keen pleasure in the immensity of
the sky, the infinite shades of gray in tune with my desire not to think. Sometimes there are bald eagles here
at this time of year. Not today. The world felt empty of
people, as if they had simply stepped off the planet, had
driven away into another dimension. For a moment the
world was empty of everyone except me and this small
dog. There were no funerals, no mysterious old lady
deaths, no well meaning aunts to wrangle me into staying. OK. Enough of that, Lyle. Back to town. Time to
face your life. Yeah, right.

Glory turned her head and looked right at me, as if
she could hear the lectures I give myself, and the inevi-
table, surly skepticism in reply.

"You're right," I said to her. "Time to go."

2

I took Wakarusa north, checking out the new strip malls, office parks, banks. This town has more banks than any place I've seen. The bankers themselves seem sheepish about it. Signs announcing new construction say, "Another bank???" Anticipating incredulity in the local population. I'd count them, but it would just be upsetting. What do banks *do*, anyway?

By the time we got to Kasold and Sixth, I remembered the empty refrigerator back at the house. Luce never ate very much and was not particular about food. I love food in all its variety, and we were getting low on basics. Crossing the intersection, I turned the heat way up so the dog would not freeze while I was in the store. I pulled into the Sun Ripe grocery store and parked where Glory could see the entrance to the store. She goes ballistic if she can't keep track of me.

The young woman at the register, "Ashley" her tag said, caught my attention with her eye shadow. Right eye silvery bluish, left eye pink-shaded. Pretty cool.

Pale skin, long dark hair. A co-ed, not too proud to work at Sun Ripe. You go, I smiled to myself. Love to see the Protestant work ethic in action.

There were two people in front of me, a woman paid with a check while I panicked, wondering if they still didn't take credit cards for groceries in Kansas. Ashley looked at the woman's drivers license and started in on her. I couldn't believe it.

"Arkansas!" She pronounced it 'ARK-n-SAW', drawing out the syllables, shooting my moment of admiration right out the window. "I hear people there are weird, marry their cousins and such? I never..." The girl was setting up for a rant, so I cleared my throat theatrically, jerking a thumb over my shoulder at the few benighted souls behind me.

The woman grabbed her ID and her groceries and fled the store. I was working myself up to ask Ashley if she wanted to be the next duct tape employee of the week when the man in front of me spoke first.

"You know, some people think that it's Kansans that are weird." He spoke gently, momentarily blinding Ashley and me with a smile that could melt feet.

"Kansas?" Ashley blinked. "Credit or debit? What d' you mean?" She practically gift-wrapped his groceries in plastic bags.

I looked over enviously at people easing through the automated check out stations and sighed one of those my-eyes-are-rolling-back-in-my-head sighs.

"Some people think it's weird that Kansans are debating whether evolution should be taught in schools." Patience in the face of idiocy. Priceless.

"Nuh uh. No sir. You teach that ev'lution to kids and you're going straight to hell." She handed him the groceries and took a step back in case he decided to burst into flames. The nice man shook his head and wisely moved away.

People think California is strange? Get me out of here!

I loaded up my groceries and treats and got through check out pretty quickly, avoiding eye contact with Ashley, my conversation consisting of "Credit."

At the car, I beeped the door locks and popped the trunk. "Never wrestle with a pig," I muttered to myself, "You just get dirty, and the pig likes it." I placed the first of three bags in the trunk. The stupid purse I'd worn to the funeral was hanging on my left arm. It tangled and got in my way. I made a mental note to switch back to my satchel as soon as I got back to the house. Shaking my head over the uselessness of purses, I stuck it in the child seat part of the grocery cart and reached for the next sack. They are *sacks* in Kansas, not *bags*.

Placing the bag in the trunk, I heard the dog barking maniacally. There was motion behind me. I turned to see that my purse had been snatched from the cart.

Instinctively pivoting on one foot, I kicked off my Merrells and sprinted after the hooded figure who dashed across the icy lot. I noted briefly that we were the only two people out there. His mistake was not looking back. He assumed because of my hair I'd flail my hands helplessly and call for help. He was Wrong.

I was so pissed off I could not feel the cold. I pushed my stride into high gear and whipped after him. As luck would have it, the idiot thief was not watching his feet and he caught a patch of ice and started to skid. The time it took him to right himself was the moment I needed to come up behind him. Silently, because of my shoeless feet.

The kid was totally unprepared when I charged him and pushed; just "encouraged" his momentum, shall we say. He flew, face down onto the pavement and I leapt on top of him as if he were a sleigh, so that his body and down jacket completely broke my fall. Totally cool.

He completely lost his breath, and I reached up with my left hand and drew his arm behind his back in a tight wrist lock, a technique learned from studying Aikido. I'm sure my old sensei would have had a few choice words about my lack of harmony, but I was definitely in the moment. I tightened the torque to see if the kid was paying attention.

"Hey!" Definitely paying attention.

"Turn your head!" I shouted.

"Nggh?"

"Turn your head, asshole! Or your face goes first!"

Getting the point, the kid turned his face to the left. I dragged off his knit cap, grabbed a fistful of lank hair, lifted his head and knocked it firmly into the pavement, one, two, three times.

"Do" (slam), "Not" (slam), Fuck with me! (slam)

"Ow! Hey, hey, hey! (whining and sniveling) That hurts!"

"No, Dickhead. THIS hurts." I bashed his head down and leaned on it, humming on adrenaline. He wasn't bleeding much, just a few scratches, really, so I shifted my attention to his wrist, tightening my grip and lowering my voice to whisper at the back of his head.

"You move, you even twitch, I will break it. Get me?"

The kid nodded.

"Name! What's your name?" No answer. I added a little torque.

"No, Stop!" He was close to shrieking.

"Dumbass." I smacked his greasy head with my free hand and patted his sides. I found the wallet in his right rear pocket. Predictable. I raised myself and placed my knee in the small of his back, making him work for air. Flipped the wallet open.

"Well, Bartholomew Rodriguez, you just made a big mistake. What shall I do with you?" It was a statement, not a question. He gave it up, totally crying now, snot on the pavement. We were both out of breath.

"Tell you what, buddy. I now have your name and address. You are what, seventeen? You mess with me or anyone else like this again? I'm showing up at your house on—" checking his ID again, "—532 Kentucky, apartment One, and I will rip your fucking ears off! Right?"

The boy nodded.

"I'm getting up now. When I stand, you will get up and run, and you will keep running until I can no longer see you."

I stood up, ready to grab his jacket and throw him to the pavement again. Wanted him to do something stupid to give me an excuse, but off he went.

I picked up my purse and noted the scratches on the leather from the fall. The kid had no time to get into it, but I checked anyway then started back to the car, eyes on the ground. I began to shake, not from the cold. A voice said something about not alarming me, and a hand tentatively took my left elbow, supporting my arm. I jumped about ten feet.

"Whoa, there. It's OK. I'm friendly."

Whoa? Friendly? Unable to speak, teeth clenched, and shaking with adrenaline overload, I looked...up. The man was tall. I didn't take in much else. The shaking was taking up my attention and all of my will. It was total, every part of me. Apparently ears and toes can shake. Clearly, my elbows could as well because the support increased.

"Let's go inside and sit you down." He placed the

Merrells in front of my feet, not letting go of my arm. Wordlessly, I stepped into my shoes and moved forward, numbly. I looked toward the car. The trunk was closed. Glory was standing at the window fogging the glass, pointing at me like a knife. I stopped and looked at her.

"Dog's OK, ma'am. He'll be fine."

"She," I said. "Thanks." I took his arm, walked into the grocery store watching my feel carefully, impressed that they could do such a good job without me.

"Coffee?" It was the man from the check out line, the guy who attempted to reason with dreadful Ashley. He handed me into a cane backed chair at the Starbucks concession and placed his olive drab jacket on the back of a chair facing mine, unwrapping his scarf. I regarded his gloves, brown leather, taking up space on the small table. A lot of space.

"Tea. Please." I glanced at his face. "Earl Gray." Nice face. Longish. Firm jaw. Eyes, brown; moustache, brown; hair, also brown. Nice combination. Age? No idea. A grown up, that's all that matters.

"Right back." The Stetson lands on top of the gloves. He walked over to the coffee bar.

My trembling subsided a bit. Familiar with adrenaline intoxication, I concentrated on my breath. Too soon to think. Let it ride.

"Didn't know they had tea. She said to let it steep a minute or two." Two packets of raw sugar appear beside my cup. How did he know?

"Anything else?"

"Milk, please. Two per cent." I put my hands around the cup. Breathe in, breathe out. Slowly. Willing the tremors to stop.

The man sat down, crossed one lean leg over the other, set the Stetson on his knee. Looked like a habit to me. He sat back in his tiny chair, running his eyes over passers by, looking up aisles of the store, giving me time to calm down. Drank his coffee. I realized he was the same man from the checkout.

I ripped open the sugars and added them to the tea. Pouring milk, I realized that I had the whole thermos. I looked at him seriously. "Won't other people need this?" I was definitely liking what I saw. Brown hair, touch of silver here and there, not too short, sort of rippled; tawny-brown eyes, dark brows; solid shoulders; fit. Too bad about the moustache. In response to my question, his eyes do that wrinkly thing that looks so good on men. Death to women, though.

"They'll figure it out."

Lord, help me. He has the Voice. You know what I mean, Lord. That clear, dark from the throat and chest of a man voice. As my eyes misted over, I realized that I had not registered the voice before, hadn't heard a word, like I just tuned in. *Ms. Hudson is back in the building.*

I sat up and smiled at him, spontaneously giving him the full wattage. I am amused, enjoying the moment, suddenly at ease. Defender of purses, Bludgeoner of thugs and hooligans, perfectly natural. He sat back abruptly, surprised into smiling back, brows raised in appreciation.

"Guess you're feeling more yourself." A statement, not a question.

"Yes, I am." More smiles. I took a lengthy draft of the tea. Lowering the cup to the table, I saw that some of my hair had fallen into the cup and now hung wetly down the side of my face. Sexy. Good move, Hudson. Shaking my head, I wiped the hair off my face with one hand, reaching back with the other to unclip my hair and reattach the barrette to keep the whole mass in place. Shiny and light, it looks great when it's not sticky and wet and stuck to my face.

The nameless Samaritan studied me. When our eyes met they held for a moment. Two people taking stock.

"Black, right?" I offered, referring to the coffee.

"Quite an impressive display out there, ma'am," he said. "I don't think I have seen anything quite like it." He's serious. His eyes took inventory: shoes, hair, face.

"Don't be fooled by the hair, the gray is premature. Runs in the family. I'm Lyle Hudson. Thanks for the tea. It's great." Ever a way with words, Lyle. Eloquent as always. I held out my hand, which no longer shook. It was swallowed up, gently, in one of the most beautiful hands I 'd ever seen. Long fingers. Large lapis and silver ring. Probably Zuni, the ring.

"MacDonald George," he said. Again, the intent, steady gaze. "I wasn't thinking about the hair. You had him down and pinned before I could get a start in your direction. At one point, I thought that boy was going to get hurt."

"Yeah. He's got a few bumps and scratches. Enough to make him think about it." I paused and shook my head. "You don't think we'll have to call the police, do you? In case the kid reports me for assault and battery?" The thought made us both laugh.

"If he does, you give me a call." MacDonald George pulled out a card and handed it to me. A detective? "I'm a reliable witness."

I turned over the small card thoughtfully.

"I was so angry, so damn mad." The anger washed back over me, and I raised my left hand to my face, fingers at the hairline, thumb below my ear where it meets the jaw, holding my head. Before I knew it, tears slid down my face.

MacDonald said, handing me a napkin, "It's shock. You're OK."

"I *know* it's shock!" I snapped. "Got it. This..." I waved my hand at the tears, "has nothing to do with that..." I took a breath, blew my nose. "It's complicated." I paused. "Got to rescue my dog. Sorry." I started fumbling with my jacket and knocked over the remains of the tea. "Shit!" I cut my eyes to the man just in time to see him throw back his head and laugh out loud.

"Lady, you are something else," shaking his head. "That boy doesn't know how lucky he is."

I sat back down, briefly. "I have to tell you, I'm not like this." Lie. "I'm not a violent person, nor so...foul-mouthed." Lie. Oh, well.

"Hey, Lyle," Oh, man, my name sounds nice. "You're entitled. That punk was trying to rob you, right? Right. He had it coming, but part of me can't help pitying him." Another slow, blinding, smile.

"Here, let me walk you back to your car. The dog's fine."

He mopped up the table, threw the debris away. I tried to remember how to button up my jacket, loop my scarf without strangling myself. Pull the gloves from my pockets, retrieve my keys. MacDonald George shrugged into his winter stuff, placed the Stetson on his head and looked at me as I stood there staring at my keys as if they were a foreign object or maybe magic beans. Our eyes meet again. I'm starting to like this eye thing, no words to mess it up. Smile again. Less wattage but warm. Nice and warm. Careful, girl.

We walked slowly. He moved close by my side but not hovering. Hey! Maybe he thinks I can walk on my own two feet. How cool is that?

Glory had shaken off the towel I put on the seat in a

futile attempt to prevent the flurry of short white hair that flies around like snow and was standing at the driver's side window in all her (I can't help myself) glory.

"What is that?" MacDonald asked, a tone of wonder creeping into his voice.

"A dog?" I'm trying to forestall his questions and grasping desperately for straws.

He waited patiently, his eyes on the dog.

"It. Is a sweater. My mother knit the dog a sweater. It's too cold out. The dog has to wear it." Glory wagged her tail so hard the garment in question slipped half off one shoulder.

"I'll be damned. I thought it was a hairball."

I regarded the mustardy sweater with its flecks of red and green. It *did* look like a hairball! I whooped and laughed, too. One or two people brave enough to face the cold were hurrying to get into the store. They glanced our way and kept moving. Clearly, we were nut cases.

I righted myself, put my hand on my left hip and took a breath. "Nice boots." They just caught my eye. Polished. Soft. The color of tobacco or mahogany. Cowboy boots. Omigod. Kansas!

"Thank you, Ma'am." A nod at my car. "Nice vehicle." Appreciation sitting right next to a whole slew of questions. How do I afford a customized, silver G35? How old *are* you? Did I just see you chase that kid down and beat the snot out of him? The questions hung in the air as he studied me. This studying thing feels not too bad, I thought. I studied him back. MacDonald removed his glove and held out his hand.

"A pleasure to meet you, Lyle."

"Me, too, MacDonald." Gloves off, hand in hand. Oh, yes. This is nice. "See you." Be strong. Do *not* give in and blurt something out.

"I hope so." He stepped back as I slipped into the car, immediately slathered by the dog. The man knocked on the window, which I rolled down enough so the dog didn't escape.

"I have to ask," MacDonald says. "What's his name?" Pointing to the dog.

"Hers," I say. "I call her C."

"Sea?"

"No, C, as in ABC, only C is her first initial." There is no way in hell I am telling this gorgeous man the dog's name. Shoot me.

"Ah. C as in...?"

"As in CLD." I am giving him as little as possible. But We're both smiling like idiots anyway, enjoying a good flirt. "Which means Creepy Little Dog. *Crazy* if she is being good." We both started to giggle again. He waved me away and stepped back, shaking his head and laughing.

I was grinning like a fool, Glory blissfully happy as her leather seat warmed up to its preferred setting. As I pulled away, I waved briefly. Checking the rearview, I saw the man looking at the license plate. Memorizing the license plate. The dog. I smiled all the way home.

3

For a while, my life in Lawrence continued to consist of avoidance maneuvers—email, cell phone arrangements and communications with San Francisco, seeing to continuity and order in my absence, however long that would be. I asked my neighbor there, Charles, to check that mail was forwarded, plants watered and fish fed. He loved the opportunity to lounge around in my flat up on Twin Peaks with its Ansel Adams view of the city. He had the identical view, but he said that getting away from Jerome once and a while made him feel like he was a single girl again.

I adore Charles. He adores me, despite my disregard for house work and my hopelessly traditional sexuality. We share so many interests: music (jazz female vocalists, nouveau folk, random spates of Jimi Hendricks and Talking Heads), food (the cooking and insobriety thereof), art (so much to love!), architecture, computers, literature (how many people do you know actually *read*?) He loves my hair, which languishes without his attention.

"Some women are at their best *groomed*, my darling, and *you* are one of them. That silver framing your face? Divine. The tawny and chestnut glimmers? You can't *pay* for that effect. Mesmerizing. Men just want to *touch* it, don't they? Yes, they dooo."

When Charles is around (*not* "Charles," sweetie. Call me Chas), I feel awesome, drop-dead gorgeous. He listens well, completely focused on what I say, and is not too hard on the eyes himself. Fit, thirty-something, honey blond hair, unbelievably green eyes. Very particular about clothes. We share that interest, too. Listening to his voice on the phone or reading his emails, I can hear every tasteful, well bred inflection. When we cook together, we get into these heated arguments over words that can get out of hand.

"Over here, Lyle. Right now. Step away from the knives. Let's just take a breath, shall we, and step out and survey our kingdom together." Pause. "Of course, that would make *you* the king, sweetie."

If there is a damp, impenetrable fog hanging over the city, we adjourn to the fireplace and sit a tad stiffly until the tension relaxes, rather like two cats.

"Sometimes, I just hate you, Chas."

"I know darling," stroking my hair down over my shoulder and back, "I hate you too. More wine?"

I missed him. Hiding out in Louise's house, I felt isolated, out of touch with reality. Not that San Francisco is the real world, but it works for me. Kansas felt cold, like outer space, casseroles included.

The morning of the day we found the gun, I awoke to a spate of crank phone calls. In response to my hello, I heard muttering, unintelligible, dark words followed by a click. Calls two and three were treated to my crank-specific "Asshole!" response, and then I just left the phone off the hook. Mental note: ignore house phone. I'd much rather deal with the assholes I know. After a grumpy breakfast, I decided to start sorting through books, deciding what to throw away. I sat on the floor of the library, packing books that would never be read again, mysteries and fantasy on tapes that would not be listened to again, into boxes and paper bags to be dropped off at The Book Trader, a shop that sells used books and will give you store credit or cash for the ones they want.

The top floor of the house, an area inhabited by servants in the last century, I now claimed as my own, but the library was my favorite room, more than the kitchen even, which strikes me as odd. It is off to the right of the front door as you enter this huge old Victorian, to the right of the mahogany staircase leading to the second floor. It has its own fireplace, a dark, cavernous affair with a black enamel mantel. The ceilings are high, the paneled walls are lined with bookcases, and a screened in porch looks out at the garden. It sounds gothic, but it's not. During the day, the rooms fill with light. Heavy green drapes shut out the drafts, and there is a brown leather couch and two worn leather chairs, regulation Hudson size, draped with warm throws and pillows. A matching leather ottoman on which to prop feet, or in this case, boxes of books, sits in front of the couch.

One entire case of shelves that had been devoted to my mother's paperbacks was almost empty. I sat on the floor, dark wood overlaid with small Persian rugs, surrounded by stacks of books, arranged according to size. Glory was curled in a corner of the couch anxiously watching me, nose tucked under one skinny leg. She's a slender dog. If it weren't for the pedigree, I'd swear there's a bit of whippet mixed in; she has a lithe appearance. Sitting, for this dog, always involves doing something about those legs. They get in the way of her image of herself as a lapdog.

Loretta gave Louise a pretty hard time when she came home with the puppy.

"If I'd known you were lonely, Lou, I'd a set you up with one a Vern's friends! Why didn't ya just go to the Humane Society, plenty of sorry-assed dog flesh *there*. Just look at the puny thing, will you." Even Lenore was outraged that a puppy that small could cost so much. I heard after the fact.

All Louise would say on the subject was that she liked the dog's smile. Then she smiled, too. "That's all there is to it, girls. And by the way, her name is Glory."

Leaning back against the smooth leather of the couch, I picked random books, looking for some kind of sign, wondering when they had last been read, what kind of pleasure or message my mother had taken from them. I stacked them by size, moving the smaller books with one hand, like poker chips.

"I'll see your John Le Carré, and I'll raise you two Ngaio Marsh." I looked up at the partially empty bookcase next to the fireplace. Strange that she would give these old books pride of place, I thought.

I stood up, brushed my dusty hands on the seat of my pants, and walked over to see what else was there. Ursula K. LeGuin. Madeleine L'Engle. Books I'd loved that she had held on to.

"You sentimental woman," I said to her, shaking my head. The last book on that shelf was *A Wrinkle In Time*. Taking it down, I saw another book stuck beside it, hidden by the beveled edge of the case. Dark blue, cloth binding. No title.

Out of curiosity, I opened it, looking for a title page.

What I found was my mother's handwriting and a page of dates from the 1980's. A diary? I flipped a few pages until I came to a page of words instead of accounts and started to read.

I don't know what to do about Ann, Louise wrote. *She's trying to pull me deeper and deeper into her problems. Where do I go with this? Her stories haunt me. Yesterday she told me that Matt wanted the house, threatened to take it from her whether she liked it or not.. I told her it was worth it if it meant she would be rid of him. Not even listening to me, she told me about her and Little Matt the night she got the call. I'm writing it down just as she told it to me. Maybe once I see it in written out, I'll be able to figure out what she's up to, get the hell out of the way before she explodes.*

She would do anything for her boy. Anything. He was the world to her.

It was the way she said those last words, Louise wrote, *that sent a chill through me. "He's my world, Lou." That woman is capable of anything.*

I still held the book, looking off at a world no longer there, when Luce stepped in the room, concern written clearly on her face. The green silk scarf at her neck brought out the green of Luce's bright eyes.

"Lyle? I wasn't sure anybody was home. Not even Glory." At the sound of her name, the dog looked up, gave a half-hearted wag of her tail, but did not move from the couch to greet Luce.

"And what have you done to Glory? She's not dead, is she?" Luce lifted a box of books from the ottoman and sat directly in front of me, folding her hands on her lap.

"I'm fine, I guess. Here, read this, Luce. Tell me what you think." I handed over the blue diary and waited.

Luce read the pages intently, brushing a wisp of

hair behind her ear. I gazed at her bare feet. Luce always kicked her shoes off, no matter what time of year. Her feet looked younger than I felt.

"My. . ." Luce whispered, looking at me with wide eyes.

"Who is she talking about?"

"Well...I'm not sure. Let me read on a few pages and I'll let you know."

"No way. I found it! But I *will* let you read it with me," I promised.

"Lou had a lot of friends. There was a rumor that somebody had killed her husband after he divorced her, but was her name Ann? Damned if *I* know!" She laughed at me over her reading glasses. I closed the small book and sighed.

"Old. I feel old for the first time in my life. No, maybe the second." I smiled up at her, if you could call it a smile.

"Honey, that's to be expected. Same thing happened to us when our Mama died. You know what I think? I think you need to get out of here; you're not in purdah, you know. No one is making you stay in the house." Luce was big on fresh air and the outdoors, no matter what the weather.

"Yeah, and look what happened last time!" I had told her about my encounter with idiot Bartholomew and meeting MacDonald George.

"Pretty lame as excuses go," she said, standing up. "Here. Let's box up these books right in front of you and put them in my truck. Come to the shop with me and we'll drop 'em off afterward, maybe go get a cup of coffee or check out that new tea place. I have not been in yet, and I would like to see what it's like."

Luce bustled about, piling books into the box in front of me, her voice playful and full of life. She moved about gracefully in her bare feet, completely at home in the moment, not giving in to my emotional weather map. In spite of myself, I perked up. Ever since I was kid, when Luce got to doing something, I wanted to do it too. Without thinking, I started picking up books, jumbling a bunch of them into a paper bag.

Glory jumped down from the couch, trotted over, and stuck her nose in the bag just as I was putting in some books. The ones still in my hands bounced off her nose and fanned out onto the floor. Picking them up again, I noticed an edge of paper in one of the books and pulled it out, intending to toss it in the trash.

"What's that, Lyle?" Luce asked. Never missed a trick, that woman.

"A playing card?" I looked at the yellowing Ace of Spades in my hand.

"I can see that, my dear. There's writing on it. What does it say? It might be something Lou wrote. If so, I'd like to see it, wouldn't you?" Her box was packed, flaps tucked in. She looked at me expectantly. The small scarf had moved up from her neck to tie back her hair, so that the loose green tips resembled Glory's ears. The dog and the woman both cocked their heads at me.

"Don't do anything stupid."

"I beg your pardon?"

"That's what it says. The handwriting is not hers." I handed over the card and shrugged.

"Looks like it's been folded. There's a crease right through the middle," Luce said, examining the card closely.

"It's a threat, Luce. Or was. Ace of Spades. Classic." Creepy-classic I thought. "It's a good thing the card looks ancient. Otherwise, I'd be alarmed."

"That's just an old superstition!"

"The hell it is. Hand it over. We'll stick it in the diary for now." I fell silent, thinking again that my mother's death had no tangible explanation. Reading my mind, Luce broke in on my thoughts.

"It's interesting, like a puzzle, don't you think? The note, the mysterious Ace! Who knows what else we'll find." We regarded each other silently, our past in our eyes, memories of Louise, of each other. Luce was side-lit by morning sun, her sandy, dappled hair shining, eyes smiling over the top of her glasses. I have never known anyone, any woman, so completely there. The phone rang. Damn. I must have hung it up out of habit on a visit to the kitchen. I shot a dirty look in the direction of the phone and waved Luce off as she moved to-ward it.

"Crank calls. Don't bother."

"What if it's Lenore and Loretta?" I hadn't thought of that. I had been avoiding everyone but Luce. It would make sense that my aunts were tracking me down. I shrugged, and Luce lunged at the phone.

"No one there," she said, replacing the receiver.

"Heavy breathing?"

"Just a dial tone." She looked at me. "Well? What do you think?"

"About the crank?"

"No, the journal! If that was your aunts, they'll call back. Or show up and tie you to a chair, make you eat a casserole." Her grin had an evil edge to it. The L&L's—family short hand for Loretta and Lenore—were entirely capable of manhandling relatives who did not bend to their collective will. I shuddered briefly and returned to the matter at hand, the Ace of Spades. Luce broke in on my thoughts.

"Let's go down to the shop and see if we can find something else!"

"Luce? Let's not. You know how I feel about the

shop."

"Pish tush. Don't be difficult. Get your coat and let's go. Now!"

"The dog stays here, Luce," I demanded.

"Of course. What a ridiculous idea, a dog in a bridal shop. Please." Having the last word always makes a Hudson woman feel good. Luce felt good. Off we went, leaving Glory to her own devices.

Hyacinth, Louise's shop, sits at the south end of Massachusetts Street, near the park. On one side is an audiophile shop and a bar; on the other is "Park Place," a gem and bead shop that actually does a fair bit of business. Luce parked the truck in back, off the alley, climbed out without a word, preferring not to notice that I was stalling, still sitting in the truck. It is an excellent truck, much coveted by me and a population of adolescent boys. Vintage Chevy, V8 engine, lemon yellow, original leather upholstery. She has had it forever and swears we will have to bury her in it. An idea that is not as amusing to me as it once was.

Watching Luce unlock the backdoor and turn off the store alarm, I sighed heavily, exited the truck, and joined her at the back of the shop.

Putting her keys in her pocket, unbuttoning her jacket, Luce moved toward the front of the shop, saying back over her shoulder, "Lyle, don't fuss. We're here to pick up the mail, check phone messages, and just see what's what."

"Fine," I called after her, feeling a habitual mulishness raise its head. I hated the place. Wedding dresses were lies on hangers, as far as I was concerned, and the shop was designed to make you love the lie.

I had to admit that it was pleasant, attractive, even. Louise had made it inviting and intimate. The back of the bridal shop was separated from the front by a pair of French doors that were usually left open to extend the sense of space. Back where I stood were a work table with a computer, a counter with a stool, filing cabinets, and a small fridge, above which rose shelves of old ledgers, large bobbins of lace trimming and other notions.

In the front is the long, airy space for customers. The place was filled with light from the tall front window. The walls were brick, a dusty rose color that complemented the blinding whiteness of the merchandise. Track lights illuminated dresses singled out for display, the Queen Anne table Louise used for her conversation/register area, and two large black and white framed photos of brides in traditional dress.

There were comfortable chairs pulled up to the table and another by the front window with a basket of magazines for friends of the bride or the odd, uncomfortable male who might find himself trapped in hostile territory. It was lovely. Elegant and understated. It gives me the creeps. My usual response is to break out in hives. Even now, the shop closed, with not a bride in sight, I felt myself drawing short, shallow breaths.

"Lyle!" Luce came back with a handful of envelopes from the front door, handing them off to me as she headed back toward the phone. "Sort through these, will you?"

I knew the drill: bills in one pile, customer communication in another, crap in the trash basket. Anything that I couldn't figure out went in the customer communication pile. It was one of the first tasks I learned back when Louise opened her store. I smiled at the recollection of adolescent sullenness.

Two bills, I tossed the rest. Luce was still listening to messages, so I moved to the chair by the front window and looked out at the park.

The gazebo where the city band plays in the summer was deserted, too cold for teenagers to sit and smoke, but warm enough for the homeless to drift through. At this time of day, they were probably down at 10th and Vermont waiting for the soup kitchen to open for lunch. My thoughts caught on nothing in particular and just drifted.

Behind me, I heard Luce start talking to herself as she climbed up on a step stool to get at the older files and ledgers. Curious, I moved to the back of the store and leaned against one of the French doors to watch her ratch around. The computer had been turned on and the tropical fish on Louise's screen saver were swimming around, reminding me of my apartment in San Francisco

"Might as well be on Mars," I muttered. Whether I meant SF or Kansas was unclear.

I sat down in Lou's chair and shuffled through a few loose papers. To the right of the desk, an antique pie rack was mounted on the wall. Its function as a filing system made obsolete by the computer, it was now a dusty object, a reminder of an earlier era.

The pie rack's dark niches attracted my curiosity and I started poking around, noting that Luce had a couple of stacks of ledgers off the shelves and ready to sort. I stuck my hand in the lower right slot, expecting to find a button box or an old pin cushion. What I found was a gun. Palm-sized, snub-nosed .38, Smith & Wesson logo clearly printed near the rosewood grip. A classic. Not so dusty, either.

"Hey, Luce?" I turned and found my aunt standing behind me, ledgers in hand.

"Oh, my." She put the books down on the desk and stared at the gun. It did not answer any questions for us.

What it did was raise the ante,

"Why would Lou need a gun?" Luce's eyes didn't blink.

My mind started buzzing, making unpleasant connections—Lou's death, the crank calls, the gun. I was getting angry and I wanted answers. Fast.

Back at the house, I put the revolver on the table while Luce pulled out one of the casseroles from the groaning fridge—an edible one. An L&L special turkey, artichoke and cheese thing. Microwaveable and great on toast. I let Glory out the back door and watched her zoom around the yard. The day was warm, so I grabbed a tennis ball to throw and went down the back steps. There was a shuffling and mumbling in the alleyway on the other side of the warped and faded wooden fence, some passer by, possibly a homeless person, I thought. Not uncommon in this part of town.

Uncommon enough for Glory. If she can hear it or see it or imagine it's there, she can bark at it. Her T-shirt in the book of life reads: "I bark therefore I am." Slamming herself against the aging fence, she knocked a slat loose and broke it, which loosened the slats on either side of it. I jumped down the back steps, trying to catch her, but was too late. She had slipped through the small opening and disappeared, howling her head off. Shit.

Cursing the dog, I opened the gate to the alley, hearing a commotion and barking off to my right. Cannot be avoided. Like Fate.

"GLORY!" God damn that dog. "GLORY!" I called in a futile attempt to catch her attention. "GLORY!"

"Hallelujah!" echoed from a nearby garage, followed by gales of laughter. People love it when that dog escapes. It makes their day, I swear it does.

I ran the length of the alley yelling "GLORY!" and stopped at the sound of cursing behind a battered fence. A small rock flew over the fence and landed at my feet. Furious barking ensued. From over my head? Oh no. I walked over to an old walnut tree, its lower branch leaning over the top of a dilapidated fence. Peering up around the far side of the trunk, I could see Glory's skinny rear end.

"Glory! Come down!" The barking and the cursing abruptly stopped. No movement up in the tree, but the gate in the fence opened and an elderly man with wispy thin hair stuck his head through the opening and glared at me.

"I could have a heart attack, you know!" he accused me.

I stood there looking up at Glory, momentarily stumped, hoping the angry man would not throw any more rocks. His face was pretty red.

Inspired by the tennis ball in my pocket, I took it out and bounced it on the pavement. Responding instantly to the siren call of thwok, thwok, Glory ran down the tree and circled around me, her eyes on the ball.

"I'm so sorry," I apologized to the latest victim. "She is usually not like this."

"The hell she isn't," the man responded. "That dog is a menace! That old lady who owns her is nuts to keep a dog like that! I ought to file a complaint!"

"Too late," I said. "That old lady was my mother. She's dead. What's wrong with you anyway?" Hudsons are expert at turning the tables. Jerk. He had it coming.

"Oh...excuse me, I did not know. Please, accept my condolences."

He seemed genuinely upset, so I let it go. The bouncing ball got Glory home.

The kitchen table was a jumble of ledgers, empty plates, notes, Lou's journal. And the gun. Luce and I kept staring at it, shaking our heads. The gun told us that Louise was not the person we knew, not the quiet woman with a quiet life who died a quiet death. Or if she was, there was one hell of a secret. As far as I knew, my mother was a small town kind of person. The gun did not belong to that world. It was the key to something and I was determined to find out what.

I sifted through the papers in front of me one more time and pulled out the scrap of paper I'd found before we went to the shop. *It will burn you... and a heart full of spite will come to know regret.*

"This is a passage from Anna Akmatova, Luce." Akmatova was a Russian poet who'd lived in a world of torment, deceit and betrayal. "It reads differently now, doesn't it." I placed the piece of paper next to the small revolver on the table. "Who do you think it's for?" I asked, referring to the poetry.

"I can see her feeling regret, maybe. But spite? Not Louise. Looks like she had someone in mind," Luce said thoughtfully. We kept digging.

The ledgers were from the late seventies, early eighties. Lou never did trust computers. No place to put the swatches, she'd complained.

It was slow going for both of us. Luce would look up from a book in her lap, and I would catch her dreaming out the kitchen window, remembering something, thinking private thoughts. I found myself impressed by how dogged my mother was, how determined to make her shop a success once my father walked out of our lives. A bridal shop. Who owns a bridal shop? What was she thinking? The aggravation made me itch. Unconsciously, I scratched an elbow and stared at the pistol.

There was occasional jotting in a margin, a note on the patience of a bride, or her *glow*. Louise believed in glows. Swore she could tell who was going to make it as a married woman or not, despite the demise of her own marriage.

"That child is getting married for the dress," she would say from time to time. Usually she was right. In time, the space of two ledgers, the store caught on. Possibly as much for its ambience as anything else. It was pleasant, Louise never rushed, and she wasn't particularly pushy. She also had taste and an eye for line, what dress would look best on what body. When women took her advice, they were always happy.

Ledger #3 had yellowing swatches of satin stuck between some of the pages, bits of lace or other trim. No changes in handwriting or notes. Nothing jumped off the page. I pushed the book aside and went for one at the bottom of the pile. The time frame looked like the late 80's, a lifetime ago, another world. Ruefully, it occurred to me that she was my age then, or a little younger. Still building that new life.

There were notes reminding Lou to check with Annette, her first bookkeeper/sales assistant. She was having a hard time sticking to her resolution to go with appointments only. I flipped past some messy pages and found a blank page or two. After them the neat figures and accounts started up again. Interesting. I picked up the book and a small velum note card slipped out onto my lap.

"Hey, Luce. Look at this." I held the note up between my first and third fingers, giving it a wave in her direction. She was on the couch in an instant, making Glory give a sleepy grunt.

"Open it."

Dear Mrs. Hudson,
The gown is divine!
Thank you for letting me bring it home
to show Mom who is still not feeling too well
after the surgery.
I will be the most beautiful bride in Kansas!
Many warm regards,
Ann
PS: I will call and find out when is the
best time to bring it back to the shop for my final fitting.

Luce held up the little note card and looked at it. "Seems like every other girls was named Ann then. It was such a long time ago," she sighed.

"The gun is recent, Luce. Mom kept it in her shop. It was there when she died."

4

Monday morning, Luce came over for coffee, a bag of Einstein bagels and a tub of chive cream cheese under one arm. Seeing the bag, I knew something was up. Food was a sure sign of bad news. Not as bad as "How's the Weather" news, but still not good.

Glory dancing in happy circles at her feet, Luce found a plate and unloaded warm bagels that smelled like heaven. Luce seemed unusually cheerful and full of local gossip. Pulling up a chair to the kitchen table, she watched me tear off a piece of bagel ("the Works", my favorite) and feed it to Glory who was showing off.

"So. Luce. What's up?" I asked, deftly slicing the remainder of my bagel and slathering it with way too much cream cheese. I took a bite, regarding her dispassionately while I munched. Bad news conversations are a lot like playing poker.

"I'm going out to Salina for a yoga retreat on Thursday, Lyle, and thought I'd ask you to look after Tetley while I'm gone." Luce was nothing if not direct. She always won the "Put-the-Cards-on-the-Table-Award" when we gave out prizes at family gatherings. It happened in February at Louise's wake. She accepted gracefully with her customary acceptance speech: "You're all drunk." Gotta love her.

"Who's going with you?" I was in no mood to capitulate, not immediately anyway. Luce knew I owed her one. Or forty. Despite my loathing for Devil Cat, I knew I would have to agree. The cards were on the table.

"Oh, just a friend." Luce evaded my eyes and took a long draw of her coffee. Luce is a terrible liar. For Luce, an omission was just a bad lie.

"Which friend?" I asked with an evil little smirk.

"Not that it is any of your business, Lyle, but William has decided he'd like to come along this time. So, I said that's fine, Will, and he said great. Will has an open mind, you know. It's one of the things I like about him, and besides, even if he can't do the exercises, the poses, you know, he will enjoy the peacefulness of it, and..." I'll be damned, Luce flustered! This thing with William is making her nervous!

"Whoa! Stop! Too much information. I think it's great, really."

We looked at each other innocently enough, so I don't know how it started. Maybe it was the vision of William Stillman doing the "Down Dog", "Cobra", or "Sun Salute" stretches at his age. We both cracked up. I tried not to pass cream cheese and bagel through my nose.

From under the table, Glory gave a sudden woof and scrambled to her feet, launching herself at the back door where she bounced off the doorframe, making excited little yips. Her frenzy could only mean one thing. I shot an accusatory look across the table at Luce.

"Did you tell..." Before I could finish the sentence, the door banged open and my aunt Loretta barged through, scooping Glory into her arms with a whoop. "Oh oh." Luce smothered her grin with one hand and ducked her head, as one would at an onslaught of wind or extreme weather.

Loretta's twin sister, my aunt Lenore, followed right behind, peering over Loretta's shoulder with twinkling eyes.

Plopping the dog unceremoniously on the floor, Loretta placed her hands on her hips and boomed at me, "Let's see the gun, girls! Where is it?"

My mother's older sisters, Loretta and Lenore, are less than two years apart. They are often taken for identical twins. They could have been Siamese twins for the amount of time they spent together. They functioned as a single unit. We dealt with them as one would a force of nature, a tornado, say. They cut a wide swathe and there was always a lot of cleaning up to do. No one particularly minded; they made life exciting. That's what my uncle Vernon always said. A token Hudson male, he had been adopted into the tribe. He was Loretta's husband and took it as a given that there would be two women in his house. When Loretta went to spend a week or two at her sister's, that was just fine with Vernon. "Good as a week in the country!" he'd say.

My aunts were regulation Hudson height, 5' 7", and described themselves as of "a distinctive age—as if it's anybody's damn business!" followed by gales of laughter, as if the L&L's had come to the punch line of a joke, the welcome return in an ongoing, unspoken conversation between them. They have flamboyant hair, a curly-wavy, wild silver that comes just to their shoulders. It flew out, as in a wind, even when they were standing still, which wasn't often. Sometimes they would tie it back in a ponytail or a cockatiel's top knot. If you want to know what's on a Hudson woman's mind, check the hair. Mine was particularly pathetic that day and needed to be washed.

Loretta and Lenore are lean, muscular women. Glowing, healthy, they hike and bike—are lovers of food and animals. Men were OK, too. Lenore had out-lived two husbands, whereas Vernon was Loretta's one and only—a hardy man, she called him, which always cracked the three of them up. It was an inside joke that always scared me. With large, gray-green eyes, they carried reading glasses the way kids carried toys—stuffed in the pockets of their jeans.

I greeted my aunts with the customary hugs and kisses, deflecting Loretta's accusations of hiding from them and trying to keep her from slamming through kitchen drawers looking for Lou's gun.

"I'm astonished, really I am," said Lenore, settling into my chair and placing a white bakery box on the cluttered table. "Get a knife, will you, Lyle?" She opened the box, releasing a cloud of cinnamon, vanilla, and untold calories into the air.

"Cake's still warm," she continued. "I just took it from the oven. Didn't want to arrive empty–handed." Lenore smiled beatifically and delicately licked a sticky fingertip.

I rustled up a couple more chairs and a knife and plates, managing to keep one object or another between Loretta and me at all times.

"Time's up, little girl! Where the hell is it? Who'd a thought sister Louise would have a gun! Makes ya proud doesn't it?" Loretta stood there and beamed at us.

"Gun?" I said coolly to Luce. "You told them there was a gun?"

"You've got it on you, I bet. Get over here!" Loretta attacked me, pulling at my shirt and groping through my clothing. The screaming and laughter and barking filled the crowded space with pandemonium.

"All right!" Loretta removed the pistol from my pants and raised it in triumph. It wouldn't have been half the fun if I'd simply handed it over.

"Puny little thing," she commented. "36LS. Fires five shots. Got a hammer shroud, too! Damn!"

"Lucky for us it's no longer loaded," Luce observed dryly. "Sit down and have some cake."

Lenore's coffee cake can reduce a room to instant silence. You want to eat the whole thing, even if you've just finished a meal. Her coffee cake gave coffee a reason to exist.

"So, what do you think?" I gestured at the revolver sitting in the middle of the table, a lethal contrast to the mugs and plates. Four sets of gray-green eyes no longer smiling regarded it somberly.

"Damn. I thought Luce here was just having us on," Loretta said. "We just came over to give you a hard time. A person could *die* waiting for an invitation from *you*, missy!"

"I think," Lenore interrupted before Loretta and I started wrestling again. "That if Lou had this..." she waved at the revolver, still pretty shocked by it, "In her shop, she must have been scared. Really afraid of something."

"Or someone," I added, "Me, too."

"Can I have it?" Loretta reached for the gun.

"NO!" a three-voice explosion. Luce grabbed the gun and placed it in her lap, out of sight.

"I'll let you know what I find out," I promised them.

"OK, then!" Loretta beamed. "Let's go, Lenore, we got some business to attend to!" I lifted an eyebrow at Luce whose eyes said not now. We stood and hugged, and the L&L's trooped out the kitchen door, returning the room to quiet. The departure of my aunts always left a room feeling smaller.

Luce and I cleaned up and returned to our argument about her wretched cat

"I'll stop by, pick up the mail and the papers and feed Tetley."

"I *was* hoping you would have him over here, Lyle" Luce said. "Tetley's been jumpy lately. I don't think he should be alone. It wouldn't be too much trouble. This house is huge!" Great. Devil Cat and Paxil Dog under the same roof. Just shoot me.

"OK. OK. When do you want me to pick him up?"

"Oh, I'll drop him off on the way out of town. How's that?" The woman was too perky by half.

"Fine. Do you want to come to the shop today? I'm meeting Nola, taking a look at invoices. I might ask if there was a firearm on the premises. You can help."

"No, I don't think so, Lyle." She made a face. "You and Nola get along just fine. Besides, I've got a few errands to run. A couple of boxes of books to drop off at the library. Have you been to The Book Trader yet?" The ball was back in my court. She really was being shifty about something.

"Today. Or tomorrow at the latest, promise." Procrastination is my middle name.

"All right then. Time to get going. See you Thursday!" And off she went. I sat listening as she started up the truck, getting my head around the fact that my aunt had a love life and I did not. *Que sera, sera.* Lyle the philosopher. Do philosophers procrastinate? I bet they do. Yeah, they procrastinate. And if they don't it's because they have wives to do stuff and look after them. And another thing...Better cut myself off before I get lost in a rant. Not a good state of mind before getting behind the wheel of a car. Calm thoughts.

Nola waved as I walked through the back door. She was listening to phone messages and jotting notes on a pad. Nola has been around forever. Louise paid her almost nothing, but that didn't seem to matter much. Nola retired early with a pension, and IRA, and a few shrewd investments that hadn't been hit by the economic slump. She, like Louise, worked at the shop for the pleasure of it, and for each other's company. When I first called her, she had to hang up the phone because she said I sounded so much like my mother. She was better now and looking quite well. 70-something, bright brown eyes, white hair cut into an attractive pixie shape that accentuated her heart-shaped face. A tiny woman, she was naturally trim. Navy slacks, navy boiled wool jacket, a russet, orangey shawl on her shoulder. Nola always looked great.

Momentarily struck that I did not feel too awful being there, I stopped and studied the latest window display. As a dress, quite apart from its purpose, it was lovely. Simple lines, a rich, creamy white silk, shot-silk, I thought. It caught subtle bluish hints from the morning sky. A matching silk shrug accentuated the shoulders and neckline. Wow. Nice dress.

"Yes, it is lovely, isn't it, dear." Nola said as I turned to greet her with a smile.

"Lyle," she said, "You look so attractive today!" A good sign. If I was unacceptable in Nola's sight due to some fashion faux pas, she ignored what I was wearing and kept her eyes unwaveringly on my face, which had the weird effect of making me feel utterly naked. How do women do that to each other? (Better yet, why?) I was not in the club. A yellow lab in a world of poodles.

"Thanks, Nola. That's generous of you." Can't resist a touch of acid on the subject of clothes. "I decided that if I was going to be dealing with the public, I should be careful, right?"

"Exactly, dear. The green of your sweater really brings out your eyes." Nola smiled approvingly. "Very nice." Christ, was she going to purr? What's up?

Nola took my arm and we walked to the back of the shop. We took care of the invoices (money in, money out), brewed a pot of tea, and consulted the appointments book. While anyone was in the shop, the door was open, but we didn't keep regular hours. Too much wasted time, Louise said. People had gotten used to the appointments set up, and it helped keep the utilities low.

"Only one appointment this afternoon, Lyle. Why don't you take it? She's a new customer, someone I haven't met." Nola flipped through her note pad. "Name of Cristobel Banks. You could take her information, date of the wedding and such, and see how it goes."

I was staggered. Usually, Nola took care of the customers, her bread and meat, as it were. Was she jollying me? Tossing a bone to the grieving daughter?

"Don't you usually do that, Nola? What's up?"

"Well, it happens that," Nola hemmed and hawed a bit, fussing with the fringes of her silk shawl. "I have an appointment this afternoon, Lyle."

I regarded her silently, a yellow lab spotting a poodle.

"It's a Mary Kay thing. Facials for my new customers. At my house, of course, not here. You don't mind, do you?"

"Relax, Nola. It's fine. Probably good for me to try

my hand. If I screw things up, you can always make it right later."

"Oh, no, dear! You'll be fine, really. It's quite simple." She did not mean to be insulting; it just came naturally to her. Poodles condescending to the big dogs. Remain calm, Lyle. Superior mental attitude.

"Thanks. So. Nola. Did Lou keep a gun in the shop, by any chance?" Not subtle, but it got the subject out there.

"Here? At Hyacinth?"

"Mm," I nodded helpfully.

"No, I don't think so, dear." She looked at me with pity. Taking a deep breath and avoiding further conversation, Nola checked her watch.

"Oh! Look at the time!" She bustled about, grabbed her keys and was gone.

Snapping out of exhaustion from behaving appropriately, I stretched luxuriously, glad to be rid of Nola for the time being. I pulled my Nalgene bottle and sandwich out of the mini-fridge and prepared for lunch, maybe a brief walk in the park before C. Banks arrives at 1:30, an hour from now.

In the quiet, I mulled over the mystery of the snubbie. As far as Nola was concerned, it didn't exist. It had sat right there where Lou could reach it. Her chair faced the front door of the shop and the street beyond. Excellent line of sight, really.

A sound caught the edge of my hearing and I sat up to listen. It came closer, a sound I had not heard for a while but recognized as one of the first signs of a still distant spring. Sure it was geese, I dropped the sandwich on the table.

Outside, in the cool air, the sound was louder, approaching from the southeast, heading north. I looked up, glad the leaves were not on the trees yet, craning my neck to see if I could catch a glimpse. How many eons have they been doing this?

I wasn't the only one out on the sidewalk. The audio guy, a few lunch customers from the bar, one or two passers-by were looking up, caught on the wheel of the turning season. The V-shaped formation passed, and we rubbed our necks and smiled. A friendly nod here and there. We've obviously done this before; no need for words. I walked back to the shop door. As I did, I heard a car slow behind me. I turned as a voice called my name.

"Lyle, Lyle Hudson!" It was a dark blue Mustang, vintage '66, MacDonald George behind the wheel.

"How are you?" he asked, smiling. I smiled back.

"Fine, just fine. How are *you*?" I walked over to the curb and looked up and down Mass street. No traffic. Time enough for a chat. It has been what, a couple of weeks? I had not forgotten how good looking the man was. Really good looking. I leaned casually (yeah, right) against the trunk of a parked car, resting a foot on the curb.

"Nice car."

"Thanks," he said, checking me out. Taking in the dark green cashmere sweater, tiger's eye necklace, brown cords, and tapestry mules. The man was totally checking me out. I decided to like him even more.

"Nice shoes. Guess you like the kind that kick off." The shoes are cowboy boots without the boot, and a reasonable heel.

"Yeah. Never know when some jerk is going to come along and try to wreck your day." I swiveled my ankle back and forth, avoiding eye-contact.

"You get that a lot? Random criminals, I mean." Definitely deciding if he was going to park the car, I could tell.

"I try to avoid those situations." I gazed at the car. It was a midnight blue, almost black—I recognized the color from my youth—with red leather seats. Customized steering wheel. The man loved his car.

"So. What's up?"

"I was on my way to some coffee, care to come?"

"I'm looking after some business right now, otherwise that'd be great."

He looked over my shoulder, read the shop window, and started to laugh. "Hyacinth? You run a bridal shop?" I smiled tolerantly.

"My mom did. Louise. This was her shop." I let the verb hang in the air.

"Ah. Sorry to hear, Lyle. Maybe another time, then. Do you have a phone number?" Steady gaze right into my eyes, to show me he was both interested and not the kind of person to play games. God, I love grown ups, especially when they're good-looking men. I took my time returning the look. Nodded my head slightly and reached around into my back pocket. While I was retrieving a card, I swear I could feel him looking at my body, like curves have outlines. This I did not mind. The card was in my fingers, held out.

"Call me. The cell is more reliable. Thanks for the invitation." He studied the card. I checked my watch. Got to go. Take it easy...Mac."

"You, too." He checked the rearview mirror and drove off with a wave. On the way back inside, I shook my head. Vanity. If we were any cooler, any more stingy with the signals, we'd still be on square one. Ah, well. Small steps. I admit to my own skittishness, a reluctance to get involved.

Back in the back of the store, I finished the sandwich and the water. Dug out a small spiral notebook from my satchel, and turned to the pages with the questions I had asked myself about the gun, the diary, the Ace of Spades, and the notes, one in Lou's handwriting. I unfolded both the bill and the note card from Ann-whoever and reread them again, wondering.

Are you the same Ann that's in the diary? I tried out a few possible plot lines in my head—happy ending, sad ending. Which way did it go? Why the gun, Mom? Not enough information to tell. There may never be enough, Lyle. You have to accept the fact that you may never know. The LS36 snub-nosed revolver mocked me with its silence. I stashed it in my satchel and checked my watch. 1:25. Just enough time to pull myself together and...the small bell attached to the front door rang prettily and I looked up to take in the full effect of the Gothic arrival of Miss Cristobel Banks.

Goth? Oh, yeah. In spades. I took a deep breath and strode forth to meet her, thinking, OK, Lyle: WWLD? What Would Louise Do?

Miss Cristobel Banks, aka Crista, was a slender 5' 6", dressed in full black ensemble: Black tulle skirt over black leggings and black boots laced to the knees; black camisole under black cardigan under black beaded sweatery type thing; black choker with black cameo. Black, spiky hair; black wrist bands, black thumb bands; black tattoo on back of hand; silver rings with onyx or garnet stones or metal spikes; black eyeliner around big brown eyes. White skin, no make up except for a purply-reddish lipstick, the only color other than black on her person. It must have taken her hours to get dressed! She sat down in the Queen Anne chair at Louise's prize Queen Anne table and pulled a small artist's portfolio from under her left arm.

I reached out my hand and smiled quietly into her eyes.

"Hi. I'm Lyle."

"Crista. Nice to meet you." We shook hands carefully. Her voice was soft, devoid of local twang. I assumed, wrongly, that she was an out-of-state student at KU. So young, I thought. Young people have no idea how lovely they are.

"Um...where's Mrs. Hudson? A friend of mine told me it was an older lady that owned this place and that she was, well, really nice, and easy to talk to?" She looked around expectantly.

"That was my mom, Louise.. I'm looking after the shop now. May I help you?"

"Well..." She hesitated, thinking it over. Not wanting to waste time for either of us, I got to the point.

"When are you planning on getting married, Crista? Maybe we should just talk for a bit and see where things go. Would you like a cup of coffee? Tea?" My guess is she either drank coffee, ink, or Lapsang Souchong. "I've got pretty much everything back there."

She smiled a truly sweet smile and said yes, did I have any green tea. I said Green Tea with mint, and we were best friends.

As we waited for the tea to steep, she told me that the wedding was planned for May, she was a local girl, a senior at KU majoring in philosophy, and that the groom was a sort-of-folk singer who made good money at computer contract work, data bases and graphic art. One of them would be making money at least.

She had definite ideas on what she wanted, namely the dress in the window. With a few modifications. The dress was in stock in her size (6), so there were no time constraints there. She had her deposit ready and had worked out a payment plan that would pay for the dress in six weeks, well before the end of April.

"I don't see any problem, Crista," I said, nodding and filling out the invoice, "Let's talk about those modifications." I should have known better than to feel comfortable with the whole bridal thing. I should have known.

"Here, look at these!" she said, completely at ease by now and growing excited. Out came her portfolio, the pages flipping to a couple of designs she had clearly modeled on the dress in the window.

"I just love the lines on this dress!" Crista exclaimed, pointing a purple fingernail at the bodice of the dress in question which was now incarnated as a postmodern construction with metallic detailing. I was speechless and could only gaze in wonder, grateful that my mouth was not hanging open.

I cleared my throat, noting that it made me sound exactly like Luce. Oh God.

"Original interpretation," I said dryly. "Are you sure it can be completed in the time you have between now and April?" I could still put sentences together. Good!

"Oh, sure! Look." Pages flipped. "I have it planned out in stages, starting with hand application of the aubergine (read eggplant), merlot, and bituminous (read black) dyes!" I followed her with a horrified admiration at her attention to detail. I could visualize the entire process. Whether I would sleep that night was another question.

"The shrug, of course, I'll have to hand pleat, giving it a Vera Wang look, you see?" Oh, yes. I saw. I wondered where this blessed event would be held. No. No need to know. Don't ask, don't tell.

"But, Crista, what if you change your mind? This

payment schedule," I nodded to the fatal document, "covers enough time that your situation might change, and..." She cut me off with a look before I could finish my plea.

"Nothing will change." Strong gaze for one so young. "I promise that whatever happens, I will buy this dress. You have my word." Oh, God, not her word. I closed my eyes, pretending to think but really praying.

"Agreed. Shake." Crista and I shook hands and finished our tea. One of us needed to use the bathroom, so we said goodbye and ended our first encounter.

After washing up the lunch and tea things, filing away my notes and Crista's deposit for her "stellar!" dress, I checked the answering machine (No messages), checked to make sure the gun was in my satchel, and locked the back door, deciding to walk up Massachusetts Street before returning to the house. I had walked to the shop this morning and knew that the afternoon would be a mild one. About time.

I set the alarm, locked the door, and headed north toward the main drag. Main drag, listen to me. It must be the effect of that Mustang.

As I walked, I swept my mind of chatter, remembering the geese this morning and savoring the clear air. Something about Crista appealed to me. I smiled as I thought about her. She took me back to high school when I drove my parents mad with my own "constructions," only I called them dresses and insisted on wearing them to proms. My Dad had a theory that boys dared each other to date me and take me to the prom; it was some sort of fetishistic rite of manhood. Quite the joker. He was probably right.

I went to a few proms before my own, a benefit of dating older guys. One year I had already made my dress, a lavender chiffon with a white empire bodice and spaghetti straps, floaty white things hanging off the shoulders. But then I found this stretch velour—velvety material, claret with dark blue highlights—that so entranced me that I cut it out and put it together the day of the prom, sewing myself into it minutes before my date arrived because I did not have time to mess with a zipper. I hated zippers, still do. Loved the dress, though.

Coming downstairs to greet my date—Gary something? — and make an elegant entrance (maybe give my date a moment to collect his courage), I was met by my father's amused comment that he could see the outline of the broccoli I'd had for supper. Ha, ha. As if anybody actually ate food the day of the prom. Idiot. I have no actual memories of the prom or the whatsisface who took me, but I loved that dress.

I smiled with the memory, then looked around me to realize I had walked to 7th Street, much further than I intended to go. I checked my watch. No need to rush right home. Paxil Dog was in the back yard behind a newly repaired fence.

The Liberty video store was right across the street. Why not see if I could find a foreign film for the evening? Permission granted, I crossed the street, satchel over my shoulder and snug against my hip.

I love to browse through DVD's; it's almost as enjoyable as a bookstore. Lost between Luchino Visconti's *The Leopard* and Kurasawa's *Dreams*, I heard someone say my name from the other side of the rack of DVD's. I felt a sudden, creepy chill.

"Hey, Dr. Hudson? Man, is that you? It is you, right? Yeah, it is, I know it's you. Cool!" and with that expression of delight (Not too loud, that's good. Nobody else in the store, even better), the owner of the

voice came around the display of DVD's to stand in
front of me. Which was good, since I was frozen to the
spot where I stood.

"Dr. H! All right! It is so good to see you. Remem-
ber me? Maybe not, that's OK. I was in your class at
UCSF, mythology? Actually, I took a bunch of classes,
you were so cool. Still are, I bet. Yeah, remember?
Um...Arts and Humanities, I think it was, and...Intro to
Poetry, British Lit. That's where you turned me on to
Blake! Get it, BLAKE?"

It slowly dawned on me. His name was Blake. Blake
Phipps. If I close my eyes will he disappear? I tried it.
Damn. No, the blond dreds, hazel eyes, almost classi-
cally arranged features—beautiful, yes, but gonzo. In a
friendly, puppyish way— and droopy clothing were real,
100% Blake.

"Blake, hello." Please let that be tepid enough!
"How are you? What are you doing in Lawrence? I
thought you were purely an San Francisco guy, or East
Bay."

"Ah, Dr. H, I can't really say, you know? It's complex. Life can be complex, deeply so."

Blake featured himself a bit of a philosopher. It was
best to humor him, speak gently. No sudden moves.

"Yeah. So. I'm at KU now. Part time. Taking some
course on Psychology of Urban Youth? Got to have
enough time to perfect my art. He indicated the skateboard under his arm, not releasing it, not presenting it to
public gaze. For Blake, the board was sacred, like Beo-
wulf's sword.

What I did appreciate about Blake, and what en-
deared him to me, was his dedication to his mother
tongue. No surfer speak for him, no rad or coolio or
crunk. Blake spoke pure Midwestern prose, obtained
from the school of Tom Brokaw and Peter Jennings.

"Luchino Visconti! All right! Did you see *The Damned?* Now that is some twisted movie! Hey, Dr. H? Want to go have a beer? Or a coffee or something? It would be cool to sit and talk. How about it?" Blake wasn't quite wagging his tail, but he was cute. Maybe I was homesick. I found myself smiling at him.

"Blake, that would be great. Really." He was getting ready to pout, anticipating rejection. "But I have to go home," Did I really say *home?* "and feed the animals, OK?" I wanted it to sound like I had Pythons and Tigers to feed.

"Tell you what. I'll feed the pets, eat dinner, and then meet you at the Brewery at 7, OK? That way we'll get to talk, and you'll still have the whole evening to spend on homework or whatever."

"Excellent! Great, Dr. H!" He fiddled with one of the dreds. "You are going to be there, right?" I try never to lie to children, and Blake was a golden child in my book. Lies I saved for people in the game. Or for people who just made me want to lie. Not Blake.

"I am a woman of my word, Blake. I'm surprised you ask."

"OK, then. See you at 7!" Blake raised his thumb in salute, I raised mine back and we went our separate ways. It is possible both of us were smiling.

5

Promising Glory that I would make it up to her tomorrow, I left the house and took the Infiniti back down town. I felt guilty about using the car, but I didn't feel safe walking the 10 blocks back in the dark. I try to do my bit for the environment, but self-preservation comes first. Idiot Bart had gotten to me.

I found a free space on Mass Street, in front of the Eldridge Hotel. It was almost as rare as finding a parking space in San Francisco! Feeling pleased with myself, I crossed Mass Street, turned left, and made for Union Brewery, close by The Liberty theater. A few movie-goers stepped through the door to buy tickets. Not quite 7 o'clock; the evening was quiet.

I had to admit I looked good, even if I was just meeting a former student. It had been ages since I had been out. A touch of *Pure* by Alfred Sung, jeans, black Merrells, French wool walking coat (guess I was my mother's daughter), white silk blouse, a string of pearls. I'm a sucker for pearls. They make your skin glow. Hair pulled back through a tube-shaped, silver holder, the swept back look accented the silver in my hair. At night, it practically reflects light. God, I love being an adult!

Musing on my mysterious maturity, I strode into the Brewery, satchel over my shoulder, remembering I'd decided to leave the gun at home. The Brewery was not my first choice as a watering hole, the place was usually busy, loud, almost impossible to talk. Students go there for the specialty beers. For me, it is redeemed by an excellent selection of single malt scotch.

A light Monday night crowd was dispersed among the first floor tables. No line waiting. Quiet. Lots of room at the bar. I walked over, slipped up onto a bar-stool and perused the list of scotches above the bar.

The bartender appeared quietly in front of me, placing a Copperhead Beer coaster on the bar. I brought my gaze down to place my order.

"Nice evening," he said. At least he didn't call me *ma'am*.

"Yes, it is." A slight, appreciative smile for him. "I'll have a Macallan. and a glass of water, too, please

Sipping slowly, feeling the smoky glow of that first taste of scotch, I watched Blake Phipps walk in the front door, eyes heading straight for me. As he crossed the stone floor, I tried hard not to gawk. What happened to the loopy skateboard dude? Blake looked...he looked...pretty!

Charcoal gray pleated slacks, thin (Italian?) leather belt around narrow hips, one of those silk blend sweaters outlining his shoulder very nicely. Tawny, brown scarf looped lightly around his neck, leather jacket over one arm. Mmm. The dreds were still there, but sort of pulled back. *This* Blake Phipps looked totally GQ. Smooth, very smooth. STOP! cried my inner voice, Remember his age, Lyle. This young man was your student. Behave.

Not bothering to say shut up to my interior debate, I greeted him with a smile. He hung the jacket over the back of the barstool and smiled back.

"Hey, Dr. H, you look great! Thanks for coming." Big hug. Sweet smile. Oh my.

"And look at you, Blake! I'm impressed! You look so...well, smooth." We sat on our barstools, smiling. He was. Blake was smooth. I was speechless.

"Blake, I have to tell you, I feel so strange sitting here, having a drink with you."

"That's because you're the only one drinking, Dr. H." Cheeky smile.

"Well, let's fix that right now. It's on me. What will you have?" A quick sip of the Macallan to steady my nerves. Blake turned to the bartender, not seeing the sly assumptions I was picking up on.

"I'll have the Wheat, with a slice of lemon. And a glass of water, please." Good boy.

Drinks in hand, it was time for a toast.

"To..." he paused, searching for some formal words he usually didn't use. "To the Heartland!" We laughed, one of us ironically.

"Indeed. Cheers." Glasses touched, we sipped and felt self-conscious. I tried to lighten things up.

"Blake, if we are to have any kind of real conversation tonight, you have to stop calling me Dr. H. My name is Lyle."

"Not Carlyle?"

"Well, that, yes. But folks who know me call me Lyle. I'm used to it."

"Lyle." Blake drank from his beer. "I think I can do it. Lyle. So. Lyle," trying it out. "How did we get here in this place at the same time. I've been thinking about it, and it seems way beyond coincidence, you know?

Something cosmic."

"Well, less than cosmic, surely, Blake. It's just...good to see you. You bring a breath of San Francisco with you. Very nice. Familiar." We were doing just fine. The awkwardness dissipated as we talked of San Francisco, the pros and cons of Kansas. We visited, enjoying each other's company.

At one point, I looked up at the drinks board again. Blake had just started his second beer, and I was nursing my second glass of water. His arm hung across the back of my chair, and we were sharing some lame joke about problems reading while on a skateboard in motion, when I glanced over my left shoulder to see Mac-Donald George approaching the bar. Oh my.

Still smiling from the joke, Blake followed my eyes and turned that angelic face to full view. There might have been a hesitation in Mac's stride, but I couldn't swear to it; I was feeling strange and self-conscious again. Blake and I sat up as Mac neared us, smile on his face, twinkle in his eye.

"MacDonald, hello! How are you?" It was the best I could do on short notice.

"Evening, Lyle. I'm fine. You?" He said this not looking at me but at Blake. Taking inventory, clearly. Blake sized him up, too. Hey! This could be cool! I was starting to feel all girly inside.

"MacDonald, I'd like you to meet a friend of mine from San Francisco, Blake Phipps. Blake, MacDonald George." I can do this, really.

"Cool." Blake shook his hand, firmly. The kid was open and friendly. Did not have a clue. The innocence took the edge off of Mac's suspicions, and he smiled back.

"Nice to meet you. Good to know the woman has some friends. I was beginning to think she was an orphan." Blake laughed, and I'll be damned if they weren't friends in two seconds. Disgusting. Women don't behave like that! They turned and smiled at me and I thought I might melt, girly-like, right there.

We asked Mac to join us, ordered some fries to sop up the alcohol, and spent a lovely time. The eyes had a separate conversation which I, after my second Macallan, found a bit hard to keep up with. Oh, well.

"Hey, um...Lyle?" Blake said. "I've got to go. I had a really good time catching up with you. I'll call, OK?" I must have given him my card earlier. A sweet kiss, right at my temple, hand lightly on my right shoulder. Nice. Very nice, I thought.

Blake ambled out of the bar, graceful and unself-conscious in his youthful beauty. He waved at the door, clearly glad I had seen him out.

I turned back to the bar, interested to find Mac's eyes on me, studious.

"Lyle, my sweet, you have to make a decision."

"Mmm." I *liked* his voice, not growly or rough but rich. Damn. Did I make that 'Mmm' sound out loud? Stay calm, don't panic. Pretend nothing happened.

"What decision is that, Mac?" My ponytail had slipped over one shoulder and he took the ends of my hair in those long fingers of his.

"Whether you are going to go out with me or not. I'm not going to ask you now. I have no wish to take advantage of your...relaxed state of mind. But think about it, please? Because I definitely want to go out with you. You know...see you again? On purpose and not by chance?" He looked me in the eyes and I looked back, calmly.

"Yes."

"Yes, you'll think about it?

"Yes, I'd be glad to go out with you. You know, see you again." No lie there. We settled on Friday night. Classic.

6

Tuesday morning I felt a sudden jolt, a kind of dread. Luce was going off, leaving me with these animals, in this house, in this town. I yearned for my Emerald City, San Francisco. Without Luce, I'd be cut loose, a stranger in...well, you get it. The chips were stacking up on another part of the table. My cards were too loose.

"Luce, hi. It's me." I paused. "Yeah. No. I'm fine, no emergency. Just thought I'd call before you drive off to Yoga Heaven. Thanks, I think I'm charming, too." This is how our phone calls went. Luce hated the phone and could get a bit testy, unless she was the one making the call.

"Yo, yo, yo! Time out, OK? I don't want anything—nada, niente, bupkis. I'm actually offering a favor, so hear me out." I gave her space to get over herself and entertained myself by balancing bits of dog biscuit on Glory's nose. She was really good at it and would play this game until I ran out of biscuits or her liver burst, whichever came first. Pate de Gloire. Now there's a thought.

Eventually there was a silence on the other end of the phone. I could hear Luce's fingers drumming on her kitchen table. Oops! Waited too long. She was at it again; I found myself drawing to an inside straight.

"Luce, Luce! Listen...Yes, I am going to the shop today; I'd get there faster if you would shut up and listen to me. Yes, I said *Shut up*. Sorry sorry. Luce? I'm hanging up the phone! Just forget I called." I hung up. I swear my ear was smoking.

"The woman can be evil, Glory, evil." The dog jumped into my lap and licked the offended organ. Glory thinks she's a lap dog.

"Lap dogs are not bony!" I explained to her. She just looked at me from behind her black, Zorro mask, as if I had started to speak Dutch. I munched on one of her dog biscuits, sharing it with her, waiting for the phone to ring, which eventually it did. I waited for three rings then answered.

"Hello?" When I pretend I don't know who it is, Luce goes ballistic. This time was no exception. "Whoa, whoa! Luce? You need a sense of humor, hon. Maybe you left it in the garage. I'll wait while you go get it, OK?" We play hang up again. See, she really does not want me to get out of the house without talking to her, so she called right back. 30 seconds, max.

My first words are scripted in the Hudson DNA.

"I apologize. That was rude of me. I'm sorry." I paused. "No, ma'am, I am not a nut cake. Can we talk now, please? I really have to get going. Yes, Glory is coming with me. It's not that cold out. She'll be fine. Yeah. Yeah. OK, stop or I'm going to walk out the door. Thank you. The favor is that I'm dropping off a final two bags of books at The Book Trader and wanted to know if I should stop by your place on the way." Another pause. "Yes, I *can* be a sweet girl." Although I'm not sure that 'girl' applies any more. Still another pause. "I called yesterday and they're glad to have the books. Louise's collection was really fine." Fourth and hopefully final pause. "No, I don't have any use for them, do *you?* Do you read paperback mysteries? No. Didn't think so. Fine, thought I'd ask. No, I can't stop by for tea because I've got a couple of appointments today. KU Barbie, the Goth Princess, and a woman with a voice like a cello, sounded like a mom. Yes, that's right. Why don't you call my cell and we can avoid the whole histrionics thing. Oh, you are, too, Luce. When I was little you'd scare the crap out of me. This gray hair? That's because of you! Did, too. Love you, bye." Whew.

The books were already in the trunk of the Infiniti. Glory's towel was in its place, though I had given up on the blizzard of white hair. Backed out of the garage slowly. The alley was a no-man's land. You had to have nerves of steel or faith in something.

The homeless guy who inhabited the alley was heading out, too. Clothed in an array of lumpy outerwear, he waved as we passed by. "Hallelujah!" he saluted Glory with a laugh and a grin.

"Hope he's on his way to the soup kitchen," I said as we turned right, out of the alley and headed downtown.

Leaving the dog in the car in the sun, I wrestled two bags of books a block and a half to the bookstore. No parking karma today. Juggled my way in and staggered to the desk before the paper bags tore. Joan leant a hand as I steadied the books on the counter.

"Hello, Lyle. This is great. I can't wait to see the

books! Cash or credit?" Joan was generous with the
store credits, kept the books moving.

"How are you, Joan? Credit is fine. No rush. I'll just
browse until you're ready."

"Great!" You'd think I handed her two bags full of
chocolate bars. Book lovers are their own breed.

It's a neat shop. No matter how old (or young) you
are, there's sure to be something there for you to discover. Old, upholstered armchairs and ottomans are
placed in likely places for reading; shelves and tables
are stacked with books; and there are small piles of
books waiting here and there invitingly. An ancient
tabby cat sleeps in one of the display windows, taking
advantage of the sun. Passersby often linger at the windows to read book titles, and small children will point at
the sleeping cat. It always feels so peaceful here.

I wandered over to the poetry section, unwrapped
my scarf, unbuttoned my jacket, stuffed my gloves into
the blue satchel slung across my shoulder to my hip. It
was the only way I could have managed two bags of
books for a block and a half without dropping something. I realized I was still sweating and divested myself
of my burden, unceremoniously dumping it behind the
counter by Joan.

"Just go ahead," she said, not looking up from the
books. Back in the poetry section, I read spines of
books, thumbed through the odd volume, tasting the
words of people I had never heard of. I tucked a collection of James Galvin under my arm. My stuff, books included, was still in San Francisco and I had no idea what
I was going to do or why. I stared out the window. Luce
was leaving tomorrow. Then there was Friday with the
lovely Mr. George. Not to mention decisions about
Hyacinth. Who owns a bridal shop? And what about that

gun? It was with me now, in my bag. The fact of it was too weird. What the hell are you going to do, Lyle?

Looking for a place to sit and read, I recognized a young woman examining title in the pet care/exotic animals section. You'd never know it from looking at her, but Caitlin was just a step away from being homeless and on the street. A group of loving friends, 20-somethings like herself, and her boa constrictor, Brunhilde kept her indoors and presentable. Caitlin is an animal rights activist. I encountered her on my first trip to The Book Trader when she was just outside the shop, confronting an abusive dog owner. Caitlin had threatened to use the dog's choke collar on him and make him eat his own vomit. The police arrived and sent Caitlin on her way. Joan told me that Caitlin isn't arrestable. She's an urban hero of sorts. Her heart is in the right place and the cops usually let her off with a warning.

"Hey, Caitlin," I greeted her, giving her time to adjust to the fact that someone wanted to talk to her.

"Hey." She turned toward me, hand resting on a shelf, keeping her place in the books she was browsing through. "Lyle, right?" Caitlin blinked slowly and looked up at me from beneath a fringe of brown hair framing her face. Petite, angelic features, but unsettling and unpredictable.

"No Brunhilde today?" I asked. Caitlin was rarely seen without the snake.

"Digesting." OK. No more questions from me. "Where's the dog? Isn't she the one that climbs trees?"

"Yes, she is. Glory's in the car. I'm in here for just a few minutes," I explained. "The sun'll keep the car warm enough for her."

"Cool."

A subtle vibration and unobtrusive "brrring!" from
my pocket. "Sorry, Caitlin. Got to go. See you."

"Cool." Caitlin resumed scanning the shelves devoted to exotic animals.

I took out the cell. One new text message waiting:
"When R U coming back? Stop. Fish are pining. Stop.
Me, too! Call!" Chas.

I pocketed the phone, resolving to call as soon as I
got back to the car. I hate cell phones other than my
own and detest being held hostage to other people's
conversations. Deciding the Galvin book would do for
now, I settled myself into a chair. Joan was almost finished. I could wait

"Lyle? Here, this was in one of your books." Joan
handed me a folded sheet of paper. "It slipped out as I
was going through them."

"Thanks, Joan." This was the second piece of paper
that had slipped out of my mother's books. No lost
moments here. Bits of something that she had wanted
hidden. I was sure of it.

"I'll take the Galvin, Joan. Put the rest on my ac-
count." No way was I going to find out which book had
held the paper, which my instincts told me would be
something, I could feel it the way you can feel what cards
are coming your way from the deck.

I checked my watch. Time to rescue the dog and go
to *Hyacinth*. In a minute. Adjusting the glasses on my
nose, I opened the note. No date. Louise's handwriting:

> *Do not apologize to me.*
> *I knew what I was doing when I agreed to help.*
> *We each make our own choices.*
> L.

There were erasures and words written over in ink.

This was a working draft to get each word just right. Too short to merit such trouble. But it looked as though my mother had put a great deal of thought into it. She wanted to be clear, but not too clear, not for eyes other than the intended recipient. Well, well. Is this when you decided you needed a gun, Mom? I stuck the note in my pocket and left the bookshop.

7

Glory greeted me ecstatically and slathered love all over my face and black wool jacket. Making sure that we were alone and no one was looking, I returned her affection with a nuzzle and ear scratch. I started the engine, pumped up the climate control to tropical, settled Glory under her towel, and pulled out the cell phone. I speed-dialed Chas' number, and my mind roamed across the plains and deserts west. I longed for the freedom of California and the home I had made for myself there. Here in Kansas, I felt so paranoid, not so much trying to fit myself into small, socially acceptable boxes as hiding out, working on my psychic camouflage.

I didn't know what it was, but I felt deeply uneasy here. Lawrence was not so bad, really; the university gave it a cosmopolitan air despite its small size, and there were the amenities of coffee houses, book stores, music venues, and lectures. And the people were friendly enough. At first. I appreciated the fact that neighbors looked out for each other and would pitch in after the random tornado to help folks get their homes back together. Yes, tornados bothered me. Loud, unpredictable...frequent. Living in earthquake territory, I felt it would be hypocritical to complain. But complain I did. Loud and clear, inside my head.

In Kansas, I felt uncomfortable every waking moment; even while I was growing up, I felt like I did not belong here. I chewed on a thumbnail.

"Helloooo!" a little tiny voice said in my ear. "Lyle, sweetie, you called me. I answered the phone and now it is your turn to say something. Unless your life's blood is oozing out of you. In which case, it is time to whisper your last words, something about a sled, or maybe my name because you love me most. Lyle?" His hyperbole charmed me and made me feel even more homesick.

"Chas! Sorry! I was sitting in my car having a past life experience of the bad kind. How are you, my darling?"

"Don't darling me, you callous woman. When are you coming home? This week, perhaps? Any time soon? Don't make me start eating your goldfish!" I imagined his lithe, well-dressed frame standing by a picture window, one slender hand brushing back silky blond hair. God, Chas was beautiful, even 1000 miles away.

"I miss you, too. I don't know." I put my head in my free hand and rubbed my forehead. "I'm so confused. I hate this, hate being here, but then I don't, totally. I hate Louise being dead forever, and I don't know what to do...about the business...about the house. It is torment! I can't leave and I can't stay!" Were my eyes leaking again? No way. Lying to myself was an old habit too.

"Lyle? No fair! You cut that out this minute, hear me? It is bad enough that you're a zillion miles away, but I simply cannot handle tears. Oh, God, I'm starting to weep. Now look at what you've done!"

"I'm sorry, Chas. It's just that I miss you, and I don't know what the hell I'm doing. Not here, not there."

"What have they done to you? This is wrong. Stop, you're totally scaring me." Silence passed along the line as we both calmed down.

"Forget what I just said, OK? I'm not myself. I'm fine. Really."

"Sure you are. Your mother died, you're surrounded by farmers and cowboys. You own a bridal shop, for God's sake, and you are *fine*. Right. I'm coming out there."

"No, Chas. You'd hate it. They'd eat you for lunch. Don't come. I'm fine. And the fish need you."

"Screw the fish, my darling. They are why God made cats."

"Look. It is cold. Very cold, lots of wind, no sun, no ocean, no Shiatsu massage. Dust, a muddy river, and stubbled corn fields. And wind. Did I mention wind?"

"Wind, yes, I heard you." Chas paused in his diatribe and switched gears. "Who is looking after you?" The question was more than just a question. Might just as well give him the information he was looking for. Note to self: Don't tell Chas about the gun.

"Luce. Sort of. And I met a guy."

"You have got to be kidding me. In Kansas? What are you thinking of? What have you done with Lyle? Where is she? What *guy*, you hussy?"

"He's not a farmer or a cowboy. I don't think. He might be. I don't know. We haven't really talked. I'll find out more Friday night." A piercing shriek leaped from the phone into my ear. Ouch!

"Carlyle Hudson! A date? You're going on a *date*? In Kansas? Does your therapist know about this? Does she? You're grounded, young lady, no ifs ands or buts. Definitely not butts. Tell me he is *not* pretty."

"No can do. He has the *voice*, Chas." I start to grin in spite of myself.

"He does NOT! You're driving me to drink... It is so early, I'll have to get out of bed to do it."

"Apologies, Chas, but the message said to CALL you."

"So you did, and look at the thanks I get."

"Listen, Chas, I have to get to the shop."

"You're not driving are you?"

"No, baby; the traffic exists only in my head." I was going for a dry tone, a touch of cynicism to reassure my friend and get him off the phone.

"I'll call you later, Lyle. We are not finished by a long shot, Sweetie."

"I love you, too, Chas. Soon."

I opened the shop, put John Mayer, Boz Scaggs, and Diana Krall on and hit shuffle, determined to lighten up my day. Mellow Lyle. Reclaim the kingdom, baby. At 10:30 on the dot, the co-ed arrived with a stack of bride magazines (titles I had never heard of), every hair, every eyelash, every fingernail in place. Insisted on my undivided attention. Mom had not arrived in town yet, and she wanted to be sure to have her say. This was not, repeat not, her mother's wedding; it was hers, thank you very much.

I looked over my glasses at her, couldn't resist. "You should appreciate your mother, Brianne, she won't be around forever, you know."

"Oh! I should be so lucky!" A pert, spoiled flip of the head, and blonde hair swished, highlights in perfectly choreographed motion, as if her hair had taken lessons for just such occasions.

"No, really. I lost my mother, you see. Just after Christmas." Eyes lowered, I looked subdued, chastened.

"Omigod! I am so sorry! Are you OK? I am so sorry, I had no idea." The child was shocked to think she could have been anything less than perfect.

"Of course, how could you. But I think you should be careful what you say, yes?" Shit! My inner poodle was on the loose! I was turning into the passive-aggressive women I despise! The bridal shop brings out the worst in me, always.

"Um, let's talk about the dress, shall we?" Brianne was grateful for the change of subject. Gave me a big, bright, orthodontically enhanced smile.

"Great! Here's what I'm thinking." And the nightmare began. Magazine pages flew open at her slightest command, notes appeared on the day planner (pink) Brianne had with her, and I was adding in my head.

"Brianne, dear? I think your idea is wonderful, really. It is so creative, so original, so you." Some people will eat my lies with a spoon. "But this is a very expensive proposition you're laying out here..." She cut me off.

"Not a problem Lyle! My dad's an orthodontist." Bingo. "He just wants me to be happy! He said so!" Big smile. My head was starting to throb.

"Yes, very good, Brianne. But we are a small, very small operation here. What we mostly do is order from local companies, and..." Cut me off again!

"You mean you don't have a seamstress on the premises?'

"Look around, sweetie." I was not afraid of losing this particular customer. 'High Maintenance' didn't even come close. "Not enough here to even call a premises, don't you agree? We can't afford to contract out." Big fat lie.

Brianne's sweet little face formed itself into a pouty mew. "But this is the dress of my dreams!" She was definitely a wedding-lover. I could feel Louise looking at Sandra over my shoulder.

"Tell you what, Brianne." I consulted the trusty rolodex and pulled a card. "Here is the address and number of a very good place in Kansas City. Very chic. You will love them. Check it out and tell me how it goes. Mention my name and they will take very good care of you." If they don't commit arson after they meet you.

She dabbed her eyes, gathered up her paraphernalia, and flounced out the door of the shop, saying how disappointed she was. I said I was too but probably it was for the best, that I wanted *her* to have the wedding dress she was meant to have, not a second best which was, sorry to say, the best that I could offer her. She ate the whole thing, frosting and all, and happily went her way. We waved bravely.

Back at the drawing table, I threw out my notes and flirted with the idea of going to the bar two doors down, to rinse the bad taste of lies and insincerity out of my mouth. I cheered up when I realized I no longer had to deal with Brianne, much less whatever form of mother she might have, and congratulated myself on a narrow escape. Setting the water on for a pot of tea and reminding Glory there were bagels for lunch, I took the dog out back to the alley for a few minutes so we both could get a breath of fresh air.

She loved to catch the ball before it hit the ground. It would land in her mouth with a thwok! and she'd dance proudly back to me a thousand times or so before getting bored. Glory was a blur of white against the faded yellow of old stone walls. The alley was cramped and dusty, no real distance possible, so we didn't stay very long, maybe 10 minutes max, which is what I told the nice young police officer who stopped by an hour later, after we had gone back inside, turned off the stove, ate our bagels, and had said hello to Crista who walked into the shop, art box in hand.

"Hi," she said, placing her supplies on the floor and stooping down to greet Glory who reciprocated with lady-like licks of Crista's face before turning to sniff the mysterious box she had with her. Laughing, Crista looked up at me and asked, "So where's the dress? Did you sell it? Mine is still hanging in the back, right? Do *not* tell me it's the same one!"

"What dress?" I was certain Brianne had left as she had come.

"The one in the window, you know, silk? White? Worn by discriminating brides everywhere?" Cute, everybody thinks they're cute.

"The window? My window? That window there?"

"The very same." We both froze as we took in my incomprehension and what it seemed to imply. I walked over to the display window at the front of the shop and peeked behind the gauze curtain that served as a backdrop. The white wire dress frame was there, but the dress was gone. Lying on the base of the dress frame was what looked like a playing card. I reached in and palmed it before Crista could see.

I looked back at Crista and Glory, both of them sitting on the floor, silent. I stepped quickly out onto the sidewalk and looked around. No one, nothing. No fleeing maniac with a white dress waving in the air.

Back inside the shop, I did what one was supposed to do when one has been robbed and called the cops. Hung up the phone to wait and sat at the Queen Anne table, staring numbly at the hands folded in my lap.

Crista came up and stood behind me, leaned over and hugged, talking quietly in my ear.

"It's OK. I'll stay here with you until the police come. I'll stay the whole time, OK? Are you OK?" I patted her arm absently.

"I'm fine. Fine." I needed a robber to chase, a face to bash in, a way to regain control. "It wasn't you, was it? No white dress folded in that back pack?" She rolled her eyes at me before half the words were out of my mouth.

"I'll make us some tea. Earl Gray, right? Lots of sugar. Is there someone I can call?"

I handed her my cell phone and said, "Press three. Her name is Luce. She's my Aunt." As Crista walked to the back of the shop with my cell, I pulled the card out of my pocket and turned it over. Ace of spades. *25G*, it read. *Tool box. Your garage. Pay up.* I slid the card back into my pocket and leaned forward and spoke to the dog, "Things are getting personal, Glory. What do you think?"

The officer arrived and double parked her patrol car with the flashers on, which, of course, drew a crowd. She wasn't really twelve, maybe it was her size. Petite, dark, perky pony tail, she had to be in her teens! That impression lasted until she walked into the shop. Officer Danielson, as she introduced herself, was a tightly coiled, self-controlled black woman. Late twenties, I revised my estimate. With one stern demeanor. Her voice was as economical and collected as the rest of her.

"Afternoon, ma'am, I understand there's been a robbery." Ma'am my ass. I raised my eyebrows politely.

Crista was a sweetheart, helped with the "description of the item in question." Telling myself to shut up and not be critical, I drank my hot tea and answered appropriately: Been out side, ten minutes, this is my dog, didn't see a thing, no 'perpetrator' to describe, as if the dress simply vanished. Yes, it was there. Yes, I'd had a customer. No she was not interested in the dress. Yes, I was positive it happened. No need to mention the card.

Then, Luce walked in the back door, and Mac-Donald George walked in the front. Simultaneously.

8

People who compartmentalize and insist on living their lives in separate little boxes experience a kind of vertigo when two or more boxes converge. Normally, compartments work fine for me. No messy feelings. For some reason, I could not absorb the fact of them both being in the shop. I felt confused and feverish; what I was seeing was not making sense to me. Clearly, I was upset, but I couldn't figure out what Mac was doing here. I heard Luce talking to me in one part of my brain, and that part of my brain was doing a good job of answering her questions, but I watched Mac out of the corner of my eye, willing myself to come up with an explanation for his presence, which I did once he walked over to the young officer who was gathering information for his report.

Fact: they knew each other. Fact 2: Officer Danielson respectfully deferred to Mac. Fact 3: nobody in the shop seemed much surprised he was here, and nobody, including Mac, seemed as upset, shocked or put out by this event as I was. Fact 4: Mac was opening his mouth and speaking to Luce.

"Hello, Luce," Mac nodded, removing his Stetson and holding it in his hand.

"Lo, Mac. This is my niece, Lyle Hudson. But perhaps you two have already met." How could she tell? Just by looking at him? Probably so. And how did they know each other? I was still confused.

"Correct. No, don't get up, Lyle." I was the only one sitting down. They looked so tall standing around me. I must have looked alarmed.

"You take this chair, Luce. I'll pull something from the back. He nodded amiably to Crista, who couldn't take her eyes off him.

"This is Crista Banks, she's a customer." Crista and I communicated with hand gestures that said she'd be in the small storeroom up the stairs in the back, checking on her dress, and would come back down later. Everyone in the room got the message.

Luce sat up, poured more tea in my cup, added sugar, and took a sip before handing it to me. Mac came back with a folding chair that seemed unusually small in his hand. He sat, dropping the Stetson to the side on the Queen Anne table. It crossed my mind, briefly, that a Stetson would be a cool hat in a magic act. *Cowboy Magician*, the possibilities were intriguing! What would be the first thing a cowboy magician would pull from his hat? I pondered.

"Lyle, Lyle." Luce snapped her fingers, bringing a smile to Mac's face, crinkling his eyes. "She gets this way under stress," Luce confided, blushing. Is she *blushing*? Luce, going girly on me? For him? I turned my head and looked at him, sitting there like...that. OK so it made sense.

"Why are you here?" I said pointedly to MacDonald

George. "How did you..." Was it those damned lights on that freaking car? I pointed to the window. "Can she turn them off, please? No one got hurt; those people need to go...away."

"Sure." He stood up in one smooth motion that held my eyes and Luce's eyes in some sort of masculine tractor beam and stepped over to have a word with Officer Danielson.

"You know him, Luce?"

"Mac?" Like there was anyone else in the room we were looking at. "Oh, I know Mac, yes. His sister's kid is my neighbor. Miguel keeps an eye on the Chevy for me, so I know it's safe. Nice people." She tucked a wisp of hair behind her ear. Smiled.

Our faces lifted like sunflowers turning toward the sun when he came back, and stayed with him while he settled himself in his seat.

"Done." The nasty lights went away.

"Thank you."

"You're welcome." Were we flirting? Luce gave me a sharp look.

"You didn't answer my question, Mac." I was quiet but not accusatory. Curious, in a Taoist, no-point-in-thinking-that-you-ever-know-anything kind of way.

"I heard the call on my radio and decided to stop by and see if you were OK." Playing his cards close to the chest. Who did that remind me of? Me? I glanced at Luce who was shaking her head at how odd life could be, definitely enjoying herself. I hated being the last one to know what was going on. Made me feel 13 years old. No one's favorite year.

"And what kind of radio would that be?" I asked sweetly, which cracked Luce up.

"I'm a detective, Lyle." Now he was curious, too. Taoists like to sit back and see what happens, a description that would fit Luce at this moment, too. Well. Weren't *we* the bunch of Asian philosophers?

"Ah." I nodded my head, sagely. Lao Tse would be proud of me. "Well. Thanks for stopping by. I'm fine, as you can see. No mess, no bruises. Right as rain." Louise used to say that all the time, right as rain...

"Luce?" I was still dumfounded that someone could get around me and rob me without my knowing it. "It just happened. I couldn't stop it, didn't even know it had happened. Just like that, the dress...was gone!" Why was I so upset? I hate the shop, hate wedding dresses. What's one dress, anyway? What was up with me? I had a sudden, vivid image of blue eyes squinting at me through a curl of cigarette smoke, my father's contempt heavy in the air. "Lose some thing?" he'd say. Inviting me to complain or accuse him of messing with my head, which he was. For years my mother insisted I'd simply misplaced things. But they never showed up. I learned not to get too attached to possessions; if I liked it, it was sure to disappear.

I came around and saw that Mac and the police girl were gone. The people outside the shop were gone. The flashing lights were gone. Glory was in her basket looking up at me anxiously. Luce looked around for a bottle of water and went to the back of the shop. I was ready for stronger drink.

"So, how'd you two meet?" She called over her shoulder.

"I asked you first, remember?" I snapped back to the present.

"No, you asked me if I knew him, Lyle. Which I do." She grinned at me, enjoying her cold, bottled water.

"We met in the parking lot at Sun Ripe. I had

smashed some kid's face into the pavement and then let him run away."

"Excuse me?"

"He tried to take my purse!" Which justified any manhandling I may have inflicted on his sorry hide.

It's not that I'm violent by nature. In fact, I avoid conflict. But when I find myself physically threatened, I may, suddenly, over-react. It's like being hit by lightning. Dangerous. When I moved to San Francisco, I discovered Aikido—a martial art that gave me the discipline to overcome my reactivity. Even now, years later, my training keeps me from inflicting serious harm. Usually.

"All right, Lyle. I just asked." We looked at each other for a moment and Luce cracked up.

"Oh, Lyle, you are a treat! No wonder MacDonald is attracted to you. He doesn't have a chance!" More laughter, sharing the joke with herself.

"I should postpone the yoga retreat. This could be very entertaining!" Big grin, deftly flipping a shock of hair behind one ear. "I am seriously tempted."

"If that means that I don't have to keep Devil Cat for you, you're on!"

"Now, I promised William. You'll just have to tell me about it when I get back."

"Tell you what?" I asked. She just looked at me. I blinked first and looked away.

"We're going out Friday night," I grudgingly revealed.

"There. See?" Last word.

Luce cleared the dishes from the Queen Anne table and straightened things in the back of the shop. I stored the folding chair and called up the stairs to Crista, to let her know that I'd be closing early and it was time to go.

She had set up her design stuff in the storage space up-stairs and would work as late as Nola would let her.

Even if my 4 o'clock appointment intended to show up, she'd probably been deterred by the police. Maybe tomorrow. Or, not. I was seriously thinking of taking the rest of the week off.

I locked the front door, set the alarm, muttering curses about barn doors, and sat down to watch the light sink from the sky, the outlines of trees disappearing into twilight. Street lights would come on any minute. Glory came over and hopped into my lap, settling her bony legs and looking out, too. I felt Luce standing behind me, her hand lightly on my shoulder. We shared the silence together.

"Luce? Why don't you come back to the house. There's something I want to ask you. And I need a drink. Glory hates it when I drink alone. Don't you?" The dog licked my face then jumped down and shook herself, sending a fine dusting of white hair into space.

"Sure, Lyle. I'd like that."

Crista came quietly down the stairs, looking around at the silent shop.

"Hope I didn't keep you waiting, Lyle." Some sort of sparkles glinted in the dark hem of her skirt.

"No problem. Your timing is good. Things going OK?"

"Outrageous!" Translated by her smile into good, very good. I offered her a ride home, but it was a nice night and she preferred to walk. I let her out the front door, reset the alarm, turned out the lights and locked up. Luce was waiting for me by her truck.

"Want to race?" she said. We had a history in that department. Hudson women and our cars. We smiled, remembering.

"No way! Some unsuspecting citizen would end up

getting hurt, and *then* where would we be?"

Simultaneously, we cheered: "Half way to Colorado!"

Glory fed, drinks poured (scotch for me, white wine for Luce), I asked her to come upstairs and take a look at Louise's room. The armoire and dresser were empty, chairs and incidental tables pushed off to one side. Knickknacks and photographs boxed and stored, paintings on the floor, propped against the walls, Persian rugs rolled up, wood floors bare. My mother's four-poster looked like a raft in a sea of change. The lights were low. We studied the room silently, Luce waiting for me to find my words.

"If I'm going to stay here for any length of time—and I'm not saying I am, mind you—I'll have to move down here. The upstairs is impractical." Luce nodded, encouraging me to continue.

"And even if the house were to be sold, I wouldn't want people in here walking around in her bedroom. I'd just as soon change things now." I paused, casting a superstitious glance over my shoulder, as if the house was listening.

"I love the light in this room, in the whole house, Luce. And in the summertime the leaves give it a sense of airiness and privacy. It's lovely. I was thinking of repainting, getting a different bed, saving this one for...later." Whatever that meant. I was not going to sleep in my mother's bed. Period.

"Sounds good, Lyle, eminently practical. I like to think of you staying for a bit. It would be quite a change, wouldn't it." A statement, not a question.

"Why don't I get you a couple of movers in to help you shift things around. I bet Miguel would help you." Miguel was Luce's neighbor, the one with the good-looking uncle. Small world.

"Excellent. It can wait till you get back. I'd like to paint the walls first."

"On your own? Wouldn't you like to have some help with that, too?" She sat on one side of the bed and swung her feet up, sipped her wine. I sat stiffly on the other side of the bed, cradling my drink.

"Lyle, relax. She went in her sleep, as far as we can tell. In this room. Quiet and peaceful, the way most people would like to go, given their druthers. Lou was a good woman and she lived a good life. I feel nothing but peaceful when I think of her, Lyle. Eventually, so will you."

"Maybe. I don't know. The gun makes me wonder."

"She kept it at the shop, not in this room. Whatever the issues were, they had no place here. Give it time, you'll see."

I nodded, non-committal. I reflected on the gun, which had a new home in my blue leather satchel. Every time I looked for something, it was there, asking me questions. I sighed and finished my scotch. Famous Grouse, my old familiar. "Got any plans for supper, Luce?"

"No, dear. I thought I'd stick around and dine with you. Unless you'd rather go out?"

"No, staying in works for me. I'm pretty worn out."

"I should think so! Let's go downstairs and you can put on some music while I root around in the fridge, OK?" I turned out the lights, closed the door, and we walked companionably down the stairs.

The evil crank calls had abated, or I just hadn't been around the house that much to notice. The neighbors had returned to their customary lives and took my comings and goings as part of the order of things. While she was cooking, Luce told me that my aunts, the L&L's, had decided to give me some space. They were busy with a number of projects and had plenty to keep them busy without worrying about me. "Just tell her the door's always open," was the message. Like I was a stray creature that needed to be humored. Maybe I was. That made Luce laugh.

Over supper in the kitchen, we talked about the robbery. "I can't believe the dress just disappeared like that, without a trace, in daylight, cars going by. And no one saw a thing," I said, wondering at the neatness of it, but holding back the 25G Ace as my hole card.

"As far as we know, Lyle. The police are sure to question a lot of people, you know. Somebody might have seen something."

"Possibly." Pork chops and sautéed mushrooms. Luce had put together an excellent Marsala sauce, and I was trying not to talk with my mouth full.

Luce said my upset was less about theft and more about the sacrosanct nature of the shop as my mother's life work. It wasn't my store, it was my mother's store that had been robbed. It grieved me that I couldn't keep it safe, untouched.

We sipped our pinot noir and ruminated on that one. Luce's look said she wouldn't put it past *me* to pull a stunt like that, and if I hadn't been so visibly moved, I'd have been her first suspect. Yeah, my eyes said back, if I weren't so allergic to the thought of marriage. Who said anything about marriage? Luce's eyes replied. Some women just like weddings and wedding dresses. Not me, my eyes shot back. Oh hush and drink your wine. Luce's eyes liked to have the last word, too.

The truth is, a good deal of my lying centers around the subject of marriage—whether I was or wasn't, how many times, death of spouse, divorce, murder, "He had it coming"—whatever my fancy devises. I'm past caring whether or not I get caught out. Whose business is it, anyway? People want a statistic to pin on me, and I resent the sense of entitlement to my personal life.

If we were at a bar having a drink and you asked me? I'd lie. If I liked you and was in a good mood, the lie would be small. Hell, I might even tell the truth. If I felt you were being nosy, the lie would be flagrant, operatic; it might go on for twenty minutes. I might even manage a few tears.

Interestingly enough, when I'm playing cards the subject does not come up. No one cares. It's one of the few things I really appreciate about the game. That and a run of good luck.

9

Thursday morning, Luce stopped by as promised on her way out of town. Tetley was riding in the Cadillac of cat-carriers, making disturbing growls beside Luce's feet. Luce's "friend", William—a big, bluff man in denim jacket and jeans—stood a few steps down from Luce, a big sack of cat bits in his arms. Not so much to be helpful as hopeful to see what might happen if the cat was released from confinement.

I was shuffling around in my slippers and robe, dewy-eyed and fresh as spring, as anyone in their right mind would be at 6:30 a.m.

"Luce, dammit! It's still dark out! What's wrong with you?"

"Tsuh! Salina is not Topeka, for your information, Lyle. It does take a while to get there and we want to arrive in time for the second stretch and second meditation of the day. It'll be light soon enough. Here's Tetley, and here's his food. Put the sack inside the door, Will."

She did not take a breath or slow down, just kept talking as William stowed the cat kibble. He beamed at me over the top of her head. "You know Tetley's habits, Lyle. The cat will be fine. I'll call you from the car when we're driving back. Sunday afternoon, I suspect. Let's go, William. Bye, Lyle!" A peck on the cheek. Gone.

I closed the door. Nothing needed to be done. Luce had left the cat pan for Devil Cat's "biologicals" in the basement the night before. I hate cat pans.

"I'm going back to bed, Cat. You stay in your box and think about life for a bit. Better than boarding at the Vet's, right? Later." Four days, I thought, I can do this.

Glory was still in bed, under the comforter. I plugged myself in beside her, mooshed the pillows, and to my great delight promptly fell asleep.

I woke up calm and hungry. Great combination! It was going to be a mild day for February, not a flake of snow in sight. Awesome! Bet it's mild enough for a run! Anything faster that a walk counts as a run to me; I like to be flexible.

Downstairs, I fed Glory and we both looked at the cat, still in his carrier. Glory knew better than to get too close and decided to finish her breakfast now rather than wait for later. I made myself a cup of herbal tea and thought I'd better run sooner than later. *Carpe diem.*

I let Glory out back, opened the cat carrier and left a dish of bits to distract his attention while I changed into my running clothes. "Rags! You mean rags!" my mother said whenever I left the house this way. SF or KS, the outfit was the same: T-shirt, sweatshirt, leggings (sort of), and shoes. Who cares what I looked like? I was going to get messy and sweaty anyway.

I headed north, then west, up towards the university where the hills were a bit of a push for me, but it wasn't as bad as hills in San Francisco. My mantra was "Just keep moving." It didn't have to be pretty. If I took it easy, I'd be fine. And I was! First time out, stick to 30 minutes, with 10 minutes to cool down. Whoever thinks Kansas is flat has a surprise coming in Lawrence. Eastern Kansas can roll quite a bit. Things don't flatten out until you're out west, well past the Flint Hills.

Kansas countryside fascinates me. God's gift to landscape painters. I like to think about the fact that these empty miles were sea bottom once. I pictured the subtle muted earthiness of it as I jogged from street to street, angling my way up to KU.

The part of town where I ran was tree-lined and picturesque, Old West Lawrence, with its cobbled streets, Victorian houses, stone hitching posts still standing by high curbs. The curbs seemed excessive until it rained. In a downpour, you could see they made sense. The water could rise ten inches in moments and fly off down hill. It could rain so hard here, with the thunder so loud, it felt like fists were pounding on the roof of your car. More people were hit by lightning than I cared to think.

Pausing at the top of Mississippi Street, I caught my breath and checked the watch. Twenty minutes out. Time to head back. College kids were walking slowly up to campus, backpacks full and more books in their arms. A random skateboard caught my eye and reminded me of Blake Phipps, the dreadlocks angel from my teaching days. It was too early in the day for cell phones (most undergraduates dislike early classes), but the iPods were in evidence. Was I ever like that, plugged in and tuned elsewhere? Nah. Probably too busy bickering inside my head, shouting at an imaginary biology professor that I would never need to know about Rana Pipiens or what the inside of a frog looked like.

I remembered one early morning while an under-graduate at a university far, far away. I had stepped out of my Dodge Dart, horrified to discover that I was still wearing my fuzzy pink slippers. Mere minutes left to get to class, the walk across campus a gauntlet of humiliation from which I still bear scars!

These days kids wear pj's everywhere, but then it was unheard of. What was I, stoned? A friend took pity and loaned me her gym shoes. I have no other memory of that day.

Back at the house, I found that Tetley had been surly, as expected. Kibble was scattered across the floor like hail, plastic bowl upside down but intact. Glory tip-toed downstairs from where she had been hiding, stay-ing out of Tetley's path. I fetched a bowl of cereal and a banana, ate on the back porch, shoes off, throwing the ball for Glory whenever she brought it back. If I ne-glected to throw the ball, she would drop it on my foot and go chase it after it rolled off. That dog would con-tinue to play with me if I had a stroke, I was sure of it.

The mindless action allowed me to mull over the demand for money. Twenty five thousand was pretty specific. Not ransom for the dress, clearly. Pay Up. A debt? Whose? Putting money in a toolbox in the garage was pretty lame. Too easy to watch. Whoever was dealing me these aces was either stupid or wanted me to call the bluff. Maybe Luce was right, maybe it wasn't about money at all.

Mr. Tetley the Poisonous stuck his head around the door and gazed at me with one yellow eye. He had two, but he didn't like you to catch him looking at you. The cat sneered and returned to swatting his food and curs-ing. James Cagney reincarnated.

The day brightened as the sun won out over the clouds. What will you do with your day, Lyle? Coffee?

Maybe later, maybe downtown. Definitely after a shower! Washing my hair, I came up with a few possibilities.

Hustling into jeans, light blue turtleneck sweater, jacket and scarf, I grabbed my satchel—gun still in it—and left the house, telling Glory to maim any interlopers. Tetley was nowhere in sight. Hooking my reading glasses onto the top of my head to keep my hair back, I skipped down the front steps and headed downtown, donning my sunglasses. If anybody ever designed a dual-purpose hairband/reading glasses item, I'd buy a hundred of them.

Just after ten o'clock, so most shops were open, the business day moving apace. I headed east on Ninth Street, took a right onto Mass, and strolled past Weaver's and The Mad Greek restaurant and into Copy Mart.

Inside, I moved the sunglasses up to hold my hair and placed the readers on my nose so I could root around in the satchel for the notebook that held the tantalizing clues to what I was sure must be some dark chapter in Louise's past. For a moment, there, I swore I heard her laughing at me, telling me not to be so dramatic.

My turn at the counter, I looked up, greeted the clerk and was about to explain my rather pedestrian request when a man started yelling behind me.

"Nobody Move!"

Of course, I turned to see what was going on.

"Stay right there! Everybody! This is a robbery!" A skinny, not-so-tall guy was waving a gun around, unnecessarily, I might add. The other two customers had left the store after placing their orders, so it was just me, the clerk behind the counter, and two guys working copy machines further back in the store.

My mouth dropped open. "You are robbing a Copy Mart? What are you, stupid? There is no money here, you idiot! This is not a bank!"

"Shut up! Shut the fuck up! Hands in the air!" An idea of going for Louise's gun flashed through my mind, but with his piece already out there and waving around, it'd be stupid to even try. Hey, hey...was this guy just a little familiar? Droopy jeans, dirty sneakers, knit cap, blue windbreaker. The bandana on the face was new.

"Shouldn't you be across the street?" I pointed. "See? Wells *Far*-go. It's a bank. They have money there. *This* place is Copy Mart. What do you plan to steal, toner?"

"I said shut up, bitch!" He moved closer with the gun, pointing it at my head.

"Bartholomew? Is that you? It is you, isn't it."

"I said SHUT UP!" The force of this last statement caused the clerk and the two guys in back to hit the floor. Bart, or whoever, was squeaking and high-pitched, like he might actually start shooting.

"Hey, is that gun real?" I asked with a demented perkiness.

"Turn around, now!" I wondered how he was going to get any money from anybody since everyone except him and me were on the floor.

"OK, OK, no need to be rude." Thanks, mom, I was wondering what would be appropriate to say to a nervous skinny guy with a gun.

He shoved the gun at me again, as if punctuating with a finger to make a point. Shifting my weight slightly to my right, as if following the metal finger, I gathered up some torque, dropped the satchel to the floor, and swung my entire body to the left in one motion, going for a full circle.

In its initial arc, my extended hand clamped on his right wrist (the one connected to the hand connected to the gun) and lifted it over his head, taking him off balance. My right arm came around and caught the guy's arm where it joined his shoulder and lifted him off his feet. He weighed nothing, the momentum did it all.

I stayed with him as he flew backwards and hit the floor with his back, lifted his arm straight up behind him and flipped him onto his belly, locking his shoulder with my foot, stretching his arm toward the back of his head. Classic move. Very firmly, I removed the gun he could no longer feel, and looked at him. Not even winded, feeling pleased with myself.

"OK, kid, you know the drill. If you move, I will dislocate your shoulder, which will hurt. He answered by attempting to move and discovered that it was not a good idea.

"Hey, guys? Anybody there?" Three Copy Mart guys stood up and looked at me, silent as ghosts.

"You didn't see that, did you? That's too damn bad. I was awesome, wasn't I, Bart? Remember me? Sun Ripe parking lot?" He groaned and tried not to move. "Thanks. So. Did we push an alarm? Do we need to call the police? I could stay like this for a little longer, but my friend here might hurt himself."

The clerk nodded.

"OK. We wait."

Not long, either. Flashing lights, two patrol cars, folks in blue, guns at the ready, entered the store and turned on me.

"Whoa! Hey, I'm the good guy here!" Their guns looked so much bigger than Bart's. "I'm just keeping this guy company until you arrived, right, guys?" This over my shoulder to the three amigos who began synchronized nodding.

"Hand over the gun, please. Ma'am." I recognized the voice instantly and turned to face Officer Danielson's ironic eyes. Hazel. I held the gun by the barrel and extended the handle to her slowly.

"Let go! Let me go! Tell her to let go! I can't feel my arm!"

"All right. Let him go," said Officer Danielson's tall partner, "And step back slowly, please. Back behind me. You! Hands on top of your head. Now."

I did as I was told and stood back while Officer Danielson got the guy off the floor and into cuffs. The hat came off the head.

"Do you recognize him, ma'am? You called him, what? Bart?"

"No, I don't know this man. Guess I was fooled by the hat, the jacket." I just assumed the robber was the same kid who tried to rob me in the Sun Ripe parking lot. Oh, oh. I had made a foolish and potentially fatal mistake. Not a first for me, and not lethal, I reminded myself. You are alive.

Whoever he was, was loaded into the back of a squad car and one set of flashing lights drove away. Officer Danielson walked me over to one of the computer stations, sat me down and took my statement, jotting notes with lean, dark hands. She was very thorough, professional and polite.

"You do that martial arts move a lot?" she asked, putting her pad and pen away, looking at me with amused eyes and a not-quite-smile.

"That move? Not in a couple years. It just came over me. I guess because I thought I knew him, thought he was this punk kid..."

"He had a *gun*, Ms. Hudson. Never a good idea to

mess with a gun, no matter who is holding it. It was loaded, you know. He could have killed you, right over there." I stared at her. Neither of us blinked.

"I could use a drink of water," I said. Officer Danielson shot a look at the counter and one of the clerks scrambled toward the back room. Please don't let her be psychic, I begged the universe. She doesn't need to know about the handgun in my satchel for which I do not have a permit. Not as if I got to use it, or knew how, I reflected.

"I'm glad you're safe, Ms. Hudson. Things turned out OK. Meanwhile, take it easy, please, no more Jackie Chan."

I smiled at that. "Who would rob a Copy Mart?" I asked. We shared a laugh, and the clerk guy brought me a glass of water, which I drank gratefully.

"Takes all kinds," she said. "Have a good day." Yeah. *She'd* have a story to tell at lunch today. Wait till you hear this one!

I pulled myself together, placed my order which the clerk promised would be free, and got out of there before the manager arrived and I had to go through the narrative again.

"Tell him I'll be in this afternoon to pick up the photocopies. He can talk to me then."

Back on the sidewalk, I did the switch-the-glasses-headband routine and looked around, deciding where to go. Coffee. What I needed was a lot of caffeine and sugar to offset the adrenaline. I decided to backtrack to Ninth Street and stop by the Bourgeois Pig, a funky little place with a few tables out front on the sidewalk to capitalize on the mildness of the day. I claimed a cappuccino and biscotti from the bar and sat outside to think.

Was it me or this place? In San Francisco I never got violent. Kansas. Bloody, bloody Kansas. What the hell was I doing here? I chased myself around the puzzle of my choices and came to the conclusion that I had no perspective whatsoever.

And why was I not shaking like a leaf? Was I expecting this stuff to happen, waiting for people to wave guns at me? No. This time, it was an accident, my being at Copy Mart. The thing with Bart in the Sun Ripe parking lot felt personal. Better not go there, Lyle. If you start to think about you-know-who, he'll probably show up and ask a lot of questions. I looked around superstitiously, then took my empty cup inside and placed it on the bar. Time to go have a chat with Nola.

10

I stood transfixed on the sidewalk, gawking at the new window display for Hyacinth. It wasn't that I couldn't believe my eyes, I did believe that what I was seeing was real, but the dress defied words. *Gone With the Wind* meets the Taj Mahal. Did it even have a frame? It looked like it was standing in the window on its own feet, daring the viewer to enter the shop. As a wedding dress, it was a Mardi Gras parade. It could enter as a float. What was that stuff hanging on the backdrop behind the dress? Pom poms? No, they were little furry hearts and...cupids? There was more of the stuff suspended from the top of the window. It looked like a Valentine's blizzard!

Teeth clenched (they were well beyond 'on edge'), I stormed into the shop, the bells on the door sounding like hail in a high wind.

"Nola! What the...."

"Ssssh. Hush, dear. I'm on the phone." Perky smile, one manicured finger raised. "Oh, yes, Ms. Wainscot,"

Nola gushed, "I would be delighted to meet with you Saturday. Yes. Appointments only, much more digni-fied, I agree. Oh!" (girlish giggles) "Not *in the least!* Four p.m. will be perfect. Yes, indeed. See you then! Bye bye!" She hung up the phone, finished her notes, and looked at me with a satisfied smile.

"Lyle, you will never guess who that was!" Nola was pink with excitement and did not pause for my obligatory lame guesses. "That was Lavendra Wain-scot!"

"Wainscot? As in an architectural element of dining room design?"

"No, silly! Wayne-Scott, as in the Arts Board, as in Lawrence Finer Gardens Association, as in M-O-N-E-Y?"

"Yeah, OK. Got it. Nola, what is that *thing* in the window?"

"Thing?" I got a blank look. "Oh!" The lights went on. "The dress! Isn't it divine! It's the very latest *thing*, perfect word, Lyle! I saw it in the latest issue of Prairie Brides and ordered a sample immediately. It arrived yesterday and I put it right on display. AND, wouldn't you know it, but Ms. Wayne-Scott drove by on her way somewhere, saw the dress, stopped the car and was just *hypnotized* by the window," she paused for breath, "and NOW she wants to buy it! Oh, Lyle, aren't you thrilled?" Thrilled? I was speechless.

"Nola, calm down. What does she want the dress *for?*"

"For? Why, her wedding, of course!" We looked at each other as one would at an alien species.

"Her wedding? Which one? How old is this woman, Nola? What size is she? Any older than 12—twelve year olds can't get married in this state, can they? Any larger than a size three, and she'll look like a....a...a...an exploding can of shaving cream! Have you looked at the dress, Nola?" I grabbed her arm and dragged her to the window display.

"Lyle! Of course I have looked at it! Have you? Can't you see the glamour? The mystery? This dress is a dream!" She sighed and we stood there a full minute looking at the bizarre confection of lace, seed pearls, ruffles, gew gaws and frou frou I didn't even have names for, the satin band around the waist, the fluffy-floaty scary stuff at the shoulders, the whole thing blinding in its perfect whiteness.

"Nola. I stopped by to ask you about something, but I cannot think with this *thing* in the window. It has to come out. It will frighten small children, Nola, give them nightmares."

"NO! Lyle! Stop!" The screech of brakes interrupted our argument. One of those new VW bugs, bright yellow, double-parked in the street and two blonde coeds—no, three (one was still pulling herself out of the car), ran to the window and started to jump up and down, hugging each other and squealing.

"Omigod, omigod, omigod!" They didn't see Nola and me, or perhaps they thought we were similarly moved by the dress.

"It's even more beautiful in person!" one sighed, hand over heart. The third girl joined her friends and they stood there in their pj bottoms, belly T-shirts, and navel rings to gaze enraptured at the object of their adoration.

"See," Nola whispered, "This is magic, Lyle. Magic! Look at those girls. They know what I mean." I was afraid they did.

"Lock the door, Nola! Don't let them in!"

"Lyle Hudson, what is wrong with you?" I get asked that a lot. "This is a bridal shop, that is a wedding dress, those girls are customers. This is a business, Lyle. We sell merchandise to our customers. We do not to lock them out. "

Maybe I should go back to Copy Mart. Life made more sense there. "Nola, You're absolutely right. I think...I need a cup of tea. Want some?"

She didn't even hear me. She was caught up in the spell along with the three girls at the window. I headed to the back of the shop wondering if my mother had an emergency bottle of scotch stashed somewhere.

The shop bells rang and the three Tinkerbells entered to be embraced by Nola's maternal regard for the inner bride in each one of them. They chatted and gushed and eventually piled back in the cute little bug and drove away. Nola came back and settled herself at the Queen Ann table.

"Sugar?" I asked. I had replaced the tea in my cup with scotch and had almost regained my equilibrium.

"Never mind, Lyle. I can do for myself." She fussed with the teapot and soon was sipping her tea, smiling her pixie at me, cheeks flushed and glowing.

"I have a gift, Lyle. I can tell when a dress is special. Just *right* for today's world."

"I guess you do, Nola," I sighed. "Never second-guess the master."

"So. What's up? Did you want to take another look at the books? At the list of appointments? You didn't come to tell me you're selling the shop, did you? Her hand rose daintily to the neck of her twin set, indicating the degree of her alarm.

"Nothing like that, Nola. Relax." I scrutinized my tea cup. "I'm still in the fog about the shop, no idea what I want to do. "

"That's quite all right, dear. It's perfectly understandable. You take your time. By the way, I hope that you know what you are doing with that girl? Crista? She said you OK'd her working in the store room upstairs, so that's OK, but she *is* unusual, Lyle. And what she is doing to that dress!" Nola shook her curly head and poured herself the last of the tea in the pot.

"Crista is fine, Nola, a creative, bright young woman."

"I guess so, if you say. She just seems Odd."

"That's *Goth*, Nola. It's a style, not a character flaw. I like her."

"I see that, Lyle, but after the robbery..." Nola was setting up for a sniff, and I wasn't in the mood.

"Nola, Crista did not steal the dress." I tried to avoid looking at the latest 'dress' in the window. Nola's eyes were drawn to it as if magnetized. She sighed softly with contentment. Time to ask my question.

"Nola, do you remember a customer from way back, late 80's maybe, named Ann Headley?"

"Before my time, dear." Nola consulted her inner social register and frowned. "No particular Ann comes to mind. You know, before I started here, oh, ten years ago, I really didn't pay much attention to weddings. Outside my own circle, of course." Nola twinkled at me. "These days, I'd say I'm very much in the know!"

The phone rang and Nola picked up. I waved and left the shop. My legs felt stiff from the morning run because I had forgotten to stretch, and I realized I was hungry. Decided to hot-foot it before the tea and scotch caught up with me.

I did the wild turkey dance at the front door, searching for the right key. Victory! I stepped nimbly around Glory, and dashed to the washroom off the library. Home free all! Made it!

In the kitchen, Glory watched me scarf down the last of some leftover chicken salad and an apple. I ate another apple, watching the dog race around the back yard. I was trying to stay away from bread. OK, I was watching my weight as part of an ancient, ingrained, irrational dating ritual left over from high school, no doubt. No-food-before-date-night, the age-old taboo.

Startled out of my refrigerator reverie by the home phone, I answered it without thinking, only to be rewarded by a crank call, another bout of garbled sound. Bloody hell.

"Get a life! Get a new phone number! The person who lived here is dead, don't you get it?" My irritation had led me into the trap of trying to reason with a crank caller. I knew it was pointless, but there you are.

"You know what to do. Five days," the gravel voice said. "Pay Up. Or else." Followed by a click.

"Well, we'll see, won't we?" I told the phone and replaced it on the hook. I looked out the kitchen window at the garage and checked to be sure the gun was still in my satchel. It was.

"Glory! C'mon, girl." I called her inside, grateful that the yard had no trees suitable for climbing. "Glory, where's the cat?" I hadn't seen Tetley anywhere and his bowl was still full of food. I had to feed the cat on the countertop because Glory loves cat food and gets dog breath that would take rust off a fender. Glory loves to play "Where's the cat." It is her second favorite game, next to "Get the possum." The dog snapped immediately to attention, glued her nose to the ground, and proceeded to hunt. Despite my encouragement and cheers, she turned up nothing. No Tetley. Wretched cat.

Taking pity on the dog, I got out her leash and took her for a walk in the neighborhood, tennis ball strategically hidden. Playing her I'm-the-best-dog-in-the-world role, Glory pranced beside me, on her way to dog heaven. To look at her, you'd never know that I was the one on the leash and she was walking me. It was the only way I could get her to tolerate the leash. Today, Glory knew where she wanted to go. The park was close by. There were no other dogs in sight. Glory had an inner Rottweiller and she would savage smaller dogs and make Kamikaze runs at large ones. She is so petite that people give me dirty looks for walking her in a muzzle. Little do they know.

At the park, Glory kept up her Little Princess act, so I threw the ball, letting her off the leash and watching her run. She returned the slimy tennis ball unfailingly, laying it at my feet like a sacred relic. When there were small bushes in the way (OK, my aim was not consistent), she would leap over them, skipping through the air like a gazelle.

Glory is both obsessive and unrelenting. When I got tired, I sat on a swing in the empty park while she ran back and forth between the ball and me, showing me where it was. When that didn't work, she'd retrieve the ball and drop it in my lap, giving my knees a sharp push with her paws. "Throw the ball, Lyle!" When I ignored her, she circled around and nipped me in the butt.

"Ouch! That's it, Glory! No more ball!" I stuffed the ball in a pocket and showed her my empty hands, glaring at her. She shivered theatrically, Glory's version of a guilt trip. I ignored her.

"It's not nice to yell at your dog, you know!" came a child's voice behind me.

"Yeah! And besides, it doesn't work!" crowed voice #2. I twisted my swing around to find two small boys standing at the next swing. Red-cheeked, denim jackets, and baseball caps, one red, one blue, emblazoned with KU Jayhawks.

"You're right, boys. But I don't know what else to do. I told her I'm worn out, but she won't stop. You saw her nip me in the butt, right?" They laughed when I said "butt", a real knee-slapper for the younger set.

"You guys here alone? Where's your mother? Don't you know you're not supposed to talk to strangers or go near unfamiliar dogs? She's a monster, she could kill you." Gales of giggles. Storms of hilarity. I was clearly more fun than roly-polies, gravel, or snakes.

"She's over there!" They pointed at a woman with a stroller sitting on a park bench, next to a diaper bag, a sack of snacks, scarves and other items heaped up beside her, a blanket-swathed item in the stroller at her feet that I assumed to be an infant.

"Hi, Mom!" the boys yelled, jumping up and down and waving. I waved, too. Mom appeared unconcerned at the vision of a long-haired, disheveled woman on a swing being stared at by a demented, small white dog.

"I am too a stranger, " I told the boys. "See how strange I am?" Hanging my head to one side, rolling my eyes back in my head, I stuck my tongue out. Totally cracked them up.

"Oh, yeah? That's nothing! Tommy! Tom-tom! Show her the Monkey Boy face!" With no further ado, young Tom puffed out his cheeks, crossed his blue eyes, and pulled his ears straight out to the sides, looking very much like a Monkey Boy, indeed. I regarded him solemnly.

"Cool. Glory thinks it's cool, too, don't you, girl?" Thinking I was about to relent, the dog moved closer, nose touching my pocket.

"That's the dog's name? Glory?" Uh oh. Sometimes I forget what a God-fearing place the Midwest can be, that even the younger generations are conversant with Biblical rhetoric. The boys, Tom and Little Tom (I never got his name), immediately started to shout this particular word of Praise at the top of their lungs. "Glory! Glory!" They alternated, a kind of miniature call and response thing going on. "Glory! Glory! Glory! Glory!" Throwing their little arms up in the air over their heads and marching around me and the gonzo dog as if we were tied to a stake or something. Soon, they started running and chasing each other around us in a tight circle, shrieking in delight a never-ending "Gloryglorygloryglory!" A distant "Halleluiah!" floated across the play ground.

I had to throw the ball to break the trance. Glory dashed off and the boys screeched to a halt, laughing and trying to catch their breath.

"Hey, boys? I think your mother is calling you." Inaudible to them, her feeble yoo hoos drowned out by their own maniacal mantra, Mom was waving a return to home base.

"OKAY, MOM!" Waves and jumping in the air, a quick "See you! Bye!" thrown over the shoulder as they pelted off. Glory dropped her filthy relic in the dirt at my feet.

"No way, Glory bird. Come here." Snapped on the leash. "You can carry it home. I am not, *not*, touching that thing! It's disgusting!" The walk home was short and uneventful. In the house I put down fresh water for the dog, glanced around for Luce's cat, and lay down on the couch in the library. Definitely time for a nap!

11

Thursday evening was spent wrapping up loose ends and taking stock of my situation, which roughly translates as a lot of running around in order to avoid the central question: What are you going to *do*, Lyle? Denial works, for me. It can be reassuringly industrious. Why think about the future when you can go to the hardware store and collect paint samples for the bedroom? There's online poker. I could work on my game!

I ran out to Copy Mart to retrieve my photocopies, assuming (rightly so) that the evening crew would have no clue who I was and that I could escape without weird looks and embarrassing questions. I picked up some Chinese take-out (egg foo yung for me, extra fortune cookies for Glory) and a DVD, "La Femme Nikita," the original, with subtitles. In San Francisco, it is part of my movie collection, as is "The Professional"' with Jean Reno and Anna Paquin. Awesome flick! No, I'm not addicted to violence; I like to think that I love movies, from "Finding Nemo" to "The Impostors," to "Scent of

Green Papaya." The litmus is a good story line. Alone in the car, I thought briefly of Chas, how we spent so much time watching movies together. Later, Chas, later.

Back at the house, I brought in the mail and threw it on the couch for later. Dropped the take-out on the kitchen counter, and kicked off my shoes. Cursed myself briefly and carried the shoes back out to the front door and dropped them on the rug in the entranceway. A standard in Hudson households is "Shoes come off at the door." The mommy-inside-of-me left me no choice but to obey the prime directive.

Returning to the kitchen, I uncorked a 2003 Castle Rock Sauvignon Blanc and stood by the counter, appreciating its sharp clarity and absolute yumminess. It deserved some music to go with it, but I never got there. Tetley. Where the hell was Tetley?

"You don't suppose the cat died, do you, Glory?" The dog's eyes indicated that she was interested only in a fortune cookie or a dog biscuit. If I wanted to put the bowl of cat chow on the floor, she'd eat that, too.

"Where could he be? We have looked everywhere." The combination of guilt and fear of the wrath of my Aunt Luce led me to postpone the egg foo yung (well, maybe just a quick nibble) and scout around for the cat.

I called "Here kitty, kitty, kitty!" in that repulsive falsetto adults use when we try to lure an obstinate animal. Who in their right mind would dignify such a call with a response? Not me, and definitely not Tetley.

"YO! Teabags! Time for supper!" No more effective, but I felt like less of an idiot. I rattled the plastic food dish enticingly, which aroused Glory's interest, but still no cat. I walked back to the kitchen, micro-waved the now-cold egg foo yung, and poured myself another glass of wine. Tossed fortune cookie #1 into the air. Glory caught it with a mighty crunch and dropped the pieces on the floor so that she could eat the cookie and avoid the tiny piece of paper. I don't know why she doesn't just eat the whole thing, paper included. She is one funny dog. Neat, too; not a crumb left behind, just a little spit of paper on the wood floor. I picked it up with my chopsticks. Moving the universal hair/eye ornament to the bridge of my nose, I read that my lucky numbers were 7, 22, 53, 84, and 19. The other side said that "The invisible is only invisible when looked at directly." Nah. Couldn't be the wine. I examined the glass in my hand carefully, looking for signs of tampering. Wait! Maybe this was a hint about how to find the cat! I cheered up and munched happily on the last of my supper.

Still no Tetley. I dug a small flashlight out of the utility drawer and decided I would reverse the direction of my previous search, working this time from the basement up. Lots of places to hide in the basement, but the lighting was bright; the flashlight totally unnecessary. Dusty things remained dusty. No cat had disturbed them. I made a mental note to talk with Luce about the quantity of junk down here. Not in the mood to think about it tonight. I had a cat to find!

Listening for the cat in the unnatural stillness of my mother's basement, my cell phone rang upstairs. Damn. Why does that always happen? Where's the damn phone? I charged up the basement steps, listening for another ring. As I reached the kitchen, it stopped. I swore again. The cell phone started ringing again. Charging into the library I threw myself across the leather couch and answered while the cell was still live, "Hello?" Silence. Not even a click. No incoming number. Maybe a salesman. Whoever it was had blocked their I.D. Was that even legal? "Asshole." I put the cell in my jeans pocket. Find the cat.

I remembered the other, earlier phone calls, coming at odd hours. Once, there was this blank sound, as if the person on the other end was listening. Then the call just ended.

I had thought it might be some random prank, but when I checked Lou's phone at the shop for messages, I'd found the same thing. Pause. Click. Dead air. I began to feel uneasy about being alone in the house, especially at night. My sense of myself as brave and gutsy disappeared like water into dry sand. It wasn't something I could even think about without shuddering. I tried to ignore the calls.

On my way back upstairs to the pantry, my cell phone chirped AGAIN. Not a number I recognized.

"Yes?" My no-nonsense voice. You never know...

"Um. Hi. Is this D—is this Lyle Hudson?" It had to be Blake, I had given him my number the other night. It was my own fault.

"Yes, Blake, it's me. How are you?"

"Oh, Wow! How do you *do* that, just know who's calling. I mean, it's not caller I.D., is it? It's your brain! It's the power of your *mind*!"

"Don't make too big a deal out of it, Blake. Very few people here have my cell number. Basic deduction, no biggy."

"Yeah it is. I think it's totally cool!"

"So. What can I do for you?" 'Do?' The question hung there while he thought about it. "Oh, DO, as in, why am I calling?"

"Exactly." I couldn't help smiling. Blake is a bit of a flake, but he's sweet.

"Uh...I thought I'd call and say hi. You know, have a conversation or something? See how you're doing. Do you want to meet for coffee maybe? Thursdays are cool downtown, there's usually stuff going on."

"Ah. I'd like that Blake, but tonight is not good for me. I'm in the middle of a project…"

"Whoa! Like research?"

"No, not quite, though there are some resemblances. Remember I told you I was looking after my mother's house? There are a few items I'm trying to find (like the freaking CAT!) and some papers I have to go through before Sunday. Maybe next week some time, OK?"

"Sure, I see. You must be, um, busy right now. Right."

"Truly, Blake. Today I'm busy, and there is nothing fun about it." My chagrin was sincere. "Tell you what. Let's plan on *next* Thursday. Maybe Reed's? If something comes up and you can't make it, just call. Otherwise, I'll meet you in the bar at 8."

"Yeah! Cool, Dr. uh…Lyle. That's great! See you then!"

"You bet. See you then. Bye, Blake." And I was off, back to tracking Tetley.

Following my intuition, I resumed the search on the second floor, Louise's bedroom. In his youth, T-Cat had spent a fair bit of time in this house, I remembered. Luce was always taking off on treks, walking tours, or hikes, leaving Tetley with her older sister. Louise had had a real affection for this ugly, grouchy cat and found him highly entertaining. She was the only one (aside from Luce) who did not bear the scars of his clawing on her ankles. When Tetley was in the house it was best to wear boots.

Standing in the bedroom doorway, I gave my attention to the cat. Previously I had been looking for him as one looks for car keys or overdue library books, not really paying attention, just going through the motions of looking.

Paying attention interests me. I hate taking so much for granted, going through days on the cruise control of habit. In my present state of denial, I was more than willing to give my attention to anything other than myself. Finding T-Cat would do just fine.

Paying attention feels good to do, once you slow down and, well, *pay attention*. It felt great, just standing there, Glory standing beside me looking around in tune with my looking around the room. It felt a lot like sitting at a poker table with a pile of chips to win. I relaxed an got comfortable with the process.

Despite the disarray of the contents, this was still very much Louise's room. The cat would not be on the bed, too obvious. Tetley was probably shocked by Louise's absence, not having been here in some time. He was an *old* cat. Avoiding his daily routines was ominous. He was probably brooding, or ill, either or both of which required darkness and solitude.

I checked the dresser drawers. Tetley was famous for slipping into small spaces, such as partly opened drawers, and spending the night tucked in someone's undies and socks. Then, in the morning, when you went to find clothing for the day, he'd jump out, fur on end, sparks flying from his evil yellow eyes! Scaring me...um, you...half to death! For some reason, folks preferred not to stay at Luce's house for the holidays. She might have taught the cat the drawer trick.

I sat on the bed and played with the flashlight for a while, my empty wine glass set aside. Click. Click. Click. On/Off; On/Off. Where are you, Tetley? I pulled an image of the cat into my mind: calico, almost brindled russets, grays, browns and black. Long-haired, with a pink nose. A tongue that could remove wallpaper. Tetley preferred a growl to a meow, and...Tetley snored. I sat quietly and listened. The house was silent, as if holding its breath. Glory held her breath, too. I held mine. We were four ears, listening. Nothing. Glory sat beside me on the bed, her nose and her attention pointed at the closet door which was, glory be, slightly ajar! Open enough for that cat.

"You stay here," I whispered to the dog. She lay down and placed her black nose on top of her paws. At the closet door, I slowly opened it wider and pulled the string for the closet light. At my feet like a discarded sweater, Tetley lay still and quiet. Sleeping? I knelt down and stroke his fur, felt his nose. Alive, but lethargic and unresponsive

"Not good, Tetley, you old plate of soup. Not good." He regarded me through silted eyes, his nictating membrane barely drawing back. "You stay there. I'll be right back." I got up, called the dog and ran down the stairs, closing the bedroom door behind me in the unlikely case that T-Cat was strong enough to drag his ass out of the closet.

I grabbed a handful of cat bits, a plastic bowl and turkey baster and rushed back up the stairs, leaving Glory outside in the hall. In the bathroom I filled the bowl with water, threw a towel over my arm and went to the closet to find Tetley still there, still breathing.

"Okay, here's the deal. I give you water, and you agree to live through the night. I'll take you to the Vet, should you choose to live. It's a good choice; I highly recommend it, T. Deal? Good. Here we go." I lifted the cat's head gently in my left hand, partially filled the turkey baster with water with my right. Inserted tip of baster into Tetley's mouth and let the water dribble out. He didn't like it but did not put up much of a fight, either. I took my time. We were both pretty serious about the whole operation.

After three relatively successful doses of water, we were both damp around the edges. I dried Tetley off and went and got a fresh towel to make a bed. He closed his eyes and resumed just lying there. "I'll be back later to check on you, T-man. You rest." I left the food and the water inside the closet door and pulled the string to shut off the light.

I retrieved my wine glass and went downstairs, Glory at my heels. Back in the library with a fresh glass of sauvignon blanc, I made a small fire, sat on the couch with Glory draped across my lap, watching the small flames, contemplating the transience of living things. Hudsons are expert at brooding.

Time passed. I listened to the sounds of the fire and drifted, not exactly "denying" anything, but not focusing, either. I guess you could say I was just sitting there. The wine was excellent and the dog was good company. I was content, sort of.

The cell phone rang again. I picked it up and answered without thinking. "Yes?" Not a demand as earlier, more a question.

"I was hoping you'd say that," said a familiar voice.

"MacDonald," I spoke three full syllables. "Hello."

"Hello, yourself." The voice was nice. Very, very nice. "I thought I'd give you a call and see if you were still agreeable to the idea of going out tomorrow night. You haven't changed your mind, have you?"

"Well, yes. I'm still agreeable, as you put it. Usually when I say yes, and a day and a time are established, I mean yes. What makes you think I might have changed my mind? Do I seem particularly changeable to you, MacDonald?"

"Yes. But I mean that in a good way."

I laughed. "Deciding *not* to go out with you after I said yes would be good?

"Don't be difficult, Lyle. Besides, there is something I need to know."

"Ah. What might that be?"

"Your address. Where you are? Unless you'd rather meet somewhere."

I gave him the address. "MacDonald, do I seem skittish to you? The kind of person who would run off, need to have her own car nearby?"

"A little. I guess you do."

"Well, why would you want to go out with such a woman?" He laughed and I smiled to hear it.

"To be honest, Lyle, I do not know. It could have something to do with the fact that you're an exceptionally attractive woman. And you're not skittish on the inside, in who you are. You have depth, Lyle, like water. When I am with you, I feel...thirsty."

"Whoa, whoa, whoa! Just a minute, there, mister! You can't just say things like that to me! I'm at an impressionable age!"

"I like that, too. Bottom line, Lyle? I want to go out with you. I thought we had covered that part already."

"Yes, but I know how I can be...and...never mind. It has been a long day, MacDonald. Bottom line? I'm looking forward to seeing you tomorrow. Why don't we move the time up to 6:30 so we can take time to sit and talk before we go out?"

"Excellent."

"You're smiling, aren't you."

"Yes, Lyle, I am. I am indeed smiling. One more question. Any food preferences?"

"No, I'm pretty much omnivorous. You don't have to choose on your own, Mac. We can talk about it; we're not teenagers, you know." Or 30-year-olds, for that matter.

"Far from it, thank god. OK, what's your pleasure?"

"Hmmm. In Lawrence, I like the Indian restaurant downtown. There's Mexican, always a favorite. How about you?"

"Indian it is. I'll make the reservations."

"Great. See you tomorrow, MacDonald. Good night."

"Night, Lyle. See you tomorrow."

That wasn't hard at all! What was I so upset about? Shaking myself, I got up off the couch, switched off the gas jets in the fireplace, gave Glory her last out. Went upstairs, stopping to check Tetley and squirt more water down his throat. Offered up a quiet prayer that he would make it through the night.

In my room, I climbed into T-shirt and pj bottoms, set a full glass of water on the bedside table, and went and brushed my teeth. Brushing out my hair, I regarded some long silver strands slipping across my fingers, the way it captured the gold of lamp light. I thought about MacDonald George, wondered about the mysteries of mutual attraction and wished I could be more relaxed about it. Let it be, Carlyle, let it be. No more thinking.

It had been a long day. I settled myself, listened for Glory's grunt of contentment from the end of the bed, and quite simply, fell asleep.

12

Tetley made it through the night. I managed to pull myself together and get the cat to the vet in Baldwin, south of town, before they opened at 7:30. Tetley kept a stoic silence in his carrier, and Glory sat beside me in her customary seat. She had insisted on coming along, and now, having figured out where we were, she was miserable. She kept shooting me nervous looks and wrinkling her brow.

"It's OK. You get to stay in the car." I ate the apple I'd brought and looked out at the cars and livestock trailers gathering in the lot around me. Ought to be interesting. Anybody here this early had to be totally dedicated to their pets, or desperate, like me. Eventually I found myself in the linoleum waiting room with sundry pets and their owners. I placed the carrier on the floor at my feet, got T-cat on the list and sat back to wait, resigned to the pace of waiting rooms.

A mother and daughter held towels full of tiny white puppies, looked like small white Labs. The

younger woman bent down, pups firmly embraced in
her ample arms, and squinted into T's Cat-Cadillac,
looking up from the cat to me.
"Zat creature alive? Hon, you should of saved
yerself the trouble. That loaf is baked!" Mom really
liked that one. The two of them chuckled, bouncing
and brimful of puppies.
"Mmm." I smiled enigmatically, trying not to roll
my eyes. They had me outnumbered and outweighed.
A denim-clad farmer who I'd seen step down from
the cab of an equine trailer, sat across from me, red tractor cap pulled low over his leathery face. An older man,
he was neatly dressed, a large buckle gleaming at his
waist, legs stretched out, one work boot propped on top
of the other. He seemed to know he was in for a significant wait and exuded an air of infinite patience. Like
me, he was taking in the people and pets, the coming
and goings of this busy office on a Friday morning. No
doubt, I had been pegged as one a them long-haired
college teachers with a scraggly old cat, possibly de-
ceased.
The puppies were ushered into the examining
room, and suddenly there was a lot more space—for a
minute. The door opened and a large, well-made man
walked in with what looked like a Mastiff to me, beautiful dog, calm-tempered, with huge paws. The man
checked in as the dog paced behind him. I reached out
my hand to let him smell it and then stroked his muzzle, rubbed behind his silky ears. The man sat down.
"Beautiful dog," I said. "Mastiff? Looks like he's
still a pup."
"Indeed he is," said the big man with his big, deep
voice. "Nine months old. Bet he weighs 100 lbs."
I had to crane to see over the pacing dog's back to
talk to his owner. "He's a brindle, isn't he? What's his

name?" The dog was clearly a *he*; hard to miss the generous package swaying back and forth in front of me.

"Chocolate brindle, Miss. His sisters are both solid brown. Name's Shadrack." Nice smile.

"Don't tell me! His sisters are Mishack and Abednigo?" I was smiling, too. The biblical tale of Daniel in the fiery furnace was one of my favorites as a child.

"Bingo! Give the lady a prize!" Shadrack wagged his tail happily and stood by the man, basking in his attention. Soon, the dog resumed his pacing, a slow, majestic, leonine gait.

Equine-trailer-man sat up and adjusted the hat on his head, signaling his entrance into the conversation. "So," he moved his shoulders in a friendly way and sat forward, leaning his elbows on his knees, watching the dog walk back and forth, "What's he in for?" A dramatic pause here and a twinkle in his eye tossed my way to see if I was listening. "A shot of Veee-aggra?"

My jaw dropped and my eyebrows hit the ceiling. At the same moment every adult in that room burst into laughter, including the Vet's assistant standing at the register.

"Heh, heh, heh." He sat back, pleased with himself, "Shot of Veee-aggra...."

Shadrack's owner smiled, a good sport about it. "No, Shadrack is here to get his inoculations. He's going to be a show dog, aren't you, boy?"

Tetley's name was called and I heaved the carrier into the examination room. The assistant, Dana, wearing a smock decorated with little cats, dogs, and fishies, reached in and dragged the inert feline out onto the steel examining table.

"What do we have here?" I recounted my adventures with the search and the turkey baster as the Vet walked in, drying his hands on some brown paper towels.

"A turkey baster?" he said, "That's inventive! Good for you. Let's start with his temperature and see what we see." Oh, my my. One good-looking veterinarian. Doc Tenent was one of those lean men with aquiline features, his gray-blue eyes catching the colors of his plaid shirt, wire-rim glasses, longish, wavy brown hair reaching his collar. Nice eyes, smooth skin, strong hands...damn. Nice! I tried not to stare and busied myself with Tetley who had come to and was not happy with the thermometer.

"105. Not good. He's pretty dehydrated. See this?" He took a handful of fur at Tetley's neck and pulled gently. The pelt practically stood where he had left it.

"That means he's too dry. Normally, his skin would go right back down. Hard to tell what else is going on till we take care of the dehydration." He washed his hands and checked Tetley's chart again. "Tetley is pretty sick, Ms...Hudson?" He looked at me, trying to place me. Wasn't going to happen.

"That's right. Luce is my aunt. This is her cat, Tetley."

"I've got that part." He smiled, charming me. "I've known Tetley forever. "Daniel Tenent." He held out his hand, which I took.

"Lyle Hudson. Nice to meet you." Dana looked on with one raised eyebrow.

"I'm going to give Tetley an antibiotic to see if it's an infection. If he doesn't respond, we'll talk about other possibilities for what might be wrong." As he spoke, he found the serum he wanted in a glass cabinet, loaded the syringe, and gave the cat the shot between his shoulders. Rubbed the medicine in and petted the cat with an expert hand.

"I'd like to keep him overnight with an IV to get

him rehydrated. Call before 8:30 and I'll let you know if you can come pick him up."

I stood there and studied the cat, petted under his chin, thinking about it. We had a rule about pets—Hudsons have a lot of little rules of life, most of which I have broken—No Extreme Measures.

"OK." Nodded my assent to the plan, pulled my escaping hair back and retied it snugly.

"Is that a shoelace?"

"Yeah, it is." I grinned at the man, switching on my flirty, tomboy look. You'd be surprised how many years the tomboy thing can work for a woman. It seemed to be working quite well for me now. Dr. Tenent laughed and shook his head.

"No offense! It is just another indication of resourcefulness. The turkey baster was most impressive."

"Oh. Well. Thanks. I see it more as a desperation move, myself. I was close to panic, if the truth be known. If I let anything happen to that cat, Luce'd kill me."

"I know the feeling," he said. "She has that effect on me, too." We smiled agreeably, to Dana's great interest, and I left so Shadrack could have his examination. I wondered if they'd even bother to try to get that dog up on the table.

On the way out, I begged a couple of dog biscuits for Glory, to tide her over until we got home. My apple was long gone; the dog treats looked good to me.

The Infiniti purred along the rolling hills back into town. The sky looked clear and the land looked dry. Water levels in the rivers were dropping, and creek beds were bone dry. People were fretting over their winter wheat. It was a drastically different mind set from SF, to see so much space given to weather and crops and cattle prices in the newspapers and on the radio. The methane from industrial hog farms in outlying districts was a huge concern to rural folks who suspected it was tied to health problems. Scientists were speculating on the impact of hog methane in the current trend of global warming. No one was laughing about it, either.

Back at the house, I set down enough kibble to keep Glory sane and promised her pancakes when I returned from my run. While I made my way haphazardly though 45 minutes of heavy breathing, aches, and hunger pangs, the clear sky turned gray and sat itself down on top of the trees. The air turned sharp and cold. In San Francisco, you expect you'll have to dress in layers. Here, the place feels so damn huge, you figure the weather will stick around for a while. The unsuspecting will be bushwhacked.

Fortunately, I had warmed up and had a hooded sweatshirt, but even the hood could not stop my eyes from tearing up or my face and hands from turning red and cold. I stepped up my pace when I should have cooled down, but what the hell, I'd cool off in the house. As I let myself in, huffing and puffing, the first flakes began to fall. Grabbing a large bottle of water (KS tap water had always tasted awful), I bounced upstairs to start some laundry and change and shower. Remembering the consequences of an earlier run, I made sure to stretch and avoid muscle cramps.

Practical to her toes, my mother installed her the washer and dryer close to the source of the laundry, the bedrooms. Go, Lou. This particular arrangement had spoiled me and made it hard for me to find housing in a tight market like San Francisco.

After I cleaned myself up, I started coffee (tea does not cut it with pancakes) and rousted out my grandmother's iron skillet. I put on a Louis Armstrong & Ella

Fitzgerald CD from my mother's music collection and had myself a Sunday morning on Friday. The only thing lacking was the funny papers. I made dollar-size pancakes, warmed up some Canadian maple syrup, poured myself a mug of medium-roast, and entered a state of gustatory bliss.

I had Glory's pancakes—four or them—on a saucer, and I fed them to her once they were cool. No syrup for her. She nibbled them delicately and then lay down at my feet. The snow had picked up and was falling in platelets, clusters of flakes about the size of a quarter. Exaggerated, like cartoon snow; backlit, as if the sun were trying to break through. Pretty.

Using up the last of the batter, I made pancakes to freeze and pop into the toaster at a later date. I left the griddle to cool on the stove and quickly wiped down the counter and table top, washing the few dishes there were and stacked them in the drainer for later. Ran upstairs to move laundry around, then returned to the kitchen and poured myself a second cup of coffee to take with me to the front parlor.

Luce and I had piled photo albums beside one of the armchairs. I thought I'd spend some time taking a look. Glory tucked herself up in the chair across from me and sighed.

The room glowed with the quiet light of falling snow. March. Had I been here a month? More or less. I felt the day grow heavy around me with the decisions I had to make. It did not help that Luce was away just now. I had come to depend on her, on the way she could make me feel that I could figure my way out of any problem.

Perhaps she was aware of that dependence and chose this weekend for her yoga retreat... 'Get real, Lyle!' said my inner voice, 'The world does not revolve around *you!*' No, but it would be like her to take a few days off from being the light of the world. My inner me nodded her head. Too true to argue.

I sighed and opened the album on my lap, seeking distraction from my mood. What was I thinking? Sitting in my mother's house, after her solitary death, a family photo album was going to make things better? Lyle Hudson, you deserve what you get.

What I got was photos of Louise from when she was young. Pictures I had never seen before. High school graduation, smooth of cheek, the way girls looked back in the 1940's, clear-eyed and hopeful. Louise at eighteen, her life unwritten, five years away from marrying my father. Was there ever such a world?

Photographs of Louise and her sisters, arranged like a circle of flowers on the lawn, skirts billowing around them, legs demurely tucked away, white gloves, each with a nosegay in her hand. Luce was draped across Louise's lap, arm flung out, gazing into the camera with a dreamy expression on her face, as if for her this was a perfect moment. The three older girls smiled for the camera, each in a set of identical pearls. How lovely they were with their creamy complexions, light eyes and fair hair. On the verge of a war that would change their world.

Unable to look through this particular album, I set it aside and gazed out the front window. The snow moved like a lace curtain. I reached up with both hands and took the holder off my hair, shook it loose, separating it with my fingers, bringing it forward and separating it into tresses, examining it, studying the silver in the reflected light of the snow as I threaded and rethreaded it through my fingers. I noted the way the silver thickened and rivered closer to my hairline. I love the mass of it, the silken feel of it sliding through my fingers.

My hair told time, too. Seemed appropriately expressive of both aspects of my being, the young and the old. *A certain age*, the French call it, to include a range of years and experience. I never tell people my age. Younger women often think that I'm their age. But, things that are hard for them—ever younger women, high heeled shoes, weight control—don't matter to me. I find younger women lovely, possessing a beauty they hardly know. High heels, Blahniks or otherwise, look silly at best, dangerous at worst. Most of womankind looks feeble in them. Ever see a woman in four-inch heels try to get up out of a chair? Case closed. As for weight, I've learned that it comes and goes, following its own inscrutable laws. I work with weights and run to maintain strength and flexibility. The endorphins are pretty cool, too.

Women my age or older know how old I am. That's how it works. We just know. In stores or restaurants, or just out and about, I always smile at these women, Unless they're poodles, they smile back. The poodles wear a lot of make up and dye their hair and wear heels too high for comfort. They hate it when I smile at them, and they always look away. Gotcha! They are happiest among their own kind.

Each to her own silliness. It is simply a matter of choice. Time to choose, said a voice in my head. Time to choose.

As if stung, I jumped up and padded back to the kitchen, following a dim memory of a steno pad I had left on top of the fridge. Yes, it was there. And a pen. You can do this, Lyle. I sat at the table and wrote at the top of a fresh page: You Have 6 Months to live. What do you Do? Extremes work for me, get the electricity flowing.

Answer: Return to SF: Sell the House. Sell the

shop. Take Glory With You. Just Go. Well. That was interesting. It looked so simple on paper. Just Go? It sounded totally me! I started to lighten up. "Hey, Glory? How about a road trip? We could have fun! My friends in San Francisco would love you! What do you think?" Glory wagged her tail and pointed at the back door. I think she was taking "just go" in a slightly different way.

I let her out and checked my watch. 4 p.m. What to do until MacDonald George showed up? My cell phone rang before I could answer the question.

"Surprise!" I could hear his big, blond, gorgeous smile in that one word.

"Chas! Where are you? This is not your cell phone number."

"When the cat's away, sweetie..." Chas purred in my ear.

"When has my presence ever gotten in your way, Chas?" My voice raised an eyebrow at him. "Don't be coy. Where are you?"

"Carmel. I love this time of year, no tourists! We miss you, Carmel and I."

"Miss you, too." I paused. "Odd you should call just now, Chas. I was thinking about you. City by the Bay, etcetera." Let the tone of voice hang there.

"About time. I was *this close* to jumping on a plane, woman, and rescuing you from some arcane, Mid-Western form of brain-washing." He paused, searching for the right words, and then gave up. "The biscuits and gravy torture, something like that. So when are you coming home?"

"To Carmel? Don't live there."

"Don't be bitchy, darling; it's unbecoming." We slipped back into old habits of conversation, a back-and-forth of teasing and talk. Chas and I went back a ways and valued our intimacy and our honesty with each other.

"The irony of your call, Chas, is that I've just decided to go back to San Francisco. It's not something you need to *make* me do. I'm there."

"I am greatly relieved to hear it, ma chère. The truth is that I miss you. Terribly. 'I've grown accustomed to your look,' as it were. You are important to me, Lyle. Jerome, needless to say, is a bit miffed about it. Says he doesn't 'get' our relationship."

"Hell, Chas, I don't get it either!" I grinned at him.

"It's a Mystery!" we exclaimed together, and cracked ourselves up. "It's more a friendship, though, wouldn't you say, darling?" I quipped. We exchanged a long, complex silence.

"Friendship. Oh yes, most definitely." I could see his sly, feline smile at that one. There were a hundred things we didn't need to say, which floated between us. With a sudden shock, I raised my hand and looked at my watch.

"Bloody Hell! Chas, I've got to go. Hot date."

"A what? Lyle, darling, you're positively aflutter. Who is this man? Why don't you just make him wait, go maddeningly inscrutable on him?" I could feel his cool green gaze on the other end of the continent, enjoying my discomfort.

"His name is MacDonald George. We met when I was beating the crap out of some jerk who tried to rob me." The story has a galvanic effect on people, apparently.

"Really? Oh, do tell, Lyle. I want to know everything."

"Chas! I don't have the time! I have to pull myself together, fast!"

"Hmmm. Would this be a *first* date, by any chance?

How delicious. Do I get to meet him?" I laughed, suspecting that MacDonald would take that eventuality just fine

"You wish! OK, I'm going to have to start tearing off my clothes and running upstairs, Chas, if you don't hang up this minute!

"Naked totally works for me, Lyle," Chas said. "But to keep you happy I shall say adieu. I'm glad you're coming home. Make it soon, please. Don't be seduced by a pretty face."

"Like yours, you mean!"

"Ciao, bella."

After a spritz of a shower, I hopped into some fine lingerie (don't leave home without it is my motto) and stood in the middle of the room, cursing. I hate the clothes part of dating. Hate dating. Shit. Call it something else, you've got to focus, Lyle. I looked out the window at dark skies and wet branches. The snow had turned to rain. Weather helps. So does knowing what you want, and I wanted MacDonald George to feel comfortable with me. Oh yes.

My body is toned. I go out of my way to keep it that way, stay flexible. I am, however, not impervious to age. Gravity shows a bit here and there, but fortunately no one has to sit naked at a poker table. If we did, most of those guys would be scarier than I!

I think my legs are my best feature. Strong thighs from running, tapered calves, ankles that look great in heels but would rather not wear them. Argh! Find some clothes before you freeze, Lyle!

I chose cashmere, black. A pair of fitted fine-wale cords, flattering and soft to the touch. Black looks great on everyone, but with me it accents the silvery hair which seems to shine. I was good to go. A splash of *Pure*, and I was on my way downstairs.

I put some jazz on the CD player, got a fire going, and opened a bottle of wine. Glory lay on the Navajo rug in front of the fireplace. She looked up as I walked in the room.

"Nothing to say?" I asked her. She wagged her stubby white tail at me. Amused and indolent.

Grateful that she was not shedding her indelible little white hairs over my black clothing, I headed to the kitchen for goat cheese and crackers to go with the wine.

There was a knock at the door. Glory scrambled across the wood floor and proceeded to make her usual racket. I opened the door to find MacDonald George shaking rain off his hat. The snow had given way to a warm front.

"Hi, come on in," I greeted him.

Mac looked at me and his eyes did that crinkly thing. "Thanks. Think I will."

We got through hat and coat, the dog's delighted dancing, and I showed MacDonald into the library. Blossom Dearie had melted into Boz Scaggs' *But Beautiful*. We stood at the fireplace and I watched as Mac looked around appreciatively.

"Nice place," he said, eyes coming back to me. "You must feel at home here."

"Yes, and No," I said. "Would you like a drink? Or tea? Coffee?" I was feeling awkward.

"Maybe a glass of water first, Lyle."

"Good idea. Let's go back to the kitchen. I need to feed Glory her supper. Do you mind?"

"Not at all." We stood there a moment and looked at each other. I smiled first.

"Come on," I said, heading to the kitchen with a

firm step, "We can do this, we'll be fine." He followed silently, but I could feel him smiling. I could also feel his eyes.

"You smell great," he said, stepping closer, tracing the perfume.

"Thanks. There's a pitcher of water in the fridge," I said, getting down two tumblers, then turned, almost walking into him.. I stepped into the pantry, grabbed a handful of kibble, and placed it in Glory's bowl.

"She's only supposed to get breakfast, but while I've been looking after Luce's cat she gets a snack at dinner time. Parity with the cat." I returned from the pantry, brushing my hands on my hips, getting rid of kibble crumbs. Oh great, now I smelled like dog food. Way to go, Lyle. Blue eyes followed the movement of my hands. Well. Maybe no loss.

Mac handed me a glass of water and took a sip of his own. I drank the whole thing down without breathing, plunked the glass on the table and took a big breath.

"OK. Time for wine!" Mac laughed out loud, ran a hand through his dark hair, and grinned at me.

"Lyle Hudson, you have to calm down. It's just me. See?" He put the glass down and held out his hands. "Nothing going on."

"Easy for you to say." I got a fresh wine glass and poured from the bottle I opened earlier. I took a discreet sip and looked up at this man standing in my mother's kitchen.

"This is my mother's kitchen. Her house. It feels a bit strange, MacDonald. Hell. I can't remember how old I am when I'm in this house. I'm... flustered. That's the only word for it. Flustered." We regarded each other, taking in the view. What I was looking at was tall and broad-shouldered. Dark shirt, open at the neck. Dark wool slacks. Mac smelled good, too, like woods and moss and something that made my mouth water.

"Okay. Here's the deal," I said. "Name your poison. I am not standing around in this kitchen another moment. You don't have to drink it, but you do have to choose."

"Red wine?"

"Good choice." I handed Mac a glass and picked up the plate of goat cheese and crackers and headed back to the library. I was reaching up to get a bottle down from the wine rack in the library when Mac came up and stood close behind me, scanning the racks of wine..

"May I help?" he asked quietly. I turned around intending to identify a really nice Shiraz when he placed his hands on my shoulders. Warm. Felt good. Oh, God, I'm monosyllabic!

"Lyle, I have a suggestion." I looked up at him, having a pretty good idea of what that might be. Unfortunately, I was not able to produce sound. I think my heart was beating or something.

"There is a little something we can get out of the way right now. That way, you could relax, I could relax, and we wouldn't have to spend the rest of the evening wondering about it. OK?" Mac's voice was slow and rich, sort of husky around the edges. I must have been holding my breath because all I could do was nod. Managed to whisper a faint "OK" just as his arms wrapped around me and his moustache headed straight for my face!

First thing I knew I was feeling pretty OK, sort of floated around in that kiss for a while. It could have been more than one kiss, I don't know. There was a lot of it. Hands in my hair, hands on his neck and shoulders; I think ears were involved, too. Catching my breath, I grabbed his arms hard and stepped back, crashing into a bookcase.

"Whoa! Whoa!" I put my hands on my knees for a moment to let the blood return to my head from its travels to other parts of my anatomy.

"Good," I said, "That was good. Kissing. I'm definitely not wondering. You?"

He moved forward and my knees commenced to feeling weak.

"Definitely still wondering." Followed by another excellent kiss.

When we broke for air, I started to talk, oxygen deprivation, no doubt. "So. This is going well, don't you think? Would you like to sit and talk now?"

"Not particularly." Mac was kissing my neck, his hands working their way under my sweater.

"We're on a slippery slope, Mac. You know that." I started working the buttons on his shirt.

"I know it, Lyle. This isn't... what I intended. I was just going to get us through that first kiss."

"I think I'm through it. You?" My answer was more kissing. I didn't think I could stand much more. I pointed to the ceiling. "Upstairs. Now."

Afterwards, we listened to the rain glazing the windows, stippling the roof, neither of us in any hurry to move.

"Lyle." I put my fingers over his mouth. He kissed my fingers and then rolled over onto one elbow. "You are amazing," he whispered.

"This was supposed to be a civilized, you know, talking thing, get-to-know-you time, not...hot sex on the first date! What the hell happened?" I sat up and looked at him accusingly, sheet held chastely to my chest. MacDonald lay back, looking pleased.

"I think it was spontaneous combustion. Or, maybe one of those chemical things."

"Pheromones?"

"Them, too." he drawled. "I think what happened was what we wanted to happen, don't you?"

"Well, yes. But it seems so out of control!" We thought about it for a minute.

"Yes, it does," Mac calmly agreed, hand behind his head, smiling at me.

"Very cool. You know something? I feel great!" I jumped out of bed and sashayed to the bathroom.

"Looking good, too, Lyle. Looking very good."

"It feels so strange, MacDonald, to feel that I know you when I know nothing about you." We were sitting on the couch in the library, drinking our wine, Glory asleep at our feet. I leaned towards him and scrutinized his face. Mac was amused and let me look.

"Part of me," I continued, "wants it to stay this way, just like this—no past, no prologue, Athena stepping fully formed from the forehead of Zeus."

"I see what you mean." He took my hand and ran his thumb along my palm.

"I feel comfortable with you, too. I guess when we reach a time of life, some of the old questions have no point. I like it."

"Me, too." We were the opposite of married people. No history, no misunderstandings, no assumptions. No possessiveness or entitlement. Not yet, anyway, I added to my self, ruefully. "How about Indian food?" he asked. Dal and nan are perfect for a rainy night, don't you think?"

"Absolutely! I'm starved!" I turned off the fire. We grabbed our coats and told Glory to guard the house.

Mac's Mustang was beaded with rain under the street light. MacDonald opened the passenger door and handed me in. We smiled as he started up the engine, enjoying the sound of 8 cylinders.

"Great car," I said. He leaned over and kissed me.

"It suits you," he said.

Dinner was great. The dal was followed by papadams, lamb gosht, tandoori chicken, and an excellent okra dish. We drank Kingfisher beer and told each other the story of how we met, reviewed first impressions, and laughed a great deal, enjoying each other's company. MacDonald asked if I had had any news on the bridal shop robbery.

"Not a thing. Nary a clue! It was so random. I don't think the police will come up with anything." Insurance covered the cost of the dress, we were more vigilant at the shop about locking the door while we were there, and I had gotten over my upset.

"You might be surprised. Our guys are persistent, Lyle, and smart." He grinned at the compliment to himself. "I'll ask around, see what I can find out."

"Thanks." We ordered a pot of tea after the dishes were cleared away. I resisted the temptation to tell Mac about the gun. Putting a weapon on the table would definitely spoil the mood.

After a brief silence, Mac asked, "Have you thought of any questions yet?"

"Questions? Oh. Questions. Well, no. To be honest, if you are married, I'd rather not know about it, so you can keep me in the dark about that one. And, I'll do the same for you." Gave him my sphinx smile.

"Wicked woman," he growled.

"Hey, that was my feline inscrutability. You're supposed to be impressed." Big grin this time.

"I like that smile better." His voice was warm, inviting. I leaned across the table.

"How about you? Any questions?" I got a measuring look.

"Just one, Lyle. You don't even have to answer it, but as a favor to myself I have to ask. You see, I find myself not knowing how to proceed. Your answer might help."

"What? What?" I was beginning to feel alarmed by the seriousness of his expression. "Have I ever been arrested? In jail? Is there a warrant out for my arrest? Am I now or was I ever...an evolutionist?"

"I was wondering how long you were planning to stay in Lawrence. That's my question." He sat back and drank his tea.

"OK. You get an A for best question." I fell silent and looked at my tea. "Since we're being honest? I have to tell you that earlier today I'd decided to take Glory and beat it back to San Francisco. That was way before wild Mac-sex." I put my hand to my cheek which was still a bit pink from whisker burn. Maybe I was blushing, hard to tell.

"I know that Lawrence is your home, MacDonald. I know that your family must be here, your life, and I respect that. My connection to Lawrence is more tenuous and more complicated. Kansas scares the hell out of me. I don't feel like myself here. I may have to go back to San Francisco, even if it's just to stay sane."

"Any idea when that might be?"

"As in how much time we have? Or, is it worth it to invest time and energy in this woman?"

"I think you know you're worth it, Lyle."

I could eat him with a spoon, my inner me said. I shook my head and sighed. "You make it hard to decide."

"Good, I'm glad." He smiled. "That's a start."

He drove me home and we sat in the Mustang in

the rainy dark, watching patterns of water trace the windshield.

"Time to say good night, Lyle."

"Yes. I had a great..." He cut me off mid-sentence.

"Not in the car. The best we can do in here is shake hands." He came around and opened the door. I stood up right into his arms. Nice. Very, very nice. A long kiss in a light rain, standing beside a Mustang. I felt like a kid again.

"Night, Lyle."

"Night, MacDonald." I ran to the door, calling over my shoulder, "Sweet dreams!"

13

Tetley Lives! I hung up the phone and took Glory with me out to Baldwin Junction. The rain had passed, the sky was clearing. There was a fresh smell in the air, as if the countryside had been scrubbed.

At the vet's, I was paying the cat's bill, chatting with Dana, scooping a couple dog biscuits for Glory, when Daniel Tenent walked out from the examining room. It was quiet in the office, a rare event, apparently. He came over and shook my hand.

"Good to see you," he smiled. "Whatever kind of infection Tetley had, it's under control. The antibiotics and rehydration did wonders." I shot a look at T-Cat in his Cadillac and deemed him significantly less than wonderful.

"He's not done with his medication; he'll need to finish out the ten days of the prescription, " he added.

Oh, joy, I thought, ten days of figuring out how to get a pill into Devil Cat. Wait! Luce gets to do that!

"He's already had today's dose. You should also try

to get him to eat, maybe some wet food, something to tempt his appetite. Other than that, keep him indoors and quiet for the next week."

"Easier said than done," I said ruefully. "But that's Luce's lookout. She'll be back tomorrow and Tetley can return to his customary habitat." I realized I was having a good time talking with this nice man.

"Why don't I carry him out to the car for you?" Dana and I very carefully did *not* look at each other, but I could feel her eyebrow raise and the antennae pop up.

"No, really, that's..."

"It will give me a chance to visit with Glory. Haven't seen her in a while."

"Oh, OK. Maybe I should make an appointment to bring her in for a check-up. I have no idea when Lou..." I shook my head and continued, "Anyway, Glory is mine now and I want to be sure she's current on her shots." As we left the office, I said to Dana, "I'll check the calendar and give you a call."

"That will be fine. Any time." She was trying hard to keep from smiling. Working for a handsome, unmarried veterinarian must be pretty interesting.

I beeped the car and Dr. Tenent slid the Caddy onto the back seat. Tetley was maintaining stoic silence.

"Things going all right for you, at your mother's place?" He asked as I closed the car door. It was an odd, awkward question. I turned and gave Tenent a sharp look.

"What do you mean?" He stood there with his hands in his pockets and shrugged, seeming to search for a reason for his own question.

"I mean it must be tough for you. Your mother was such a great person." He paused and gave another small shrug. "She's been coming out here for years, took an interest in animals..." his voice trailed off. A wry chuckle followed. "Words are not my strong suit. Just hope everything is going OK for you."

I went around to the driver's side and lowered the window for Glory, wondering what was going on.

"It's really muddy out here. Think she better stay in the car," I said.

The dog would have climbed through the window to get at him, if she could. What was it about Glory and men? Hell—what was it about me and men? 'Good question, Lyle!'

Daniel greeted Glory and rubbed her ears and she looked up at him expectantly. Clever girl! She had decided that since she wasn't *in* the office this must be a happy visit. He pulled out a biscuit and fed it to the dog, observing her with a proprietary pleasure. I gave him a look as Glory shed crumbs liberally over the leather seats of the G35. He made a gesture of apology that I waved aside.

"No prob," I said. "It's only leather."

Nice car."

"Thanks." I stepped back and ran my eyes over the sleek lines of the Infiniti, taking in anew its elegance, its silvery grace. It felt so much a part of me now, more a friend than a machine.

"Must've set you back a bit." Tenent stepped to stand beside me, the spontaneity of the movement in contrast with the edge of his unstated question. He wants to know about money? What was he after?

"No, not really." I smiled, enjoying the memory. Tenent's inquiring gaze asked for more information, which punched the big-fat-lie button in my consciousness.

"Gift from an admirer," I told him. "Generous guy." My eyes twinkled.

"Lucky you!"

"Yes. Very." And not another word to *you*, I thought. The man was a bit of a mystery himself, definitely flirting, but something else underneath that I couldn't read.

"Dr. Tenent? Hal Gruber has a question about inseminating his cows!"

"Got to go. Maybe we can pick up the conversation...soon?" He headed back to the clinic and called over his shoulder, "Call me!" Big grin and a wave. A confident man asks you to call him and doesn't insist on your number. A no-pressure sort of pressure. I smiled to myself and my inner bitch spoke up: What the hell are you thinking? How many men d'you need in order to make your life a living hell of indecision, Lyle? Wake up!

"Shut up," I muttered sullenly and got in the car.

I needed fresh coffee and time to think. Glory made a bee line for the kitchen. I followed slowly with the cat carrier. Tetley made a feeble growl as I lifted him from the carrier, but he seemed content to be in my arms. No sarcasm from me, no attitude from him. A truce.

I set the cat down and went to the pantry, finding food for both animals. T-Cat walked to the water bowl, sniffed it and sat back, mesmerized by the water.

"Are you stoned?" Briefly pondering the mysteries of veterinary pharmaceuticals, I put kibble down for Glory and placed the bowl for Tet at the cat's feet. A stay at the vet's is traumatic for any animal. I suspect they come home deaf from the noise. Takes a while for their hearing to readjust itself. Tetley was decidedly in a befuddled re-adjustment zone.

I placed the anonymous demand on the table and got the coffee going. I appreciated the economy of Louise's French press, little fuss and smooth results. I put a slice of bread in the toaster and reached into a jeans pocket for a ponytail holder, pulled my hair back and sat down, frowned at the piece of paper.

"Pay Up," I muttered. "Who the hell are *you*?"

The toast popped up and I slathered it with Lenore's plum jam while the toast was still hot. I was sharing the last bits of crust with Glory when the phone rang. So did my cell.

"Whoa!" Somehow I managed to answer them both at the same time. "Hello?" I focused on the cell first.

"Good morning. How are you?" Mac asked in that warm voice of his.

"I'm great. Really." A smile in my voice if not on my face. "Just got Luce's cat back from the vet, grateful the evil feline decided not to kick the bucket on me while she was away. Hold on a minute OK? I've got someone on the land line."

Turning my attention to the other phone, I recognized Nola's voice. She was in the middle of a rush of words that had started when I answered, not a clue that I wasn't listening.

"Nola, stop. Back up. You're talking too fast and I missed…OK. Hold on. I turned and spoke into the cell. "Um, MacDonald? I have to go. There's a bit of a situation here at the moment. Can I call you back?"

"You bet."

"Thanks. I had a great time last night. Talk to you soon. Bye."

"Nola!" I began. The rest of the conversation was hers. I listened. Tried to stretch the cord far enough to reach my coffee. Glory asked to go out again, but I signaled "Wait," at which point what Nola was saying finally got through to me. I stood perfectly still until she finished.

"It's OK, Nola. Just calm down. I'll be right there.

Maybe not *right* there, but as soon as I can. Hold tight. Yes, Bye." I hung up the phone and let Glory outside. "This is crazy!" I said to the sky. From the back steps it looked like a normal day, pleasant, really. But there was that "Pay Up" business and news from Nola. "Bloody Hell!" I cursed in frustration. "Glory!" I called the dog with my no-nonsense voice and got no answer. "Shit. Glory!" I heard a snuffling in the bushes beside the garage, near the back fence. What now? I stomped down the steps and over to Glory who was wedged into the bushes, her nose stuck through a gap between two decrepit slats.

"Glory! Bad girl! Get out of there!" She wagged her stubby little white tail but did not move, didn't even look at me. What the...

"Hallelujah, baby!" said a friendly voice from the alley side of the fence.

Peering over the top of the fence, I saw the home-less guy squatting down on his haunches, offering some-thing to Glory's nose. Her pink tongue flicked out helpfully. There was a pink and white bakery bag at the man's raggedy feet. I groaned.

"Please. Do not feed the dog donuts, OK?" I pleaded.

He turned his weathered face up to me and grinned. "Share the wealth, baby. Want one?" He held up a do-nut with white icing and sprinkles.

"No. Thanks. It' nice of you to share, but sweets are bad for her."

"Yeah, prob'ly so. Love that dog, though!" The man laughed. "Hallelujah! Makes my day!" He closed up the paper bag, stood up, and walked away, chuckling. "Glory Hallelujah! You have a nice day!"

I waved at his retreating back and then sternly es-corted Miss Glory back to the house. "No more sweets for you, Miss."

The phone was ringing as we entered the back door. What NOW?

"Hello?"

"Not answering our cell?

"Chas! No—I was out back begging a homeless guy not to feed donuts to Glory."

"Interesting neighborhood. So. How was the date?" He drawled the last word in that girly-way of his that I hate. I decided to punish him.

"It was excellent," I said. Simple. No games. Chas hates it when I won't play.

"Excellent? Great." Pause. "He's gorgeous, isn't he. I can tell." Pause. "You had sex, didn't you."

No response. I let the silence hang there.

"You bitch! Lyle Hudson, what the hell are you *do-ing?* Do not tell me you changed your mind. Again. Do not tell me that you are staying there—in Kansas?" His voice rose sharply. I could see Chas pacing back and forth, throwing his arms about, green eyes flashing dangerously, as clearly as if he were in the kitchen with me.

"Chas, I..." He cut me off.

"Do not presume to think that I'm jealous, Lyle. This is about you, not me. YOU—your life... I thought you were out of the woods, finally. No more going over to the dark side, tempting the fates. Shit!" I heard him slam his hand on a table. "Wake up, woman!" There was a brief pause while he gathered himself for the rest of the rant I could feel coming. I took the opportunity to sit down.

"Have you told him how you make your money? How you win your daily bread? The gambling, Lyle? Does he know about that? Or are we in the sweetheart phase? You'll tell him when you're ready to move on. Move onto what, Lyle? San Francisco? Poof! Gone, isn't

it? You will have burned the bridges. You are a dilet-
tante, Lyle. You walked away from teaching. You have
money now, but you do not have a life. Your mom died.
Boo Hoo. You are using it as an excuse. To do what?
Cocoon yourself in delusion? You will die if you stay
there. You know it and 'I know it. Lyle, I will not be
around to watch." Click. He was gone.

Glory whined to be let out again. I opened the door
and looked up at the sky as she trotted down the steps.
"Be a good girl this time!" I called after her. The
weather was lovely. Clear. How ironic. I closed the door
and stood with my back against it.

Potrero Hill, a lifetime ago. Sunny afternoon. Hot.
I'd driven back to San Francisco from Reno in time *not*
to miss Chas's birthday. I rolled in grimy and sunburned
after three days of a walkabout at Pyramid Lake. Fresh
bass cooked over piñon, an ocean of stars at night, the
stray lizard during the day, the heat and the silence of
stones. I was buoyant in the way one is transparent from
the walking away from psychic crap that can happen out
in the high desert.

I had stopped hating myself that day, found myself
on the lighter side of the leaf, changed, scoured out with
solitude and meditation and poetry. I came across an
eagle feather and tied it in my hair, pulling the mass of
it up and off my neck.

I walked in from the sun to the roomy coolness of
Chas's then apartment, barefoot, carrying a sheaf of poems and a perfect snakeskin, fragile and translucent.

"Who is *that?* I heard someone say, waiting for my
eyes to adjust from the glare.

"Dear God," Chas whispered, and came over to me.

"Lyle Hudson, you are a vision! You radiate light!
Isn't she fabulous?" Chas's usual friends were inter-

spersed with people I did not know but assumed to be friends of the then boyfriend. I was one of two women in the room.

"Happy Birthday, Chas," I croaked and held out the snakeskin like a sacred relic. He kissed me and licked salt from my temple.

"Where have you been? What have you been up to?"

"Talking to God. Taking dictation." I shook the roll of poems at him. "Could I have some water?"

"Dear girl, have some champagne!"

"No, Chas, better not. I'm pretty dehydrated. After the water, I'll go. Doesn't look like my kind of party."

"Now, now. Don't assume. There are people here you would like and who would like you."

And so it was. I took a shower and borrowed a white silk shirt and pants from Chas. Stuck with the water and ate fruit, avoiding the birthday delicacies. There were wonderful conversations, talk about art, poetry, deserts, perception, that sort of thing. I felt so unself-conscious, so free. My friendship with Zandra began at that party. Zan and Diego, new friends for a new me. That day is luminous in my memory. How ironic that I should re-visit it just then, standing on what felt like the edge of an abyss. I shook my head, as if to clear it and stepped back inside the house.

I decided to leave Glory out back for a while. She liked to sit at the top of the stairs and keep watch for Viking pillagers, or donuts. I didn't anticipate spending much time at the shop. Told Glory I'd make it up to her later. Tetley was coming back to his old self and lay sprawled across the kitchen table, snoring.

It was complete deja vu down at Hyacinth: another

empty window, another set of flashing lights, and a random crowd drifting away down the sidewalk. Nola was fluttery and excited. She had seen the theft in progress, called 911, and had run into the street yoo-hooing to passers-by to stop the person with the white dress. The wedding dress got away despite her best efforts.

Officer Danielson was on the scene again, taking Nola's statement with calm competence. A young black woman, trim, fit, she had an innate confidence that did not come from police training—it was all hers.

When Nola introduced me as the owner of the shop, we both smiled.

"Call me Greta," she said. "We seem to be seeing a lot of each other."

We chatted briefly about the likelihood that theft of dress #2 was related to dress #1. No message left, as far as I could tell. I received a terse lecture about locking doors, and then she was gone, the bridal shop suddenly empty and still.

"Is Crista around?" I asked Nola as I headed for the back of the shop.

"Should be, Lyle. She came down to talk to the police and then went right back up. Very upset by the fuss, apparently. But the, young people can be so sensitive, don't you think?"

I nodded agreement, not voicing my opinion that it was the hideous dress that would've made Crista cry, not its absence.

Crista sat at the long work table, her back to me, the Goth wedding dress in progress laid out in two sections in front of her. The bodice was positioned above the full skirt but not connected to it, reminding me of that old magician's trick of the sawed-in-half lady.

"I think the graduated purple dye really works," I said as I stepped beside her. Crista's response was to turn aside, still giving me her back.

"What's up?" I asked, pretty much picking it up from the atmosphere in the small workroom.

"I'm going to finish the dress and pay for it, just so you know." She turned toward me but kept her eyes on the dress lying there on the table.

"Want to talk?"

"Not really," she said softly. "This morning we just looked at each other and...woke up. It wasn't going anywhere, just stopped. I don't know. It was just over and we both knew it. Nobody's fault..." Crista shrugged one shoulder, still gazing at the dress.

"I'm sorry to hear it."

"Yeah. Me, too."

There's always this long pause when there's nothing else to say. I looked around the room, searching for a way out of the sadness. "Listen, why don't you stick around for a while. Keep using this space as a workshop? No rush on the dress, or the payments, OK?"

"You mean it?" A ray of hope returning.

"You bet. Put the space to use. besides, I think Nola likes the company."

"That would be great! I really like it here." She turned and took her sketch book from a nearby shelf. "And I've got some cool ideas."

"OK, then." I gave Crista a quick hug and went back down the stairs thinking dark thoughts about the failure of love.

"Nola, let's close the shop for a while."

"Oh, no, dear. I think this would be a good opportunity to promote our line!"

"What line? This is a small shop, Nola. We've been robbed twice! Not exactly a recipe for success."

"Now, now. I can see you're upset, Lyle. Never you mind. You just go and take care of the ...um...business at the police station. They're open Saturdays. I'll look after things here and see that Crista's alright? There's a dear." Before I knew it, she had ushered me out the door. Promote the line, Pssht! The woman's crazed.

In the car, I checked the cell for messages. There were two. The first was dark and garbled, the disguised voice saying "Pay up, pay up, pay up, pay up" over and over, angry and threatening. Again, the blocked I.D.

"Fuck you." It crossed my mind briefly that this might be some bizarreness of Blake's. Or not. Whatever it was, I was not in the mood.

I brushed my hair back from my face and exhaled, asking the universe for a little sanity. Message two was from Mac. OK, much better. I called him back.

"Hi, MacDonald. If you see a wedding dress running down the street, grab it, will you? It belongs to me."

"Another robbery?" He was trying no to laugh.

"Yeah. A lucky day."

"Are you still at the shop?" His voice sounded so smooth, like corduroy and leather.

"Sort of. I'm in my car, getting ready to leave."

"I'm downtown, too. Can I buy you coffee?" I was definitely tempted

"Sorry. I've got to go rescue Glory or rescue someone from Glory; I'm not sure which."

"All right. How about I call you later? I have a plan. Glory can come, too. She'll be your chaperone." I could see him do that crinkly thing with his eyes, inviting me.

"Reassuring. Thanks. Talk to you soon." We said our goodbyes and I drove the Infiniti back to Lou's

"How do people get through days like this?" I asked the universe as I gathered mail and walked through the kitchen to let Glory in. I opened the door and turned to put water on for tea. Flipped through assorted catalogues still addressed to Louise. What was it, six weeks now? More? It could be years, so slender was my grip on time.

Instantly aware of the absence of dog, I looked around for Glory.

"Glory?" Remembering I'd left her in back, I went to the door. No barking from the back yard, either.

"Glory!" I stuck my head out the door and yelled. No answer.

"GLORY!!"

"Amen, sister!" came a shout from the alley. But no dog. No barking.

Not wanting to instigate another Hallelujah chorus, I walked down the back steps into the yard. Around the side of the house I heard a skittering and a thwok sound. As I headed over in that direction, Glory scooted by in a white flash, turned a tight circle and zoomed back around the side of the house. Was she having a fit? Before the question was fully formed in my mind, she flashed by again. Silence and speed. I was intrigued. On the other side of the house, behind a large lilac bush, a gas meter guy was throwing the ball for the dog. Sweet! She had him trained! I broke into a big grin and the man smiled back sheepishly, picked up his apparatus and let himself out the side gate. Glory ran over to the fence and stood there expectantly, tail wagging, waiting for him to come back and play.

"Come on, Glory-B," I called to her "In the house. You have had enough excitement today." Inside, I sat down in the rear entryway with an old towel and cleaned off her feet. A fragment of Chas's angry diatribe rose in my memory, making me wince, as did a moment's vision of Crista's sad face. Glory licked my cheek and I hugged her warm little dog body to me. Then I got up to find some tissue.

Lou kept paper products on the top pantry shelf near the stairs to the basement. I had to jump up for what looked like the last box of tissues. I heard a clank—a short, sharp noise as I groped for the box. After wiping away dog slobber and blowing my nose, I dragged over a kitchen chair so I could see what was up there. I found an old tin box, a pattern of forget-me-nots on the lid, about the size of a box of stationery. I took it down and dragged the chair back to the table. Not bothering to brush off the layer of dust, I opened it, breathing in the fragrance of old paper and time.

Inside were a number of yellowed newspaper clippings, a blurry black and white photo of what looked like swans on water, and a book of matches. Whatever this stuff meant, Louise wanted it out of sight. I turned the book of matches over in my fingers. What was my mother hiding up there on a back shelf? Was there a connection to the mysterious notes? To the "Pay Up" invitation? The gun? I sat down and started to read.

14

I woke up early with a growing sense of uneasiness, feeling that my procrastination over decisions, geographical and personal, was catching up with me. Storm clouds this big usually produced tornados. In my life, anyway. I threw on some sweats, brushed my teeth, and examined the stranger in the mirror. Where's the spark, Lyle? Where is the person who does not hesitate to go all in, who reads the tells, plays the game? The face in front of me wore doubt like a shroud; her hair had more will power than she did! "Christ, you're pathetic," I muttered, and left the room.

In contrast with my dark mood, the animals were getting along, waiting for food, purring. Cheerful little creeps. Sun and blue sky proclaimed me an idiot, and birds contributed their share of racket and joyful mayhem. I was outnumbered and outclassed. I took my cup of tea out onto the front porch and stood at the rail, surveying the neighborhood. The church-goers were already up and out. Godless humanity slept in or hid out, like me. The image cheered me up.

It is a beautiful old neighborhood of spacious Victorian houses, small yards that, just weeks from now, would erupt in an abundance of iris, lilac, tulips, hydrangea, dogwood and crabapple trees. Ornamental pears, profuse in the newer areas of Lawrence, are absent here. They needed more sun than the ancient oaks and occasional elm would permit. The houses were well-cared for. People respect each other's property and privacy.

There was a rumbling, clacking noise coming down the sidewalk. A skateboarder, no doubt, taking advantage of the downhill incline of the street. Lawrence was a hotbed of skateboarding, I remembered. The town council had had to put restrictions on their use in order to protect the more elderly pedestrians, not to mention small children. Renegade teenagers on the loose! I thought skateboarders were cool and observed them the same way some people watched birds, looking for markers of dress, style, and technique.

Yes, this one was an authentic Dude! Baggy cargo shorts, assorted layers of shirts and sweaters and unidentifiable outerwear; a long striped scarf trailing over his shoulders, knit Rasta hat, iPod wires plugged into his ears, wrap-around sunglasses. Definitely a dude. Who was grinning at me. I waved and opened the door, hitching up my sweatpants.

"Docta H!" No. It couldn't be. I turned. I looked. It was. Blake Phipps.

"Hey, Blake. What are you doing up so early on Sunday?"

"Making my way back from a friend's." He took off the shades and surveyed the architecture. Grinned at me, happy as a Lab puppy to see a friendly face. "Cool house! You live here?"

"At the moment," I said acerbically. "Would you like to come in for coffee, Blake? I could probably scare up bagels and cream cheese, as well." Well, hell. A friendly face wouldn't hurt me either. He hopped off the board, kicking it deftly off the ground and tucking it under one arm.

"That would be awesome!"

He left the board on the porch and followed me into the house, back to the kitchen where I put on water for coffee and introduced Blake to Glory who thought he smelled just great. She started to nibble on his socks, and I had to pull her off before she started making a meal of his entire left foot.

"Sorry, Blake. She usually does not eat guests." I got her out the back door only to find that Tetley had emerged from his stupor to jump up into Blake's lap. There was a loud purr. At first, I thought it was Blake. Blake did not seem in the least perturbed by animal affection and was leaning back against the table, amused and nodding at the huge cat that had claimed him.

"Animals dig me, especially cats. They go nuts. You just have to go with the flow, let them lay a little love on you. This dude is a big guy, isn't he." He scratched T-cat's haunches and the cat growled and started to bite his own leg.

"OK, that's just weird. Stop!" I grabbed Tetley and put him outside, too. Both animals sat by the door and looked at me.

Coffee poured, bagels toasted and smeared with cream cheese, Blake and I had a friendly breakfast. I asked him about his classes and he said he was doing well, actually getting grades! His roommates were cool, nightlife was cool, music was cool, and the boarding was awesome. Was he making ends meet? Oh, yeah, no problem, this and that. Hmm.

"You know, Blake, if you could spare me some time, I could use some help moving furniture around. Nothing too heavy."

"Why not now? Lead me to it!" He stood up and waited for me to lead the way. I put the dishes in the sink and told Blake we'd come back for coffee later.

"No! You're not coming in!" I yelled at Glory who was whining at the back door. I took Blake upstairs and into Louise's bedroom, which was still in considerable disarray.

"Whoa," Blake said, "You want me to call in some help?"

"No, I think we can handle it. You might want to take off a few of those layers, Blake."

"No prob." Off came the Rasta hat, and the dreds flopped onto his shoulders. He pulled out a band and tied his hair back. Off came the sweaters and shirts and he was down to a "Life is Good" T-shirt, reddish, and khaki shorts. I took the pile of clothes down to the kitchen, told Glory to shut up, and went back upstairs to find Blake, hands on hips, surveying the room.

"What's the plan?" he asked.

"I'm thinking."

I hate decisions and this was going to be a doozy. If I was going back to San Francisco, there was no point in rearranging the room. If I was staying, I had to turn the room into a space that did not remind me of Louise.

"Still thinking?"

"Yeah. Give me a minute." I could feel sweat form on my upper lip.

"Hey, Lyle?" Blake turned and put a hand on my shoulder, looked at the room then back at me.

"Don't stress on it, OK? It's just a room. Look at it.

See?" I looked. Perhaps I should breathe, too.

"Just a room." The other hand came up onto the other shoulder, and Blake proceeded to nod encouragingly.

"Now, tell me what you want to do. Just try something, OK? We're not nailing anything in place. Dude! If you don't like it, we'll try something else. Piece of cake."

I nodded back. We were nodding in rhythm, catching the movement of possibility. I smiled.

"Blake, I have an idea."

"Let's do it!" We high-fived and I told him my idea and we went to work.

In the process of dismantling Louise's four-poster, I bumped into a small bedside table, momentarily losing my balance. I grabbed the table and shook a small drawer open in the process of righting myself.

"You OK?" Blake asked. He was standing the headboard against the wall and couldn't really turn to look.

"Fine. Practicing my table-tossing skills." I shoved the bedside table out of the way, causing the drawer to snap itself shut. Something small clattered to the floor and I went to investigate. At first I thought it was a matchbook. A playing card folded in half. It must have been stuck to the underside of the drawer.

"Find something, Dr. H?"

"Just an old book of matches, Blake. It's Lyle, OK?" I slipped the card in my pocket .

"My bad!"

Two hours and four bottles of Dasani later, we stood back and gauged the results. Not bad. The four-poster had been dismantled and relegated to a back bedroom. With some minor changes, the bedroom had become a sitting room. There was plenty of space, art on the walls. It looked great—no need to think of it as Louise's *or* mine. It was a new space.

"Crazy." Blake said. "It looks like it's always been this way. Hey, Lyle? You are one strong woman!"

"Thanks, Blake." I leaned over and stretched out my lower back.

"Cool tattoo. That new?" I had stripped down to a camisole; the sweatshirt had grown too warm. Both Blake and I had the slight sheen of sweat that comes from moving furniture. I ran my hand over the tattoo, looking at the top of my right arm.

"Got this the day after her funeral," I told him. I forget it's there. You're the only one who has seen it." I smiled and he moved in for a closer look.

"Nice work. Old School. That's your mom's name, right?"

"Indeed it is." A red heart not much larger than a quarter, with a banner across it that reads "Louise" in old-fashioned letters. Blake ran his thumb across the tattoo.

"Feels like skin."

"It is skin, Blake."

"Yeah."

We looked at each other and I slowly pulled his hand away. I kept the hand and led him out of the room.

"Let's go downstairs and get some coffee." He silently pulled me back to him and kissed me on the lips, asking.

"No way, Blake. Life on earth as we know it would end. Nuclear winter would set in. We would be smitten with flaming swords, and our livers would be eaten by eagles." My tone was dead serious.

"A total no."

"Fraid so, Blake." I stepped away from the beautiful young man, for once at peace with myself, no nagging inner voices sneering at me.

In the kitchen, fully dressed, if not hygienically perfect, we sat with hot cups of coffee and listened to Glory's whining. Blake reached across the table and took my hand.

"But why not? It's not an age thing, is it? I mean, you are gorgeous and wise and deep and totally sexy. It'd be great, you and me."

"No, Blake. You know that's not true. It would be damaging to both of us. Disastrous. It is an age thing, decidedly so." He shook his head and I held my breath for a moment; the young are heartbreaking in their beauty. His face was painted by the morning sun—smooth complexion, a halo of sunlight around his blond head.

"Blake. Look at my hand. Look at it." I made a fist and opened it a couple of times. We watched the flexion of tendons and the articulation of knuckle bones against skin, the way age reveals itself in a woman's hand, where no cosmetic surgery is possible.

"I'll always find you attractive, Lyle." Blake's voice was soft and tender, registering resignation.

"And I you, Blake. Always. Let's leave it as it is, OK?" He picked up my hand, kissed it and held it to his face. I stood up, and kissed the top of his head. Then I let Glory in the house. We definitely needed a change of atmosphere.

Glory danced around ecstatically, climbed into Blake's lap, licked his face. A sharp knocking on the back door interrupted Glory's love fest. Silently cursing the fact that no good act goes unpunished, I opened the door to find Luce standing there, Tetley wrapped around her ankles. Taking advantage of the open door, the cat charged inside and coiled tightly around Blake's much more acceptable ankles. The cat's purr sounded like a tractor engine."

"Morning, Lyle." Luce said. "You certainly look like Hell on Earth. What have you done to my cat? Won't give me the time of day! Oh, hello, young man." Blake beamed at her and tried to reach his coffee. A sharp look flew from Blake to me.

"Coffee, Luce?"

"No time for that. William is waiting in the car."

"Suit yourself." I went to the pantry and dragged out the Cadillac and the antibiotics. I filled her in on Tetley's overnight at the vet's. "One a day until they're gone. Good Luck getting him into the cat carrier."

Luce scrutinized that label on the pills.

"Possum, no doubt. Cat can't resist messing with possum." The cat in question refused to be removed from Blake's person, so he helpfully picked the cat up and carried him to the carrier. Glory stood behind him and licked Blake's leg.

"Thank you, young man," Luce said.

"No problem."

"Luce, this is Blake Phipps; Blake, this is my Aunt Luce." If she wanted an explanation, she'd have to ask.

"Pleased to meet you. Ma'am."

"Likewise." Luce hated being called ma'am more than I did. I grinned.

"Bye, Luce," I said. "Mustn't keep Yoga Man waiting."

"I'll talk to *you* later," she said and made her exit.

"Should I help her with that carrier?" Blake asked. It looks pretty heavy, and that is one big cat."

"No, she's fine. Luce likes to do things for herself."

"All right. Guess I better be going."

"Probably so. Thanks your help, Blake." Out on the sidewalk, he threw the board down in front of him, hopped onto it, waved, and rumbled noisily down the street.

I washed the breakfast things, straightened up a bit, mulling over how smoothly things went with the dreaded bedroom, how grateful I was for Blake's moral support. Changing into my running clothes, I took a moment to unfold the card I had found in the bedside table. An Ace. "Don't forget" scrawled in angular letters across the face of the card. It did not feel like a friendly reminder. Gave me the creeps. I flipped the card onto the dresser, resolved to deal with it later. I'm the queen of procrastination.

I picked up my Nalgene bottle and clattered down the stairs, calling Glory and asking her if she wanted to go for a ride. Yeah yeah yeah was her response. Leash, ball, dog biscuits, hat & gloves, water bottle and jacket, granola bar in the pocket. We were good to go. Checked twice to see everything was properly locked up. The robberies had made me anxious. I backed out of the driveway and headed north toward the river.

I parked the Infiniti by the levee, just east of 2nd and Elm. Checking my watch, I was surprised to see that it was afternoon already. I looped Glory's leash around my waist in case we ran into dog-phobic people, and we headed up the slope to the top of the levee. The dog waited for me at the top.

We stood together quietly, taking in the rushing sound of water coursing over the dam and down the four shallow steps below. The only other sound was the occasional faint cry of a gull high overhead. The movement of the water generated a soft breeze. Perfect. I stretched, checked the laces and kicked off into a slow lope, giving my muscles a chance to warm up. Glory ran off ahead, delight in motion.

We were the only ones out on the levee, the wide gravel path spread out before us. We ran past the modest houses and back yards of north Lawrence on the left, with the occasional play structure in back yards. On the right was the river, its muddy green water throwing off light in silver flashes. We were completely alone. But my creepy I'm-being-watched radar went off. I looked around, raking my eyes across the streets and jogging path. Not a soul in sight. I shook it off, kept going.

The sound of the dam receded, and I listened instead to the rhythms of my breath as my stride lengthened. I was glad to have the hat and gloves. It was not spring yet, and when the sun hid behind a cloud the air cooled considerably. Glory ran back and forth, checking on me then sprinting ahead. Unencumbered by my sense of immanent dread, she would occasionally drift off the path to the right, but the slope of the levee was pretty steep, so she didn't go too far. I took out the ball and tossed it ahead, giving her something to chase. I wasn't as adept as the meter man, but that was OK with her. She'd leap into the air, catching the ball before it hit the ground. I laughed out loud, loving the little dog.

Eventually the path narrowed as it turned into a dirt trail. It led away from the river toward train tracks and open land. You didn't have to go very far in Lawrence to meet pastures or farmland. The houses grew farther apart, and the sky took over. There were always hawks or eagles to see if one took the time to find them. Trains whistle off in the distance or rumble past on nearer tracks. I'd wave at the engineers and they'd wave back. It was like going back in time.

My feet slowed and then stopped. There it was again, the feeling watched sensation. I made a slow 360 and stood totally still. Glory trotted back, tennis ball in her mouth, tail wagging. I was mystified. "Let's book it, little girl," I challenged her. Kicked off and sprinted into some hard running.

After half an hour, Glory and I stopped and caught our breath. I drank from the Nalgene bottle the offered her some water, pouring it slowly into my hand so she could get a good drink. When she stuck her wet nose in my face I knew she'd had enough.

Jogging back the way we had come, I felt the sun full on my face. I could smell the river before we got to it, a rank humus odor that disappeared as the currents of air caught it. I slowed to a walk to cool down, and Glory stopped her frantic back-and-forth.

We approached an area of stones that had been piled up to protect the levee from floods. In the middle was a mosaic of smaller rocks arranged in a design of sunflowers and daisies, I think. There was a surface flat enough to sit on, so Glory and I sat, looking down at the river and sniffing the breeze. She leaned against me, an invitation to scratch ears. Before I could move to oblige, the ears perked up and Glory whipped around and stood beside me, nose pointed behind my back. I stood up to see what she was looking at. Nothing. The streets beyond the levee were empty. The dog stayed on point for another moment and then gave it up.

"You can be a spooky dog, you know that?" All on her. As if I'd had no creepy intuitions myself.

Glory and I had some more water and returned to the car. Before I got within beeping distance, I could see a mass of white material draped across the windshield of the Infiniti, cascading down onto the hood. The message scrawled in red marker across the bodice read, *Time's Up.*

Dragging the ruined wedding dress off the car, I wadded it up, jogged back across the levee to the river and threw it in. If the watcher was still around, he now knew that I was angry. And not a person who went through the proper channels. All bets were off.

15

Dressed in a clean pair of jeans and pale yellow turtleneck, I stood by the old dresser and examined the playing cards that had come into my life from two different directions. The Ace from Louise's bedside table was worn. It was scuffed, and the crease almost cut the card in half, as if it had been open and closed many times. "Don't forget." Forget what, mom?

The card left in the shop was brand new. Same Ace, different deck. Hadn't been folded, no marks of any kind other than the strange, angular writing, written with the same ballpoint pen. *25G*. For what? Ace present was threatening enough; with Ace past, the message was complicated, ominous. How did the cards connect to the two dresses? I was expected to know something I didn't know. With two days left I had a feeling I was about to find out. Lying side by side on the dresser, the Aces gave me no hints.

I sensed something missing and looked around. No Glory. The duvet on the bed showed signs of her presence, but the room was still and unnaturally silent. Without Glory, I was a foreigner here, I thought. I sat on the bed and looked around the room again, at the afternoon light shining on the dark floor. The furniture, the room itself, was as familiar as my hand, but it was not mine. I was a transient presence, a passer-through. Nothing here was part of me. Nor I of it. Temporary. When had I become so impermanent? The question applied to more than the room. Brooding about it, I grabbed my watch, stepped into the Merrells and went downstairs to find Glory. I could have called her, but I enjoyed sneaking up on her and seeing what she was up to. I did not often catch the dog unawares, but when I did it was totally cool.

The Hudsons are a family of sneaker-uppers. We sneak up on each other in grocery store aisles, in movie theaters, even at Mom's funeral. Librarians had learned to look out for us and threatened not to check out our books. They actually banned Loretta and Lenore after one particularly raucous incident in the main reading room. Family get-togethers could get out of hand with so many people sneaking up on each other. The funny thing is that even though we each knew we were sneaking up on each other, we were usually so distracted by our thoughts that we were pretty easy to sneak up on. And we always jumped about six inches into the air. Must be armadillos in the family genome.

Smiling in anticipation, I walked into the kitchen to find Luce sitting at the table, Glory at her feet.

"Earl Grey?" I asked her.

"It might need some heating up. Why don't you put the kettle on." I did and took the time to make myself some toast and honey. I was starved.

"So. How was the weekend, Luce?"

"Peachy." She narrowed her eyes at me. "What are you up to with that young man, Lyle? Is he out of high school yet? Does his mother know about you?"

"Whoa! Good to see you, too. Calm down. Not that it is your business, but there is exactly nothing between Blake and me. He helped me move some furniture."

"I should hope so. He is a mere child…"

"Before I start to get insulted, Luce, why don't you tell me why you're here?"

"I have reason to worry about you, Lyle. The whole time you've been here you have been flighty and indecisive, a dangerous combination."

I shook my head at her and wagged my finger. "Do not avoid the question." I added hot water to the tea, poured myself a cup and munched on the toast, licking honey from my fingers. Putting my chin in my non-sticky hand, I looked at her and waited.

"The weekend was fine," she began. "Like the place, the pace of the yoga sessions. The peace of it…nice. Very Zen," she added, sourly.

"Why the long face?" I was curious about the black cloud hanging over her head and the crabby vibes that were so unlike her. Luce is the avatar of equanimity. I was shaken to see her so…put out.

"Lyle, I am so mad I could spit nails. Honestly!" she exclaimed in exasperation, "It was fine, just fine! And then he ruined it, shot the whole damn thing to hell! Peace of mind? Gone! Oneness of being? Gone! Meditation? I don't think so!"

"My God, what happened?"

"The son of a bitch asked me to marry him! Oh! I could have smacked him right in the kisser." She burst into tears, causing my jaw to drop off my face. I could not have been more surprised if Glory had sat up and asked me for a cigarette. Luce, crying?

She stood up and went to get some Kleenex. I waited quietly, giving Glory a scratch behind the ears to reassure us both. Taking a deep breath, my aunt came back to the table and sat down.

"I tell you, Lyle, I have never been more disappointed in a man in my life." She sighed. "At least not as far as I can remember."

"Why are you so upset? I think it's sweet!"

"Sweet, my ass! What do I want with that old coot cluttering up my house, creating smelly laundry, asking me to look after him? I like my life *the way it is*. I like William just fine. Don't you see? It will never be the same. It's over. He'll be mopey and disappointed and feel rejected and I'll be the villain, the guilty party! No, thank you."

"Well, was it a romantic proposal? Did he declare undying love and all?"

Luce's eyebrows shot up in complete surprise and she burst into a peal of laughter.

"Not hardly!" More laughter. "It was more like whether we should have waffles for breakfast. In fact," she leaned forward for emphasis, "We were sitting on the veranda of the ashram, watching the sunset and he up and says, plain as a post,

'It's time we got married, don't you think?'

'The hell I do!' I cried, 'I tell you flat out, William Henry, if I were dying of cancer, I wouldn't marry you! I am not lonely, I am not sick, and if you had the sense that God gave a flea, you'd never suggest such a thing! You were a lucky S-O-B to have me and *now* you've gone and torn it, just threw it away!'

'Now, Luce,' he said, 'No reason to go off on me. If the answer is no, just say no. What has got into you?'

'The kiss of death has got into me, you old plate of

soup!' "

"I admit it, Lyle," she took a breather here, "It took me a while to cool off. But, really, I was that exasperated. Now what are we to do? Greet each other like strangers? Exchange inanities at the post office?"

"I don't get it. Why can't you go on as before, just get on with it?"

"Lyle, once a man has proposed to you, he can't be trusted, pure and simple. It is over, O-V-E-R. Over." She was getting her color up again, so I suggested we let the subject go.

"Easy for you to say, Carlyle. William was a good friend, one of the best. Played cards well, talked about things going on in the world, read books. Damn. I'll miss that!"

"Well, Luce, why don't you just let it be for a while. Like you're always telling me. Maybe things will turn out differently than you expect."

"Trust you to throw my own words in my face."

"Now, Luce, clam down. I meant no disrespect. Would you please just think about it? I suspect Will wouldn't mind a 'time out' either, not with you chewing his ears off all the way back from Salina."

"Bloody Hell." That was usually how Hudson women ended a conversation when they unwilling to give ground.

"Do you have anything stronger than tea in this house?"

"You bet." Without either one of us realizing, it had grown dark outside. The kitchen was mostly shadows now, and Luce's face was itself a study in shadows—as beautiful as a Rembrandt, had he taken pains to make his women as noble as his men, which he had not.

Neither of us needed a light in that house. We moved by instinct into the darkness of the library where my hand knew where to find the small Tiffany lamp and bring to life its gem-like colors.

"You throw a few sticks on that gas fire, Luce. I'll get the wine."

"I think I'll have a scotch if you don't mind, Lyle."

"Luce, you don't drink scotch."

"I do tonight. Hop to it." She almost smiled at he look on my face.

"Straightaway," I responded, giving us both a grin. Straightaway's what we use to avoid the dreaded *yes ma'am*. It worked just fine.

"Here's your scotch. I've got a couple of phone calls to make before it gets any later. I'll be right back." I took my drink with me out onto the front porch, as much for the fresh air as the privacy. Pulled out the cell and a piece of wrinkled paper and dialed a number.

Through the window, I watched Luce fuss with the blue scarf at her neck for a moment. She sat forward to engage Glory in conversation, shaking her finger at the dog, clearly instructing Glory in the unreliability of men. The dog wagged her stubby little tail and scotched closer, big grin on her black and white face. Luce laughed. I folded the cell—no answer, no message—tossed the ice in my glass over the porch rail into the bushes, and walked back into the house.

"Get yourself another drink," Luce greeted me. "You've got some catching up to do!" Clearly, my aunt was in better spirits.

"Don't mind if I do," I smiled at her and fetched a plate with goat cheese and crackers so Luce would have something in her stomach.

"Maybe it's one of your, you know, gambling buddies," Luce said, munching a cracker, when I showed her what were now two envelopes that had been left.

"I don't have any gambling debts, Luce. I want no

baggage attached to my play. It's that simple."

"A dare, perhaps?" she continued, undeterred by the hand on my hip and my steely glare.

"A what?"

"I don't know, Lyle. You're the one who..."

"Time out! Stop right there. It was one thing for Lou to cop an attitude about my source of income, but I won't take it from you. I live a respectable life, and, though it pains me to say it, I play by the rules. Period."

My words were abrupt and could put a crimp in our relationship that might last a week. When Hudsons disagree, we give each other the silent treatment, which, for me, only made things worse. To avoid this particular eventuality, I quickly changed the subject..

"Would you like to stay and scare up an omelet or two, Luce?"

"No, I am not in a mood to spend much time in your mother's house, Lyle. Let's go out." She untied the blue silk scarf at her neck and used it to catch her hair back, then raised an eyebrow at me.

"Out it is! I think we're both presentable enough," I said.

"We are if we keep our mouths shut," Luce replied. We clinked glasses in agreement. I filled Luce in on recent events—the ones I felt like sharing—and discussed with her my changes to Louise's bedroom and possible plans for the house.

"What say we save the larger issues for another time, Lyle. I'm glad to see you making headway. Well done." Luce always did appreciate difficult decisions as a means to building character. "Shilly-shallying," as she called it, resulted in more harm than good. "Just makes folks mad at you," she claimed.

We put ourselves to rights, "Enough so as not to scare people," Luce said, and left Glory snoozing on the couch, the fading embers of the fire winking into darkness.

"Reed's?" I asked once we were in the car.

"Just the thing. Let's go!" And go we did.

Reed's is a trendy, San Francisco-style restaurant and bar in what once was a bank. Saturdays it would be a major singles scene. But Sunday evening it is a quiet, transitional space. Since Lawrence had passed its no-smoking ordinance, Reed's had become a much more pleasant place in my book. No more cigarette smog drifting over into the dining area. The appeal of the place was more its ambience than its menu, which was less than impressive. Perhaps I was spoiled by San Francisco. High ceilings, marble floors, the wrought iron and glass lamps one would have found in a 19th Century bank. The restrooms were located in what was the bank vault, the heavy doors and barred grillwork still there, a classy combination of high-tech and retro black marble.

Luce and I chose a table by one of the tall windows overlooking 8th Street. We ordered bruschetta, mushroom soup, and asked for a bottle of Petit Syrah.

"Did Louise ever play cards, Luce?" The question just popped out. My aunt just stared.

"Excuse me?"

"You know, cards. Games of chance." I took the cards out of my jeans pocket and Luce put her reading glasses on to inspect them.

"No she did not. Not that I know, anyway. She never did say very much about your...livelihood." Luce pushed her hair back behind her ears and leaned forward across the table, eyes bright with curiosity. "These cards may say something about the messenger, but I doubt they tell us anything about Louise."

"Mmm. Maybe not. I just have this feeling." Luce rolled her eyes and changed the subject. What I might be up to and what she might have to say about it was far more attractive than used Aces. Before I knew it, I was explaining my behavior to my aunt.

"The truth is, Luce, that I've made some decisions, finally. I'm going back to San Francisco. I have to see what I would be giving up, whether moving back here would make sense. Chas thinks I'd go postal here. I'm not so sure. Mom's death has...has changed something in me. I don't know if I can explain it."

"No need, honey, no need. The important thing is to do something, to get you thinking again. Right here, right now? This is the most *you* I've seen in a while. It's reassuring." She smiled and signaled the waiter.

"We'd like some coffee, young man. You can bring me the bill, while you're at it."

"No, Luce. This is my treat."

"Too slow! You are clearly out of practice, girl!" The waiter cleared the dishes and we regarded each other appreciatively. Outside the windows passersby were strolling at a leisurely pace, and window shoppers moved in and out of the light cast by displays of Spring merchandise.

"I'm not leaving tomorrow, you know," I said, continuing the conversation. I have to work something out about the shop, among other things. Nola and I are meeting to discuss it this week. I am still here for a bit."

"What *about* the shop?"

"I think I'll sell it. If not to Nola, then to someone else. I'm not much on absentee landlords. Besides, the place gives me the willies."

Luce regarded me seriously. "I'd like to think, Lyle, that you would talk to me and to the L&L's about it first." She usually referred to Loretta and Lenore as the "aunts", making our relationship something else, apart from her sisters. Looked like she was shifting allegiance on the subject of property.

"It never crossed my mind that any of you would ever be interested. I'm surprised!"

"No offense taken. I'll bring it up with the girls and you can move on to Nola or whoever if we decide to give it a pass. But I'm pretty sure that Loretta and Lenore would be interested. Hudsons hate to let go of property or business once it's in the family, remember." She placed her chin in her hand and smiled.

We finished our coffee and I arm wrestled Luce into letting me leave the tip for what turned out to be rather decent service.

We strolled down Mass Street for a bit, enjoying the evening and each other's company, looking in store windows. As I beeped the car door, Luce laughed at a stray thought that had caught her attention.

"Carlyle Hudson. You are one bad woman!" More laughter. Luce was feeling no pain. "When I think of how you got this car..."

"Hey, hey!" I admonished her, "Don't start on me, Luce! We have had what Louise would call a *dandy* evening. Let's just leave it that way, please?"

"All right, but it is still a good story." She avoided my pointed look by taking the scarf out of her hair and retying it, humming a little something under her breath.

"Am I driving you home or what?" I asked testily.

"Get in the car." She giggled the way we do when a button has been well and thoroughly pushed.

16

Next morning, I found Glory downstairs standing at the front door, her taut little body rigid, inhaling heavily through the mail slot. I opened the door to find three dead cats on the welcome mat, painted silver, eyes gouged out and tails cut off. Gagging, I covered the small bodies with a paper towel, fighting dry heaves.

I picked up the phone and called MacDonald. I hated playing the frightened female card and going to the big, strong man for help and protection, but Mac-Donald George was a cop, sort of, and he knew other cops.

"Something is going on, Mac, and I have the feeling that I'm supposed to know what it is but I don't and this shit is getting to me!" I told him the progression from phone calls to notes to dead cats. I should've told him about the money and the ultimatum, but I didn't.

"What makes you think this is about you, Lyle? Why couldn't it be unfinished business about Louise?"

"Come over and take a look at the cats, Mac;

they've been deliberately mutilated." My hand on the phone was sweaty and clammy.

"Oh, I will, but..."

"Cats! They are silver cats! That's how I know it's me!" MacDonald let the silence hang there until I filled in the gap. Which meant that I had to stop hyperventilating.

"Cat is my table name. That's how I know." I didn't want to tell him more just then. On the gambling circuit, people have these stupid nick names. Fallout from late hours, adrenaline overload, whatever. You get one it sticks. Trying to change it only makes things worse. Silver hair, silver feline. You figure it out. I didn't care one way or the other until now.

"A name from childhood?" He sounded confused, not getting the gambling thing because I hadn't told him. Yet.

"Whatever. Sorry. This is getting on my nerves."

Between the time I hung up the phone and MacDonald arrived at the door, another note had arrived. I looked at it incredulously. What? The cats weren't enough?

"Fine guard dog you are!" I snapped at Glory. She looked up at me as if to say she hadn't heard a thing, honest!

I collected the blank envelope and stood by the door, staring, feeling my breath go shallow. I was still standing there when Mac's knock on the door made me jump and sent Glory into a scramble of barking and spinning circles around me.

"Hi," I said in a small voice.

"Hi, yourself. What's the matter?" he asked Glory. The dog looked spooked.

"We're having a bad day." I showed him the most

recent envelope. We went into the kitchen to open it.

"Sure you don't want to see the dead cats first? I saved them for you." The cats were in a plastic bag out by the garbage.

I tore the end of the envelope and extracted the usual sheet of photocopied words. Only this time two more words had been added: OR ELSE.

"Why can't these people just tell me what the fuck is up?"

"What do you think is up?" MacDonald stood close to me and spoke quietly, but the words came as a revelation. I stared at his questioning eyebrows and let my gaze travel to the soft flannel covering his shoulders, an inviting reddish, brick color. Still in my trance, I reached up and placed my hand where my gaze rested, feeling the warmth and muscle beneath the fabric.

"I don't know. For some reason, I have not asked myself that question, MacDonald. Weird." I sat down at the kitchen table and looked at the note. Mac sat quietly, giving me plenty of space to think.

"It's the cats that have me confused. That part has to be about me. Before the cats appeared…the crank calls…I thought that had to do with my mom. The notes…. It's me, now. I'm being threatened." I put my chin in my hands.

I felt better with MacDonald sitting across from me. Maybe I could figure this thing out.

"OK," he said, "That's a start. Show me the cats." Right.

MacDonald George took the mutilated cats with him, and the envelopes, saying he'd look into things for me. He took the threat seriously and advised me to be careful.

I needed to see normal people doing normal things. I grabbed my iMac and satchel and headed for the car, taking Glory with me. I was in the mood to head back to San Francisco and take Glory with me. But then I'd have to deal with the wrath of the Hudsons, which would make the poor mice look like chump change. SF. I started calling San Francisco SF because of computers. Between IM's and cell phones, I hardly ever used the full name of the place any more, not even when talking. SF was wired in my brain. Random thoughts like these are good, a welcome release from mutilated mice and vague threats.

Neo is a cyber café on 8th Street, downtown. Good latte, people minded their own business, and I could take Glory with me. The only dog there, she'd quickly curl up on the smooth tiles at my feet and go to sleep.

Placing my order at the counter, I gave the barista guy a double take. Who did he remind me of?

"Excuse me, but do you have a...cousin? Someone in your family looks like you? Without the height? I think his name was Bartholomew." I tried to be cute about it, but turns out it wasn't necessary, he got that a lot.

"Tolo?" He shook his head sadly. "Man, that kid gets around. He cause you any trouble? Here, it's on the house."

"No, not necessary! I ran into him not too long ago. The only reason I asked is the resemblance." I put the money on the counter and smiled at him.

"Maybe I should dye my hair! You let me know he causes you problems, OK? I sic my mom on him!" The thought made him laugh.

I logged on and thought about Tolo, short for purse-snatching Bartholomew evidently, who I called Bart. Bad news is right. Just thinking about that punk made my hand itch.

Nothing in my inbox, I moved on to the news services I used to keep me up to date. What with the war in Iraq, the most recent airline disaster, avian flu, and terrorism in London, there would be something to take my mind off my own worries. The latte was excellent.

"what r u waiting 4? horse head in bed?" Usually I like IM's.

"who r u?" I typed.

"PAY UP" I choked on my drink.

"pay what?" I typed.

"25G"

"for what"

"times up"

"how about a clue" I shot back.

"check her computer"

"what r u talking about" Silence.

Bad news, wacko has my email and knows where I live. Good news, maybe the dead cats will go away. Bad news, threats were escalating. I did not have a good feeling about this.

"Luce?" I called her after a fruitless search of the house. No computer. "Do you know if Louise had a computer?"

"Hello to you, too. No. The only computer I know of is the one at the shop, why?"

The shop! Of course. Louise would have kept her records in one place, home as well as business.

"I'm trying to find something, a record? That she might have hidden somewhere." That sounded pretty lame, even to my ears.

"What kind of record?" She asked with some asperity. "What are you up to, Lyle? What's going on?" Luce never raised her voice, she just polished the edge until I gave in and told her everything.

"I tell you later. I don't have much time. Bye!" I closed my cell phone, packed up the laptop, and piled Glory in the car. I hate driving downtown, especially when I'm less than ten blocks from my destination, but I had to hurry. If Luce beat me to the shop, I'd have to wrestle her to the floor to get to the computer first.

At the shop, Nola was talking to a customer, her pixy eyes twinkling. I gave her a breezy wave from the back door and headed to the computer, in what I hoped was a nonchalant manner. Glory watched my back, and I got to work. "C'mon," I told the computer. "Let's back into this hand and catch some luck!"

Luce walked in the front of the shop as Nola's customer was leaving, just as I admitted to myself that I had found nothing.

Luce and Nola had a brief conversation, then turned toward the back of the shop in tandem. I felt surrounded. In a moment I was.

"You are looking for a particular file, are you, dear?" Nola was nothing if not helpful.

"Yes, but I don't know what it is. Personal accounts, personal information? Something like that." I sat back and pushed my glasses back onto my head.

"Hmm." Nola shook her head and looked at Luce who had trained a laser glare on me and was willing me out of the chair. "I wouldn't know about anything like that, Lyle. Louise was such a private person." She paused, tactfully. "But I'd be glad to help you look. May I?"

"Help yourself. I scoured the files and found nothing." Trying not to sound petulant about it.

"How is Crista?" I knew Nola would know about the breakup, and I wanted to know without intruding on the young woman.

"Oh, she'll be fine. A bit preoccupied just now, but she's almost finished with her gown. Not in today, though. Taking a bit of personal space."

Nola seated herself and Luce and I hovered over her shoulders, peering at the screen.

"Well," Luce said, "if it was a file she wanted hidden, she'd have stashed it six folders down, with some misleading name, maybe even encrypted. That's what you'd do, wouldn't you?"

"I thought about that, Luce. But that would mean going through every file in the system. And we're not even talking passwords." I leaned over her shoulder and watched Nola's fingers commune with the keys, her gaze locked on the screen.

"You're holding your breath, Lyle," Nola said. "Why don't you go. I'll call you if I find anything."

"Since when did you get so proficient at computers?" I asked resentfully.

"Since they started offering free classes at the senior center. You should come over to the house and check out my new software. It really keeps me entertained!" Luce laughed and scooted out the back door.

I mumbled something juvenile under my breath and said I'd take a walk, clear my head. Made sure my cell was charged before Glory and I left the store.

We crossed Mass Street and entered South Park. I pulled a tennis ball from my satchel and made Glory delirious while I mulled the problem over in my mind. With a ball in her mouth, she wouldn't even think about barking at kids in the park. Ball: small, round object of desire and obsession.

Something about the whole "Pay Up" demand disturbed me. What if this situation *was* about Louise and not me? What then? What about my mother did I not know? How did it involve me? I was chasing myself in mental circles when I felt a sudden splat strike the side of my face. It felt like a hard slap, a water balloon, maybe, and my head pitched to the left. There was gooey stuff oozing down my cheek, and I was hit three more times. Splat, splat, splat. I lost my balance and tipped over, fell to my knees on the sidewalk and tried to protect my face from the barrage of the attack

I caught a quick glimpse of a guy on a bicycle, and I heard the gears shift as the wheels brushed by me, the kid's voice calling over his shoulder, "The message is Time's Up, bitch," as he sped away. I gasped for air, choking on paint fumes. Was that Bartholomew, my Sun Ripe nemesis? I couldn't be sure.

Glory was no help at all. She came over, stood by me, and barked at the retreating bicyclist but she was not willing to abandon her ball. The bike was gone in an instant. I sat down on the cement to survey the damage.

My knee ached from the fall, but not much. The rest of me felt like I'd been hit with big marbles, or small rocks. I hoped my arms had kept my face from serious bruising. I wiped my face and my hand came away, sticky with turquoise green paint that had made it past my arms. The stuff oozed thickly down my back. When I stood up, a puddle of green, orange and purple paint formed around my shoes. I'd been shot with paint balls! The thick glop was nasty and cold. My shoes, jacket, pants—everything I wore—was ruined. The Merrells were a mess, as was the satchel. Glory kept her distance but whined her concern..

I dripped my way back across the street to the shop.

In the middle of Mass Street, in front of Hyacinth and tried to get their attention. God knows what people in passing cars thought. They made wide arcs to move around me. I was getting very cold. Glory sat at the curb in front of the shop, protecting her tennis ball, watching me as I pulled my cell phone out of my coagulating satchel. The phone turned turquoise blue as I punched in the number of the shop.

"Hi, Nola. Look out the front window, will you?" Pause. "Yes. That *crazy person* is me." I waved at Nola peeking at me from behind a particularly bouffant wedding dress.

"Ask Luce to find a trash bag and bring it out front, please." Pause. "Yes. Now. It is getting cold out here." Pause. "Nola? I don't care whether it will snow or not." Pause. "Yes, it really is me and I really need help. Unless you want me to drizzle this paint all over the fucking shop!" The obscenity got through to her.

Luce came out with a box of trash bags and waved me over to the curb, where I proceeded to disrobe and place various items of clothing into separate bags. Some customers from the bar came outside to watch my Blue Man show.

"Back off! You take one step out that door, any of you! And I will break your fucking necks!" I shook my paint-soaked shirt at them like a wild woman.

Luce, who had been doing a pretty good job of keeping a straight face, lost it

"Honey, you tell 'em! You run out of wet clothes, throw rocks!"

The sight of Luce trying to talk and laugh—it was more a howl, really—went through me like lightning. Half naked, I laughed so hard I jumped up and down. When I hugged my sides to stop the laughing, my skin literally turned bright blue. I thought Luce would have a seizure.

Nola ran out to see if she could help, took one look at me and froze. Both hands over her mouth, she doubled over and ran back inside. Great, I thought. I'm about to die of frostbite or get arrested for indecency and all they can do is laugh.

Nola returned with a ratty old afghan she'd found upstairs and wrapped it around me. She helped me into the shop after checking to see that I would not mar the wood floors with paintball footprints. Luce picked up the plastic bags, occasionally pausing to give in to a fit of the giggles.

An hour or so later, I was dry enough to drive home. My skin was still a greenish mermaid color, but I could drive. Not too many welts and bruises. Nola graciously offered me the loan of a wedding dress, but I told her the afghan would do quite well. The thought of me in a wedding dress left Luce sitting helplessly at the computer, leaning her head on her arms, howling.

Mustering what dignity I could, I picked up the baggie that held the contents of my purse and swept out the back door of the shop where another surprise awaited me. All four tires on my Infiniti were slashed to ribbons. My long, nasty day had just gotten longer and nastier.

"Bastards!" I yelled at the top of my lungs, tearing the afghan with my teeth.

17

"Ann Headley?"

"Yes?"

"My name is Lyle Hudson. I'm Louise Hudson's daughter?"

"Yes?"

"I…" I wasn't quite sure how to continue and the lack of response on the other end of the line was not making it easy for me.

"My mother left this box, with some things I think she wanted returned to you. There were no specific instructions, but I'd like to give you the box in person." Absolute silence. Not even breathing.

"Ms. Headley? Are you there?"

"Yes, Ms. Hudson. I was just…thinking. I'm not quite sure what to say."

"It's pretty simple, really." I kept my voice light and unconcerned. "I'm pretty flexible in terms of time. Are you interested in having the box returned to you?" A sharp intake of breath was my response. And then the conversation shifted gears.

"What are your intentions, Ms. Hudson? What exactly is it you want?"

"I would like to meet you, to talk about the box."

"Are you sure that's wise?"

"Listen, Ms. Headley. You were obviously a friend of my mother's. This box has gathered a lot of dust over the years. I do not intend to betray any confidence between you and Louise. What's over is over." Another significant pause.

"In which case, Ms. Hudson, why meet? Why not just throw it out and have done with it?" A bitter tone in her voice made me uneasy. Maybe she was right. But then, I never could resist temptation. I just came out with it.

"To tell the truth? I'm curious about my mother. About the secret she kept, about who she was." This time, I paused. "If you knew her, you know we did not get on well. There are gaps. I'd appreciate it if you would meet with me."

"Later on, we did not see much of each other, Ms. Hudson. But, yes, your mother was a friend. How about tomorrow. Four p.m. Best not to put it off. I might take a change of mind."

"Thank you."

"Let me give you directions to the farm. There aren't any signs out here, you know." She gave directions, and the conversation ended with a degree of civility, if not warmth.

"Carlyle Hudson," I addressed myself in tones a disapproving Luce would use. "People who play with fire deserve what they get. Be careful, my girl." I took my mother's Smith & Wesson out of the blue satchel and checked that it was loaded and that the safety was on. Insurance, I told myself. I pointed the gun at the kitchen door, elbow tucked against my side to keep my hand steady. The rosewood grip warmed in my hand. At close range, my lack of experience wouldn't be a problem. My temper might.

"Ann Headley? Where do I know that name from?" MacDonald and I were on the phone making plans to get together. It had been a while.

"She was a friend of my mother's, "back in the day." There are some odds and ends that Louise wanted returned to her, so…"

"I don't know, Lyle. The name nags at me."

"Anyway," I said brightly, changing the subject and avoiding any intimation of knowledge on my part, "I'm calling to ask you out, MacDonald George. Go out for a drink or coffee, or such like?" Oh, my God! I was getting a twang? Where did this old-timey diction come from?

"When?"

"When?" I am lousy at this kind of thing, setting up appointments, making dates. My sense of time is tenuous at best.

"Lyle? You there?" I could not read his tone of voice, not on a phone at any rate.

"Sorry, MacDonald. I got lost there, trying to make up my mind. Luce considers it the worst of my many and manifold character flaws. Why not just say what works for you and I'll show up." The sound of his laughter was reassuring, and sexy. Very, very sexy. I called to mind his stupendous skill as a kisser and felt a little light-headed.

"What are you doing tonight? For simplicity's sake, that is. Wouldn't want you to think I had designs on you or anything. I happen to be free. You might, too."

"Tonight. Tonight works. I've got Glory with me.

We're driving out to the Headley farm and then coming back into town. We could meet at the Union? Or Reed's?"

"If you'll be out at Headley's, you could just stop by here on your way back to town. Bring Glory with you."

"Here?" I was having this echo syndrome. Airhead city. But I was listening hard, too. Feeling flustered and anxious, and totally green.

"My place, Lyle. It's comfortable. I'd like you to stop by and visit. What do you say?" Give the devil his due, MacDonald George was a cool customer, very smooth. He wasn't pushing at all, just setting it out there to see what I'd do. What the hell.

"OK." Sometimes you just play your cards and try not to think too hard. "How does seven sound?"

"Great." He gave me directions from the Headley farm and signed off. I closed the cell and slipped it back in my pocket. Glory sat up in the passenger seat and looked at me. She stood up and shook herself, sending her ears flapping and the leaned across the console and licked my ear. I stroked her smooth head a couple times, for comfort.

"Great. I get to go to his house and tell him I can't see him again. Should be a fun evening."

I looked at the old metal box with its design of faded forget-me-nots, lying on the floor at Glory's feet. I started the engine and headed south out of town. A fun day all around, I thought.

As I drove up the gravel drive, my brand new tires slipping around to the side, the woman stepped out onto the porch and watched the car approach. She held her arms crossed in front of her, not a hint of welcome in her posture. This was one angry woman. Oh, well.

I left Glory in the car, window open for air, and

walked up the stone steps onto the porch, the metal box tucked under one arm, mostly obscured by the tweed sleeve of my jacket.

Ann Headley did not strike me as a farm wife; in fact, she was well-groomed and dressed in an understated sophistication. The woman was younger than my mother, but she looked younger still, middle sixties, I guessed. Short, gray hair swept back from her face accentuated fine bone structure. Small, gold earrings, a green crew neck sweater over gray flannel slacks, black leather pumps with low heels. A trim, smart woman with eyes black, like marcosite; hard, like flint.

"I see you got here all right," was her sharp greeting from the porch.

"Yes," I began in a light tone, "Your directions were fine." She cut me off with a shake of the head, indicating the door behind her.

"Well, let's get inside, shall we?" Her voice was tight and sharp as knives. No pretence, no charm. I had yet to prove I deserved civility.

I followed her into a spacious, warm living room, and she motioned me to a couch.

"I've made some lemonade," she said, indicating a pitcher and glasses sitting on a coffee table. "Would you care for a glass?" The rituals of hospitality tempered the charged atmosphere.

"Yes, please." I placed the box on the polished table and sat back. We sized each other up. The box lay on the table like a loaded gun. Neither of us even looked at it. We knew it was there. We knew what it said. I felt curiously relaxed and at the same time completely alive, alert. Life didn't get much more real than this. The thought made me smile.

Ann Headley poured the lemonade with a steady hand, gave me a glass and took the wingback chair to the left of the couch. She watched me take in the features of the comfortable room, the contemporary furniture, the art on the walls. Patient and collected, she had the dead calm of an experienced card player. There would be no rushing, no confusion, no tears today. I had the distinct impression that I'd be lucky to get out alive. The lemonade was perfect. I drank deeply.

"All right, Ms. Hudson. What is it you want?" Cards on the table. Fast.

"Two things. I want to know why. And I want to know about my mother. Why I never heard of you until after she died." People find honesty disarming, upsetting, even. They rarely know how to respond. Ann Headley had no such problem. She laughed.

"That sounds like three things to me. But never mind. What do you intend to do with the information, Ms. Hudson?"

"Nothing. Knowing is enough for me." We paused, taking a break from words to read each other. She relaxed a notch. Fiddled with the single gold charm on her bracelet. I noted that her nails were manicured but not painted. Like mine.

"I wonder. Knowledge is overrated, I think. Rarely as satisfying as anticipated. Some knowledge is burdensome. What I may tell you about your mother may take away more peace than it provides." It was my turn to laugh.

"Hardly! My relationship with my mother was not the peaceful kind, Ms. Headley."

"Call me Ann, please." Was she warming up, just a little? "You look a bit like her. Around the eyes and the mouth. But you are a different creature, aren't you, Lyle."

"Very." The irony was mutual.

"I, too, have a request. Not that I'd be in any posi-

tion to make a fuss if you refused, but I must ask." She
paused. I waited. No charade of geniality here. What we
were about was utterly serious. We both respected that.

"Please. Do not tell what you learn to my son. I
could not bear to lose him, not like this." She folded her
hands with composure and placed them on her lap.

"Why would I want to? And why would he believe
me?"

"Oh, he'd believe you, all right. We'll talk about
that later. As to why you might tell? People engage in
cruelty for many reasons. To relieve their own suffering,
perhaps. It may even be more random than that. One
tells because one can."

"Louise didn't tell, Ann."

"No. Remarkable, isn't it?" We considered her, almost as if she were present in the room.

"I give you my word that I will not tell anyone.
Least of all your son."

"Thank you."

Ann Headley took a sip of the lemonade and then
looked out the window. She collected her thoughts in
silence, and when she began to speak it was with the
voice of someone far away in time. As she spoke, her
words were well-chosen, her narrative complete, as if
she had memorized each detail. Perhaps she had. There
was no self-pity, no judgment, either. She relayed
events dispassionately. It was I who was moved, disturbed by her story.

"I had sent my son over to spend the weekend with
a friend who lived in town," she began. "It was summer,
and it was our custom to bring boys out here for fishing
and horsing around and for Matt to be invited into town
for softball and movies. A nice way to break up the mo-
notony. Which fit into my plans seamlessly. It would be

a good three days before he would come back to the farm.

"I called Matt Sr. and told him I'd like to discuss his proposal, that I was tired of fighting him and just wanted Matt and me to be left in peace. He'd better come over before I changed my mind. He said he needed to clear up some work at the office but he could meet me out at the farm around four. I agreed and suggested we meet over by the old sheep pen. It was a pretty place, surrounded by old apple trees, with a view down the hill to the pond. Sure, sure, he said and hung up. I made myself a cup of coffee and walked through my plan, the outcome of which you already know. So let me back up a bit.

"Your mother, Louise, had helped me out years ago when I was planning to marry. Life's full of irony, once you get a little perspective on it. Anyway, I'd had to cancel the dress I'd set my heart on. It was my mother's illness..." Ann paused, visiting an old distress.

"But Louise generously set the dress aside and arranged for a series of deposits. As I stopped by the shop to make my payments, we got to know each other pretty well. She was a few years older and found my romantic idealism touching. I suspect she worried about it.

"She'd take the dress out so I could visit and dream of my wedding day. I'd go on and on about Matt Grimer, and she'd ask me questions. Was I sure I really knew him, Did I know how he was going to make a living, practical questions.

"One day I came in with a bruise on my arm, and she just looked into my face and knew that Matt had made the bruise.

"You cannot marry that man, Ann. If he will treat you this way now, he will treat you worse later. Just walk away. I'll give you credit for another dress at some other date to some other man.

"Of course I didn't listen. Oh, I bruise so easily, and so on. Louise did not believe me for a minute. She did the best she could to help me see sense, but then my mother died of cancer, and Matt insisted that we move the date up so he could *rescue* me from my grief and loneliness. Which meant him moving in with me at the farm. Louise warned me that he was taking advantage, but I married the son of a bitch and she came to the wedding anyway.

"In the miserable years of our marriage, your mother was a true friend. She comforted me when I found out about his affairs, when he would lose his temper and take it out on me. When I was pregnant with Matt Jr., she kept me from doing harm to myself. I mean, I was so moody and depressed and lonely that I stopped eating. I knew it was bad for the baby, but I didn't care. By that time, the bastard had started selling off pieces of the property and I was beginning to catch on to how I'd been used.

"Louise found me out in the barn one day, staring at a dead chicken. I had just wrung its neck, originally planning dinner, but the dead bird seemed so pathetic I wept and couldn't stop. She took the bird from me and led me into the house, washed my face, and made me some tea.

"Ann, she said, it's time to pull yourself together, girl. Sit up now, and drink your tea, and listen to me. Listen well. Are you listening?

"I nodded, numbly. Felt the baby moving inside.

"Here it is, Louise said. Number one: you are a prize for any man lucky enough to have you. Number two: Matthew Grimer will eat you alive if you let him. You chose poorly, dear. You need to protect yourself, Ann. You need insurance against that day when he will

try to take the last penny you have. Agreed?
"I nodded some more, beginning to really listen to
her. Louise was so serious, so angry. I don't remember
anyone ever being angry *for* me. It was a revelation."
Ann continued, "All right, Louise, I said. What do
you want me to do?
"I want you to prepare for that day. Will you practice?
"Why yes, I think I will.
"Good girl. Now, eat this sandwich. So I ate the
sandwich, probably the first meal I'd had in days, and
listened and nodded, beginning to see the plan. Every
couple of days, Louise would show up when she was
sure my husband was in town or somewhere, and she
would bring a hand gun with her and some ammunition,
and we would have target practice out by the pond,
shooting pop cans that she'd brought with her and
which she would take away when she left. Your mother
was one careful woman, Lyle.
"I never asked her where she got the gun, and she
never volunteered the information. While I improved
my aim over several weeks, she explained what she
meant by insurance. By then, I had started to feel better
about myself, thinking maybe I was not as pathetic and
useless as the bastard had led me to believe. I had also
begun to fall in love with the idea of a baby. Matt was
already pleased about that and was promising me jewelry if it was a boy. He couldn't wait to name the child
after him."

Ann poured herself another glass of lemonade. The
gold charm on her bracelet clinked against the side of
the glass. I asked if I could bring Glory in, and she
agreed. Glory danced around for a bit sniffing the room,
walked over to give Ann a sniff or two, and then curled

up at my feet.

"Cute dog," Ann said. "What's her name?"

"Glory. She belonged to Louise."

"Really. Well, well." Her thoughts drifted back.

"Insurance, as interpreted by Louise, meant being able to stand up for yourself, not having to count on anyone.

"Cops are men, lawyers are men, judges are men, any system is a system by and for men. Women do not have a chance, she'd say. Domestic violence? Who the hell is going to step in there? Aim a little higher next time, Ann. A man can take your land, your child from you? What does that leave you with? Squeeze the trigger, dear. Don't jerk the gun. Louise went on to explain that I probably would never even have to use the gun, that just the idea of it would support me when I was alone with the opportunistic son of a bitch. But if I did, he'd have it coming.

"I learned well. And I remembered. I practiced just enough to keep my aim. When I ran out of ammunition, I'd stop by Hyacinth for a cup of tea. It was the most natural thing in the world to stop by with the baby. Probably you noticed the bracelet. My reward for having a boy. The only piece of jewelry the bastard ever bought me. I keep it as a reminder of my freedom."

My head was reeling. My sweet, passive mother a guerilla feminist? Provider of fire arms to disgruntled, downtrodden housewives?

"Hey, Ann? Could we do the rest of this story some other time?"

"We're in it now, Lyle. I warned you. Besides, there's not much left to tell."

"I put up with my husband's crap for years," she continued, "thinking somehow things would change. That Matty and I deserved to have the bastard come to his senses and be a good husband and father. From time to time I forgot I had the gun.

"When we went through the divorce, I resumed practice. I shot the hell out of cases of soda cans.

"The woman Matt Grimer had left me for was only the first in a series of young women he would take up with. Never married any of them, so I felt that Matt Jr. and I were pretty secure. I was unhappy, but I had a life, of sorts. I took back my maiden name as a gesture of independence.

"Then, when Matt Jr. was a freshman in high school, the bastard decided he'd get married, start a new family. He'd met a dental hygienist and fell hard. Started talking about how my house, the house I'd been born in was really his, that as my husband he owned it, some such crap. Said he had legal documents drawn up by his lawyer that I'd signed as part of our divorce that gave the house and what little land was left to him. And now he was going to claim it and start life over with his bride to be!"

Ann's voice trembled with a cool rage as she remembered the deception, the humiliation of having been taken advantage of yet again.

"So, I called him, as I told you. He drove out to the old sheep pen that resided on property that had not belonged to me for about a decade. I was there waiting for him. The plan was in place: shoes, shovel, bullets ready to go.

"I was wearing a yellow sundress with white sandals, my right hand held behind my back, my left hand on a basket that looked like it held muffins. The man sauntered over to me, a big smile on his face.

"Ann! Glad you came to your senses! He crowed.

"So am I, you son of a bitch. I dropped the basket, pulled the gun from behind my back and shot the bastard in the face."

Shit. What have you gotten yourself into here, Lyle? I watched Ann's face closely, hoping mine did not betray my surprise.

"I must admit, I never felt so good in my life." She allowed herself a thin smile and picked up the thread of her narrative.

"I took the old farm boots out of the basket and put them on. I dropped the shoes and the gun in the basket, and walked around to cover any tracks made by my sandals, then I walked over to the woods. About half way back to the house, I stopped and put the sandals back on. I made sure to walk on fallen leaves and pine needles. At the edge of my property, I took the sandals off and walked barefoot, just in case. I found another pair of boots in the barn and took the shovel and basket round back to the compost heap and dug a hole. In went the boots and sandals. The hole was deep, considering I was just burying shoes and boots. So it took a while. I covered the spot with compost.

"Back in the barn, I cleaned the shovel and set the work boots out to dry. I then got in the truck and drove into town, where I was sure to be seen picking up a few groceries. Before I left town, I drove over by the river and threw in the gun. The police investigation blew over after a while. My life's been peaceful since then." She paused. "Until you showed up."

Ann Headley gazed at me, steady and cool.

"Is that it?" I asked.

"Not quite."

18

Where the hell did that gun come from? I was so startled that I laughed out loud.

"Are you nuts? You think you can just kill me and get away with it?" My laughter died when I saw she wasn't smiling. Ann's face was blank. Dangerous. That sobered me up. Got my full attention.

"Is that the gun?" I asked, sitting forward and looking closely. Ann now stood across the table from me, her grip on the gun firm and steady; her left hand supported the right, as if she could stand there forever.

"I thought you threw it in the river."

"I lied." She was shimmering with intensity. I wondered what it would take to get her to not use the gun. Odds were slim to none. Then she surprised me.

"The police looked everywhere and never found it." A small smile of satisfaction. Maybe I could keep this going, stay connected long enough to think of a way out, away from the gun that was way too close for comfort.

"Where was it?" I asked. The question broadened her smile. She was enjoying this.

"This isn't a novel, Lyle. The gun is real. I am not going to tell you where it was, and I am going to use it." We looked squarely at each other. I had to think clearly, without moving my eyes to the satchel, which I very much wanted to do. I could not afford to have her read my mind. Ann took my silence as some kind of acquiescence. She took a small step back.

"It was interesting, really. They didn't even find the body for three days. Matty had just come back from town when the police showed up at the door with their questions. Endless, repetitive questions. I told them I hadn't seen or heard from my ex in a while; that I'd spent the weekend around the house and the barn, aside from a trip into town for groceries. Told them where and when. Said they were welcome to look around as much as they liked.

"They let me tell Matt Jr. about his dad and they stood there and watched as we both wept. I told them it was such a shock. I couldn't imagine what had happened. They believed me. Eventually, they had to. There was no evidence to connect me to the scene, no clear motive, despite their suspicions. I told them it was a tragedy. I had wished Matt Grimer well, with his new fiancé and all.

"Even the lawyer said I had no motive, as the bastard had agreed to let me stay in the house for my lifetime. I tried to look grateful. Sure, we had our problems, but he was a decent man, I said."

While she was talking, Ann kept her hand as steady as her voice. This was no nostalgic visit to the past, no getting lost in memory for her. She knew exactly where she was. She shifted her weight and continued.

"My son always suspected, though. I could see it in

his eyes, and it killed me to see the shadow between us. But he knew I loved him, and in the days that followed whenever his father's death was mentioned, I'd be sure to look sad enough. Our life was quieter, no other change occurred. I saw to that. And Matt Jr. did the things most kids did in high school, had a job, dated girls. I was a good mother through it all.

"But he went away to college instead of staying here and going to KU. He wrote regularly but did not come home much, lives out on the East coast. I see him occasionally. Not often." Her face softened with the thought, but she never wavered, never took those eyes off me.

"Damn it, Ann. Why did you take out the gun? Louise stayed silent—all these years—I planned to stay silent, too. Let you *keep* your secret. It seemed to me that my mom thought he had it coming."

"Perhaps she did. I never asked her. But trust is a fragile thing, Lyle. I could not take the risk of trusting her, even after her help." Ann chuckled softly to herself.

"It must have been quite a shock after she put it together."

Suddenly Glory started growling, the hair rising on her hackles, each growl accompanied by a shudder through her small body.

"Hold your dog, Lyle." I leaned forward and put my hand on Glory's collar, trying to quiet her. The growling had raised the tension in the air. I dropped my left shoulder, slowly reaching for the bag, wondering if I'd have time to get to the gun and use it.

"Stop! Don't move! Why did you come here? Why push me to it like this? Did you not *think*? Think, Lyle: Why do you *think* Louise kept silent? Trust? Kindness? Is that what you *think*?" This was one scary woman. I felt out of my depth here.

"I threatened *you* if she told." Ann said quietly, as if the words coming out of her mouth and going into my ears were completely logical. "You were my insurance, Lyle. And now you leave me no choice."

Ann's revelation brought to my mind the inexplicable occasions of tension and difficulty between Louise and me, the times I could not understand why we were not getting along, the subtle ways my mother pushed me away, encouraged me to find my own life in another state. That San Francisco was so far away clearly worked for her. She made one visit. We walked along the overlook at Seal Rock, when she was as happy as I'd ever seen her. I remembered her laughter and the sky full of seagulls.

"Stand up. Slowly." Ann's voice was heavy and lethal as an axe. I did as I was told and rose slowly, shaking my head, keeping my eyes on her, taking a step closer to the satchel and my mother's gun.

"You can't kill me, Ann." My voice was soft, reasonable. It felt like my heart was going to leap out of my throat. Not one inner voice complained; the object of survival was universal in my consciousness,

"Oh, but I know I can. I did it once…" her voice faded. "I just have to think."

NO, NO! NO THINKING! This was me talking to me. One voice, one chance.

"The car? The dog?" I was raising obstacles, I hoped.

"Disposable." Her tone was implacable.

"People know I came here, Ann."

"You left. Simple. It all can go away, you see."

This was not going well. Ann had this glassy look in her eyes. I felt wired from my eyelashes to my toes. If my hair could have stood on end, it would have.

"Let's go." She nodded toward the door. I looked at the door and then back at her. My eyes were exclamation points. Something snapped.

"No way, you crazy bitch! You think I'll wimp along and make it *tidy* for you? I don't think so! You do it, you do it here. Blood everywhere, Ann—messy, messy, messy!" Much better. Pissed off feels much better than scared shitless. Glory jumped up on the couch behind me and started barking outright, a high-pitched bark that took the skin off your ears. Ann Headley didn't even blink. She had entered a different time zone.

"All right," she said, barely audible over Glory's hysteria, "Have it your way. Messy it is."

"WHAT?" I was outraged. I stamped my foot on the floor in frustration and rage and swatted behind me at the dog, not wanting to see her shot dead in front of me.

"Glory! Shut UP!" Instead the dog jumped up and down, bouncing off the back of the couch, howling her head off.

"You wacko!" I yelled at Ann, "Nut job!" I could not believe it. I was drawing dead, with no hope for a winning hand.

"Get the dog out of the house, Lyle!" she yelled, "Or I shoot her now!" Ann waved the gun toward the door and started spinning explanations for events to come.

"The dog was fallout from the brawl we had. Collateral damage. You attacked me, Lyle. The stuff in the box belonged to Louise. She killed my husband, and you found out and now you were trying to kill me, something like that, I'll work it out.

"The dog will be a mystery, perhaps. Or, I can shoot her—a crossfire thing, from the struggle for the gun. Or, I can break her neck later, as if we fell on her. More convincing that way." She was practically panting, talking herself into it. Freaking me out!

"Whoa! Wait a minute, will you? I'll get her out!" Ann stepped closer, the gun pointed squarely at my chest. Shit! She wasn't even sweating! I twisted behind and reached across the frantic dog, lunging for the bag. What the fuck, I thought, might as well go out fighting.

It's amazing how when things happen all at once, the mind slows it down, and little pieces take on the clarity of splintered glass as they catch your attention in a random chaos.

I was a bystander, not at the center of madness. The front window shattered into the room, and I felt a stinging sensation on my hands and face. Even though I was falling, I took note of the fact that night had fallen. There was nothing on the other side of that window but black.

The room was filled with sound that was way too loud for a little gun. On the floor now, and immobilized for a reason I could not figure out, I couldn't see much of Ann, who had fallen across the table and down, beside the couch. There was lots of blood over everything. I could smell it. The sound was followed by a silence that was almost shocking in its totality. I closed my eyes and tried to breathe

I heard someone walk across the porch and the crunch of shoes on broken glass. When I opened my eyes, MacDonald George was kneeling beside me, a rifle held by the barrel in his left hand. Still trying to sort out what had happened, I wasn't even phased to see him.

"I can't move, Mac." Could hardly get the words out.

"The ambulance is on the way." He must have called from his cell outside.

"What are you doing here?" I whispered.

"Checking up on you, Lyle. You have a way of getting into trouble." My eyes wouldn't focus, but I could hear the smile. He sounded relieved. "I remembered who Ann Headley was. The whole story. How do you fit into this...mess?"

I groaned. He pushed a strand of blood-soaked hair from my face and felt my neck for a pulse. I could hear Glory whimpering, but it seemed far away. I couldn't open my eyes, and I was very, very cold. The last thing I heard was Mac's voice.

"Damn. There's too much blood." He reached inside my jacket sleeve and clamped my upper arm, hard. The pain was incredible.

"She must've got your artery. Hold on, Lyle." There were sirens and the sound of flying gravel out in the yard, feet thudding on the porch. The strangest floating sensation came over me.

"Don't go, Lyle. Don't go."

Whose voice was that? Mom? Mac? I couldn't tell. I dropped into darkness.

19

It was a shock, waking up in my own bed. I'd been sent home from the ER in a sling, left arm strapped across my ribs, doped to the eyeballs. Thirsty and aching, I dragged myself out of bed and into the bathroom. Whatever you do, do not look in the mirror, Lyle. There be monsters. Washed my face, drank some water, took a Percocet.

I shook my head, trying to sort out the memories of getting shot and time in the ER with police asking endless questions. Everything disconnected, like a dream.

Working my way slowly downstairs, leaning against the wall with my right shoulder for balance, I remembered my dream. Can you dream on painkillers? Guess so. Monsters. My father. Not so much his leaving as the aftermath. Me walking through wreckage, a house or a shipwreck, smoking ruins. Nothing left intact. I climbed over piles of rubble, my hands shredded and bleeding at my sides.

At the foot of the stairs I held up my right hand and looked at it. Speckled with scabs and scratches from flying glass. "I'm still here," I said, refusing the damage and looking on the bright side, grim or not.

"Lyle?" Luce called from the kitchen. "You sit down. I'll bring you some tea."

I smiled at the sound of her voice and went into the library, my eyes drawn to the window.

Spring had blown into town while I wasn't looking. The old trees along the street were studded with buds, the grass had greened, and the flowers were out in Louise's yard—daffodils, jonquils, hyacinth, and, peeking out from slender leaves, tiny grape hyacinth. The forsythia blazed like a fireworks display at the side of the front porch. Around back, the pussy willow would be in full swing, the tulip tree, as well.

Louise loved spring flowers and would force a spray of forsythia to get her through the bleak days of early January when she was hungry for color. I missed her so much. Upset by the damage Ann Headley had inflicted in the past as much as by the gunshot wound, I sat mute. My eyes burned.

I had never felt so weak in my life, physically and emotionally. I also felt old, broken, used up. I gazed out the window and watched branches bobbing in a spot of sunlight, the new leaves translucent, as if illuminated from within, pure as alabaster. The beauty of their moving with the wind in an eternal present of spring gave me strength to open the car door and get on with life.

A small, warm body leaned against my legs. Uncharacteristically quiet, the dog had snuck up on me, tail wagging.

"Here, girl." I patted my knee and she leapt up onto the couch beside me.

Glory is not really a "small" dog. Smooth-haired fox terriers have strong, straight legs and move a lot like compact greyhounds. I took one of her front paws and held it, feeling the rough pads. She licked my face. Sticky with dog saliva, I told her to get down. I really needed to wash my face.

Glory shook herself, turned around and tucked her hindquarters under herself and sat delicately, at my feet. We shared a look and then I lifted my eyes again to look out the library window. Wind had blown clouds in. I could hear wind bells on the porch next door. The house around me was completely silent. I felt awkward. And tired. Very tired. Luce came into the room with a mug of tea in one hand and a small, cobalt glass vase full of mixed daffodils in the other.

"I'll just set these here," she said, "We can bring more in later."

"Thanks, Luce," I said.

She sat across from me, slipped her shoes off and tucked her legs under her, unconsciously slipping into a half Lotus posture in the big leather chair. She huffed a big sigh and sipped at her tea. Her silvery, sandy hair held by a feather-shaped, silver clip, her face down turned and thoughtful. I was unnerved by the uncharacteristic quiet. Time for a diversion.

"Why is that?" I asked. "Why do people *sip* tea and *drink* coffee?" She smiled at me almost as if she were considering the question.

"It's a matter of attitude, I suspect," she offered. We both laughed. I ran a hand over my eyes and my face and looked at the hand, as if expecting to see green slime.

"Let me get you a cloth, Lyle." She was up and back in no time, it seemed. I was so tired, I could hardly talk. I took the cool, damp cloth gratefully and washed my face, so tired I could ignore the lump in my throat.

"I think I'll lie down, Luce. Don't know if I can keep my eyes open."

"Here?" she suggested.

"No. I can make it back upstairs." I was going to lie in my own bed if it killed me. Luce heard the determination in my voice.

"Good girl. You take your time. We'll get there." Glory ran ahead of us. Luce gave me the space and time to move at my own pace. As we went up the stirs, she told me the plan.

"The L&L's called and said they'd be over later with some supplies and a casserole for supper." Loretta and Lenore's casseroles were legendary. People injured themselves just to get one. At a church auction, the bidding on one of their casseroles could grow fierce. It was a pasta-and-whatever casserole, but what they could do with cheese was sinful. There was a secret ingredient of some sort, but I never asked.

"Good girl!" They exclaimed once they had caught on to my lack of curiosity about the recipe.

"We'll leave the recipe to you in our will!"

"Oh, no!" I exclaimed in the mock-horror of a dramatic 13-year-old, "That means I'll have to learn how to cook!" "Guess it does, Little Miss. You better get started!"

The memory took me up the last few stairs, as Luce continued: "I've got some errands to run, Lyle. You rest. The car keys are in the bowl in the hall, not that you'll need 'em. I'm taking the truck. There's a carafe of water by the bed, the phone's off the hook in the kitchen, Glory will take care of any invaders. We'll talk when I get back, after you've rested."

"Thanks, Luce."

"No thanks needed." She kissed me and left the

room. Glory settled on the bed at my feet, and I lay back gingerly, placing one of the softer pillows under my left arm which was still in its sling. I hate sleeping on my back, I thought briefly. Say goodnight, Gracie—I was gone.

I felt like I'd slept a month. Something woke me up, not a sound, a feeling. What was it? A brief inventory told me it was not pain, although my left arm felt stiff and sore. Glory was softly jiggling the bed, wagging her tail, it felt like. I groaned and opened my eyes, not wanting to move.

MacDonald George was sitting at the foot of the bed, beside Glory, his hand on her head.

"Can I get you anything?" he asked.

I blinked my blurry eyes a few times to get a clearer view. "Did you break into my house?"

"Maybe." He smiled that sexy smile of his. "How are you, Lyle?" His hand shifted from the dog to one of my feet, the right one I think. I wasn't sure.

"How'd you get in?" I queried grumpily.

"It's good to see you, too! Luce said she'd leave the back door open. She did and it was."

"Oh. OK. Hi. I can't keep my eyes open, Mac."

"Go back to sleep."

I did. When I next woke up, he was still there, had moved the rocking chair over beside the bed and was reading a book by the daylight coming in the window.

"What's the book?" I asked inelegantly.

"Violence in Women and Other Deviant Behaviors," he said.

"What chapter are you on?"

"Gun play."

Not funny!"

"No, it isn't. But we'll wait till later for the lecture."

"Thanks."

"You're welcome."

"What is it, really, the book?" The whole conversation had gone on with my eyes closed. I opened them.

His legs were crossed, one denim knee over the other. The book lay open, face down on his knee. His hands folded loosely over the spine of the book. Mac regarded me steadily over the top of wire-rimmed reading glasses. He looked like a bronze statue: "Man Reading in Rocking Chair", or some such title. Side-lit by the window, he was beautiful.

Shifting up onto my right elbow, I looked at him—checked him out thoroughly, one might say—and he looked right back. I knew which one of us had the better view.

"You are a beautiful man," I said. Looking at him was like going to the movies. Or, maybe it was the drugs. I didn't care.

"Thanks. Want to know about the book?"

"What book?" I'm easily distracted. Blame it on my impressionable age. Or the drugs.

Placing a leather bookmark, he held up the book so I could read the title on the cover: *By The Sword*, by Richard Cohen.

"I have that book! It's great!" I said approvingly.

"This is your book, Lyle. I found it on that shelf by the door." He smiled enigmatically.

"Oh. Well, you should read it, Mac. It's excellent, very well-written."

"It's a history of swordplay, from Gladiators to Olympic champions."

"I know. I've read it. What's your point?" I was feeling a bit testy and struggled to sit fully upright and twist myself around to reach for the glass of water.

He moved over to sit on the side of the bed and

took my hand, turned it over and looked at it, both sides. There were small cuts from the broken glass of Ann's window. I was well aware that there were similar small cuts on my face. I turned my head away, suddenly self-conscious. MacDonald reached up and turned my face back to his.

"They said you died, Lyle." Flat statement. "That for a few seconds while they were trying to get blood into you your heart stopped."

"I know that, Mac." I had successfully avoided thinking about it, and now here it was again.

"Why did you go there?" His blue eyes were dark. His voice was earnest. He wanted to understand.

"Why didn't you tell me what was up *before* you went out there? This whole mess could have been avoided." Pause. "Why?" He gestured to the book. "Do you think you're some sort of *swashbuckler*? Or a *samurai*? Invincible?" Mac ran a hand through his dark hair, a gesture of frustration. He stood up and looked out the window, revisiting the scene.

"She had a gun. That I expected. You had one, too, apparently. I call that looking for trouble, Lyle."

I looked away from his intensity. "Mac. I can't do this now."

"You have to give me something, Lyle." The ultimatum was implicit in his tone.

"Are you *threatening* me?" My voice wasn't much more than a croak, but I could still muster up incredulity.

"Hardly. What I am worried about is whether you are a threat to yourself. That it's part of your character. I'd like to know."

"Me, too." I held my hand up and felt the tiny cuts on my face. I leaned back against the pillows, very tired.

"Truth is, Mac," I said slowly, looking him right in

the eyes, "I misread the whole situation. I misread the stuff in the box, misread my mother's silence, misread Ann Headley, I admit it. I thought it would be harmless, something long over—that a secret had been set in stone and I was going to leave it alone. But I just had to see her." I paused. "I'm no teenager. I know full well how fragile life is, how lucky I am to be alive after what I'm sure looks like monumental stupidity." I tossed my head, casting about for the right words. "Who knows? If I had never contacted her, things might have been OK..."

"Or not," he interrupted.

"Or NOT!" I shot back at him. "And if I had never found that damn box? What then? She could have simply assumed I knew and come to this house and shot me here! Am I right?" Mac was listening hard.

"I'm right. So. What do I want—a sadder, wiser *me*, who is very much trying to figure out who I am—or, an ignorant, well-behaved, *dead* me. What to choose, what to choose?" I was pissed off and glaring at him, ready to start spouting inappropriate verbiage at the drop of a hat.

"I see your point. No offense intended, Lyle."

"The hell you say, MacDonald George! Offense is bloody well taken! You come here, to my home, when I'm at my most vulnerable, and you want to what? Scold me? Hold me to task? Now? What the *hell* is *that* about?"

"That's enough, Lyle," said Luce from the door to the room

I jumped out of bed despite the sling, oblivious to the fact that I was in my skivvies. The medication was kicking in and I had to fend off the wobbles, too.

"You're not my mother! I'm not a child! Last time I looked, this was my fucking house, and I can cuss, swear, shit fuck, piss, at the top of my lungs if I want to!" I raged around the room, flinging my hair out of my face, looking for something to smash. Luce stood stock still, watching me. MacDonald snuck up behind me when I had my back to him and wrapped his arms around me, holding mostly to my good arm.

I turned to his chest, intending to give him a nasty head-butt to the sternum, but instead I stood still, like a horse that suddenly finds itself gentled. I leaned into his shirt and let his arms stay around me. I felt safe, a feeling I hadn't experienced in some time.

"I'm sorry, Luce," I muffled over his shoulder. "So sorry…" I let Mac lead me back and sit me down on the bed, and wrap a blanket around me. Luce came over and sat by my side. Mac took the rocker. The three of us were pretty shaken up. Luce spoke first.

"I'll go get you a sandwich and bring it up."

"No, Luce." My voice was dull. "I'll come downstairs. You said the L&L's were coming over, and I don't think there's enough room for all of us up here."

"I'll go," Mac volunteered, and stood up.

"Please stay," I asked him. "You and Luce can bring the stuff into the library…" I was starting to feel that I actually had a grip on things again, weak or not.

"Well, one of us has to help you get some clothes on," Luce pointed out.

"I choose him," I said, pointing, and we laughed, tension broken. Luce chuckled and shook her head and headed downstairs, where I assume Glory had fled to avoid my rant. I picked up the jeans from the floor and looked at Mac.

"Let's work from the bottom up," I said. He took the pants from my hand and pulled me to him for a nice, long kiss.

"Lyle." His kiss moved to my forehead and my hair.

"Sssh." I put my hand to his lips. Then I reached up

and kissed him back. Perhaps we were starting to get somewhere. Not all men are monsters.

Somehow we managed to get me dressed without too many setbacks. A light blue shirt to go over the jeans, a navy wool sweater to wrap over my shoulders, some wool socks, and a quick visit to the bathroom to run a brush through my hair without peeking in the mirror, and I was downstairs before I knew it, feeling almost human.

Luce and Mac and I were sitting at the kitchen table, having decided against the library—too much balancing of plates involved. I was munching potato chips when there was a thumping clatter on the back steps. The kitchen door banged open, and in tumbled the L&L's in full tilt.

20

My twin aunts bustled through the door. Lenore first, carrying a large blue casserole dish covered in foil. Loretta followed, arms full of small white pastry bags. They looked up from their bundles and saw Luce and Mac and I sitting at the table, watching their entry. Even Glory stood back, her short tail wagging expectantly.

"Well, Look who's here!" Lenore said in tones of delight. "Let me put this casserole down, Lyle, and I'll give you a hug!"

"I'm losing my grip on these packages! One of you come help! Woo-eee! Good to see you, Lyle!" she exclaimed over Luce's shoulder. If what you had to say didn't have an exclamation point on it, it wasn't worth saying, as far as Loretta was concerned.

Packages were off-loaded, the casserole set on the stove, and we got to the business of hugging and kissing hello. Glory received her portion—"God, I love this skinny little bitch!" Loretta laughed as Glory licked her face. "Isn't she just too sweet?"

"I'll put her outside and give us a bit more room in here," she said and pushed me back into my chair.

"Mac, get down some more mugs, please. One of you girls put on some more water," Luce continued.

"Is she trying to get bossy with us?" one L asked the other.

"Would she dare?" Lots of laughs.

"MacDonald George! Is that you? How's the weather up there? C'mon down and give us a kiss!"

"Stand in line, Loretta, I got here first!" Lenore rarely competed with her sister. Guess she thought MacDonald George was worth the extra effort.

Kisses and hugs all around. I suspected MacDonald was having a rather good time. The L&L's were not much for a peck on the cheek.

I sat grinning, as if someone had just set off fireworks just for me. After appreciating Mac, the L&L's clucked over me, with delicate pats on my good shoulder, brushing my hair back with their hands and covering my face with kisses. They reminded me of Glory who was whining to be let in.

"Lyle! Hospitals are the devil on hair! Whyn't ya let me wash it for you right now?"

"If it were a wig and not attached to my head, I would, Loretta, but I don't think I have the strength for leaning my head over the kitchen sink right now."

"Fair enough!" She stood behind me and gathered handfuls of the offending stuff, twisting it into a French braid. It felt good.

The teapot was filled and emptied, sugar and milk passed around, the aroma of Earl Grey and cookies filled the kitchen. The L&L's took down folding chairs Louise kept hung in the pantry for visitors to her kitchen, so there was always a place to sit. Loretta removed a holder from her pocket and untangled it from her reading glasses—the purple ones. She finished off the braid with a kiss on the top of my head.

"You come over to Lenore's tomorrow, Lyle, and we'll take care of that hair."

"I think she's looking a bit bony, don't you, Luce?"

"You're not used to seeing her without her hair flying loose," Luce contributed.

"You should let me wash your hair, Lyle. I've got some new biologicals!"

"Not biologicals, Lenore, we're not talking about piss! You mean *botanicals*!"

"Whatever! The rosemary and mint, Lyle, you'll love it!"

The L&L's were born-again entrepreneurs. Passionate, eclectic, embracing any scheme that caught their interest, of which they had many. One field was hair care, organic products in particular. Lorena made her own shampoos and conditioners. The pine tar shampoo experiment is best forgotten. Lenore had to cut her hair down to sprouts because the stuff wouldn't come off. But the rosemary-mint was a success.

Lenore had acquired an old-fashioned salon chair, the kind with a foot pump and reclining back. We referred to it as Lenore's throne because it sat at her kitchen table and she would sit and drink her tea in it. The chair was easily dragged over to the sink where, oddly enough, it reclined to a comfortable angle for washing hair. The thought of sitting in it gave me a fit of the giggles, something Mac watched with interest. The man was clearly enjoying observing the Hudson pride in close proximity.

I agreed to stop by Lenore's the next day, in the afternoon, two probably. Mornings were rough at the moment, I explained, and I had to begin physical therapy at ten a.m.

"So what have you L&L's been up to recently?" I asked. "I haven't seen you in a while." Not since the funeral, if the truth be told. "I'm a terrible niece, I apologize."

"And so you should!" they declared in unison.

"Getting yourself half killed, selling the shop!" Their white pony tails quivered at me as they shook their fingers.

"Whoa, please! I told Luce I was *thinking* about it. I won't do anything without consulting with you, OK? Promise. Now, tell me what's up. I'm listening." It was like waiting for a story. Luce rolled her eyes.

"You visit with your aunts, Lyle. Mac, would you come help me bring some stuff in from the car? I didn't unpack when we came back from the hospital." Mac complied politely, but I was pretty sure he'd move quickly enough to catch the gist of the story.

Loretta brought a few of the small white pastry bags to the table, smiling to herself. "You start, Lenore."

All right." Lenore opened one of the bags and took out a handful of delicate, pastel shapes. "Hand me a plate, Loretta, I don't want these to melt on me." I found myself looking at handmade candies in the shape of delicate eggs, flowers, and rabbits. I popped one in my mouth.

"Mmm, chocolate!" They were delicious.

"We make these for specialty shops like Au Marché," Lenore explained.

"They are totally yummy! Bravo!" I popped a small, pink bunny into my mouth and let it melt.

"We have a bunch of molds, all kinds!" Loretta interjected, with a meaningful look at her sister. "And we use white chocolate, peach, pink, lavender, as well as milk and dark chocolate," she said.

"How's that going for you?" I asked.

"So-so," Lorena admitted. "The chocolate is expensive, and what with the initial outlay for molds, the amount of chocolate, the time involved, we just haven't recouped our investment in these seasonal chocolates. It's mostly Easter—like now—and Christmas. Halloween and St. Patrick's Day are not worth the effort."

"No one especially likes orange or green chocolate," Loretta whispered.

"But then we had an *idea*!" Lenore exclaimed. The sisters nodded their heads vigorously, which was adorable. They reminded me of Kewpie dolls, mischievous Kewpie dolls. Each sister opened up a white bag and started to laugh.

"Here are our best sellers, Lyle!" Slowly, each reaching into her bag, the L&L's displayed their wares along one side of the table: pink breasts, peach-colored breasts, white chocolate breasts with red nipples, chocolate buttocks in pink and milk chocolate, miniature, anatomically correct torsos in a variety of colors, and penises, diminutive and large, in shades of pink, red, milk and dark chocolate.

"Impressive," I smiled up at them.

Luce and MacDonald walked back into the kitchen, just in time to hear the entrepreneurial pitch.

"You see, Lyle," Lenore explained, "Loretta has this friend, Candace, who owns and operates an adult video and book store out on 23rd street. She does a good business, apparently, what with trucks passing through on the way to route 10, not to mention college students, so we asked her if she thought adult chocolates would catch on. Candace said she'd give it a try, and what do you know? In the past month we've paid for the molds as well as the extra chocolate we need..."

"The penis molds take *a lot* of chocolate!" Loretta

broke in.

"And We're starting to show a profit!" Lenore concluded. I picked up a tiny chocolate derriere and bit into it.

"Cool!" I looked over to see Luce with a pained expression on her face. Mac had stepped out of the room briefly. The sound of his laughter roared in from the library.

"We have our ups and downs, though, experimenting with color, haven't we, Lenore?"

"Oh yes," she sighed. "You can't make one of these penises in lavender chocolate. Or any other body part, for that matter. They just look dead. No one will touch them!"

"Except Vernon. But he eats the rejects. Breaks them into little pieces. Got sick to his stomach not so long ago, says he's off chocolate for a while."

"But the peach-tinted breasts are popular. Candace says even women like those."

"Don't mind if I do," Mac volunteered, reaching over my shoulder for one of the little tits.

"We do special orders and cakes, too, for events like showers, engagement parties, bachelor do's. Have a couple of steady gay customers, too!"

"And lesbians!" Lenore chimed in.

"Does your business have a name?" I asked, genuinely curious.

"Oh, no, dear. We're staying with L&L Enterprises."

"Candace asked us what it stood for," Loretta shook her head disapprovingly. "She thought it meant Licking & Loving or Lashes & Laces, something like that. I told her it's our initials. I worry about Candace, though. The business might be getting to her."

"L&L can mean Loretta & Lenore or Lenore &

Loretta!" They nodded at each other, pleased with the arrangement. "That way we get to have it both ways!"

"As it were," I muttered.

"What dear?"

"Oh, nothing." I thought Mac would choke on his second chocolate.

"Well!" Luce walked over to the table hands on hips. "I suppose I'd better try one."

"You go ahead. Tell us what you think."

"I will." Luce selected a dark chocolate penis, large size. Very pleased with herself.

There were bawdy jokes and whoops of laughter from the L&L's, but eventually the naughty chocolates found their way back into the pastry bags, and from there into the refrigerator.

I sent my aunts off with a promise to show up for the hair washing. Luce dithered a bit about the casserole, but I assured her that I'd be fine. If I got stuck, I could give her a call, but she had her own life to look after.

"Well, yes..."

"I'll be fine, really. You go home and tonight I'll think about how to deal with my temporary impairment." We smiled at each other, two independent women in total agreement.

"Sounds good, Lyle. Do you still want me to drive you to the store tomorrow?"

"Please. Whenever it's convenient."

Luce said good night to Mac and went out the kitchen door. MacDonald and I sat at the now spotless table and listened as she started up the truck, engaged gears, and drove away.

We sat silent for a minute and then looked at each

other and broke into laughter. We'd calm down, then remember something and crack up all over again.

"You Hudson women are something!" Mac said.

"It even surprises me, sometimes!" I replied.

"So—When are you going back to San Francisco?" Mac asked, "I assume that's what you wanted to talk about the night you went to the Headley place."

"What makes you say that?"

"Well, if you'd rather risk death than talk to me..." He let it lie there. I was not amused. "Besides, you were behaving like a wet cat. What else could it be?" Ball in my court.

"Smart ass," I grumbled. "You're right, yes, that was my plan."

"Why the sour face?"

"I wanted it to work out, you know? I wanted it to be OK, that you wouldn't be hurt or upset. That I'd go back to San Francisco and see where I was, where I really want to be.

"Sounds reasonable. Why would I be hurt?" I squirmed around in my seat and looked at him. He didn't seem upset at all. Not compared to our little drama upstairs.

"Well, I thought we had something going, sort of. With something going, I assumed you'd want me to stick around."

"Of course I want you to stick around. But, 'Something going' takes two, Lyle. So does 'sticking around.' We're both grown ups here. You go back and do whatever. I'm staying here. This is where I live my life." He paused and looked at his clasped hands resting on the table.

"Would I like to see more of you? You bet. Aside from the fascination of the Hudson tribe, you are an attractive, intelligent woman, as I have noted before." He smiled at me.

"Present circumstances might contradict you."

"That's temporary."

I smiled back. "Maybe I'm tired or something, but I thought it would be harder…talking to you, telling you I had to leave. Your being OK with it is confusing me. I don't know what to think."

"Don't over think it, Lyle. You'll be fine. You never did make it out to my place. I'd still like you to come see it."

"I'd like that." I shot a quick look at the casserole.

"How about you take a day of two to rest and work on that shoulder. Sunday? Glory is still invited. I'll pick you both up, what? Say five? That way we can look around, sit and talk, get you back early if you're tired." Mac sat back as Glory nudged him, asking to sit in Mac's lap. He let her up, petted her head and let her lick his ear. Very nice man.

"Great. Thanks."

"Anything I can help you with before I go? You're looking pretty tired."

"Feeling it, too," I admitted. "If you'd put some kibble down for Glory, that'd be great. I can manage the rest." I planned to transfer some of the casserole to a bowl, put it in the microwave and nuke it. Then bed. Life pared down to basics.

Mac came back from feeding Glory, lifted my chin to inspect the damage. He ran his hand over the braid at the back of my head and leaned down to kiss me. Tender and sweet kiss, just like chocolate.

"I'll just go out the back, and you and Glory will have the place to yourselves." He dug car keys out of his jeans and waved as he went through the door. Glory and I looked at each other as we listened to his steps recede.

21

Glory did not make her usual fuss and let me sleep in, not that it helped a whole lot.

I woke up with a knot in the middle of my back from sleeping flat to accommodate the sling. The arm was not broken, but with the surgery, the general opinion was that I should wait for a bit before I could sleep without the sling. I had to rearrange and re-secure it before I even got out of bed. The process made me grouchy.

Eventually, I got Glory out the door and slowly started making toast and coffee. Thought I'd bypass tea today and save a few ergs for movement. My slowness induced an almost Zen-like stupor. I watched my right hand as if it were a circus performer doing amazing feats in mid-air. My left hand stayed close to my ribs, looking after the arm. It felt weird.

I left the back door open, letting in light and air. It was going to be a mild day. I sat at the table, feet up on a chair, drinking my coffee and looking out the window.

The trees were moving from flower to leaf. the Red-buds glowed a full, extravagant purple. I could discern the busy voices of blue jays, cardinals, robins, and mourning doves. The morning conversation of crows in the high treetops echoed from the end of the alley. Worse than teenagers. If they spied a cat, they'd start cursing.

Glory slipped in to see what I was up to and then made a tight U-turn and went back out onto the porch. I knew she'd sit there in the sun and gaze out over the fence, keeping an eye out. We were both hoping a squirrel would appear, Glory so she could chase it, and I so I could watch her run. Today I particularly envied her speed and ease of movement. I hated having to move so slowly, caring for my body as if it were some frail, elderly relative. Already the sling was driving me crazy. I fiddled with the buckles and decided to take a look around.

I got the sling off and set it on the table. Moving carefully, I set my left hand on the table edge and studied it. I dropped both arms so they hung straight sown at my sides, measuring the difference in agility. Which was considerable. Move without pushing, I told myself. Try it out. Resting my hand on the table again, I felt the blood moving in my veins and marveled at the complexity of tissue and bone, of the way we are and are not aware of our physical construction. We live so much in our heads that impairment, even temporary, comes as an insult. How dare my body do this to me!

I wanted my arm back. But my body would have its own timetable for healing. I remembered my mother telling me not to scratch my chicken pox. "You'll have scars!" Well, the scar was a given in this case. Instead of scratching, I had to avoid taking chances. Yeah, right.

I eased back into the sling. There were things I

could do to keep my mind employed. I could stretch, but exercise was on the back burner for now—even the thought of jogging made my arm throb!—but I could plan; I could anticipate; I could...devise! I began to feel better.

I was in the middle of an experiment at the kitchen sink when the doorbell rang and Glory charged off in full cry. Catching up with her at the door, I threw a handful of dog treats into the front room so I could answer the door. The ruse doesn't always work, but this time it did. Flower delivery. From Porterfield's in Topeka. My My. Somebody knew flowers! I was impressed. After determining my identity as the intended recipient, the man offered to put the vase somewhere for me. I pointed with bright green fingers to the library.

By this time, Glory had finished her snack and came to check out the delivery guy. Not worth harassing, evidently. Flowers placed, he wished me well and briskly took himself off. No chat about the weather, no questions about the arm, no wisecracks about what the other guy must look like. I'd have had to say "dead" which is always a conversation ender. Apparently, my green fingers had the same effect.

Huge bouquet. Stargazers, the pollen carefully removed from open blooms to protect the petals from decay. I love stargazers and I know who knows I love them. So. What clever bon mot does Chas have to say? The note read: "You didn't HAVE to take me seriously! XXX. C." Bastard. Loved the lilies.

Back in the kitchen, I let Glory out for her biologicals and was cleaning up at the sink, trying to get the green stain off my fingers. Hard to do with one hand, but I managed. Most of it came off, and I didn't get any on my blouse or jeans. When the phone rang, I knew it was Luce.

"Have you had lunch?" she said to my hello.

"Yes, " I lied, looking around for the pain pills. "What's up?"

"I've got some errands to run before I take you over to the L&L's. Need anything? Would you like to come along?"

"That'd be great, Luce, I'd like to get out of the house."

"Sure you're up to it?"

"You bet."

"Fine. I'll be right over." Just enough time to brush my hair, pack up the experiment, lock up the house and say good bye to Glory.

I met Luce in the driveway and told her I was fine to ride in the truck, which made us both happy.

We headed west on 6th street, across town to Lenore's house. She used to live in undeveloped countryside, but Lawrence was growing rapidly in her direction. Luce wanted to stop at Sun Ripe for groceries. I pointed out that it would make more sense to stop on the way back, but she shushed me and said that I could put my stuff in Lenore's fridge while I was there.

"I will figure out what 's going on, you know. I always do."

"Oh. Do you?"

"Yup."

I got out of the truck and adjusted the sling, checking to see if everything was OK. I had switched to a man's wallet instead of a purse and checked it, too. Secure in my back pocket. My keys in the right side pocket where I could reach them easily. I was good to go. Hairs rose on the back of my neck. I looked around. Nothing. The feeling of being watched had tracked me down.

Half an hour later, we were back at the truck. Luce placed plastic bags in the back of the cab, behind the driver's seat. I told her I'd be the good citizen and return the cart. "No you don't. You wait here. It'll only take me a second." Luce doesn't like to park near other vehicles, says people have no conscience when it comes to scratching up her truck. So we were a bit away from the cart rack. I was feeling pretty good and leaned against the back of the yellow truck and closed my eyes to feel the sun.

"Now, look at that, Bubba. Ain't that sweet?"

"A generous old lady, man. I can tell!" They thought they were pretty funny. I started to laugh, too. A bit incredulous, I must admit. I opened my eyes.

"Howdy, boys. Can I help you?" I straightened up and looked right at them. What was it about me and this parking lot? I was almost amused.

"See? I told you, man. Generous. You, lady, are going to give your money to us. Isn't she, Dial?" They were teenagers, more gangly than threatening. No gun, a good sign.

"Asshole! Now she knows my name!" Dial proceeded to swat his buddy on the shoulder, and I turned and moved to the front of the truck.

"Hey, bitch! You stop right there!"

"Excuse me?" I asked, conversationally. "You are going to do what—rob me?" They nodded.

"Well, yeah!" Pointing at the sling. "You look pretty helpless!" I saw Luce sneaking up on them in the distance and shook my head. The lads thought I was talking to them, but Luce caught on, stopped where she was, and pulled out her cell phone.

"We got you two to one, Granny, so give it up. We'll be nice and polite about it. Sorry I called you bitch." He seemed almost apologetic, like the whole situation was my idea.

"I'm sure," I said dryly, reaching in to my sling to pull out my secret weapon.

"What the hell is that? We plants? You gonna *spray* us? Woman, you are seriously strange!" They practically fell out of their droopy-assed jeans they were laughing so hard. I calmly adjusted the nozzle on the sprayer and explained what they were really looking at.

"I had a gun, but the cops took it because I didn't have a permit." I shook my head in disgust. "This," I continued conversationally, "Is my best substitute. The twist nozzle keeps the vile stuff in here from leaking." I twisted the nozzle to demonstrate. It was open and ready to go. I smiled at the kids, enjoying the anticipation.

"What stuff? What you got in there?" They seemed genuinely curious.

"Cat piss. And green dye."

"No Way! That's nasty! You gotta be shittin us! How you get cat piss?" Curiosity combined with hilarity overcame their survival instincts.

"Well," I explained to my two students of urban oddities, "You take prime clumps of used cat litter and dissolve them in water. You pour the liquid through a strainer, very carefully. You do not want to get any on you. Then you add green dye. Which means that if I spray you, you stink, and the green splattered on your clothes is a clear indication that you have fucked with me, whether you get my money or not!"

They stepped back hurriedly at the change in my tone of voice, still not quite believing.

"See those white shoes? The ones with no laces and that expensive swoosh insignia? A little dribble, just a drop of this evil green juice and you will never be able to wear them again. You will instantaneously become a suspect in an attempted robbery."

"The hell!"

"You do *not* have cat piss in that itty bitty thing!"

"Ah! You desire a demonstration." I shot straight at them. A sprayer, regardless of size, can be adjusted to a narrow beam of water. Any cat owner knows this. Clearly, I was not dealing with cat fanciers. The liquid formed a gleaming arch in the sunlight. My two gentleman callers jumped straight up and back as if I had lifted them with hydraulics. They stood there, mouths agape as the stuff missed their shoes and hit the hot pavement, giving off a pungent, ammoniac odor. It was indeed bright green.

"You crazy? WE'RE NOT EVEN ARMED!" The outrage was music to my ears. I menaced them with the sprayer. There was more where that came from.

"Better get going, boys!" Sharon Stone had nothing on me. They ran off so fast, I didn't even have time for a zingy one-liner.

Luce walked over with a suspicious look on her face. "What did you do to those two boys?"

"Gave them a civics lesson." I tucked the little sprayer back into the sling. "You called 911?"

"No, dear. After your last adventure, I put the police department on speed dial. There should be someone here in just a minute. Phew! What is in that thing?"

"I told my visitors it was cat piss." I hadn't told a good lie in a while. It felt great.

"You did not! Pause. "Is it?" Apparently I am capable of anything.

"I don't have a cat, remember? I mixed up a solution of water, ammonia, bottled garlic, and green food coloring."

"What on earth for?"

"Well, Luce, as you can see, I'm a walking magnet, some sort of GPS device, for the disgruntled youth of our fair city. Call me paranoid, but I thought, given my present physical condition, I had better be prepared for any excursions. Seems I was right."

She was still looking at me, trying to think up something witty to say so she could have the last word, when a cruiser circled the parking lot. Luce flagged them down.

"Might as well be polite," she said.

"He didn't even crack a smile," I complained.

"They're trained professionals, Lyle," Luce said. "I'm sure there's a class for facial expressions—like those palace guards in London."

" He should've smiled at least. It's not natural. Either that or he's showing off!"

"Showing off—pssht—you better not spill a drop of that evil brew in this truck, Lyle! Not one drop!"

I smiled serenely. Felt like the Queen of fucking England. I raised my hand at the open window, swiveling the wrist slowly in a regal wave.

22

Lenore doesn't have a front porch. Instead, she has a rock garden that marches straight up to the house. Redbuds grow in profusion. "Too much trouble cutting them out. The damn things grow like weeds!" So she lets them stay. In the spring they provide a cooling shade beneath their dark green leaves. The stone is local, too. Sandstone chunks turned up in construction. The walk to the door curves around a Japanese assemblage of stone and native grasses. There are no weeds. At this time of year there are minute sprinklings of grape hyacinth and tulips. Cushions of sedum are coming up, and a succulent creeper I can never remember the name of. Later on there'll be pink coneflower, daisies, columbine, and day lilies. Come fall, she'll let the chrysanthemum bloom. There's an old-fashioned breeze-way between the house and the garage which is really pleasant twice a year. The rest of the time the wind roars through, either too hot or too cold.

Luce and I walked through the breeze-way onto the

deck where we were pretty sure we'd find something
going on. The deck spans the entire back of the house.
Over the dining room and kitchen entryways, a grate-
like arbor provides shade. The arbor is covered with
climbing roses and clematis that Lenore has woven into
the slats of the grate overhead. By the end of May, it
will be a riot of pink, red and deep purple.

Beyond the deck is a picturesque, decaying potting
shed, and beyond that is the greenhouse that houses
Lenore's "botanicals" business. There was evidence of
gardening in the back yard—tool bucket, work gloves,
and the small green stool that Lenore uses to "Save the
Knees!" Everything was unnaturally quiet. Luce and I
exchanged glances that asked who was brave enough to
enter the house first. Into the silence came a soft inhala-
tion of air. "Oh...no..." We turned simultaneously to the
kitchen sliding doors to see Lenore and Loretta staring
at each other in horrified recognition. They were frozen
in place, looking like mimes doing one of those annoying "mirror" routines. They held two white pastry bags
in their hands.

"How did...?"

"I don't know! Let me think!" Just then Loretta
caught sight of us out on the deck and gestured us to
join them in the kitchen. Luce put my groceries in the
fridge and brought out a pitcher of iced tea. The L&L's
were seated at the kitchen table, back lit by the bright
day behind them. Their hair was in nimbus mode today,
soft white clouds around their concerned heads. The
girls looked as worried as I had ever seen them, which
was rare. They stared at the white packages that most
likely held chocolates.

"When..?" Lenore began.

"Probably when the church secretary bustled us out
of the office! We must have handed over the wrong

bags!" Luce set out four tumblers and poured the tea. Lenore absent-mindedly tore mint leaves from the small vase of summer mint on the table and distributed them among the glasses.

"What's up?" I asked. It seemed like a reasonable question. The L&L's looked at Luce and at me and busted up. They could not stop giggling.

"It's...we..." Loretta could not get her breath.

"...Candy delivery!" Lenore's eyes were watering, she was laughing so hard.

"Oh no!" Loretta handed Luce one of the bags. She looked inside and brought out a small lavender bunny and a white chocolate cross. Innocent enough. The L&L's let out a strangled shriek and stood up so they could hang on to each other. Luce and I were mystified.

"We took some Easter candies to church," she got out, and then paused to catch her breath. "Pastor White got the wrong candy!"

"Father Bob, too!" Lenore chimed in. Luce and I got the picture and could not believe our ears. Evidently two of Lawrence's clergy had received sex candies for Easter. Little buttocks and breasts and penises in appetizingly tinted chocolate.

Lenore and Loretta looked at each other, aghast.

"What will we do? If we drive over there, it may take too long! It may be too late!" Lenore said.

"Wait! Let's call the secretaries! They got us into this mess!" Loretta picked up the phone and punched in the numbers.

"What will you say?" Lenore gasped. Loretta shushed her with a quick gesture.

"Mrs. Reynolds? Hello, dear, this is Loretta Hudson. Fine, thank you. Could I ask you to tell pastor that the package of Easter candy..." Pause. "Oh, he has. All gone, is it? He what? On the phone? Oh. No, I couldn't!

Pastor White?" Loretta's face went pale as Pastor White came on the line. We sat there, horrified along with her. "Pastor White, I am so sorry! It was at terrible mistake! I hope you ....Ah. Well. Thank you. Was it? You are very kind. Lovely. Happy Easter Pastor." She put down the phone as if it were made of glass and did not take her eyes off it. "Well, well," she reflected.

Our eyes were genetically identical question marks. Loretta cleared her throat.

"He liked the chocolate. Said he figured we'd made a mistake, was chuckling, actually. And that he'd had to eat fast—to protect his own reputation as well as ours! Said the dark chocolate was his favorite. A very understanding man, isn't he, Lenore? I doubt I'll have such luck with Father Bob," she sighed as she reluctantly picked up the phone again. Frankly, I thought she'd have better luck if she just ran him over with a car.

"Yes, hello. Could I please speak to Mrs. McClure, the parish secretary? Oh, she is. Could you tell me when she'll be back? This is Loretta Hudson and I'm worried that Father Bob might have gotten the wrong..." pause. Pause. "Oh, Brother Phil! Oh, no!" Pause. "I'm mortified, truly I am. This is quite beyond me, I must say." Long pause. "Oh. I see. No, my dear, I think you're taking it too hard. The way I look at it, you saved me from the wrath of Father Bob." Pause. "Yes, exactly. You must have been so shocked and upset! No, brother Phil, not at all. Bless you. Thanks." She hung up and turned to her audience.

"The way I see it, as long as Pastor White doesn't blab to Father Bob, we're safe! But you can't trust clergy, you know. They tell each other everything!" Loretta's first husband was a preacher, she should know!

"What happened? Tell Us!" Lenore pleaded.

"An act of God, surely," Loretta said, quite relieved. "Father Bob had to rush out to the hospital for some reason, and Mrs. McClure, that awful woman, took the opportunity to extend her lunch hour, leaving dear brother Phil to man the phones. He became curious—He gave up chocolate for Lent, you know—so he took a peek inside the package! Said he felt horribly guilty giving in to temptation and all, and was worried someone might have set him a trap! Poor boy! He was so embarrassed, and so comforted to learn that he had saved me from a fate worse than death!" We laughed and applauded and proceeded to toast the day with iced tea.

"Can you believe it," Lenore said, "That both secretaries would be so pushy and mean on the same day?"

"It is no wonder we got confused!" Loretta said.

"Well," Luce interrupted, standing up and putting her glass beside the sink, "I'm off! You'll see that Lyle gets home?"

"You ARE up to something!" I crowed.

"Not a bit of it. Bye!" and she was gone.

"It's that man she's been seeing," Loretta said, "I'll bet you anything!"

"She said it was over between her and William," I said.

"Luce? Through with a man that's good in bed?" Loretta laughed out loud.

"I don't think so!" The sisters declared simultaneously, cracking themselves up.

The throne was dragged over to the sink and my hair was duly washed and conditioned. During this procedure, Loretta reminded me about Louise's gun.

"Now if you'd a had that snubbie with you, it would've evened the odds!"

"I was lucky, aunt. If it weren't for MacDonald, I'd be dead." I paused at the thought. "Lou knew how to use that little Smith and Wesson, not me. It wouldn't have helped me at all."

"Stop going on about the gun, dear. Just drop it." Lenore sternly admonished her sister.

"I'm interested, is all. Where is it, anyway?" My eyes were closed against the shampoo getting scrubbed into my scalp, but I could hear the eagerness in Loretta's voice. She wanted that gun. Not gonna happen, I told myself.

"It's locked away, Loretta, and it's going to stay there for a long time." Or until I decided to take lessons, I thought. Helplessness was not my long suit.

We dropped the subject when Lenore dried my hair with a towel.

It smells wonderful, Lenore. Thank you." It felt like being reborn to have clean hair.

"Why don't I trim this up for you, Lyle? It's raggedy at the ends," Lenore stated. I knew she was right. In SF, Chas cut my hair. No one had touched it in months. Even if she took off four inches, I'd never miss it.

"Thank you, Lenore. I'd appreciate it if you would."

"Ooooh! Listen to that, Loretta! Gratitude!" She smacked me on the side of the head. "Where's our uppity, in-your-face Lyle? The woman we can be proud of?" She teased.

"You haven't eaten, have you," Loretta stated, flatly. "Hudson women get puny if they haven't been fed! I am making you a sandwich and *you* are going to eat it!" Oh, boy. The only thing better than a casserole was one of their sandwiches. I was in Hudson heaven. I acquiesced and said I'd like to take off the sling and stretch my arm a bit. Lenore waited while I moved around and started in with the scissors after I settled down. I was pretty sure the sandwich would be ready at the exact moment the hair was done. The L&L's were always in sync.

"What's that little sprayer doing in your sling, Lyle?" Lenore asked when I had both items off and lying on the table. I told them the story and we started to laugh again. Lenore said she had to be careful or I could lose an ear.

"Honey!" Loretta cried, "You are a Hudson par excellence!"

With my Hudson creativity, I wouldn't need a gun. I was doing quite well without it.

23

Loretta volunteered to drive me home so Lenore could work on one of her herbal infusions. She was fussing with different varieties of mint, which smelled wonderful, but Loretta said it could get pretty intense and made her eyes water.

"Did you want to make any stops on the way, Lyle?" Loretta asked as she stuck my groceries behind the passenger seat of her Toyota RAV.

"No, thanks. It's been quite a day already. A nap is about all I'm up to right now."

"Well, OK then!"

Inside the house, Glory practically climbed Loretta like a tree, she was so glad to see her.

"Lyle! This dog is pathetic, she's shameless! Look at this display!" She watched Glory chase herself from one side of the house to the other.

"She hasn't been walked in a while, has she," Loretta stated.

My mouth fell open. I was the picture of guilt.

"No blame!" She held up a hand and shook her head. "I'll just take her with me and give her a good run. You head off to bed and take that nap." She gave me a quick hug and swept blissful Glory out the door and into the RAV.

I waved them off and trudged upstairs. God knows where they'll end up, I thought. There's bound to be a good story whenever they get back. I stripped off the sling, put the sprayer on a shelf by the door and got into bed. The last thing I saw was new leaves, tiny points of green against the electric blue of the sky.

I take two kinds of naps—those from which I emerge catatonic and hung over with sleep, and those which release me from sleep as from a shower. This time, I awoke feeling refreshed and fifteen years younger. At least! Even my arm felt better. It was still pretty much a foreign object to me, but we were getting reacquainted and feeling friendly.

I poured a bath in the old, porcelain tub and checked my face in the mirror. I was still speckled with small scabs, but the redness had gone. I was healing. Lenore had given me a small plastic bottle of something she called "Recovery Serum." Said it would get rid of the scabs in no time and the rest of my face would like it, too. I carefully dabbed it on my face, enjoying the feel of it and the green fragrance of kiwi or cucumber or eucalyptus—I couldn't tell.

I soaked for a while, adding hot water when it cooled. The stiffness gone, I pulled the plug and dried off before stepping out of the tub. Wiping condensation off the mirror, I saw that Lenore had "trimmed" a good four inches off my hair. Not that big a deal, I thought. There was plenty left. Brushing hair back from my face, I liked the feel of it and the movement. Yes! I was starting to feel younger—as in no longer ancient and decrepit!

Did the arm exercises, replaced the bandage, and looked around for fresh clothes. Not that I had much to choose from. I stepped into my jeans and pondered. Too warm for sweaters. The silk blouse was at the cleaners. In a panic, I opened and closed drawers in the dresser, finding nothing but old T-shirts I had collected from various places. Casinos, mostly.

I sat on the floor in front of the open bottom drawer and laughed as I realized that the shirts spanned 25 or 30 years. There were a lot of them, some never worn. Black and orange Harley shirts? Asbury Park? The old Flamingo Hotel in Vegas? So many places and so few memories. Eventually I settled on a vintage, azure and pink Key West T-shirt. Bright colors! And, it fit fine! Must have been buying them large in those days, I mused. Black linen jacket and the Merrells, and I'd be fine.

Downstairs, I started to wonder where Loretta and Glory were when the phone rang. It was Lenore. I explained about taking Glory for a run, but we both knew they should have been home by now.

"I'll call you when they get back, Lenore. Not to worry, OK?" Right.

It was still light out, but MacDonald would be showing up soon, and the house was unnaturally silent. To keep myself from pacing, I went into the library and flipped through Louise's CD's looking for something soothing. Settled on baroque lute music—what the hell—I was desperate. I looked out the window into the quiet yard. Suddenly inspired, I grabbed the pruners from the junk drawer and went out back.

The kitchen table was covered with lilac branches, and I was pounding them with a hammer when I heard the RAV pull in the drive. Hallelujah! I arranged lilacs in two large white vases and was disposing of twigs and leaves when the kitchen door swung open and a dog vaguely resembling Glory padded in. This dog was filthy. Loretta wasn't much better, streaked with swathes of mud, a wild look in her eyes.

"Scotch. Now," were the first words she spoke.

"Stop right there!" I commanded her. "Take it all off. Just step out of it right there." I ran to the library and fetched the throw off the couch.

"Loretta, whatever it is, it can wait. C'mon." I led her up to Louise's room and on through to the bathroom, sat her down with the throw wrapped around her, and turned the water on in the tub.

"Right back, don't move." She didn't even blink. I grabbed a glass, poured a hefty measure, plopped in some ice, and told Glory to sit tight. The dog was nose deep, inhaling her water bowl as I climbed the stairs.

"Here, Loretta." I handed her the drink and turned my attention to the tub so she could just sit there and adjust to this particular moment in time. A kind of custody of the eyes, allowing a person a degree of privacy when they should not be left alone. It is only polite. I threw in some bath salts, Lenore's "Peaceful Moments" blend, and checked the heat of the water. Hot. Good.

"It's good. Put a hand on my good shoulder." I took the scotch and let her use me for balance as she dropped the blanket and stepped into the tub. No bruises. Good.

Loretta drew a tight breath between her teeth as she stepped into very hot water. Her face looked worn out and old as she held on and set herself down in the steamy water. Damn, sometimes life just sucks. I hated her being old and me being old and the way life kicks the snot out of you and could care less. Asshole, I said to

Life, or God, or Whatever. Fuck you. I started to sweat from the steam. Good.

"Lala?" I had helped her sit down and had handed back the drink, addressing my aunt by the common Hudson name that applied to each and every one of us. Except my cousin, Brett, that is. Bitch. Do not get sidetracked! Pay attention! The harpies were back inside my head.

"Lala, I'm turning off the water. You soak. I'll be back with another drink after I check on Glory, clean her up a bit. We'll talk later." Loretta nodded, her eyes closed, and sank back against the tub. I studied her. Tan in places, pale in places; some wrinkles, but one hell of a beautiful woman.

"Here's a wash cloth for your face. Back soon." I left the bathroom door ajar. Safe space. Clean. I'd be right back and I knew she'd be OK.

On the way downstairs, I pulled out my cell and called Lenore.

"Lala?" I said. Instantly she got the message. It was a childhood name I used for both of them, a signal that something was wrong.

"Yes, Lyle?"

"Loretta's fine. Bring a change of clothes. We'll talk when you get here." No answer necessary. We hung up at the same time.

In the kitchen, Glory was sitting by the pantry, trembling. I made soothing noises while I filled the kitchen sink, found a towel, and piled kibble in her food bowl.

"So, you had a big day," I began conversationally. "Bigger than both of you, by the look of it."

Glory shivered and huddled close to my feet. I sat down on the floor, waiting for the sink to fill. She climbed into my lap, and I embraced one spooked dog.

The day was worse than thunder and lightning, she informed me.

I bathed Glory in warm water as best I could, washing off the dirt, murmuring old Beatles' tunes, and telling her I loved her, and gradually the shaking subsided. She licked my face as I wrapped her in the towel, and I sat on a chair with the dog in my lap. My arm throbbed, but I disregarded it, told Glory stories of when she was a pup, and carried her into the library wrapped in a fresh, dry towel.

Upstairs, I handed a cleaner version of Loretta a fresh drink with more ice. We both liked a lot of ice in our scotch. Our own heresy

"Fresh duds on the way. You OK?"

A nod.

Downstairs, the doorbell rang. Great. I chased myself around, getting a robe for Loretta and hot-footed it downstairs. Bell. That meant MacDonald. I dashed down and opened the door as Lenore roared into the driveway. No Glory. She had taken a rain check to bark another day.

"Hi," I said, impulsively tipping up on my toes, kissing his cheek. "Life is strange. You'd better come in."

MacDonald pulled me into his arms as he came through the door and held me gently. Oh man did it feel good. I started laughing at myself and told him to stop.

"Stop! MacDonald! Something's happened to Loretta. That's Lenore coming in the back door. I've got to..." He let me go with a shake of the head and said, "Go. I'll catch up."

"Pour yourself a drink! I'll be right back!"

Lenore charged through the kitchen, jeans and shirt over her arm. Glory started to follow us but I asked MacDonald to divert her for a bit. Lenore started up the stairs with me hanging on to her shirt, pulling her back with my good hand.

"Lenore! Whoa! Stop!" She turned on me and I raised my hand, letting go.

"Take a breath," I ordered. "She's upset and I do not know what has happened yet. So you have to slow down. Do not spook her, got it?" My aunt slumped down and sat on the stairs, the breath right out of her. I patted her shoulder.

"It's OK. Let's go in and you can help Loretta pull herself together. You just be there for her. I'll ask the questions." Lenore nodded and took a deep breath.

We walked in to find Loretta in Louise's cotton robe, a towel on her head, sitting in one of the arm chairs by the bay window.

"I like this new arrangement, Lyle!" She grinned at me and Lenore.

"Sister mine, I am A-OK! Glory and I had an adventure! Think we're both done adventurin' for a while. Do you girls have a drink?" I admitted that we did not, that MacDonald was downstairs,, and that she needed to put some clothes on."

"OK, I'll get dressed. You bring Mac up and a plate of something to munch on. Got any popcorn? Maybe we should phone for a pizza!" Loretta was feeling no pain and Lenore visibly relaxed.

"I've got her," Lenore said. "You come up whenever. If you run out of scotch, vodka will do for me!"

I left the sisters to themselves and went down to find MacDonald in the kitchen fiddling with ice and glasses.

"Can I take your order, Ma'am?"

"Ma'am yourself!" I punched his shoulder with my good hand. "You smell good!" He grinned at me and leaned against the counter.

"And you look terrific. Like the hair. May I?" He slowly reached out his hand and stroked my hair back behind my ear. "So smooth. Very nice." I had to swallow before I could speak.

"Thanks. Lenore had her way with some scissors." I was blushing.

"Anyway," I took a step back, "If you could put some scotch on those rocks, I'll make popcorn and take it upstairs."

"Do we need to try another night?" MacDonald asked.

"No! Not at all. I want to see your place, MacDonald. Besides, it's not even night yet. We'll find out about Loretta and Glory's Great Adventure and then we'll go."

"Excellent." He headed off to the library for scotch and I watched him go. For a big guy, he stepped lightly, in long, smooth strides. His white shirt glowed in the shadows of the dark room. Some women like to look at men's butts. Not me. I like shoulders, especially in starched white shirts. Or in T-shirts. Or just on their own, out there in the sun. Whoa, Lyle. Find the popcorn.

In exactly three minutes and thirty three seconds, the corn was jumping in the microwave. I opened a bottle of white Bordeaux and poured myself a glass. Mac stood in the door to the kitchen, holding up the two drinks and asking me with his eyes "What now?"

"Take those to the L&L's. I'll be right behind you with the popcorn. What'll *you* have, MacDonald?"

"I'll have what you're having," he quipped.

Upstairs in the sitting room, drinks were passed around, popcorn placed near Loretta, and MacDonald and I moved with our wine to the window seat. Glory trotted over and settled at my feet with a little grunt.

Loretta had on a fresh pair of jeans and a denim shirt with pearl snaps. Her hair was still damp, so she'd run a hand through it every so often to help it dry. Lenore was visibly relieved to be there with her.

"She's mostly just embarrassed," Lenore confided. Which irritated Loretta no end. Loretta like to bide her time and choose her words when she had a story to tell.

"Lenore, dammit! Do not do that! I'm more confounded than anything. I mean, nothing actually happened. But it must be something because I'm so upset. It's just not anything that has happened to me before." She shook her hair with her right hand and frowned. I leaned forward and looked at her closely.

"What was it? What happened to the two of you?" I asked

"Well, it started out normal enough. I took Glory out to Clinton Lake—you know, that off-leash area they have out by the golf course? I thought I'd just let her run. I had a couple of tennis balls with me, so I knew she wouldn't go too far. Glory is not too friendly with other dogs, so I knew I had to keep an eye on her."

We looked at the dog lying quietly at our feet and nodded. Yep. Glory loved people, and could tolerate cats, but she hated other dogs. Had a real mean streak that could kick in suddenly.

"It wasn't much of a risk," Loretta said defensively, "The place looked empty. She hadn't been run in a while and that open area is neutral territory. She's better there than in her own back yard!"

"True enough," I replied. The police had come to the house once or twice when Glory got her head through the fence slats and had bitten somebody's dog passing through the alley way.

"Where was I? Oh, so I let her out, tossed the ball a few times and watched her run. You know how she pronks right up into the air sometimes?" Loretta laughed. "We had a good time. A Shepard and a Pointer and a few other dogs showed up, but Glory outran them all. She pretty much stayed with me and came when I called. But then a throw went into the bush," she continued, "And I knew I was in trouble. I heard some thrashing around and then she just disappeared."

I took a swig from my wine glass at this point and shook my head. I knew what happened next.

"Now, Lyle, it wasn't that bad! Yes, I had to call out after her, repeatedly. But There were other dogs around so calling out Glory! Glory! Glory! Was not as bad as calling out some other dogs' names, like Princess or Tinkey, or Bull! Bull is a boxer, I believe." MacDonald thought that was pretty funny.

"I knew I had to go in the brush after her. Which I did. The creek bed was damp and muddy and stank to high heaven. I stayed above it as long as I could, but I heard Glory crashing around on the other side, so I had to follow.

The creek circles back to the car park, thank God, so I knew I wasn't lost. I was cursing Glory to a fare-thee-well when I noticed she'd gone quiet. I called and heard a whining off to my right. Thinking she'd gotten stuck is some brambles or something, I charged over to her and practically stepped right on the body." Loretta drained her glass and waited for the explosion.

"THE WHAT?" I shouted. MacDonald was startled, too.

"Dead person. A man. Rumpled and wet and that not-healthy color dead people get." Loretta added. "Now that's what upset me. Dead people shouldn't be left lying around. What if a child had found it?" She shuddered. Her eyes filled with tears. So did Lenore's. She stood up and sat down again, knowing Loretta would hit her if she tried to give her a hug.

"Did you..." Mac began

"Oh, yeah! 911, put the dog in the car, waved people in another direction to walk their dogs, the whole deal. I told my story and the nice young man asked me if I'd like a ride home. Told him I was good to drive. And I was fine until I got back here." Loretta paused and collected herself. "Sorry."

The three of us made a hubbub of comforting noises.

"Just wait until Luce finds out," Loretta sighed. "I'll never hear the end of it!"

24

Glory slept on a blanket in the backseat of the Mustang. She was glad to be with us. The windows were down, the sky was settling in to its first shades of violet after a muted sunset. Lawrence receded behind us and we headed west, into open country where hills roll a bit and dirt roads melt into farmsteads, pastures, and grasslands. I was enjoying the sound of the V8, the feel of the car.

"It's as if this car jumped out of some forgotten memory, MacDonald, and materialized in the present. Forty years compressed in the blink of a moment. Don't you feel disoriented driving around in it? Wondering if the road is real?"

"Not at all. It must be that car gene men have." He smiled, looking at me out of the side of his eye. "For me, this car is familiar. I work on it, drive it, appreciate it almost every day. She's an old friend."

"Friend have a name?" I teased him.

"Not one I speak out loud." He paused. "Mostly I

call her Babe." His smile grew larger. I smiled, too, and watched the landscape stretch out in the evening twilight.

"What do you think about that body Loretta and Glory found today?"

"Too soon to speculate. But it is interesting that in a place full of dogs and people that it wasn't found sooner. From Loretta's description, I'd say it had been there a couple days. We'll have to wait and see. I'll look into it and let you know what I find out. Wouldn't want you Hudson women snooping around and getting into trouble with the police."

"You're probably right," I conceded. "We're an inquisitive bunch." Unconsciously, I ran my hand over the wound in my arm. Still tender, but sound.

"I don't remember ever seeing Loretta in such a state." I said. She was really shaken up."

"It's not like on TV. It's not part of daily life at all. It's unnatural. I admire Loretta for not pretending to be brave. She's right to be frightened." He turned his head and looked at me. "A little fear might be a good thing for you once in a while, Lyle."

"No lectures, please." I said tartly.

"That was just a friendly reminder. I never lecture when I'm driving." He was dead serious.

The road took a wide curve up and around a small rise. MacDonald crossed the left-hand lane and coasted into a gravel pull off. He turned off the ignition and got out of the car. Coming over to my side, he opened the door and held out his hand.

"Come on, I want you to see this." I took his hand and we crunched across the gravel to a lookout that had been cleared in some scrub trees. Glory stayed in the car.

"Very cool." I said.

The horizon was a thin peach-colored line beneath a blanket of heavy purple clouds. Beneath us, the land had fallen into darkness, and off to the left was a moving line of low flames. The smoke looked ghostly and blue, rising behind teeth of fire. Farmers were burning off their fields. I had not seen this ritual in years. I stood entranced. The smoky tang in the air said the burn had been under way for a while. Down in the darkness, the fire would be carefully monitored, but up here it had an ancient, primal feel. MacDonald took my hand, and I sighed with the pure contentment. There was no need to say anything.

When we were full up with the prairie fire, we walked slowly back to the car.

"Hungry?" MacDonald asked.

"Very!" I laughed.

"We're almost there."

Glory stood up and shook herself as we turned off a wooded side road and pulled into a curving gravel drive. Tree roots and clay earth buckle in harsh winters, so gravel makes more sense than cement or any other kind of pavement. It also makes a very pleasing sound.

All I could see was light spilling out across a wide porch. The house was filled with large windows and wood beams. Glory jumped out MacDonald's side of the car and started sniffing around in the bushes. She followed us up the stairs and into Mac's house. He stood back and watched us both look around.

"It's beautiful!" I breathed. High ceilings, honey-colored wood, books, rugs, paintings, small bronzes, an eclectic mix of styles that blended into a space that was both sophisticated and welcoming.

"Thank you." A soft rustling sound announced the appearance of an Irish Setter who emerged from a hallway at the back of the house. She stood at the edge of the living room and waited.

"Come here, girl," MacDonald said. The color of deep mahogany, the dog walked slowly over to the man who placed a hand on her head. Her graying muzzle gave away her age. I sympathized.

"This is Jesse. Jesse, this is Glory." The setter gazed adoringly at Mac, not the least interested in meeting visitors. Glory looked up at me and then over at MacDonald and his dog. She was on her best behavior and wagged her tail, not leaving my side.

"Glory is not usually shy. In fact, if I had known you had a dog, I'd have left her back at the house. She doesn't play well with other dogs." I was clearly surprised by Glory's good manners.

"Jesse's unusual that way. She has a calming effect on other dogs. Of course her eye sight is going, but around here, she knows where she is." He walked over to the kitchen area, and the dog followed just a step behind.

"Looks like setter love to me!" I laughed. "While you are near, no one else exists."

"Could be," he agreed. "Wine?"

"Maybe with dinner, Mac. I need food in my stomach."

"All right! Come on in and let's throw something together."

The house was one large open space, the kitchen defined by the placement of counters and appliances. There was a large butcher block over which were hung a variety of cooking pans and implements. Everything was well used and well cared for.

Mac put me in charge of salad. The dressing he had already made. He pounded veal scallops into a papery thinness and confessed, "I know it is not politically correct to eat veal, but sometimes temptation is just too much!" He gave me a knowing look that caught my breath. Glory sat up and regarded him suspiciously.

While we talked and went through the rituals of cooking, he told me about the house, and how much he enjoyed being "sort of" retired, spending more time here.

Glory quietly approached Jesse for a friendly get-to-know-you sniff and was tolerated. The dogs kept out of the way but stayed near to hand.

"There is a view out that window," MacDonald continued, "that is deceptive. At first, you only see trees, but if you keep looking, you'll see the land dip and rise again behind it, with more trees in the distance, and then the sky. Some mornings there is a ground fog that shimmers with light." His voice trailed off and he looked at me. I looked back.

"It must be lovely."

"Yes. It is." He shook himself. "Let's eat!"

The meal disappeared, and MacDonald watched me wipe the plate with a heel of French bread. I sat back and sighed, placing the linen napkin beside my plate. I put my chin in my hand and looked at him. His face was relaxed yet watchful. He seemed so complete in himself, a man who was definitely present and not thinking of other things.

MacDonald had to be the most attractive man I had met in a long time. The kind of man who made you wonder about how different men are from women, who made you feel grateful for the difference. I took in his long hands, his stillness. His eyes looked black tonight, deep, with a web of lines that deepened when he smiled, as he did now.

"What?" I asked. "I'm not the only one looking here, Mac."

"Oh, I'm looking, all right."

"So, what's the question?"

"Soon," he said, mysteriously. Got to love a man who does not rush things. A very good sign. "Let's step outside. Just leave the dishes where they are." We rose from the table and stepped through the kitchen sliding doors, out onto the back porch.

"That is a serious telescope," I said walking over to it.

"Not going to see anything tonight with these clouds and the smoke in the air, but I love to look at the stars. Mars has been very close to the moon recently, and Jupiter is as close as it's been in centuries. That's what the astronomers say—I'm not arguing Intelligent Design, or anything." He raised his head and looked up, seeing what lay beyond the clouds and the smoke. I looked up, too, at the strong neck and line of jaw. I shivered and held my arms.

"Cold?"

"Mmm."

He stepped over and put his hands on my shoulders, stroking my arms to make them warm.

"How's the arm?"

"It's fine. I hardly notice it." I turned my head away, struck with a fleeting image of splintering glass and noise." "The after images are not much fun," I said.

"No." Mac lifted my face so I was looking up into his eyes, which held mine. He ran his thumb up across my cheek then back down the line of my jaw and over my lower lip. I opened my mouth to speak and he kissed me. He pulled away and the came back, slowly, his hands in my hair, his mouth moving across my brows and to my ear and back to my mouth.

I stood up on my toes to meet him, holding on to his shoulders and then his neck and ran a hand through his hair. He smelled wonderful, felt wonderful, tasted wonderful. My heart was pounding. We broke for air. What the hell was I doing?

"Mac..."

He looked at me. "Shall I stop?"

"No, I guess not!" We laughed and went inside. What is a scruple, anyway? A sharp stone in the road. The road goes on. One has adventures which the scruple would have prevented. Something like that.

The dogs watched us walk down the hall and stayed where they were. They knew we would return eventually.

"A tattoo? How did I miss that last time?'

"Maybe your eyes were closed. My eyes are closed," I said, smiling, "and I don't think I'm missing a thing." I opened my eyes and reached over and traced the lines of his face. "Well, maybe I am. Did you have that moustache last time?"

"Cruel woman!" Mac leaned over me and went for an ear. I squirmed and wriggled enticingly.

"Stop! If you kill me, Lyle, we won't be able to do this any more!"

"If you die, you die!" This was the line from an old, old joke. A good line that I had never had the opportunity to use before. MacDonald was clearly familiar with the line. He took his revenge by tickling me mercilessly.

"Take it back."

"Okay, okay. No dying. Not today, anyway." I was rewarded by a long, deep kiss.

After showering, Mac loaned me his robe and climbed into a pair of jeans. Towel around his neck, he sat on the bed and pulled me down to sit next to him. Time to talk.

"Three questions each and then we'll move on?" MacDonald said.

"I go first because it's my house," he smiled. "And you don't want to do this, but we both know that something is going on between us that feels very ...good, frankly." He adjusted the towel around his neck and looked at his hands, formulating his thoughts. I waited silently.

"You know, Lyle, it's the guy who is supposed to not like to talk about *feelings*. But I need some clarity here. Not a declaration—God, no! But, a...a...timeline. I'm getting used to you and your strange, Hudson ways. I like the chemistry, the surprises that come up when you're around." This was a lot of "talking" for MacDonald, and I could see he was having a hard time of it. Jesse quietly appeared at the doorway and looked in. A telepathic signal if ever there was one.

"Me, too." I volunteered. "Not that you're full of surprises, or anything, but your timing is excellent." I smiled wryly. "Since that night out on the farm, things have changed with us, and I like that, too, Mac. I never expected to want to be close to someone. I guess we both need to know what to make of it. Clarity, you said. So. This is like "Truth or Dare," right? A Russian Roulette with dangerous questions?" I was starting to sweat. I have, as they say, a shady past. What was I getting into?

Mac laughed and shook his head. "I don't think it has to be so anxiety-producing. Unless you're hiding something from me?" He raised an eyebrow. Sexy and teasing.

"Could be. It depends on the question. Do we get to pass? What are the rules, anyway?" I stopped him, "And who says *you* get to make the rules!" I had that defense/offense thing kicking in for me and was feeling a bit more secure. Be wily, Lyle. On your toes. Battle of the sexes, bring it on!

"What are you doing?" MacDonald asked, watching the changing expressions cross my face.

"Thinking up a few rules of my own!" I grinned at him.

"This is not a contest, Lyle. I simply want some basic information—about you, about the future, if there is to be one. You're an incredibly secretive woman."

"A Hudson trait. It's genetic. Can't be helped. Sorry."

"Sorry, my ass." He narrowed his eyes skeptically.

"OK. You want me to answer three questions. I get to ask you three questions. That's it. Right? No sub-questions, no follow-ups, or right to cross examine. Correct?"

"Correct. Just the facts. Basic." He smiled. "After which you get to decide if you want to sleep over. Or go home." He was grinning, now.

I let out a breath and slapped my hands on my knees. "OK. Let's do it."

"When are you going back to San Francisco." It was a statement, not a question.

"You get right to it." Deep breath. "Next week. I..."

Mac held up his hands to forestall explanations. "We can save explanations for another time. Your turn." He sat there in front of me, so completely open and trusting it broke my heart. I am an evil person.

"This is a beautiful house, MacDonald. But it is totally you, only you. Has it always been that way?" Listen to me. If he played by my rules, I'd get a big lie right about now.

"I was married once. No children. Nan and I divorced years ago, once we discovered that we lived separate lives, had separate schedules. An RN and a detective." MacDonald paused. "You'd think it would have worked out. But she needed more regular hours, more of *me* than was available. For a long time, I blamed myself. Then I got over it. She's got a good life in Kansas City, and I'm happy with my life here. Family. Friends. This place. The land. The occasional interesting woman." His smile settled around his eyes, doing that crinkly thing. Not just the smile, though. What made the man really attractive was that he liked himself. Didn't take himself too seriously.

MacDonald gazed at me for a while, thinking. Shuffling through his questions, making a few choices. I could read the signs as if he held a deck of cards in front of him.

"Since you have been here, I have had the sense that you're not currently involved with anybody. Who you are in San Francisco is unknown to me. There is too much there to even get a start on a question, so I guess what I want to know is if you are coming back. I have told you that my life is here, Lyle. It's a good life, full of good people." He looked down at his hands. Jesse walked over and sat beside him and nuzzled his hand. MacDonald stoked her soft ears and neck and waited for my response.

"I have been asking myself that same question. My family wants me back. My feelings about Lawrence have changed considerably since I learned the truth about my mother. Her death…caught me off guard, MacDonald. So much has happened." I paused and he continued to wait, looking at the dog.

"Do I want to be with you? Yes. Despite appearances, I am not casual about men." I made a face at myself.

"Relocating here permanently?" I continued, "Is still a question." I shrugged. "I don't know. My plan is to go back, take care of unfinished business. I told Luce I'd be back in a couple of months. I have to decide about the house, for one thing. Do we have a future? I think that's what the real question is, yes? I don't know. Do you?" I was starting to feel frustrated and put on the spot.

"I mean, what if I say yes and I come back and whatever it is we think we have going falls apart? What happens to me then? I have burned bridges while you're cozy in your good life? I tell you, MacDonald, I have been there, done that, once too often. No more giving up everything for a man. Yes, I think you are terrific, OK? The most I can say right now is that I'm ready to walk down a path with you and see where it goes. If there are risks to be taken, I would like them to be shared."

I had gotten up in the midst of this statement and started pacing, over to the dark windows and back, arms wrapped around myself. Glory came trotting into the room and jumped up on to the bed, looking at me anxiously.

"Glory, get down!" I snapped. The dog obediently bounced off the bed and waited for a signal.

"She's fine," Mac said calmly. "Your second question?"

"I don't want to do this! It is painful for me, Mac. Maybe I'm not a *Questions* kind of person. Why do you need questions? Why can't you just let things...evolve, or whatever? So, yes. That's my question: What is that about?" I turned and faced him squarely.

"Good one." He nodded his head and thought about it. "I'm a planning kind of person. Plans can change, but I need a starting place, something to go on. Or I feel hung out there, uncertain. It's funny. I like surprises when I'm around you, but deep in my heart, surprises are not my thing at all." He shook his head, self-deprecatingly.

"Too much structure makes me claustrophobic, MacDonald. I need choices and options and open doors or I can't breathe." I ran my hands through my hair, which produced an involuntary laugh. At my age, silver hair and all...feeling like a teenager.

"Door's open, Lyle. I just want a little reassurance that you'll be more walking in it than walking out of it!" We both laughed. Nothing like torturing a metaphor to make you feel foolish. And relieved. Mac stood up, walked over to me and pulled me down beside him on the bed.

"Ready for question number three?"

"Please, Mac, can't we just stop? I think I'm breaking out in hives!"

"Question number three," he said, whispering into my hair. "Tell me about the car."

I didn't blink. Didn't move a muscle, possibly I did not breathe. Inside, I was cursing and stomping around, tearing my hair, and screaming "Shit!"

I cleared my throat. "Well," I said, "We could be up all night with that one."

25

I turned and squinted up at him, not the most attractive picture at this time of night, at my age, with moisturizing products located elsewhere. MacDonald did not seem particularly put off. His face was relaxed, his eyes curious. The man was definitely interested. I sighed.

"I knew the minute Luce made her first crack about the car that it would find a home in your head. I can answer the question pretty quickly, MacDonald, but it won't answer your *question*." I rubbed my eyes and shook back my hair.

"I'm leaving it here. Flying to San Francisco, which means I'll be back for it. That said, the story of the car and how I got it may change your mind about the whole 'relationship' thing." I made quotation marks with my fingers and lowered my hands into my lap.

"Why don't I just tell you that I won the car, the Infiniti, which answers the basics of the question, and just leave the rest until tomorrow? Mmm?"

There was a slight breeze stirring nearby trees, no other sound. The lamps glowed. Mac sat there like some dark-haired sphinx of Kansas, waiting.

"Reading your face, I'm guessing *No*. Right. Make yourself comfortable."

"Playing cards, Mac. Poker. I was not nice about it. I knew what I was doing when I took the G35. So did Chas." I paused, trying to figure out how this would go. Just follow the story, Lyle. If the man has questions, he'll have to open his mouth and not just sit there looking at me.

"I'm good at cards. It was not something I particularly thought about. Or, perhaps I'm good at reading people. *Was* good at reading people. I haven't won much, not since before Christmas. A losing streak, I guess you could say."

Next to me on the bed where we sat crosswise, MacDonald put his hand on top of my right foot, just let it rest there. I sat up straight and made a T with my hands, closing my eyes.

"Time out. OK. Back up. I moved out to San Francisco and was a teacher in a private school for a while. Cushy job, great kids, but it felt confining after a while. Too regimented. So, I tried the adjunct professor route. More flexible in terms of time, but dirt for pay and little control over which classes I taught. I kept at it for a while because of the perks—intellectual climate, art, poetry. But one day I saw that I was never going to get anywhere. I was breaking my neck just to pay the bills. I had no time, no life. San Francisco is teeming with hordes of the preternaturally young! I was turning into this ghost of a person. Did I say I was depressed? I was depressed."

Chas lived next door. He had been a neighbor of mine in Noe Valley, but then he got this great place up on Twin Peaks, incredible view of the city. It was a side-by-side, modernist duplex with sheets of glass and light and terraced gardens. He offered me a deal on rent in return for house sitting, gardening, pet care—and I said yes. We grew close over time.

"Anyway, between semesters not so long ago, I went into hibernation and stopped communicating with the outside world. Chas called it my meditation on darkness. Eventually Louise or Luce must have called him, asked him to check and see if I was dead. He let himself in with the master key. I had managed to keep the fish alive, but any plant not out on the deck was past saving. Chas opened the blinds and dumped a sack of mail on the dining room table."

"Oh, Ms. Hudson? Where are you? Are you dead, sweetie?" I did not respond. Not that I didn't want to, I was probably dehydrated, on the wrong end of two weeks of psychic paralysis.

"Dottore? Professoressa!" Chas warbled lightheartedly. I heard him put the kettle on and survey the wasteland that was my eternal present.

"Dear God, Lyle. What have you done to yourself." He entered my bedroom and opened the windows. "Fortunately, it is a windy foggy day or I would choke." He came over to the bed and looked at me. I felt as if I were underwater and looking up at him through the surface of a lake. He was serene in expression, but I could detect a banked anger. I don't think I blinked.

"Every resurrection begins with a nice hot shower. Instead of angels in the tomb we have fluffy white towels and a cup of tea." Somehow he got me out of bed and into the shower. Poured a mound of shampoo on my head and said, "Deal with it! And don't forget to brush your teeth!"

I dealt with it. The whole process must have taken hours, but Chas managed to bring me back. He talked and gossiped and told me about city politics, the latest exhibition at the Legion of Honor, how glad he was to be between boyfriends, and what a shitty, selfish bitch I was. Which made me laugh.

I thanked him for being such a good friend, for rescuing me.

"Oh, shut up. You have no voice at all. Have more tea."

Surveying the dust and the silence for a bit, Chas declared the need for a road trip.

"I have just the thing! A week in Vegas! While we're away, I'll get someone in to clean this mess up, feed the fish and replace your poor plants."

"No plants," I interrupted him. Too much responsibility." I was not yet in the holiday spirit.

"Fine. I have a friend..." Chas always has a friend. He could start his own underground spy agency with that network.

Two days later, after a facial, massage, and manicure for each of us, we toddled off to Vegas—two small bags for me, two big bags for Chas—in a black Mercedes belonging to a "friend". We left the windy fog bank of SF for the arid desert sun.

"Why not Reno, Chas?"

"Oh, darling, It is so small town. Vegas is the real thing. Totally elsewhere. You'll love it!"

I never did love it, but it was so out there, so strange, that I felt normal. Sort of. We shared a suite and could be together or not, as we chose. Chas loved slots and roulette and black jack, so he was off on his own with my blessings. I read and swam and slept, charging my batteries in the sun. After a few days of this I started to feel bored.

Chas and I went to see the Cirque du Soleil, the nude version. But it was that weird music that finally pulled me out of my funk.

"They manifest a degree of mystery that is missing from our lives, don't you think?" I was musing on the sense of being in the moment.

"Lyle, dear, you're waking up. Welcome back!"

"What am I doing in Vegas, Chas? What is this?" I waved my hand abstractedly

"Are we bored, darling?"

"Yes, we are." I said decisively.

"OK. Let's go play cards." And we did.

I chose poker, and Chas just looked at me. "Oh, really? It is so slow, Lyle. You go find a game and I'll join you after I visit the craps table. It is calling to me and I must answer!" He kissed me on the cheek and dashed away.

I wandered around for a while, looking for a likely table. Thought I would start out modestly and not throw away money I could not afford to lose. Some Gambler, huh? I found a quiet table with a fifty dollar ante and sat in. I was curious to find out how much I remembered.

"You see, MacDonald, Hudson women loved playing poker together. Not Louise so much, but her sisters and my cousins were crazy. We would play for dried beans, matches, toothpicks, buttons, golf tees, pretzels. Green acorns one year!" I laughed.

"We excelled in bluffing. Avoiding the trap of a killer bluff meant paying attention to the cards and the people who held them. I loved being dealer so I could watch everyone, including those of us watching over shoulders. It took years before I could beat the L&L's! They were merciless.

"People came and went at the table, a new dealer

came in, and I started winning. I apologized self-consciously, declaring 'beginner's luck,' but by the time Chas joined me, I had a sizeable stack of chips. I used his appearance as an excuse to leave the game. I could feel the cards moving elsewhere. I tipped the dealer and we walked over to the teller.

"Actually, we were escorted to the teller. The floor manager complimented me on my play and asked if I was interested in higher stakes. Chas's eyes popped out of his head when I said 'yes, why not. Tomorrow night perhaps.' I was calling it a night or a morning or whatever it was. 'Very good,' the impeccable man said. He handed me his card and asked if there was anything that would make my stay more comfortable.

Chas nodded his head vigorously and pantomimed opening a bottle of champagne.

"Champagne?" I said. 'My friend and I would like to celebrate.

"Certainly," he said and disappeared. I received twenty five thousand dollars in an assortment of denominations and we headed for the elevator.

"He didn't ask the room number, did he?"

"I think they know which one it is, dear." Chas said.

The champagne was waiting in the room. Dom Perignon, two glasses, caviar and smoked salmon, and a basket of fruit.

"Lyle, they must think you have great potential!"

"It would appear so, Watson. Open the wine, please." .

"That was my glorious start. What do you think so far, Mr. George?"

"It's a very entertaining story, Ms. Hudson," he grinned. "Why are you so reluctant to tell it?"

"Well, I'm not a gambler!" He barked a laugh at

that one. "I'm not! I disapprove of gambling. In spite of the fact that I made more at cards than I ever did teaching."

By this point in the discussion, Glory and I were clearly staying the night. I had not even gotten to the car yet.

"I don't have a system, which means that I'm not predictable. It gives me an edge. I don't cheat. Casinos know if you do and they invite you not to come back. With me, they started inviting me out. Anywhere I felt like playing, they would fly me in, comp me a room, send me flowers. There are lots of people out there like me. Casinos like us; we *encourage* other people to play just by doing so ourselves. It was fun. For a while. Until I started feeling that my play—the *encouraging* part of the equation—was not a good thing. Hence my distaste for the word—gambling.

"I guess what works for me is that I pay attention. No detail is too small. But it is its own kind of awareness, like peripheral vision. You do not know where the information comes from, but it comes and you sift it through. It got so I could feel the cards go cold for me, and I walked away. I won more than I lost, and I never lost very much. I just let the cards go."

I fell quiet for a while and drank my tea. A wry smile crossed my face. Tea. If I were Hemingway, it'd be bourbon. Or gin. If I were Hemingway, I'd be dead. Stick with the tea.

I gazed at MacDonald George sitting across from me in his kitchen in the middle of the night. In Kansas. It felt every bit as weird as being in Vegas. Who is this guy? Why am I telling him about my life this way? The questions brought me back full circle to myself. There is a mystery here and I am it, I thought. Back to the story.

"Meanwhile, Chas was amazed. It was as if I had grown a second head or something. I know he told Lyle stories to his coterie of acquaintances, embellishing them dramatically, but he never told one in my presence.

"He'd go with me sometimes, Idaho or wherever, to take notes for his stories about me.

"What you have going for you, my silver-haired fox," he told me, "Is that you can look like so many different kinds of people. There's your Venerable Artist look: black cashmere and turquoise jewelry; your Professor look: tweeds and pearls; your Outdoorsy look; tan and denim. The most insidious is the Absent-minded Granny, though. You use that one on people you don't like. Let them think you're befuddled, let them win a little, then...ZAP! You're on them like a cobra!" Chas would sip his Cosmopolitan and raise his eyebrows over the rim of his glass. It was a particularly irritating habit of his. There was one sure way to shut him up. It always worked.

"So, Chas," I would say sweetly. "Interested in a little game of cards? That way you could tell me who I am, in the moment as it were."

"You know, Lyle, some day I will. Just to know what it feels like!"

"But not today."

"No, dear. Not today." And the subject would change.

"The car?" MacDonald asked.

"It's almost here. Listen and you'll hear the engine purring."

We moved into the living room and sat in the dark,

under a wool blanket, our backs at opposite ends of the couch. The dogs were still asleep in the bedroom. I was completely awake, caught up in memory, almost reliving the past. A past not that distant, either.

"What is it now, May? June? It was about a year ago, before Louise ...died. I was down in Carmel, visiting an artist I know who had an opening at a gallery. I own a couple of her paintings, oils, and I wanted to see her new work. I had spent the day by myself, on the beach. Zandra had to be at the gallery early, so I had the luxury of her studio, deck, and the sunset, and a solitary scotch before I joined her and Diego at the show. My cell rang while I was dressing. Chas was in Carmel.

"What are you doing here?" He asked in tones of delight. I told him about Zan's opening, and he asked if he could come."

"Meet me at the door, you can be my guest. I'll be there in half an hour. If you're late, I'm going in without you, Chas." I was not in the mood to stand around waiting for him.

"You are such a guy, sometimes, Lyle."

"Bite me," I said sweetly and hung up. We drive each other crazy every now and then. This was a now.

"There is no parking in Carmel, none that can be found when something is going on, anyway. But Zan had arranged for me to borrow space in a friend's driveway. I alerted the friend to my arrival and told her I'd be back for the car by ten. Chas was standing by the front window of the gallery, mingling with the crowd. I can never stay mad at him for very long, and that night he went out of his way to be charming.

"The place was so packed it was almost impossible to see the art. I found Zan and Diego, introduced Chas. That I would know people he did not was a first for him. I asked Zan if I could stop by the next day to see her work. It was hopeless in this crowd. She nodded and then she and Diego were swept up by a wave of well-wishers.

Chas and I grabbed a couple of glasses of champagne and made our way to the back of the gallery where people were not so crowded together.

"Bet you they think I'm a kept man," Chas suggested.

"You are such a vain child," I scolded him.

"Well, why not? Look at you in your black silk and silver hair! Very dashing, Lyle. Full of allure!" He nuzzled my ear.

"You're gorgeous too, my sweet." He was. Blond and breezy and meltingly beautiful. We hadn't seen each other for a while. Strange to feel so distant and so close at the same time.

"Where are you going after this shindig?" He asked.

"Back to Zan's and to bed. I want to get up early and walk on the beach. Soak up the scenery before heading back to the city.

"Why not come out with me? I know where there's a party. Some heiress's birthday. It'll be fun!" We bickered about whose car and the usual annoying details but ended up deciding to go, sooner rather than later because of the crowd. I left Zan's car back at her house, jumped into the little canary yellow TT Chas was driving and headed down the coast a few miles. It was a lovely evening, the champagne was excellent. All was well with the world. Until we joined the party.

"Chas picked up a pair of maracas he found in an antique wood bowl in the foyer and slipped past the butler right into party mode. I lingered at the door, admired the décor, asked *Jeeves* to point me to some food and let Chas be Chas. Quickly bonding with other hungry people, I had a couple of fleeting, politically correct conversations about environmentalism in California, the paintings of my friend Zan, and the death of California cuisine. Pebble Beach aristocrats like these love to think that something is always dying, that the golden age has dimmed and passed. If it hadn't been for the enhanced hair, skin, and jaw lines, I'd have sworn I was in a Henry James novel.

Out of nowhere, Chas zooms up, minus maracas, and sweeps me away to a group of elegant young men wearing Ray Bans and Rolexes. Post-modern with expensive cologne.

"Here she is! Isn't she fabulous? Every word I told you about her is true! Cross my heart! I saw it with my own eyes!" Since none of the boys was reacting, his gushing seemed forced and made me uncomfortable. I put my hands in the pockets of my slacks and looked them over.

"Are you sure they know you, Chas? Perhaps they'd be more interested in meeting... one of their own kind. Good evening, gentlemen." I turned to walk away, less than impressed.

"But, darling, I've been bragging about you!"

"I hate when you say that Chas. I have never heard you say a thing about me. I'm going back to the food. See you later."

"Wait." A brown-haired boy took off his sunglasses and looked at me with his big blue eyes. "Charles says you play cards. Is that true?"

"Poker, not cards. But I'm on vacation." I waited but no more words were forthcoming. I turned to Chas. "Whatever you're up to, the answer is no. N.O."

"Wait." One syllable, confident as money.

"No. You wait, Mr. I-make-films, or I-make-money,

or I-own-the-Monterey Peninsula. I do not like your style, your affected silence, your clothes, or your singular lack of manners. I'm not playing cards tonight, period. Good bye."

"Wait." He put up his hand and then extended it to me. "Please accept my apologies. Charles' effusiveness was a bit off-putting. I thought he was up to something. Sorry."

"Nice friends, Chas. Let's leave. I think I can find you some better ones."

The boys took this as some sort of humor, and they relaxed. It was too weird.

"Chas, let's go. Seriously."

"Lyle. Let me introduce you. This is Chandler Royce-Gibbon." I blinked at him and shrugged.

Chandler held out his hand and said, "Pleased to meet you, Ms. Hudson. In fact, I do make films, I do make money, and I do own a bit of the Monterey Peninsula. Clever girl." The smile was cold, tightly smug. If I played this man, I warned myself, I was playing with big trouble.

"That's *Dr*. Hudson. I'm obviously well beyond girlhood, and I was making that stuff up."

"Obviously, you are a woman of some intuition."

"Not as far as I know, Mr. Royce..."

"Gibbon. Are you sure you can't be persuaded to play?" The suits sat up and took notice. Clearly, our Chandler never asked twice for anything.

"Very. I'm not in the mood, I still do not like you, and I would be surprised if I had a hundred dollars in my pocket."

"Just one hand, perhaps?" The suits were shifting around uncomfortably. I decided to up the ante.

"What, so you can say you cleaned me out? How sporting is that? Who are these guys, anyway? Can they speak?"

"They are business partners, here at my invitation."

"Whereas I am not. Got it. But then I am trying to leave," I whispered.

"It is not necessary to like someone to play cards with them is it? Why don't we just sit down and see what happens?'

"Good line. I've used that one myself. What's in it for me?"

"To be sporting, if you lose the hundred right off, I'll front you another hundred so play can continue."

"Cheesy deal. Do not insult me. Good bye." I was not liking Mr. Royce-Gibbon.

"Five hundred. If you lose the hundred, I'll give you five hundred for your time. Better?" He was still polite, but the danger smoke around him like a cloud. If I took this guy, he might come after me. If I made it out. What the hell.

I nodded. Besides, he was irritating. I wondered if it was a tactic. We adjourned to an upstairs room, and Chas was allowed to stay. Jeeves arrived with two sealed decks of cards, poker chips, and a couple of snifters of brandy.

"No thanks," I said to the brandy. "Got any Schweppes Bitter Lemon?"

"Indeed, madam," said Jeeves and I smiled up at him. "Nice manners. You could learn from him," I said to Chandler.

As the set up rituals began, I cleared my mind and took inventory of myself: posture, breathing, heart-rate, facial muscles, marshalling self-control. I asked for a cloth to wash my hands, took off my jacket, rolled up the sleeves of my blouse, sat down and shook out my hair, letting it fall across my shoulders. I could feel Chandler checking me out. He took a sniff of his cognac then tasted it, wetting his lips. I sat back and relaxed, waiting for him.

"Do you care to deal?" He asked.

"No. Let's ask Jeeves to deal." Dead silence.

"His name is Malcolm."

"Cool. I want him." More silence.

"Malcolm? If you would be so kind?"

"My pleasure, sir." The man had the face of a first class poker player. If I ever had to play him, I was in for it. Meanwhile, Chandler settled his ruffled feathers and pulled the high card.

"Five card stud?" I asked. "I like the privacy of it, don't you? Texas Hold 'em is so…transparent."

In reply the bastard anted in with a C-note. Thought he could take me. I smiled and shook my head. I looked at my cards once, placed them on the table and anted up. It turned out not to be a short game.

There was a hefty pot sitting at my elbow three hours later. Cash, two checks (his) and I was ready to go.

"Wait." No flat voice this time. The anger was barely contained.

"We are done, here, Chandler."

"Lyle, you have to give me more time." He was sounding exasperated.

"That's what we did with the checks, Chandler. I do not take checks, OK? That was a favor. I still have to cash in my chips and I'm not in the mood for any more checks. The checks make me a sucker. It is not done." I felt I could speak so frankly because the retinue were pretty much asleep. I still wasn't sure they spoke English.

"Wait! There must be something!" He slammed his palm flat on the table.

"What? What something? I am tired. I played until the end, and now I am going."

"I know. My car. Here." He threw the keys on the table. "Infiniti G35, brand new, silver, mag wheels, fully loaded." Chandler's eyes bored into me; he could not just let it go. I sighed in exasperation.

"That hand? You think you can clean me out with that hand? That you will get all your money back and the car?" I looked at Malcolm who resembled a stone Buddha.

Then I looked at Chandler. Chas was not making eye contact. Like Malcolm, he hardly blinked.

I sighed. "All right. Two cards." The hand slid my way. Fate.

Chandler stood up and left the room. I picked up the keys and put them in my pocket. The sooner I got out of there, the better.

"I shall get Mr. Royce-Gibbon's signature on the title to the car, madam, and bring it to you at the door. You may present the checks to the bank tomorrow morning. Masterly play, madam. A privilege." Malcolm bowed and turned to leave the room.

"Malcolm, wait."

"Yes, madam?"

I stuffed a wad of bills into an inside pocket of his jacket.

"Not necessary, madam," he said, placing his hand to stop mine.

"My pleasure, Malcolm. My pleasure."

"Thank you, Dr. Hudson." We smiled.

26

The next morning, I could tell without opening my eyes that the room was full of sunlight. I was in that drowsy state that comes after a long sleep, a not-quite-there before my eyes opened and the day began. I was alone in the spacious, rumpled bed. Fresh air and morning sounds came in through open glass doors I hadn't noticed last night. They must have been hidden by the drapes that were now drawn back. I sat up, pushed my hair back from my face and looked around for a glass of water. No water. Damn. Got out of bed and picked the robe off the floor and put it on. Found water in the bathroom, drank it, and washed my face.

MacDonald had set out a toothbrush for me. But I needed to get my hands on a hairbrush. I did the best I could with my hands and then went to see what kind of a "day after" it was going to be. I think people probably get married and stay married just to avoid this particular variety of suspense. Step One: remember where the kitchen is. Step Two will eventually reveal itself. There are a number of possibilities after Step One.

The kitchen, too, was bright with sun. Make that the whole house. The space was divided into areas rather than rooms. No walls to speak of. Way too much light. I found my satchel, pulled the brush out and walked around looking for MacDonald and the dogs.

The house was silent. Open and quiet. Very nice, I thought. Rather like the man. I found tea bags, English Breakfast—yes! Put the kettle on and kept brushing my hair. In addition to bringing order, it was soothing. My injured arm was aching a bit, stiff. Nothing that acetaminophen couldn't handle. I raised my elbow, extending the stretch, gritting my teeth.

Outside, beyond the deck, a flash of white caught my eye. I smiled and walked onto the deck, feeling the wood warm under my bare feet. Glory streaked back the other way, her mouth grinning around a yellow tennis ball. I waved to MacDonald who nodded and smiled in return, lifting his arm and throwing the ball across the yard. Glory sprang up and turned in midair, the picture of a dog in bliss.

Jesse sat calmly watching Glory's antics and slowly followed MacDonald. The man walked up onto the deck, his eyes on me the whole time, as mine were on him. Some men are a just pleasure to look at. Bare feet, jeans, pale blue shirt open at the neck, cuffs rolled. They make you feel so good you have to smile. So I did.

"Morning, glory," he said.

"No, baby. Glory's the dog.

"Well, Sleeping Beauty, then."

"Not with gray hair, Mac. Try again." I looked up at him, admiring his face as if I hadn't seen it before. He kissed my hair and looked at me.

"Glory, Beauty, Queen of the Morning...you choose.."

"Very smooth talk, Mr. George."

"Honest appreciation, Ms. Hudson. How about some coffee?"

"I have water on for tea." By this time, Glory was hopping around us. A maniac wanting to bark for attention but not willing to let go of the ball.

"You two stay out there," Mac told the dogs and followed me into the kitchen. The dogs retreated to lie in the shade. I made tea, Mac coffee. If this was a Day After, it wasn't half bad. I smiled at the thought, and MacDonald raised an eyebrow at me. I laughed and shook my head.

"I just feel so relaxed. It amuses me, you know?"

"Perhaps." He regarded me for a moment. "That was quite a story, *is* quite a story, Lyle."

I interrupted him with a slight wave of my hand, dismissing the topic and trying for a self-deprecating, explanatory tone.

"Mm." I was feeling self-conscious.

"What," he said. "What is it?" More a demand that a question.

"I...It makes me feel self-conscious."

"What does? The story? Telling me the story? Or gambling?"

"I play cards."

"Oh, Lyle, playing cards for money is gambling. That's a fact. You can look it up in a book. What's the big deal? If you were a guy making money that way, you'd be totally OK with it." I was starting to squirm. "Look at you, you're squirming." I gave him a look then gazed out the window.

"Look, I guess I feel guilty that it feels so natural and comes so easily to me. I keep it up—have kept it up—because I make good money." I nodded thoughtfully. "Very good money. What kind of person talks about money?" I put my chin in my hand and looked at him, thinking about it.

After breakfast, Mac drove Glory and me back into town. The day was moving on, and we both had plenty to do. At home, I checked messages, called Luce and arranged to stop by for lunch, then spent the rest of the morning paying bills, watering plants, and brooding about what to do with the house while I was away. I'd have to ask Luce about someone to look after the yard. My list of things to do before I left was growing.

Glory and I walked through Luce's screen door just as she was putting together chicken salad sandwiches. A plate of sliced tomatoes and a pitcher of cold water were already on the table, along with a small bowl of green olives. Hudsons love green olives. All olives. But then I suppose most people do. Random thought for the day #22. Sneaking a few olives from the bowl, I popped one in my mouth and gazed out the window at a spotless blue sky.

"What are the L&L's up to? Still in the custom chocolates business?" I glanced around the kitchen, hoping for a glimpse of illicit goodies.

Luce placed slices of bread on plates and shot me a pained look. "Yes, they are," she said slowly. "They appear to be branching out. Something to do with frosting and chocolate, I believe. They're quite busy."

"Chocolate frosting? What do you mean?"

"You'll have to ask them yourself. I prefer not to discuss it." Luce turned back to constructing sandwiches, and I decided to drop the subject. Made a mental not to call the Aunties. Whatever it was, Luce found it less than amusing. I ate the other two olives and let my eyes wander around Luce's bright, spacious kitchen.

"Hey, Luce," I said, leaning on the counter as she washed her hands, "I have been spending a lot of time in kitchens lately." She looked at me, waiting for the question. "Hey, Luce" always meant a question and had done since I was five years old and she told me I could call her Luce.

"When so much of life gets lived in kitchens, why do people even bother with living rooms? What *is* a living room, anyway? It has always struck me as wasted space." Luce dried her hands.

"Sit down, please, Lyle. And don't bother me with useless questions. *You* are the one with the Ph.D." She dried her hands on a towel and folded it, her face the picture of distraction.

"What's up, Luce?"

"I got a call last night from the vet, Dr. Tenent. It was so odd. He asked after Tetley and then started asking questions about Glory, and you. He didn't come right out and say it, but he seemed to want to know about you." Luce leaned an elbow on the table and rested her chin in her hand, eyes full of questions. "Have you got something going with him?"

I was speechless.

"Hear me out, Lyle. I do not believe for a moment that you are playing the field. Besides that's not my business. I'm just wondering, why call me at night? Why not from the office? What's going on?"

"What's going on? I don't know." But I'll damn well find out what's going on, and then, then what? Like I need another man in my life. I jumped out of my chair and raked my hair, drama queen.

Luce looked up at me and gestured to the chair. "Sit down and think, Lyle. There has to be a reason. Did you encourage him? Maybe he's too shy to tell you how he feels."

She was right. Something was definitely going on.
"Last I knew, Daniel Tenent was just flirting with
me. Asked me to call. He was quite charming, really." I
looked at her. "Guess I will. Call him. At the office, of
course." I fell silent, searching for a clue. "I'll let you
know what I find out."

"Be careful." I leaned over and hugged Luce, getting ready to go, when Luce's cell rang. She went over
to the counter and picked it up.

"Hello, Will. No, you know I have caller I.D. If I
were a psychic, I'd…What?" Luce's face shifted into an
expression of concern. "Right. OK, Will, right away.
Thanks." She hung up the phone and moved to the
computer.

"Will says there's a tornado watch in effect, that
they're about to call it a warning in this area. There's a
storm to the south and west of us that dropped a couple
of twisters near Emporia." She pressed a few keys and
came up with a weather map. Looked like significant
amounts of orange, red and purple moving slowly across
the screen, much faster in real time.

"Hard to believe, with everything so sunny just
now," Luce said conversationally. Instead of answering,
I leaned closer to the screen, masking my panic by putting on my reading glasses which were definitely not
needed.

"Oh, hell!" I yelled right in Luce's ear. She swatted
at me over her shoulder, still contemplating the screen
and the nasty little hook that was forming to the south
of Lone Star Lake.

"Glory, get in here!" I called, just as the siren
sounded. I'm terrified of tornados. My worst dreams
always have tornados in them. I'm haunted by the damn
things.

Outside, I scooped up the T-cat and looked at the

sky. A sudden wind came up, tossing the branches of nearby trees, and darkness crept overhead. I bustled the animals indoors and down to the basement. No such thing as a false alarm in my book, not when it comes to tornados. Luce was right there with me on this one. She closed the doors, left the windows open, shut down and unplugged the computer, and walked slowly and majestically downstairs.

I knew Luce had supplies: blankets, flashlights, a transistor radio, water. Like most older homes in the area, the southwest corner of the basement was walled with cinder blocks, sort of a cozy waiting room with cots, folding chairs and a first aid kit.

I paused to look out the back door before going down to join her. The wind had died and everything was absolutely motionless. Not a sound, no birds, no leaves moving, nothing. The sky turned a bruised, purplish green and the wind came back, hard. Then hail, bouncing white marbles of it.

I dashed downstairs and joined Luce who was listening to the radio. She held Tetley on her lap. Glory lay shaking on one of the cots. I covered the dog with a towel and rubbed her back. The only way Glory got through any storm was under a blanket or a bed. It cut down on the emotional turbulence.

Hail pounded on the roof and then passed, followed by what sounded like rivers of water. Some storms blow up so fast, it takes your breath away; others are giant cruise ships that troll past like a long thought. This storm was hell.

"I will not die here!"

"No one's going to die, Lyle."

I hadn't realized that I'd spoken out loud. Patting Glory, I was starting to feel a bit jittery myself.

I had been in SF for both the '89 earthquake and

the '93. No warning there at all, a sudden undulation of the ground, as if it had developed waves, the terrifying roar of it, like mountains chewing up other mountains. It was followed by hundreds of aftershocks. How ironic that I felt physically safe there, more than I ever did in Kansas. As beautiful as the immense sky can be, I could never bring myself to trust it. Today was why. The all-clear sounded and I stared at Luce.

"They have got to be kidding! That was what, ten, fifteen minutes?"

"It's over. C'mon, Let's go up and turn on the TV and check it out."

The TV footage made me slightly ill. I looked at the sunny sky and felt dislocated, as if the pictures were taken on a different planet.

This tornado was a mile wide when it hit the lake. Then it divided in two and sprouted a bevy of small white spinners, little baby twisters snaking off to the side. One of the two tornados veered west and north, then jumped the river before heading east to Tonganoxie. The remaining twin touched down on the west side of town, a newer area inhabited mostly by college students. A few buildings were smashed to splinters, but so far no one was killed. The storm sucked itself back into the sky and left to go tear up a wide swath of farmland, plus a church near the airport, over in Missouri.

I tore myself away from the TV in a panic. MacDonald! I grabbed Luce's phone, but the line was dead (duh). Scrabbling around in my bag, I finally found the cell. It had one bar left. OK, hold on! I told the phone and punched in Mac's cell number. My hands were shaking. When I hear MacDonald's voice, I teared up with relief.

"My phone's about to die. You OK?"

"Fine. It was loud and hairy. Got a lot of chewed up trees out here, but the house was not touched. How 'bout you?"

"We're great. I'm with Luce. No damage. Talk to you soon, OK?"

"You bet."

"Bye!" The battery held out long enough to keep me sane.

"Luce. I could use a drink."

"Sounds good. How about some of Grandma's lemonade?" We grinned. When I was quite small, I had gotten rather drunk emptying a glass of lemonade my grandmother had left on the porch. My mother never spoke of it, nor my grandmother, but my aunts tell me I sang my favorite songs for them, starting with Twinkle, Twinkle Little Star. Grandma's lemonade would do quite nicely, thank you.

27

Tornados are frighteningly random in their effects. A flattened house surrounded by others still standing leaves a queasy feeling in the pit of your stomach. Apart from the coming and going of demolition trucks and clean-up crews, you could not tell that a tornado had struck Lawrence. Then, you'd turn a corner and pass a street where trees were stripped of their branches or had been uprooted and tossed around. Next moment, you'd drive into an untouched, sunny day. I found it eerie.

I finally got in touch with Mac who was going to be very busy for the next few days, supervising clean-up of his property. Then I called Nola who told me that the shop was untouched. We agreed to meet that afternoon to talk about Hyacinth.

There was a text message on my cell from Chas, brief and to the point, "R U nuts? Come Home! Bring Toto w. U" Feeling more than ready to leave, I set to work wrapping up loose ends, one of which was the

L&L's. I called them, and after hearing that they, too, had been spared by the storm, I invited myself for breakfast the next day. The rest of the morning was spent arguing with no fewer than four airlines about purchasing a plane ticket for Glory. Not even first class, no way, no how, good bye. Bastards. I was not going to place her in cargo. She'd never forgive me. Besides, I'd heard too many stories of pets dying for unexplained reasons. Short of chartering a private jet, I was not going to get Miss Glory on a plane. My plan required air travel, driving would take too long. Which left me one option.

"Max. Lyle Hudson. How are you? Yes, it has been too long. My mother's estate...Thank you. Much appreciated. Still in Kansas, but I'm getting ready to return to San Francisco, which is why I'm calling. Yes. What do you have in Tahoe the week of the 30th?"

I didn't have to sell my soul, just a few days of my time. A limo would pick me up in Lawrence, treats would be waiting for Glory. I would be traveling with five other players, Max informed me. I mentioned items of clothing I'd like to have waiting in my suite—this would be high stakes play, after all—and we were done.

I found a parking space in the shade on Eleventh Street and decided to take the corner to the sidewalk rather than the alley way to the back door of the shop. I paused for a moment outside the bar next to Hyacinth. No. Better not. Talk to Nola first. Maybe later. Internal debate finished, I turned toward the shop and heard a whistle behind me. Whipped my head around, sending my hair flying, like fringe.

"Blake? Did you just *whistle* at me?"

"Whoa! Dr. H? Is that *you?* Oh, man! I'm sorry. No! No, I'm not! You deserve that whistle! Look at you!

You look great!"

"Thank you," I began politely. "Whistling is *wrong*, Blake! Wrong. It is demeaning, Neanderthal stuff. Shame on you!" I scowled for effect, but he couldn't see it through the sunglasses and the hair.

"No way! I would love it if some babe whistled at me."

"You're hopeless. What's in the bag?" He carried a rather bulky grocery bag.

"Margaritas! I'm celebrating surviving the tornado! I got a friend who works over in that bridal shop, so I thought I'd see if the ladies would like to join me in a celebratory libation!" He grinned.

"That bridal shop? *My* bridal shop? You are planning on getting my employees drunk?"

"*Your* bridal shop? Whoa! Strike two!" He shook his blond dreadlocks in mock despair. "I can't believe it. My gothic princess works for you?"

"Crista? Well, no. But she works in my space which is close enough. I feel responsible for her. What are your intentions, Blake?" I narrowed my eyes at him, but he couldn't see that either. The irrepressible spirits made me smile in spite of myself.

"True Love! True Love and Glad to Be Alive! Look! I even have limes! You have to hear the story, Dr....um...Lyle. For real!" It looked like full blown infatuation to me. Ah, youth.

Inside, Nola looked up as we entered and gave a friendly wave to Blake who was still bubbling over as a result of his yet-to-be-told, near-death experience.

Assuming that Blake and I had entered the shop coincidentally at the same time, Nola moved forward to the door and asked if she could help me. I gave her the high wattage smile and said, "Nola! Good to see you!"

Taken aback, she said, "Excuse me?" Then I removed the sunglasses. "Oh, my! Why, Lyle I didn't recognize you! Oh, my." She covered her mouth with one hand and we both laughed.

"It's a new look, Nola. How are you? Did you get through the storm intact?"

"The storm! Oh, my. Wasn't it terrible? The closest call in years! Our neighbor's tree crashed into our roof! Fortunately, it was one of the back bedrooms, but still! You wouldn't believe the racket! Our insurance agents are working it out."

I let her ramble on for a bit and kept my eye on Blake who was setting out drinks supplies in the back of the shop, complete with plastic margarita glasses.

"Planning a party?" I asked Nola. It took her a minute to catch my drift.

"Oh, Blake!" She whispered conspiratorially, "He's an admirer of Crista's, stops by quite often. She seems to like him, *and* he's very polite to the ladies. In fact, when he's here, they like to chat him up to get his impression of their gowns." She whispered conspiratorially.

"Really."

"You're not angry are you, Lyle? He doesn't hurt the business at all. Oh, and speaking of business, Crista and I have an idea we'd like to run by you." 'Run by you' was spoken with quotation marks. This was Nola trying on new lingo. Very with it, our Nola.

My cell rang and I answered, grateful at being spared further confidences from Nola.

"No more excuses. Payment is due. Pay or Die." Followed by silence. Bloody hell. The creep was back but not coming any closer. Wait! It couldn't be Blake. He was in the back of the shop. I could hear him moving around. No...Pay Up Man had to be somebody else. Show your face, mister. I pocketed the cell and headed to the work area at the back of the bridal shop.

"Margaritas, Nola?" Blake quickly grabbed ice out of the fridge and started piling ice cubes noisily into plastic glasses. The sound reminded me of hail. Nola returned from fussing with the drapes in the dressing rooms.

"Crista!" Blake called up the back stairs, "It is I, your Merlin! Come enchant me!" I heard a giggle and then boots clomping down the wooden stairs. Crista was still a devotee of Dr. Marten.

Nola turned to me and explained how this little celebration came to be. "We're having a slow day; the tornado, you know. So, I thought 'Why not?' You were coming anyway, we'd just close up early, hear the dear boy's story, and enjoy a festive aura for our talk. Aura? Is that the right word? Well," she waved a hand, "You know what I mean." Mm, maybe not. But it was shaping up to be a more entertaining meeting than I had anticipated.

After Nola locked the front door and checked that the 'Closed' sign was facing the right way, we headed to the back of the shop. There we found that Blake had temporarily abandoned his bartending duties to give Crista the proper greeting, which involved being wrapped around her rather tightly. And she around him.

Nola clapped her hands at them as if they were stranded on a raft in the middle of a river.

"Helloo! Helloo, my dears! Lyle has come to join us for drinks!"

Blake managed to extricate himself from the folds of Crista's flowing robes and turned to fill glasses and hand them around. Crista, meanwhile, started talking as soon as she got her breath back.

I admired Crista's Goth attire. Her maroon eye shadow complemented her tulle under skirting. Net and tulle and sparkles for June. I smiled at her resilience and beauty as much as her enthusiasm. Blake handed round slices of lime, and we raised our glasses.

"Chin Chin," Nola exclaimed.

"Love and Friendship!" Blake yelled. We toasted each other and drank.

"Excellent Margaritas, Blake. I'm impressed."

"Cuervo! For life and for my Lady!" He smiled and blushed at the same time. Very sweet. I hoped that this meant that Blake would no longer be stalking me.

Margaritas in hand, Nola and Crista asked if we could talk business for a bit. "Fine with me," I said. "What's up?" Crista ran up the stairs for her drawings and then they both started talking at once.

"You tell it, dear," Nola said, "It'll be less confushing." Good thinking, Nola.

The story was, as Crista put it, that she was minding the store one day, working on her sketches, her Dark Designs as she called them, for wedding dresses. Nola had gone to the bank or something, and a mother and daughter walked into the shop, asking to see some dresses.

Long story short, Mom loved everything, the daughter hated white dresses and out of sullen boredom looked over Crista's shoulder at her drawings.

"Why can't wedding dresses look like this?" she whined.

"Oh, these ARE wedding dresses," Crista said. "Check out the veils!"

The rest was kismet. Nola knew a market when she saw one; Mom just wanted the daughter of Eve to get married in a church; Sybil pointed a black fingernail at drawing number one and said, "No dress, no church!" Voila! Crista's first commission.

"So, dear," Nola piped in as I saw where the plan

was going, "We want to buy the shop and go into business together."

"Yes, I can see that, Nola. Crista. Let's order in pizza and some beers and talk about it." Crista and Nola high fived, and we were on our way.

28

A few days later, after supper, I took Glory for a short walk. It was still light, but the heat of the day had cooled as the sun declined behind the hill that was the university. It was cool on the shady sidewalks. People were visiting on porches, puttering with rose bushes, or just out for a stroll.

A young woman in flip flops and cut off jeans walked up the sidewalk towards us, a large snake draped around her shoulders. She wore a bright pink bikini top that was mostly invisible beneath the folds of serpent, which made her appear half naked. Barely 5' 2", she had the straight-cut bangs and round face of a cherub. Glory growled and backed up to hide behind me.

"Hey, Caitlin. How's Brunhilde?" The boa's flat head rested on Caitlin's right shoulder, its tongue lazily tasting the air. When she's not hanging out at The book shop, Caitlin lives in various places around Lawrence, is more of a nomad than a couch-surfer. In a couple of houses, she even has her own room. Everywhere she goes, except work, the snake goes with her—bars, grocery stores, Copy Mart, the bank. No one messes with Caitlin about the snake.

"Hey, Lyle. How are you? Cool hair. You still staying at your mom's?"

"Yes, I am. Glory said she needed a walk. She was cooped up inside all day. Too hot to leave her outside."

"For real. Brunhilde, here, was put out with me for leaving her in the tank at Lewis's." Caitlin stroked her hand along a muscular stretch of boa constrictor. "But it's way too easy for her to get dehydrated, you know?"

"I bet." I studied her for a minute. That snake had to be heavy.

"Hey, Caitlin?" Her attention had wandered off down the street. "I have to go out of town for a couple of months. Some business to take care of back on the coast." She nodded casually.

"Would you be interested in house-sitting for me? You could set up an entire room for Miss B, and I could use the help."

"Definitely possible, Lyle. Let me think about it, OK? I don't like to jump into things. I move around, you know. But it could be cool. It's a good time for me right now, astrologically speaking."

"Take your time," I reassured her, pulling a card from my jeans pocket. Here's my number. Or you can reach me through any Hudson."

"Cool." She grinned. Caitlin had lived in Lawrence her whole life and was a fan of the L&L's. "They still making that mint shampoo?"

I laughed. "If you house-sit for me, I'll give you some conditioner, too!"

"Awesome. Later, Lyle."

"Have a good evening, Caitlin." She strolled off in

time to her own music, her sinuous mind wrapping itself around my proposition.

"Good girl, Glory!" I leaned over and petted her approvingly. She had sat at my feet the entire time, her eyes glued on Brunhilde.

"No barking, no sudden moves, way to go!" We looped around the neighborhood back to the house.

I put fresh water down for the dog and sat myself down at the kitchen table with an unopened deck of cards. I dealt four hands and played hide-and-seek poker with myself, compartmentalizing information and examining four sets of odds as if I didn't know which cards were in which hands. The hand directly across from me won the first round, and I was reviewing play to see how that had happened when my cell chirped. I'd have to postpone the card practice till later.

"MacDonald! I was going to call you tonight."

"Beat you to it. How's it going?" He yawned into the phone. "Sorry. That one snuck up on me."

"You must be exhausted."

"Pretty much. Making headway, though. Thought I'd call and see if your plans were any clearer. I didn't want to miss you because of some broken trees."

"I'm leaving Tuesday."

"Ah."

"Mmm."

"Need a ride?"

"No, that's covered. Listen. I have to go out to the L&L's tomorrow. Why don't I stop by in the afternoon? I can bring you something to eat and fill you in on what's been going on while you've been clearing the land."

"No need, Lyle. I'm fine. You do what you have to do. We are where we are. It's OK." His voice sounded warm and relaxed.

"OK. Maybe I'll stop by anyway."

He laughed, "OK. Maybe I'll be glad to see you!"

"OK."

"OK."

I looked at the cell and sat there smiling. You certainly are a lovely man, I thought. I closed the phone and picked up the cards again. Dealing hands, drawing cards, I loosened up and felt reassured about my game. I worked myself to the point where the hum turned up a notch.

"Enough," I said to the empty room and headed up to bed. I had to be up early enough to have breakfast with the L&L's. Just to be sure, I set the alarm for six.

29

Loretta and Lenore are both as playful as little kids, but coming up against the united front, the combined force of their personalities is daunting. I had to brace myself. Glory was delighted to have me up and about so early. She went with me on my jog, happily chowed down on her kibble, and went out in the back yard to sniff for bunnies while I showered and changed into jeans, sandals, and a white T-shirt. Physical therapy would have to be postponed.

On the drive over, I had the windows open to the morning air. There was a lot of moisture in the atmosphere, so the grasses and wildflowers were beaded with dew and gleamed in the soft sunlight. Distance was veiled in mist, and low lying fields held patches of ground fog, shreds of which would shroud curves in the road and dissipate as I drove through them. I recognized the songs of birds I could not see, cardinals, mourning doves, and meadowlarks. My antipathy towards Kansas had nothing to do with the natural beauty of the place.

This morning I felt a downright affection.

The car crunched the gravel of Lenore's driveway. I parked under a catalpa tree that was dropping its last blooms and headed for the house, Glory coming to heel on my left. We were practicing polite dog behavior, which Glory seemed to find hilarious.

I walked from the car to the house sniffing the air for signs of chocolate. Glory's nose was on the ground, seeking out eau de rabbit. Each to her own.

The air around the front door was definitely sweet, but not chocolate. Vanilla? Cake?

"Hey!" I called, stepping inside. "What's up?"

"We're in here, sweetie!" Lenore called from the kitchen

"Sweetie," Loretta snorted. "That's rich."

The table was covered with cupcakes topped with fluffy white frosting. There were bakery boxes stacked on the counter next to the sink. Loretta had an accounts book open in front of her, reading glasses perched on her nose. She was hemmed in by the swarm of cupcakes. Lenore stepped out of the pantry as I entered the room, a tray of tiny pink breasts in her hand. The pink was enhanced by the blue of her jeans and denim shirt.

"Lyle, dear, how good to see you!" Lenore greeted me, bright eyes beaming.

The twins were in topknot mode today, tendrils framing their faces. Angelic, avian, possibly. The air around them shimmered with industry. Something was definitely going on. I grinned in anticipation, delighted I'd stopped by.

"Let me guess," I said after leaning down to kiss my Aunt Loretta and giving a big hug to my Aunt Lenore.

"Hold the tray, Loretta, so I can get a *proper* hug!"

"Oh, for the love of Pete!" Loretta complained, but she took the tray anyway, helping herself to a tiny pink treat. Lenore swatted her on the head.

"Stop that! This is the last tray!" Lenore retrieved the chocolates and started placing the delicate, pink breasts, one per cupcake.

"Cute. What's the occasion?" I asked.

"Betty Campbell is celebrating her 85th birthday over at Presbyterian manor. We thought we'd surprise her," Lenore said quietly, concentrating on her task.

"Breasts?"

"Well, why not?" Loretta countered, "That crowd's half blind anyway. Besides, it's the thought that counts."

"So, those boxes are full of cupcake breasts? How many are there?"

"Oh, about a hundred, I think." Lenore said.

"Won't the staff ask questions?"

"Why would they, dear?" Lenore asked kindly, as if speaking to the mentally challenged.

"Never mind. Won't this birthday surprise cut into your profit margin?" Loretta cracked up.

"Not really!" she said.

"We just made a big sale," Lenore smiled proudly.

"Full out inventory clearance!" Loretta crowed. "We are cleaned out!"

"Really?" I was intrigued. "What was it, a pharmaceutical convention in KC? Viagra, Celebrex reps handing out candies with their brochures?" The aunts burst into laughter, which, of course, got me going as well.

"Not hardly. A local sorority tracked us down. Candace found us a co-ed who was doing research at the adult video store out east on Route 10," Loretta explained.

"The girl called, stopped by the house yesterday with a couple of sorority sisters," Lenore continued the story, "and bought everything we had." My eyebrows asked for more information.

"The Tri-Delts are having a 'Girls Gone Wild' party tomorrow night," Lenore explained. Loretta shrugged as if to say, "Go figure."

Took 'em a while to get so many boxes and paper sacks into their...What was that thing?" she asked Lenore.

"A Hummer, dear."

"Ugly damn machine. Bright yellow."

"Congratulations!" I gave them a standing ovation. "Bravo!"

"Thanks!" Loretta rubbed her hands together and closed the accounts book in front of her. She put both hands behind her head and smiled up at me. "This chocolates business is a lot of fun!"

Over coffee, Loretta brought me up to date on the dead-body-at-the-dog-run adventure she and Glory had had.

"I got tired a waiting and just called 'em!" She explained, referring to the detectives that worked the case. "Turns out the dead guy's wife was divorcing him and the dog he was walking—one a those snivelly, yappie.. what are they?....Yorkie dogs? Was the center of a custody case, if you can believe it!" My aunt clapped her hands, delighted by human folly of this magnitude.

"Now, the woman did not kill her husband," Loretta explained. "Macular degeneration. Couldn't a done it. Man was shot with a .22, apparently. Ya gotta have a good eye. Anyway, best the cops can tell, this looks like a dog-napping gone bad. There'd been a spate of them recently. Expensive little dogs disappearing, no ransom notes, weepy women wanting their doggies back driving 'em crazy, Donnie says."

"Donnie's one of Pearl's boys, isn't he, Loretta?"

Lenore asked.

"Nice kid," Loretta nodded. "Didn't have to use his grandma to get information out of him. Did promise not to tell anyone, though. It's an ongoing investigation." She leaned her elbows on the table and narrowed her gray-green eyes at us.

"I told Donnie it's most likely coyotes; they been bold this year." Loretta stopped and sat back in her chair, preparing her summation.

"I kid you not. Finding that body creeped the hell out of me. Gimme a cupcake, girls! I need cheerin' up!"

30

I stopped at Sun Ripe on the way back to the house to pick up a few things before heading back to the house. It was too hot to leave Glory in the car, so I sat her in the shade outside the door to the grocery store. "Don't talk to strangers, Glory!" The command was a signal in our new bag of tricks, and Glory responded correctly by lying down and placing her nose between her paws. It looked adorable and would like as not encourage people to fuss and coo over her, which would take their attention off me and make Glory pretty happy at the same time. We both thought it was a neat trick.

I returned not long after to find Miss Glory was still sitting there, quiet and demure. People moving in and out the sliding doors told her what a good dog she was. Glory was sweetness itself.

"Good job!" I told her, and gave her time to eat a green chewy for her teeth before going back to the car. I still felt a little jumpy in grocery store parking lots, so I took the time to scrutinize the scene before moving away from the shady spot by the door.

"Whew! Glory, I have got to calm down," I told her as I started the car and listened to the door self-lock. "Ready?" She wagged her tail in reply. I was chatting with her more than usual to get her ready for our trip. On the road we would be acting in a way we never behaved around the house. My hope was that she found the change entertaining.

"Tell you what. Let's skip going back to the house and just head out to MacDonald's. See what's up." I picked up my cell and called Mac, telling him that I'd be out earlier. Invited him to a picnic lunch.

"You might find it too hot at this time of day, " he said. "But come ahead."

It was indeed turning into a hot, humid day. How did people manage to live out here before air conditioning, I wondered, not for the first time.

I turned in at MacDonald's place as a couple of cars and a truck full of debris were heading out. Interesting.

Mac said it was too hot too keep working, so he told the crew to take off. They'd come back the next day, early, when the temperature would be cool enough for a couple hours' work. I looked at him skeptically, wondering about ulterior motives.

Mac laughed and said, "Just stand here for five minutes and tell me how you would feel about clearing brush and sawing up fallen trees." I didn't make the five -minute mark.

We walked up onto the porch, and I showed him the food I had bought— hummus, goat cheese, French bread, olives, and cherries for dessert.

"That looks great, Lyle! Come inside and we'll get some iced tea to go with it."

MacDonald poured some cold tea into a thermos

and said, "I have an idea. Let's take a little walk; there's something I want to show you. The dogs can stay here." Both Jesse and Glory were lying on a rug in the living area, currently on the cool side of the house. No argument from the dogs.

"I'm not going to sweat myself to death, am I? I've already had a big day, and I'm just not up to it."

"Lyle Hudson. I am shocked. It must be that new city-girl hair do you have going. I cannot imagine you turning down a challenge."

"Please. No challenges." I just looked at him.

"You'll have to tell me about your big day," he said, leaning over to kiss me.

"OK. Talking I can do, but do we have to go out in the heat to do it?" Careful, Lyle. That was very close to a whine. I told myself to shut up and almost missed what he said.

"Where we are going is not far, is cool and shady, and that you'll like it. C'mon." He grabbed what looked like a painter's tarp, picked up the thermos and went out the door.

"Cool and shady. I can do cool and shady. Hey, wait for me!" The man did not wait, so I had to scoot to catch up with him.

"Hey, MacDonald! Not everybody has nine-foot legs! Slow down!" Instead of answering, he slipped into a stand of trees.

Entering the shade of the densely packed trees, I immediately felt better. The sweat on the back of my neck cooled off, and I thought I might live. There was a bare dirt track, no more than a deer track, really, that was easy to follow. It was quiet in the dappled light and the soft shushing of leaves. I did not want to break the silence by calling out. I'd find him eventually, I thought; and if not, I had the food. So there.

I walked down a slight declivity and saw that the trees had thinned out a bit. More sun was breaking through the trees, and the air was filled with perfume. I couldn't quite place it. Then I saw Mac, standing by a patch of dark green grass that he was examining. Above his head stretched a cloud of whispery flowers. It was a mimosa tree! The source of the aroma that drifted around us.

"Oh, MacDonald! What a beautiful tree!"

"See? I thought you'd like it! I was relieved that the tornado stayed over on the other side of the property. Here, look at this, Lyle." He knelt down and took an old, metal cup—chipped, white porcelain it looked like—of a branch that had been stuck in the ground as a hook for the ancient cup.

I walked over to him and saw that there was a small spring, a pool no bigger than a soup pot, hidden by the tall grass. An oak barrel had been shoved into the ground to provide protection for the water, keeping it mud-free and stable around the rim of the spring. Some water quietly trickled off, back into the trees. It was lovely.

MacDonald stood with the cup full of water. "I have no idea how pure it is," he said, "But none of us have died from drinking it, yet." He took a sip and extended the old cup to me. I took a sip and felt the cool of the water, tasted a mineral quality that was not unpleasant.

"The water tastes old," I ventured, "As if icicles melted here ages ago and formed this little spring."

"I know what you mean," MacDonald smiled, "It invites imagination, doesn't it?" We stood there silently, as if in the presence of time itself.

I was enchanted. "This place is like a dream, or a memory of a world long gone. It is magical. Really." I turned to him, trying to convey how sincerely I felt and meant my words."

"I feel that way, too. Here. Try this." He reached up and broke one of the mimosa blossoms from the tree. It looked so tiny in his hand. Mimosa flowers are hardly there at all; they are just wisps, small brushes of white tipped with pink. The pink grew brighter and deeper when you held it lose, almost magenta.

MacDonald moved closer to me and held the flower to my nose, smiling mysteriously.

"Oh! Oh!" I couldn't catch my breath. I was overcome by the most profoundly sexual response I had felt in a hundred years! The utterly indescribable fragrance was so intense. That combined with the frisson caused by the soft hairs of the flower when they touched the tip of my nose. I thought I was going to faint. MacDonald circled his arm around me and brushed the delicate brush of the mimosa across my lips and my eyes.

"You. Are a wicked man," I whispered in his ear. He kissed me. An otherworldly, transcendent kiss. I was incapable of speaking afterwards and just leaned against him, feeling the beat of his heart, inhaling the salty tang of the day's sweat mingled with the scent of mimosa.

I have no idea what happened after the kiss. Perhaps we had lunch. Anything is possible in a place like that.

31

"Veterinary Clinic. This is Dana, how may I help you?"

"Hi, this is Lyle Hudson. Could I speak with Dr. Tenent, please?"

"He's out of the office right now. Can I take a message?"

"No, that's fine. I'll call back…"

"OK, Ms. Hudson. I'll tell the doc you called."

"Great. Thanks."

"Bye now."

The tornado had pushed aside Luce's questions about Daniel Tenent for a day or two, but they returned with a vengeance. Now that I'd called, what was I going to say? "Hi, you think I'm mistreating Glory?" What kind of a game was I getting into here? I prowled around the house feeling at loose ends, edgy. I rummaged in the pantry, looking for one of Glory's tennis balls, unconsciously running my hand over the scar on my arm.

"Come on, girl!" I bounced the ball by the back door, underlining the message. Glory came scrabbling down the hall, her feet moving too fast for the polished surface. I opened the door before she got to me, grinning as she lifted into the air and sailed down the back steps. Glory danced side to side, waiting for me to throw the ball. Catching it in the air, she made a victory lap around the yard before I got to the bottom of the steps. She lay the ball at my feet and waited for me to make my move.

Glory and I use the back yard as a kind of squash court. I'll throw the ball against the garage, or bank it off of the back fence, and we'll race for it. If I catch it first, I keep the ball moving. If Glory catches it, she runs in circles, mostly around me.

Between the sound of ball on wood and the razzing we gave each other, we were making a racket. But in the middle of a work day, no one was around to complain.

"Evil dog!" I yelled at her. My hands were filthy with dog slobber and dirt. "Take this!" I turned and slammed one onto the garage. But before Glory could run over from the opposite side of the yard, something extraordinary happened. The garage exploded.

The force of it knocked me to the ground. I rolled onto my face, shielding my head with my hands. Glory yelped nearby and I reached out, grabbed her, and rolled again so I was on top of her. Stuff stopped falling, but the yard was full of dense black smoke. I grabbed the dog and ran up the back steps.

Inside, coughing and choking, I grabbed the wall phone and dialed 911. I put Glory down and ran back outside, praying that the neighborhood was not going up in smoke. The house was OK, but the back fence was on fire. Who knows what was going on next door. I grabbed a garden hose, turned on the water and raced for the fence. I was making some headway when three firemen crashed through from the front yard, fire hose on.

It was over pretty quickly. They saved the neighbor's fence, but our garage was a shambles, the back fence not much more than charred wood. A police officer walked across the smoking remnants of the back yard and approached with a serious look on her face.

"Ms. Hudson?" A sharp voice to go with a sharp look.

"Officer Danielson. Hello." I was rubbing soot out of my eyes. At first didn't see the object in her gloved hand.

"A man was killed in the fire, Ms. Hudson. Homeless it looks like, but we're not sure. Do you recognize this phone? We found it on the body."

I was shocked. "Somebody died?" Officer Danielson just looked at me. I forced myself to look at the small silver object in her outstretched hand. A few scratches, but otherwise intact. "It looks almost new. I don't understand."

"We found it under his body. It is not yours, I take it?"

"No."

"We'll be in touch." She turned on her heel and stalked away as if she couldn't get away from me fast enough. I looked around the ruined yard, a sinking feeling in the pit of my stomach. What a mess. Firemen were milling around, collecting their gear.

I asked the guy in charge to come inside with me so I could check on Glory. The police came with him. Glory had a nasty scratch on one ear, which had bled across the floor, but she was up and around. We were

glad to see each other. I wrapped her in a towel and sat
her on my lap while I answered questions. Out back,
yellow tape was going up around the area and men were
poking through the debris. In a daze, I answered the
best I could, but it was clear that I was shocked and
having a difficult time. After reassuring everyone that I
was fine, we agreed to meet again and review events
leading up to the fire. The first impression was that the
fire was arson.

Arson. Must be aimed at me, but why? The phone
rang, the wall phone, not my cell. I stared at it as if it
had just landed from Mars and then walked over and
answered the phone.

"Yes?" My voice was thick. My throat ached.

"Lyle? Lyle Hudson?"

"Yes."

"Hello! This is Daniel Tenent. I understand you
called." His voice was friendly. "What can I do for
you?"

"Oh. Hello. I called…" The words were sluggish. "I
called to see…how… you were. How things are going…after the tornado. I'm sorry. We just had a fire
here, and I'm not sure…can I call you back? Tomorrow
maybe?"

"A fire? Your house? Are you all right? Lyle, is anyone there with you? I'm concerned!"

"No, I'm fine. I'm just not thinking straight yet."

"You need someone there with you. I'd be glad to
stop by."

"You're very kind. And I do want to talk with you.
I'll call tomorrow. Promise."

"All right. In the meantime, if I can be of any help,
please call." His voice sounded warm and kind. I could
not reconcile it with the insinuations he presented to
Luce. Luce. Oh, God.

"I will, Daniel, thanks."

Postponing the phone calls and explanations for later, I dragged myself upstairs to clean up. I piled Glory into the tub and went to town on our collective grit, grime, and smoke residue. The process took time, and afterward the bathroom was a mess of wet towels that I'd deal with later, after a good, long nap.

Dried off and in a fresh set of clothes—khakis and oxford shirt (I wanted to be able to get up and leave in a hurry if I had to)—I lay down on the bed and rubbed my hands across my face. I was tired and my eyes still burned. Glory was already asleep at me feet. I checked the clock on the bedside table out of habit and saw the two playing cards lying side by side. Two Aces, one bent in half. Was the garage a message too? Was the dead homeless guy supposed to be me?

"Nasty thought," I mumbled. "Later for that one." I closed my eyes and fell into sleep.

I awoke to complete darkness. There was a noise, followed by the clamor Glory made as she leapt off the bed and crashed downstairs, howling her head off. I switched the light on so I wouldn't kill myself stumbling around in the dark and went downstairs after her.

Instead of settling down as I'd expected, Glory's barking crept to a higher pitch. She was excited and angry. Sounded like she had something cornered in the kitchen. I hurried down the last few steps and groped around for another light switch. As my hand reached out, a dark figure rushed past, slammed me hard against the wall and tore out the front door, Glory hounding their heels furiously.

What was that smell? Foreign, sweet. An almost cloying scent, it hung in the air despite the residue of smoke. Musk oil? Who...? An image of Blake in the shop recently, standing close to me. It couldn't be

Blake. Glory wouldn't attack him. Unless he raised her hackles, upset her somehow. Breaking into the house? That would upset her. Damn. I had to find out.

In a daze, I managed to turn the lights on, get my hands on something (an umbrella, it turned out) and run out the door after them. I followed the sound of Glory's barking down the street, running barefoot in the middle of the road to avoid the cracks and broken pavement of the sidewalk. Even with streetlights, the night was dark, and I struggled to keep moving, keep track of the dog. Crazy, fearless, and on the hunt, it passed my mind that I probably looked totally demented.

Suddenly a set of headlights flashed on in front of me, high beams blinding. It must have been moving before the brights came on because the vehicle was moving fast, coming right at me. I dove between parked cars and hit the ground just as the car caught up with me. Brakes squealed, but it hit a car anyway, making a hideous metallic gashing sound and screeching off before I could get a good look.

I sat on the curb, nursing a stiff arm and scratched face. I waited for a full minute in the absolute silence, waiting for Glory to find me. No lights came on. No cars drove by. I sat and tried to remember details. It might have been an SUV. It felt like a lot of vehicle rushing by. Not a clue about the intruder, though. A man? Could it have been Blake? Hard to tell.

"Glory!" No answer. I struggled onto my feet and padded barefoot down the rest of the block, calling her. I found the dog half under a parked car. She was conscious, panting, but not even trying to move.

"Oh, baby girl, please be OK." I lay flat on the pavement, praying I would not be run over in the dark. Running my hands along her back and legs, I could feel no broken bones, but my hands felt a lot of blood from a gash on her back leg. Sitting up, I tore off my shirt and lay it on the ground next to Glory.

"Easy, girl. Here we go." I bit my lips, fighting back tears as I dragged the dog onto my shirt. She yelped when I got to her hindquarters, but she didn't fight me about it. I dragged Glory out from under the car, tightened the shirt around her so I could lift her into my arms.

We walked back to the house and in through the door that had been left open to the night. I took Glory into the library and checked her out thoroughly. The bleeding had stopped. I made a nest of blankets for her, got her some water and decided I probably needed to replace my shirt that was now a bloody mess. In a fresh T-shirt, I made the call and sat down to wait for the police. Then thought better of it. I wanted, no needed a drink. Sorry. The day my garage blows up; there's an intruder in my house; I almost get run over, my dog is hurt. I'm having a damn drink! It was going to be a long night.

By the time the police arrived, I had scouted around, trying to figure out where the intruder had been. I also called MacDonald.

"You what?" Mac was coming to pretty quickly, I thought. Faster than I would if he has called me at three in the morning.

"An intruder," I repeated. "Might be some connection to the fire. I'm sure the police will ask."

"Fire? Police? Where are you?" He was definitely awake now.

"I'm at home, waiting for the police. There was a kind of hit-and-run, too. Aimed at me. Glory got hit. Got to go, MacDonald. The cops are here."

"I'm on my way."

"OK Good." I went to find more scotch.

MacDonald's arrival calmed everyone down, especially the police who were starting to regard me with deep suspicion if not downright hostility. I might attract trouble, he assured them, but I didn't actually go out of my way to start it. He hoped.

We had a very lengthy discussion about the fire and the intruder and the damage to the innocent parked car, as well as the likelihood that the driver intended to kill me. I promised to be around the next day for further discussion. I had already signed up to lead a discussion group on the topic of the fire. Tonight's investigating officer said he'd confer with the other team and left with a respectful if somewhat dubious "Good night" to Mac. As the designated Lucy, I had some 'splainin' to do.

Even in the middle of the night, the man looked good. I doubted the same could be said of me. Just sitting there made me wince.

"I need to get horizontal, MacDonald, I'm not feeling too swell. Care to stay over?" I was trying to muster up some charm, but mostly I was feeling desperate. Glory lay at my feet, a dirty bandage hanging off her ear, looking pathetic in her sleep.

"There is not much night left, Lyle. But let's see what we can do." He held out a hand and I took it so I could stand up.

"I'm sorry about the trouble, MacDonald." I looked up at him, still holding hands. "I don't know what's going on. This... mayhem, it has to be connected, has to be directed at me, but nothing is making any sense." I went to rub the back of my head and groaned at the pain in my elbow, stopping me midway. Then I laughed.

"Pretty pathetic, aren't I?"

"No ma'am," Mac smiled. "I'd say you're pretty

tough. If they're running cars at you, you must be pretty scary. C'mere." I thought I was going to get a nice hug. Instead, Mac stepped around and picked me up in his arms.

"No. You are not!" I tried to hide the fact that I was taken by surprise, bordering on speechless.

"Yes. I am. You don't think I'm going to listen to you moan and groan all the way upstairs, do you? It'll be noon before we get there." He swiveled around, and I hit the lights as we left the kitchen. "Don't you fuss, Lyle Hudson. We're going upstairs."

He climbed the stairs silently, and in spite of the bruises and fatigue, I had to admit it was just about the sexiest thing I'd ever experienced.

"Thank you," I said, simply, as he set me down.

"Welcome." It was a sweet, tender, kiss. If I did not love the man, I was a freaking idiot. Full house, aces-over-kings-idiot. I hope MacDonald slept well. I felt as safe and cared for as it was possible to be. For me, it was not so much sleep as a new order of being. Sweet.

I awoke to find Mac gone, a note on the bedside table: *Glory's hanging in there. Gave her water. She needs a vet. Call me. M.* Glory! Christ, what time was it? Almost ten. I ran down the stairs to find Glory asleep on the blankets in the library. She opened her eyes and closed them again. Her breathing seemed shallow to me. She felt hot. I sat on the couch and called the vet's office.

"It's Lyle Hudson. Glory has been hit by a car. She made it through the night, but…" I stopped and let Dana ask her questions. "Great. We're on our way in."

Upstairs, I struggled into my clothes, avoided the mirror, brushed my teeth, dragged a brush through my hair. The phone rang as I pulled my Merrells from under the bed. It was Nola.

"I did it, Lyle! I found those files you were looking for! You'll never guess what her code was."

"Great, Nola. I can't talk right now. Glory was hit by a car last night. I've got to get her to the vet."

"Lyle! Don't hang up! You have to hear this."

"OK. Make it quick." I had a *duh* moment that faded fast as I listened to the rest of what she said. *Enlightening* doesn't come close. Mother of God. Swearing her to secrecy, I made tracks to take Glory in, but not before gathering up a few items and stashing them in my satchel. Too bad I didn't have Louise's gun. Reflecting on the situation, I decided that a gypsy shirt with billowing sleeves would be appropriate.

"Let's go, Glory girl, you're going to be fine." I wrapped her in one of the blankets and managed to get her into the G35 without inflicting too much pain. I hauled ass south to Baldwin and peeled into the parking lot, spewing gravel. Dana came out to help me get Glory into the office and saw to it that Glory was set up with an IV before Dr. Tenet even came in the room. Office policy was that emergencies came first. I threw my satchel onto a counter. I was stroking Glory's neck, murmuring to her when Tenent came into the examining room, Dana at his elbow.

"She was hit by a car?" Tenent's eyes were full of concern. He didn't wait for an answer but went right to work. Dana changed the bandage on Glory's ear while he worked on her flank. The dog growled at him and started to struggle.

"Pain," he commented. "She's pretty stressed by this injury. We'll need to sedate her so I can get and x-ray." I nodded my approval. Glory needed no further injury. He quickly found a vial, a hypo, and injected the dog, rubbing the spot to disperse the drug into her system.

"How far under is she?" I asked, narrowing my eyes.

"Not very. She'll come round in a bit. No need to worry." Dana came back in wheeling a portable x-ray unit. Tenent slipped a film holder beneath the dog. The man moved with economy, efficiently, always gentle with his hands.

Glory didn't budge. Dana left to develop the film.

"The x-ray will tell, but I don't think Glory's worse than bruised. Still, I'd like to keep her overnight for observation," he said, washing his hands and drying them with meticulous care.

"I don't think so, Daniel. I need to have her with me right now. There's too much going on." I stepped back and put one hand on the counter behind me, next to the satchel.

"Lyle, don't be difficult." Difficult? He had no idea.

Door closed, he turned to face me. "Glory's condition needs monitoring, Lyle. I think she should stay." I nodded, skeptically, turned and retrieved one of the items from the bag, the voluminous sleeves obscuring the line of his vision. I adjusted my sleeves and turned, throwing a bent playing card onto the metal examining table, near Glory's feet. Ace of spades.

"I'm here to Pay Up, Daniel. When we're finished here, Glory comes home with me."

Give the man credit, he didn't even blink. Just took a step and picked up the ace with two fingers. Looked at me over the top of his glasses. The vain bastard took the opportunity to turn on the charm. His smile was actually quite attractive.

"Clever girl. That satchel doesn't look large enough to hold the money to cover your mother's debt. Where is it?"

"A couple of answers first, Daniel. How were you involved with Louise's gambling? And why the threats?

Why didn't you just tell me what you wanted? And why did you hit my dog with your car?"

"You guarantee payment?'

"I do. Talk."

"We don't have time. There are people out there." He was starting to fidget.

"Tell them I'm distraught. Whatever. I'm not leaving." Tenent stuck his head out the door, had a word with Dana, and turned back to me. He took off his glasses and cleaned them with a tissue. Looked at me with ice in his eyes.

"I loan money to old ladies with small dogs. Ladies who regularly hit the casinos in Kansas City, who hide their gambling from their families. I did it out of sympathy at first. Then it became quite lucrative. They always pay up. The dogs are excellent collateral. I get paid or I take the dog. It's not wise to get in my way."

I felt a chill as he spoke, remembering Loretta's story of the dog run.

"Louise owed me $25,000. I was willing to take Glory. She said she couldn't part with the dog." He shrugged, leaving me my conclusions.

"What? You killed my mother?" Was he bluffing? His eyes rested on the anesthetized dog on the table. My blood started to boil.

"Yell all you want, Lyle. The office is empty. Dana thinks you're hysterical. Who knows what you might do."

"And Glory? What happens to her?" Tenent laughed at my concern.

"You don't get it, do you. Glory is the point. Did you ever *read* her pedigree? She's worth a fortune as a breeder. Louise wouldn't breed the dog. I did manage to talk your mother out of having Glory spayed. God, she was a stubborn woman." He shook his head. "*You* weren't supposed to be part of the picture. Glory was practically *mine* when you showed up." He slammed his hand down on the steel table. Glory stirred in her sleep.

"And the threats, the aces? What was that about?"

"You were supposed to be frightened into an anonymous payoff. When that didn't work, I went after Glory. The garage fire was a diversion, of course. Clumsy of me."

Death. No bluff. "A man died in that fire, you shit!" I could not believe his arrogance.

"Time to pay up."

"Are you completely nuts? You killed my mother?" My voice shook; I was trying hard not to lose it.

"Who will believe any story you tell them? People will believe you set the fire and injured the dog yourself. Plenty of evidence and witnesses to your bizarre behavior."

I yelled to get the action rolling. Tenent was not the only one playing a game here. "All right, you son of a bitch. I am *so* going to get you!" I stood rigid, fists clenched, eyes glaring, practically foaming at the mouth. "Feeling lucky, Dr. Tenent? How about a game of chance?"

Tenent laughed. He was relaxed, in control of the situation, enjoying my rage.

"Cards. Got a deck of cards? Let's do it. Right here, right now. High stakes? We got 'em!"

Tenent walked over to where I stood and reached lazily into one of the cabinets, eyes on my face, inquisitive, wondering how far over the edge I was. He pulled out a pack of Bicycle playing cards, already opened. He removed the deck, shuffled the cards, and placed them on the counter. My luck was in play, apparently. The deck was blue.

"What shall we play? Not enough time for poker."

"In a rush, Daniel? OK. High card takes it."

"High card gets the dog," he said, mildly.

"I want another shuffle." I picked up the cards, ruffled the deck, and shook the sleeves of my blouse, freeing my wrists. Reshuffled the deck with a snap and slammed the deck down in front of him. Daniel ran a hand through his curling brown hair, and I thought what a pity it was the man was such a fish.

"You take first cut, Daniel."

Not bothering to glance my way, the man focused on the deck of blue playing cards sitting before him. With a smooth, practiced gesture, he cut the deck and came up with the queen of hearts. Not bad. He held my eyes knowing only eight cards could beat him. Tenent returned the card to the deck and placed in gently on the counter. Stepping back, he turned and placed a hand gently on Glory's neck.

"Hands off, murderer. She's still my dog." As if stung, Tenent withdrew his hand.

I shook the sleeve of my poet's blouse again, and cut the deck. I held up the draw so he could see it. I watched his eyes bulge at the Ace of Spades.

"So, fish. Did I win?"

The man snapped and lunged at me. I expected him to be a sore loser, but the attack surprised me. He grabbed my throat.

"A fish always loses," I gasped. The grip on my wind pipe was fierce. I twisted and grabbed my satchel, pulling from it my small spray bottle and letting him have it, right in the eyes. Green cat piss. It could make you go blind and ruin your shoes at the same time.

Tenent wrenched himself away, cursing and clawing at his eyes. He grabbed blindly at the waiting room door. I caught a glimpse of long gun barrel behind stacks of kibble as I swept Glory up off the table and fled. Knowing the front door would be locked, I swerved behind the cash register and through the kennel. Kicking my way through the back door, I staggered around the side of the building toward my car.

Before I could get there, Tenent came through the front door of the office, red eyes streaming, a 12 gauge in his hands. He opened it and loaded. There was no cover. He stood between us and the G35. Glory was still out cold, dead weight in my arms.

"What are you going to do, kill me? Out here? See the traffic going by? You are not invisible and neither is that shot gun, Tenent. Give it up."

"Give me the dog." His voice was insistent, almost making sense. The barrel of the gun was rock steady.

I looked down at the dog in my arms and let my shoulders droop slightly, hoping it'd make him over-confident. Ignoring Tenent, I looked down at my feet, careful to place them as I slowly knelt to put Glory on the ground. He was two steps too far away but I couldn't chance seeing the river card turned over. It was time to go all-in.

I had one knee on the ground, my weight on the foot by Glory's belly, when the man did me a favor. He took two steps and pointed the gun barrel at my head. Before he could get the words out--"Don't do anything stupid"--I came up at him, pushing the barrel up and aside with my left hand.

The gun exploded over our heads, and the recoil pushed him back. I rammed his chin hard with my right hand, knocking him off his feet entirely. Not pure Aikido, since my objective was not to harmonize with my opponent. But I was applying principles of Kokyu-ho, "Heaven and Earth" technique, capitalizing on my own center of gravity while blending with the momentum of Tenet's movement, encouraging his center of balance to move upward, destabilizing it. It feels a lot like dancing; and like dance, once the steps are learned they stay with you.

Most people do not know how to control a fall, and Tenent was no exception. He flailed his arms and let go of the gun which I caught with my left hand and swung aside in a wide arc, letting it sweep low and behind me onto the rough pavement and out of play.

Tenent hit the ground hard, the back of his head bouncing off the pavement. Caught up in a cold fury, I jumped down, grabbed his hair and gave his head a second hard push, knocking him out. Turning him onto his face in my own version of a quick pin, I sat on his back and pulled out my cell phone to call the police.

Looking around I could see that Glory was still breathing and that the shot gun was out of reach, I passed the time watching traffic pass what must have been a bizarre scene if anyone took the time to see it. Cars passed, blank and unregarding, like the look on Glory.

Finally, a patrol car pulled into the lot, spitting gravel. I was not surprised to see MacDonald in the passenger seat.

"Is he dead?"

"Not yet -- Glory -- Tenent will live." I pushed hair out of my eyes and stood up.

MacDonald got busy with the handcuffs, and I went over to Glory and sat down, holding my dog.

Officer Danielson emerged from the cruiser, came over and crouched beside me, asking if I needed help.

"Ms. Hudson...Lyle. You've got to cut out this ninja shit, OK? You're going to get yourself killed."

"Wrong, Greta. It saved my life. But I'm not sure about Glory." She patted my shoulder and helped me stand up, keeping Glory in my arms.

Psycho veterinarian and shotgun stowed safely in separate parts of the patrol car, MacDonald came over and had a word with Danielson, who nodded and turned briskly to the business of getting Tenent to jail.

"He killed Lou, MacDonald." No response. Struck by a sudden thought, I looked up. "How did you know?" I asked.

"Nola called me," he said quietly. "She thought you might be in trouble." He held me close and took some of Glory's weight with his other arm.

"She thought right."

We stood alone in the empty parking lot, Mac looking at me looking at Glory who was only now starting to come round.

"She's got to see another vet. I can't take her home like this."

"No problem. Give me the keys," Mac said, steering me toward the Infiniti. "We'll find something." I leaned against him as we walked. Glory was heavy and warm in my arms. The G35 shone in the morning light, a point of refuge in an alien landscape.

It felt weird to sit on Glory's side of the car. Stranger, still, to see MacDonald's hands on the rosewood steering wheel. I felt a tug of jealousy but was too numb to tell if I was jealous about the car or jealous *of* the car. The man's hands spoke to me, reminded me of...

"What? Sorry, Mac. I didn't catch that."

"Are you sure you're OK?" He shifted his body to see me better, his shoulders seeming to fill the car. "I said there's a veterinary clinic on Clinton Parkway we can take her to. Vet's a friend of my nephew, Miguel."

"Sounds good."

Mac pulled the car onto Highway 59 and we headed

north, back to Lawrence. I settled back against the seat
and closed my eyes, comforted by the small movements
of the dog in my lap.

"Really nice car, Lyle. She's even sweeter in person." He chuckled. "I bet that boy's still crying in his
beer over her."

"Martinis more likely." I looked over at him,
drinking in his dark hair, the smile lines, thoughtful pro-
file. More than just a friend, Lyle, I counseled myself.
Be careful.

"Nola lit a fire under me without supplying much in
the way of details," Mac said. "What was in the computer?"

"There was a protected file," I shook my head in
wonder, "Named *OnLoan*. A secret stash of information." I hesitated, not wanting to rat out my mother to a
cop. For a long time Nola couldn't figure out the pass-
word to get into it.

"What was in it?"

Bloody hell. I suppose he was entitled. It would
come out in Tenent's investigation. "Gambling accounts. Debts, mostly. I don't know what to make of it.
Possibly my success at gambling *inspired* her," the word
tasted sour in my mouth, "To give it a try. Hell, if I
could do it, how hard could it be?" MacDonald listened
without comment.

"Nola said there were some comments with the last
entries. Lou was worried about Glory, didn't want to
lose her dog." At the sound of her name, Glory struggled to sit up. She licked my chin and lay down again,
with a muffled groan.

"She needs water; her tongue's dry."

"Ten minutes, max," MacDonald reassured me.
"She'll be fine. Why did you always drive so far out to
Tenent's place anyway."

"Louise liked him and he liked Glory."

Mac paused. "The man kept a shot gun in his office?"

"Apparently. Behind stacks of kibble. Completely invisible if you didn't know it was there." I shuddered that I might have been shot—again.

"I got him, too!"

"Clearly. Face down and whimpering. Looks like 'got' to me." He gave me a sideways look.

"No. With cards. One cut, winner-take-all; in this case, Glory." The dog hummf'd. Was she listening?

"Your luck held?" MacDonald asked. "You gambled on Glory?"

"Hell, no! I have no luck—had no luck I guess. My losing streak is pretty spectacular." I paused, remembering my misery in Colorado. "I cheated."

Mac burst out laughing. I explained about the Bicycle cards, the Ace of Spades slipped from my loose sleeves with a simple sleight-of-hand.

MacDonald kept his silence until Highway 59 turned into Iowa Street. He flicked the left turn signal and bowed his head.

"There is no point in lecturing you. I suppose."

"Not needed. I'm crazy. I know it. You can stop right there." I reached up and brushed my hair back with my free hand and looked out the car window at the passing traffic—people out on their weekend errands. The scene looked so unreal. I let out a sigh.

"One thing gripes me, tough," I said.

"Just one?" The traffic arrow flashed and Mac turned the Infiniti onto 23rd. The veterinary clinic was west, off of Kasold, about a mile. Almost there.

"Tenent…. If he keeps his mouth shut, he'll get away with everything." I paused. "Psycho bastard."

Mac cracked up again.

"It's not funny! Thing is, Mac, that he was so deranged, so out there, I don't know if I believe he did it. I don't know if it wasn't some game he was playing with my mind. Torturing me about my mother." I stared out the window.

"Relax. He's in custody. And there's some good news. Sort of." I cocked an eye at him expectantly, if a bit dubious.

"That cell phone we found on the homeless man belongs to Tenent." Mac turned left onto Kasold and left again into the veterinary parking lot. I hate parking lots.

"Asshole will say it was stolen," I grumped.

"Don't be so cynical. C'mon. Let's get her inside and taken care of."

Playing the 'emergency' trump card, we were seen right away. No major trauma found, they wanted to keep Glory overnight to re-hydrate and observe. I declined, vowing I'd see that she got plenty of water. Dr. Vasquez OK'd the plan only if we gave the IV another half hour before we took Glory home.

Sitting next to MacDonald in the busy waiting room, I leaned forward and put my face in my hands, giving in to a full load of grief.

"He was such a sweet guy. I don't even know his name. He loved Glory, MacDonald. Fed her donuts." I didn't know whether to laugh or cry.

Mac put his arm around me and drew me to him, held me close. "It's OK," he murmured softly in my ear. "We'll learn his name, you'll see."

"Bastard," I gritted my teeth, changing subjects.

"He certainly is," Mac agreed. "Certainly is." I put my head on his shoulder.

"Lyle, I have one more question."

"What?" If I sounded irritated it was because I

didn't believe it was the last.

    "What was the password, to the file, I mean?"

    "4Glory"

32

It took two days for Caitlin to settle herself and Brunhilde the boa in the house. Day one was spent setting up an arboreal habitat in the spare room next to the redecorated sitting room. No trees were involved, but Brunhilde needed branches sturdy enough to bear her weight and considerable length. We took down the curtains to avoid confusion on the part of the snake, and Caitlin brought in an assortment of tropical plants for atmosphere and a specially made cage for occasions when Brunhilde needed a time out. She used the cage for feeding time, as well. I asked to be spared the details, which elicited a customary shrug from Caitlin.

There was more than enough time to arrange for Mac's cousin Miguel to collect and store the G35. The L&L's dropped off a chocolate care package for Chas and traveling samples for me.

Caitlin herself moved in with far less fuss the day before Glory and I were to leave. She asked if she could stay in the sitting room, originally Louise's bedroom.

Caitlin liked the light in there and the proximity to Brunhilde.

"No problem," I told her. "Shall we set up a bed for you?"

"I don't think so...but thanks, anyway. I like to sleep on a hard surface, you know, like the floor? I'll just lay out my bed roll by those windows. Beds always feel so...permanent." She said the word as if she were talking about a root canal.

"Hey, Lyle! Check it out!" Caitlin stuck out her tongue. Clearly, I was to admire her most recent piercing. It sat on her tongue like a steel pearl on a bed of pink flesh.

"Trendy," I nodded. Did that hurt?"

"Leth ith bib," she said, the item still on display.

"Won't it chip your teeth?" These were questions I always wanted to ask. Caitlin was glad to oblige.

"Not really," she said, returning her tongue to its function as an instrument of speech. "It is not right at the tip, so my teeth will be fine. It was sore for a while though," she admitted thoughtfully.

"So, if I may ask, what is the appeal?" She cracked up and looked at me from under her bangs.

"When you kiss? It feels awesome! Want to try? Just to see what it feels like?"

"Um, no thanks, Caitlin. I appreciate the offer, though. "So, when two of you kiss, do teeth get bumped then?" Caitlin though I was pretty funny.

"You got some dental obsession?" She giggled. "There are things to do beside kissing, you know."

"How about if I send you some vintage postcards from San Francisco?" I asked her, changing the subject to protect my mind from unwelcome albeit intriguing images.

"Very cool!" She nodded.

"Remember, you have my contact numbers over there by the phone."

"Yeah, yeah," Caitlin reassured me. "And the aunties if I get lonely."

"Correct." I smiled and we shook hands.

Caitlin would be out late and I would be up early, so we said our good byes and she and Brunhilde stepped out for the evening. Then I called Chas.

"You rang, madam?" he answered.

"Like a bell, Chas. Like a bell. How are you? Are there people living in my place, or is it safe to come back to the raft?"

"Your castle awaits you, my queen. Hmm. Or are you the princess and I'm the queen, I forget."

"Baby, you can be anything you want. Wait! I know! How about I be me and you be you?"

"Brilliant! So, my darling, when exactly are we to expect you?"

"We?"

"The royal we, Lyle, don't be a bore."

"Possibly...." I drew the word out, not exactly stalling—but editing how much I would tell Chas about my plans. "A week."

"A week," he stated flatly. "You're leaving Kansas tomorrow, by plane, if I'm correct, and it is taking you a week to get here. Very small plane, is it, sweetie?"

"In point of fact—Chas hated it when I used that expression, which made it irresistible—yes. Glory and I are making a stop or two en route."

"Miss Glory! Delicious! And I'll have *a week* to find her some kibble!" Chas and I paused, dancing around each other the way fencers do to study each other. "May I guess where you are stopping?"

"No. Maybe you should just ask me." Chas made a

pouting sound. "Chas?" I was going for a diversionary tactic. "You don't have a pierced tongue, do you?"

"Eeew! I'm offended you would even ask! How revolting! I'm wounded, do you hear me, deeply hurt!" Pause. "You have not…"

"No, I have not. Remind me to tell you about my house sitter."

"Lyle?"

"Yes, darling?" We were both smiling by this time, slipping back into what Chas lovingly called *badinage*—playful bantering on the surface with an acidic undercurrent.

"You sound exactly like this woman I used to know. What was her name? Ah! Carlyle Hudson! You have the same wit, the same delicious timbre of the voice…you wouldn't be stopping off to play poker, would you?"

"Clever boy! I would indeed!"

"Oh, tell me, tell me, tell me!"

"Not for blood nor money! You ruin my concentration. But I'll tell you about it when I get there, OK? And, if you're a good boy and do not nag me, I'll bring you a bit of chocolate, and some bling as a gesture of my esteem and affection."

"Oooh. Tempting…"

"I'm serious, Chas. Do not go snooping around. Do not track me down, please. It has been forever since my last game."

"Very well."

"Sapphires are nice," I volunteered. Lyle was planning on doing well indeed!

"Emeralds are, too, dear. They match my eyes."

We made our peace. Well worth the price, I thought. Time to finish packing.

Because I would have some clothing waiting for me in Tahoe, I didn't have to pack a whole lot. Everything I needed fit into one piece of carry-on luggage. Not that I had to worry about it. Flying privately has its perks, I thought, looking at Glory.

I'd take the dog's vaccination records with me in case she got into a tussle with man or beast, but if she stuck to her recent training, she'd be a peach.

"Who's a peach, Glory?" I cooed at her, and she jumped up where I sat on the edge of my bed and proceeded to lick my face. "All right! Enough!" I leapt up and tried to rid myself of the white hairs that were now covering my black jeans and sleeveless shirt. Perhaps I'd wear white on the plane in case Glory didn't like turbulence.

I woke up before the alarm went off and took the luggage downstairs on the way to a quick breakfast for Glory and me. She had half kibble rations, and I had a cup of coffee and a banana. I let the dog out and sat on the back steps with my coffee, taking in the morning sounds from the alley and mapping the day. It looked pretty good from where I sat. I smiled at how one can surprise oneself.

We think we know ourselves so well, I mused. Not so. There are millions of opportunities to take a step to the left or just a hop to the right, into some other way of being in the world. Most of us are either too chicken or too habit bound to take that step and find out what else might be out there for us.

I felt good. I already knew this particular territory, but I was going back to it in a new way. It felt more playful this time, less abstract. I was going to surprise a few people, possibly myself. I threw the dregs of the coffee into the pachysandra and went in. Glory came with me; neither one of us wanted to miss a minute of this day. Which was likely to be very cool.

All in white linen, black, cross-grain ribbon sandals, and turquoise, I wrote a quick note for Caitlin and went downstairs to wait for the limo. I parked my new purse by the bag at the door, and Glory and I went into the parlor and practiced a few bits from our new routine. When I said "Showtime," Glory would be on alert for her signals.

We were having such a good time practicing that I almost missed the limo pulling up at the curb. I had a minute before the driver came up the steps to carry the bag for me.

"C'mere, Glory!" I knelt down and pulled a rhinestone choker out of my jacket pocket, a new collar for the Babe. "Bling for Glory Baby!" Not too outrageous. Really.

I had a huge smile on my face when I opened the door.

"Dottoressa! Que bella!" He bowed and kissed my hand.

"Armand! Good to see you!" Armand was half French, half Persian. Why he spoke Italian was a mystery. Charming, but a mystery. For one spectacularly successful poker tournament, Armand had been my personal chauffer. He looked like those portraits of a young Byron, exotic smoothness and dark eyes. "Meet Glory, she's traveling with me."

Armand smiled at the dog and they bonded. "Can she sit in the front with me?"

It was such an impulsive, innocent request. And seriously, I doubted that any woman anywhere was capable of denying Armand anything. I put on my oversize sunglasses and beamed at him. "Of course."

On the way to KCI, I sat behind Glory, looked out the window, and dreamed a dream of the next few days. Armand drove us onto a runway reserved for private jets, and we pulled up next to a Cessna with markings that were familiar to me.

Armand opened the door for me and then for Glory, who sparkled in the morning sun. The driver passed the bag to a waiting porter and handed me up the steps of the plane.

"Always a pleasure, Armand," I said.

"Buona fortuna, Dottoressa!" Armand made a sleek return to the sleek car and drove away.

A diminutive Phillipina flight attendant greeted me, introducing the three other passengers, all of whom I knew. I was pleased by the raised eyebrows at my new look. I gave Glory the window seat and settled next to her, luxuriating in leather upholstery and extra leg space. Buckled my seat belt. Took a long breath.

"Who is your beautiful friend?" a voice asked. I looked up to see Julian, a world class poker player, talking to Glory. Sweet. Julian is bad-boy British, significantly less than impeccable, rugged, deep blue eyes set off by dark brows and black hair.

"Her name is Glory, Julian. Good to see you." I held out my hand and he brought it up to his lips, giving me a little nip somewhere near my wrist. I removed the sunglasses and gave him a look.

"Carlyle Hudson," he drawled, "What have you done with your already amazing self? You look like heaven." He stood there and smiled appreciatively, mostly at himself, judging from his next words. "Heaven and Glory. Not just appropriate, darling, positively inviting."

Oh, yes. It was going to be an interesting trip.

"So," I asked, "anyone care for a chocolate?"

Elisabeth Lee earned a Ph.D. in Victorian Literature from the University of Colorado at Boulder. A private school administrator and teacher, she lives in Lawrence, Kansas. It figures prominently in her work, along with San Francisco, Denver and New York where she has also lived.

377131